To Margare

CW00351612

MELODY

OF RAINDROPS

by Annie Ireson

Best Wishes

Annie Ireson

www.fast-print.net/store.php

MELODY OF RAINDROPS
Copyright © Annie Ireson 2015

A catalogue record for this book is available from the British Library

ISBN 978-178456-210-6

First published 2015 by
FASTPRINT PUBLISHING
Peterborough, England.

For my mum, Margaret Rose Beasley
(1932-2006)

Acknowledgements

Melody of Raindrops is the second book in the Jeffson Family Trilogy and can be read as a stand-alone novel, although it is obviously preferable to read *Sunlight on Broken Glass* first.

I'd like to thank a few people for their help in various ways.

Sue Lyons and Sarah Wilkin were readers of the first draft of the novel and I'd like to thank them for their time and feedback.

I spent a very pleasant hour or so with John Ives, a lovely gentleman who was a child in the 1930s and remembered with precise detail the delicious food he enjoyed at fetes, carnivals and fairs and gave me a fascinating account of his childhood in the east end of London. Thank you, John, for your input.

Andy Sipple and his meticulous attention to detail was the cause of an enlightening conversation about the origins of various idioms and slang, even if it did mean a further, late edit to make sure my characters were talking to each other in the language of the day. I'd like to thank him for taking the time to help in this respect.

I am fortunate in having a fantastic family: without them I doubt I would have ever had the confidence to publish my writing. Thank you Bob, Emily, Garry, Nicky, Lee, Kelly and Christie for all your support.

Many years ago, my grandma suffered a tragedy in her life so terrible she could never talk about it. I can't say too much without giving anything away that might spoil readers' enjoyment of the novel, but I'd like to acknowledge it here, and apologise if any reader in a similar situation is offended by the way I have dealt with this harrowing subject. I can only express relief that, when the same thing happened to me, I didn't live in the 1930s.

Finally, I'd like to thank Ellie for being such a lovely model for the book cover, Jamie Ray and Craig Hayward for the cover design and, last but not least, all the local Kettering people who have given me so much wonderful support over the last year.

Melody of Raindrops is a work of fiction. Any resemblance to any living person is entirely coincidental. The third book in the trilogy, *Ashes on Fallen Snow,* will be published on 1st November 2015.

A Divine Image

Cruelty has a human heart,
And Jealousy a human face;
Terror the human form divine,
And secrecy the human dress.

The human dress is forged iron,
The human form a fiery forge,
The human face a furnace seal'd,
The human heart its hungry gorge.

William Blake
Songs of Experience, 1794

ცშ

Chapter One
Desolation and Curiosity

The chilly autumn morning was frosty, still and quiet.

Inside the house, the atmosphere was frigid and motionless, everyday life repressed into a state of hibernation and enforced inactivity.

Years later, when nine year-old Violet Grey was an adult, the day would often spring to the forefront of her childhood memories, dark and mysterious with ominous overtones, even though very few words were spoken. It was the type of day that was littered with innuendo, flickering glances and faraway, distant daydreams reflected in bright, watery eyes.

No one had uttered a word since Uncle Tom had shuffled out of the front door, shutting it behind him almost silently, and the sounds created by her aunt going about her daily housework routine boomed inside Violet's head until she thought her ears would burst if she didn't say something.

'Auntie Liz.'

It was a few seconds before her aunt answered, in a

tone of voice that reminded Violet of the way her Headmaster said *Amen* at the end of the Lord's Prayer in assembly each day at school.

'Yes?'

'Did you know that William Blake wrote the poem *The Tiger*?'

Again, her Auntie Liz paused before answering. 'Yes, I did.'

'Have you ever read it? We are learning it off by heart at school.'

Violet bent her head over her exercise book, and audibly scratched a few more words on the first page with the sharp pencil Uncle Tom had given her when he had told to be a good girl while he just popped out on an errand. He had rubbed at his forehead, as if it was hurting him, and pulled on his flat cap so tightly it almost covered his eyes. Silently, he had stepped in front of the mirror in the living room, lifted the peak of his cap and studied his reflection for a long time, before shaking his head slowly from side to side. Then, hunched over, with his chin almost touching his chest he had crept out of the house without even a backward glance, a *"goodbye"* or saying what time he would be back. Auntie Liz had not looked up at him, pretending to clean the kitchen sink.

Violet put down her pencil, swung her legs around and twisted her torso so that her chin was resting on the wooden chair back. She moved her jaw from side to side grinding her teeth as she watched her Auntie Liz, who was still wiping around the kitchen sink with a dishcloth, scrubbing hard at imaginary stains, even though about fifteen minutes had passed since Uncle Tom had left.

Liz Jeffson stiffened, grimacing at the irritating sound of Violet grinding her teeth.

'Don't do that, Violet – you'll ruin your teeth,' she said, drying her hands on a tea cloth before turning around.

Violet sat up. 'My teacher says that some people thought William Blake was mad. Did you know that, Auntie Liz? Isn't it scary that some people can be walking around, looking quite normal, but really they are as mad as a hatter?'

Violet wasn't supposed to know her Uncle Tom was mad, but one of her favourite pastimes when she wasn't reading stories or writing about people was listening to grown-up conversations, followed by peeping through keyholes as a close second. There had been lots of interesting things happening in her family recently and plenty of opportunities to eavesdrop.

'Can I see what you've been writing?' Liz said, looking away as she hung the tea cloth on the oven door and shut it with a heavy clunk. With a deep sigh, she picked up Violet's exercise book, closing her eyes momentarily.

Violet's handwriting was unusual in that it didn't follow the copperplate script style that had been taught to her in school. The pressure of the pencil varied on the page, and her strokes were embellished with artistic flourishes and serifs. She was always getting into trouble for her untidy handwriting, but she didn't care. She wanted to be different. Most little girls were shy about their writing, but Violet wasn't. She knew she was good. She knew she could spell and use long words way beyond her years. She waited for the usual compliment from her aunt about her poetry, but instead there was a fragile silence that hissed in her ears like heavy rain on a windowpane. She began to grind her teeth on the chair again, watching her aunt's eyes, trembling hands and troubled expression as she read her poem.

'Do you like it, Auntie Liz?'

Liz's glance shifted slightly and she stared at her over the top of the exercise book, but her dark eyes betrayed a bewildered reticence and Violet felt a sudden rush of awareness of the supreme power of words. She shouldn't have made the comment about people being mad, not with all the whispers she had heard about Uncle Tom recently.

Liz shielded her eyes with her hand, slumping forwards as if an unseen, heavy hand had pushed down on the back of her head. The pages of the open notebook fluttered like a bird and Violet shivered. Was it her poem that was upsetting her aunt? Or could it be something to do with the reason she had been dispatched across the road to Uncle Tom's house while something that she shouldn't know about was happening in her house?

'It's not really about having your eyes eaten away until there are just holes in your head,' Violet said, her voice sounding much too loud as she tried to explain her work. 'It's about being frightened and not being able to see into the future.'

'It's a bit morbid,' Liz commented. 'Depressing, even.'

Violet's discomfort grew and she fidgeted in her seat. Her Auntie Liz looked up, and she noticed her eyes were glistening with tears as she stared through the open door into the living room, a strange faraway look in her eyes. Violet turned her head to see what her aunt was looking at. It seemed to be a framed wedding photograph that sat in the centre of a collection of photographs on the sideboard.

The silence became so heavy it was crushing her ears into the side of her head, and Violet felt an urgent need to fill it with words to ease the pressure.

'It's only a metaphor, Auntie Liz.' She stood up and pointed at the words.

'See ... it's not real. It's just a comparison.'

Liz shook her head. 'Why have you written about ants eating away someone's eyes, Violet?'

Violet wiped her mouth on the back of her hand. 'Just because it came into my head to write it,' she said shrugging her shoulders.

Violet sat down again, placed her elbows on the table and cupped her chin in her palms. It was a bad idea to be writing about ants when her Uncle Tom had suffered such an unfortunate accident involving swallowing some ant paste, which was another thing she shouldn't know about.

'I want to know why you wrote this. Is there a reason?' Liz asked, her voice beginning to tremble as if synchronised with her hands. 'Has anyone said anything to you?'

Violet tried to pin an innocent look on her face. 'No ... I just thought of it.'

Her Auntie Liz looked up from the book and began to stare at the photograph on the sideboard again. She wiped each eye in turn with her forefinger and sniffed before fishing a handkerchief from her apron pocket.

'I should get on with the dinner – your Uncle Tom will be back soon.' she said before blowing her nose.

Violet gulped, feeling slightly sick. Something very

important and grown-up was going on. Something that Auntie Liz was worried and nervous about. Something to do with Uncle Tom and his little errand.

Earlier that day, Violet's mother had planned to go to the butchers to buy the Sunday joint of beef, taking Violet with her. Her sister, Liz, had called round unexpectedly to say she would look after Violet so she needn't go outside in the cold air on account of having been away from school with a sore throat.

Now, with Violet out of the way and her husband, Walter, at work, Doris Grey was alone in the house, waiting for her brother-in-law to arrive with a shopping list from Liz. Unable to settle, she paced from room to room, peering frequently out of the front room window, hardly able to believe the unexpected turn of events which would give her some time alone with Tom.

Doris squinted at her reflection in the mirror, licked her forefinger and ran it lightly over her eyebrows. It would make a nice change to be able to spend some time with her lover in a perfectly legitimate, unscheduled visit. She had missed him so much when he'd been ill in hospital, and although she had visited his bedside and had been a frequent visitor to her sister's house once he had been discharged, it seemed like months ago since they had spent some intimate time together. Some days, she wasn't sure if her heart was actually aching, starved of its regular injection of happiness, or heavy with worry for Tom's state of health.

Her eyes widened and her cheeks flushed slightly with

anticipation as the back door creaked open.

'Is that you, Tom?' she shouted from the hallway, where in a kaleidoscope of multi-coloured shafts of sunlight from the stained glass above the front door, she was fluffing up her hair in the mirror.

'Hello,' she called again, when there was no answer.

Frowning at her reflection, she opened the door to the living room and was startled to find Tom standing silently before her, his suit jacket hanging off his once robust frame. It was hard to believe that he could have lost so much weight in just a few weeks.

'Are you going out, or have you just come in?' Tom said, his gaze locked somewhere above the top of her head. 'I haven't got long.'

Doris patted her hair with a nervous hand, and her fine, fluffy blonde curls sparkled red and green in the sunlight. 'I'm going shopping in a while, but it doesn't matter – I can go later. Have you got Liz's shopping list?'

Tom nodded and handed it to her. 'What time will Walter be back?'

'About twelve thirty. He's ...'

'Right,' Tom interrupted in a business-like voice, turning his back on Doris as he stepped away from her. 'Violet's settled with Liz: she's writin' a story or summat.'

Doris felt a growing unease. She had expected to dissolve in Tom's strong arms and now he had turned away without even looking at her properly.

'It was good of Liz to offer to have her for me. She's not been well and it's too chilly to take her shopping with me.'

'She's perfectly happy over the road,' Tom said.

Doris stared at Tom's back, willing him to turn around.

'Perhaps she'll be a little bit better behaved with Liz. She's been dreadful this week: so disobedient. Oh, Tom, what I am going to do with her? She's so difficult and stubborn and asks too many questions. I'm living on my nerves because she's been poorly and not been to school. I just can't cope with her endless whining.'

Doris's head began to throb with overpowering inadequacy. Grimacing, she lightly massaged her temples with her fingertips. She wished her life could be different. Her disjointed and distant marriage to Walter Grey was a burden that squashed the life from her. She hated deceiving her sister, but her affair with Tom had been going on for so many years, it had become like an addiction she couldn't resist, no matter how strong her resolve. She knew Walter suspected she was having an affair, but he didn't seem to care that another man was stepping into their marriage and performing his marital duties for him, while he immersed himself in his own, secret world, able only to discuss banal topics in polite tones over the dinner table. In a state of permanent discontent, she wandered around a world colonised by shielded eyes of sordid secrets and tongues well-practised in the telling of lies. As a result she was a nervy, jumpy woman who never completely relaxed because her affair with her brother-in-law lurked in a brilliant luminosity around every dark corner of her life, whichever way she turned.

It was all she lived for.

Tom turned and gave a brief smile, taking her slender hands in his. 'I can't stay for long.'

Doris took a step closer to him, gazing up at him in a

rush of love, relieved that, at long last, he seemed to be recovering from his illness. Doris noticed straight away that his rough palms had softened with weeks of enforced bed rest. Usually his skin felt tough and leathery against hers, like the hides he handled in his job as manager of the clicking shop at Webb and Wilkinson's Boot and Shoe Makers. She had always loved the warm, masculine feel of his hands.

Tom led her back into the living room. He still hadn't looked at her properly.

'Sit down,' he said, gesturing towards an armchair. 'We've got to talk. Things have ... er ... changed a bit since ... since ...'

His voice faded away and he turned his back to her so that he was looking out of the window. He thrust his hands into his trouser pockets and jangled the loose change.

Doris's scalp prickled with a dark foreboding and she spoke quickly, nerves transforming her voice into a breathless witter.

'How are you? Are you feeling better now? It's a nice day today, if a little cold. Would you like to walk into town with me afterwards? It might do you good to have a gentle stroll outside.'

She glanced out of the window at the watery blue autumn sky, holding her breath, waiting for his reply. In the back garden a gnarled, ancient apple tree was giving up its dying leaves. With a peculiar feeling of imminent sadness, she watched a solitary leaf fall from a branch, which was now almost bare. While Tom's life was in the balance, it had felt as if part of her was also dying and withering as the hot summer sun evaporated into autumn. The loss of the leaf grew to a disproportionate size inside her, and the blood flowing through her veins became as cold and frozen as the approaching winter, with no prospect of an early spring to burst through grey clouds of trepidation that were gathering within her.

She shivered, suddenly cold. Why didn't Tom turn around to look at her? Was he, too, looking at the tree, watching the leaf fall to the ground? He was wasting precious time, just standing looking out of the window. She wasn't used to looking at the back of his head; instead she yearned to be staring up into his eyes and to feel the security of the weight of him on her.

He didn't answer her questions. The metallic sound of coins in his pocket fused with unspoken words that hung like dark confetti, suspended alongside sparkling dust motes in the air. Whatever Tom had come to talk to her about was obviously very important, because usually they wouldn't be wasting precious time by talking.

'Don't you want to go upstairs?' Doris said in an attempt to smooth away the awkwardness, knowing that her request was pathetic, weak and devoid of even a thread of self-respect.

Tom coughed, his chest bubbly with the aftermath of pneumonia he had suffered. His loose jacket swayed on his fragile body. Doris shut her eyes and bit her lower lip as, again, he didn't answer or turn around to face her.

'Tom?'

He bowed his head and shook it slowly, but didn't speak.

'Shall I put the kettle on, then?'

10

'Aye,' Tom eventually said, filling the silence with a grave resonance. 'I think that might be a good idea.'

'Do you want a tot of scotch in your tea?'

'No, I can't. The doctor says I have to give up the drink completely. Doris my sweet, we have to talk, because there are other things I have to give up too.'

'Oh, what's that?'

Doris edged past Tom into the kitchen without touching him. She knew what was coming. She knew Tom was going to pluck the confetti of unspoken words out of the air and end their affair.

The wireless in the corner of the living room burst into life, making Liz jump and almost drop the wedding photograph of herself and Tom she had been clutching to her chest.

'Can I listen to some music?' Violet said, having turned the knob to switch on the wireless before waiting for permission. She had needed to take urgent action to stop her Auntie Liz from bursting into tears. It would be just too embarrassing for words if that happened.

'If you like. But not too loud.'

It being a Saturday, the voice of a racing commentator discussing the afternoon's races, riders and form filled the living room. Violet was disappointed there was no music, but relieved to see her aunt replace the wedding photograph on the sideboard.

Liz sank down into an armchair, grinding the heels of her hands into her eyes, her head bowed, muttering something about the horse racing on the wireless.

'Violet, can you go into the front room for a while? I

have a headache ... I don't feel well ...'

'Why?'

'Just do as I say ... please. And switch that blasted wireless off.'

Violet switched off the wireless set before sliding around the door into the hallway. Auntie Liz was upset by the horse racing: that was obvious. She was upset about Uncle Tom: that was certain. Uncle Tom must be over the road at her house with her mam: that was a fact.

She sat down on the piano stool in the front room, uncertain as to what to do. Should she obey her aunt's instructions and stay in the front room? Or should she go back into the living room and put her arms around Auntie Liz and try to comfort her? With a sigh, she stood up again, lifted the lid on the piano stool and withdrew some sheets of music. It was probably best to stay out of the way and pretend she hadn't noticed that her aunt was crying.

After a few minutes of sitting in silence, she stood up and tiptoed out of the door to peer through the crack in the living room door. Her Auntie Liz's face was contorted, her nose red and bulbous as she dabbed at it with her handkerchief and she rocked backwards and forward in her chair, her cheeks glistening with moisture.

'Auntie Liz?' she whispered, pushing the door open a little wider. 'What's the matter?'

'Nothing, Violet. I'm just not feeling well.'

'Is it me? Is it my poem?'

'No, it's not you, Violet.'

'Oh. Is it Uncle Tom, then?'

Liz didn't answer. She dabbed at her cheeks with her

12

handkerchief.

'Is it because he's been poorly?'

When Liz looked up at her, something about the look told her to keep her distance and not step into the room.

'Your Uncle Tom's more ill than people think. Violet. I don't know if he can ever be cured. And God help us all if he can't.'

Violet stood still in the doorway, while her Auntie Liz maintained her strange stare. It was the same look that teachers at school gave her when she had been sent out of the classroom for being spiteful to one of the other children in the class. It was the same look her mother gave her when she was accusing her of *"being difficult and asking too many questions"*. But just why she deserved it at that precise moment, when all she was doing was trying to be nice to Auntie Liz, was completely beyond her comprehension.

'Please, Tom. Just one last time ... please?'

Doris's face was flushed as she lost her grip on the frayed edge of self-respect and flung herself into his arms. Her eyes shone bright with relief as his arms encircled her shoulders and she buried her head into his chest. Now Tom had told her that he was to receive specialist treatment for his newly-diagnosed psychopathic condition, it would hopefully explain why he was acting in such an odd manner.

'No, Doris. There can be no last time,' Tom whispered as he gently took hold of her by the shoulders and pushed her away from him. 'If I am to have any chance of putting things right with Liz, we have to stop this ... right now.'

'But Tom, who would know? We can't just stop, not after all these years. Please?'

Tom gave a slow shake of his head. 'I have to mend my marriage, Doris. I want to put things right. It's the only way.'

Doris ran trembling fingers through her hair and tried to pin a seductive smile on her face. Why couldn't they just carry on as normal? After all, no one was getting hurt by their arrangement. No one knew. They had been impeccably discreet. She couldn't lose him now, not after all this time, but the solemn vow to try and mend his broken marriage to her sister was cutting so deep into her heart, she felt fatally wounded.

She began to cry.

Tom patted the air in front of him, as if trying to damp down his confusion.

'Look. I do love you Dolly. You know that. I always will. And if things had been different, it wouldn't have come to this.'

Doris bowed her head and covered her nose with a lacy-edged handkerchief. Her eyes screwed themselves shut as she attempted to stop the tears flowing. He had never once been hurtful towards her in all the years of their affair, even though she knew her sister had suffered terribly because Tom didn't love her. Liz annoyed him in so many ways: they argued frequently and Tom would become frustrated and lose his temper, but in contrast he had always treated her gently and their love-making had been passionate and fulfilling.

Did that not prove he loved her more than he loved his

wife?

'Couldn't we just carry on, Tom,' she pleaded. 'No one has ever discovered our arrangement. We've been so careful. You'll need to relieve your tensions while you are recovering from your illness, and I've missed you so much. Please, Tom. Don't leave me in the lurch. Please? I'm begging you – don't just abandon me when we have meant so much to each other.'

She sobbed, covering her eyes with her hand. 'Oh, God, I just can't bear it!'

Her eyes shut, she waited for Tom's arms to encircle her again as a sudden realisation hit her with the force of a steam train. At least while she was still seeing Tom, there was a chance she might become pregnant again. She shuddered with revulsion at the thought of Walter touching her. Dark and repulsive, his secret life cast a permanent black shadow over their marriage. There was no way she could even consider a physical relationship with him, yet she craved constantly for another child to love.

Violet didn't love her. Violet had never loved her. Violet didn't love anyone. If she wasn't seeing Tom regularly to keep the dream alive, she would just have to find someone else to have an affair with. Another man to give her the baby she craved as a consolation prize for having such a difficult and unloving daughter.

Tom cleared his throat. 'Actually, Doris, I know this is going to come as a shock, but you need to know that Liz knows about our ... er ... arrangement. That's why I'm here. She made me come.'

Doris opened her eyes and took a startled step

backwards. Her knees buckled and she fell back into an armchair.

'She knows? Oh hells bells! How?'

'She's known since the end of June, apparently, but didn't confront me with it until ... er ... just before I ...'

'Was that why you got so drunk that day? Was that why you stole all that money, backed it on a useless horse and then ate all that ant paste poison to do away with yourself? I just can't believe this, Tom. So it was really Liz's fault you ...'

Tom interrupted with a wail of anguish and a hopeless shrug of his shoulders. 'She's made me promise, Dolly. She told me I had to come over here this morning and finish my affair with you, or else she is leaving me for good. I can't be on my own, Dolly. I'm not a well man.'

'How did she find out? We've been so careful. I can't believe she's known since the summer. She's never said anything to me.'

'I let it slip to my brother, apparently, when I was drunk. Liz overheard me. She didn't say anything at the time, but she was sly and sneaky and just bided her time, Dolly, until she knew for certain.'

Doris clamped her hands over her face. 'What shall I do, Tom?' she wailed. 'How on earth am I going to face her? What shall I say to her?'

'You don't need to say anything. Liz doesn't want to speak to you ever again. After today, she doesn't want to have anything to do with you.'

'But she's my sister! She can't do that. What will folks think?'

Doris's voice was thick and nasal as helpless tears filled

16

her nose. She sniffed and looked up at him. She had almost lost him forever five weeks ago. She had prayed so hard for his recovery as he lay, gravely ill from the effects of an attempt to take his own life. It had been agony not to go to him when he had needed her. She had been stunned by his wife and daughters' cold attitude towards him, though. None of them had shown even an ounce of compassion for the despair he must have felt to have driven him to such a dreadful act. She supposed she could understand his daughter, Rose, to some degree: after all, Tom had betrayed her in the worst way possible by stealing her money, but even Liz had turned her back on him, strutting off to assist as his youngest daughter, Daisy, gave birth instead of sitting by his bedside at Kettering General Hospital where he'd lay unconscious for days, balanced precariously on the brink of death. She'd never forgive her sister for running away from her wifely responsibilities and publicly declaring that she didn't care whether Tom had lived or died.

Doris flinched as Tom spoke in a voice gravelly with emotion. 'I have to start to put things right. You don't understand, Dolly, it's the only way. My psychiatrist says so.'

'You've been for your first appointment already? And you've told him about us?'

'I went yesterday. And it's a *her* not a *him.* Of course I told her about us. I'm not paying out a bloody fortune in fees to tell half-truths. I didn't say you were my sister-in-law, though, so you needn't worry. She says our affair is part of my illness.'

Doris gave a high, brittle laugh. 'What? Loving me for

17

all these years has made you ill? Come off it Tom, that's ridiculous – it's the only thing that's kept you sane. Liz has put you through hell over the years.'

Tom gave a cynical chuckle and looked up at the ceiling. 'Sane? I'm not sane. I'm a basket case ... round the bend ... doolally.' He pointed a forefinger at his temple, circling it around and around. His voice cracked and broke. 'It's not my fault. I can't help myself. I supposedly have some sort of psychopathic disorder that makes it difficult for me to control my behaviour. I have no conscience, and so you are part of my illness. It's Liz who I really love. I know that now.'

'You just said you loved *me*.'

Tom's eyes rolled upwards, bright with tears of confusion. 'I don't know. I'm all confused. I can't think straight.'

'You did love me, though. I know you did.'

Tom shrugged and covered his face with his hands. 'I don't know,' he repeated. 'I don't know about anything anymore.'

Doris's desolation turned to anger. 'So, we have meant nothing? You don't love me at all? You've never loved me?'

'No,' Tom said a little too quickly. 'Well yes ... I said I did, didn't I? Just now? But I want my family back. I want to be cured now I have two baby granddaughters to consider. If Liz chucks me out, I'll never see them. Gawd knows why, but Liz is giving me another chance. I know I don't deserve it, but I want to feel at peace with myself and live a good, decent life now I've been given a second chance. She'll go, Dolly. She'll leave me for good if we don't stop seeing each other. Just think of the scandal.'

18

Doris's voice rose, tears bubbling out of her nose and mouth. Her thin hand trembled as she swiped the handkerchief across her nose.

'It's just words to you, Tom, isn't it? Loving someone is just words.'

Tom turned his back on her and didn't answer.

'Will you look at me? You at least owe me that Tom Jeffson. You've used my body for years – at least turn around and look me in the eye. Leave her, Tom. Leave them all. They don't deserve you. I'll tell Walter to sling his hook, and we can make a fresh start together. You, me and our Violet. We can move away from here ... go to another town ... start a new life. We don't have to rush into anything. We can take some time to make plans. None of them care about you, Tom. You must surely see that. Liz only wants to mend your marriage because she wants to avoid more scandal. We could be so happy together. Please? Just think about it and don't be so hasty.'

Tom turned around slowly. 'I love her, Dolly. And I love my family – it's as simple as that.'

Doris retaliated, sneering as she dropped her eyes from his piercing gaze. 'Well, Liz doesn't love you. She HATES you. She's always hated you. She told me so with her own lips. What about when she hit you over the head with the candlestick and almost killed you? You don't do that to someone you love.'

Tom's face turned a blotchy red, and he thrust his hands into his trouser pockets again, furiously jangling the loose change. 'Shut your bloody mouth, woman. Don't you dare talk about that.'

'No. I won't keep quiet about it any longer, Tom. You

have obviously forgotten how she made up that story about you molesting your Daisy?'

Doris sniffed as she wiped her nose and eyes again. 'How can a woman who loves you make up something as dreadful as that about her own husband? She tried to make out you were some sort of pervert ...'

Tom's voice rose with terrified panic. 'Doris, stop it. Please?'

'No. I won't. That was a terrible lie to make up about your husband.'

Tom stepped forwards, pulling one hand out of his trouser pocket and clenching it into a fist. 'Please stop talking about it. What are you trying to do to me, Dolly? You know I can't bear to even think about that awful time.'

Doris shrank back against the wall as the short-lived bubble of anger popped and dissipated into the air. Her eyes widened and she took a sharp intake of breath at the sight of his balled fist and the angry expression on his face. The man who stood before her wasn't her Tom. This was the Tom who lived over the road with her sister in a loveless marriage, not the Tom who whispered words of endearment in her ear and ran his fingers lightly over her body, telling her over and over again how much he loved her, how incredibly beautiful she was and how she was the only woman for him.

This wasn't the kind, gentle man who had fathered her only child.

Chapter Two
Forgiveness and Despair

The clock on the living room wall ticked too loudly.

Liz sat in silence, watching the pendulum swing back and forth, almost hypnotised as she waited for Tom to return. After a few minutes, the movement of the clock calmed her and the monotonous sound faded into the background as she regained her composure. Domestic normality resumed, she shut her eyes in relief.

She hadn't meant to cry in front of Violet, but when her niece had turned on the wireless set and the voice of the racing commentator had filled the room, she hadn't been able to hold back the tears as the memory of the dreadful day Tom, in a drunken act of pure stupidity, had gambled every single penny of their daughter's savings and lost the lot.

Liz shuddered. It had been the worst summer of her entire life.

Violet's voice brought Liz out of her daydream. 'When can I go and see Daisy in her new house, Auntie Liz?'

'I ... I don't know. She only moved in a couple of weeks ago, so you'd better leave it for a while until she settles in.'

'Why doesn't she come home anymore? Did Uncle Tom

21

chuck her out because she was in the family way?'

'Who told you that?'

'Dad.'

Liz's eyes narrowed and she flinched. It wasn't appropriate for a child to know such things – she'd have to have words with her brother-in-law, Walter. Not that he would listen. Violet's father was a strange man: he never said two words when one would suffice.

That morning, Rose had taken flowers for Daisy and gone to visit her in her new Council house in a gesture of reconciliation. Tom's actions over the past year had stretched the sisterly bond between her daughters to breaking point and the tenuous connection remained weak. Liz gulped in a futile attempt to swallow the hard lump that had manifested itself behind her breastbone. Tom had hurt Rose even more than he had hurt Daisy, and the terrible things he had done to them both had damaged their relationship with each other, something Liz could hardly bear to endure. Dare she allow herself to hope that the red roses Rose had chosen to give to her sister would work their magic and her daughters would make up their differences?

At least Rose and Daisy had each other, she thought to herself, hoping they would allow her to be small part of their lives even if they wouldn't have anything to do with their father.

Liz continued to stare at the pendulum. Was it possible to feel worse than at this moment? Was this the beginning of an uphill struggle to save her marriage, or was it the end of it? Would Tom do as he had promised and end his dirty little affair with her sister, and even if he did, how

22

would she know if he was being truthful? Trust was a funny thing – it took lots of time to build up, but only a few seconds to tear down and shatter so completely, it was almost impossible to rebuild.

If Tom kept his word and ended his affair, the chasm of a future spent alone with him stretched endlessly before her. Although he had vowed to give up drinking, Liz doubted he could. He had tried several times before and had always failed. There was one thing he absolutely must give up, though. If he didn't stop tomcatting with her own sister, she was leaving him for good. She had made it perfectly clear to Tom that morning: today was his last chance and that she was walking away from their marriage if he didn't break off his affair with Doris. She was well organised: she'd even packed a suitcase in readiness and showed it to him before stowing it away beneath the bed. She'd prepared herself mentally, too. She was ready to face the deprecating stares, tutting tongues and gossiping behind her back. She would do it, and she would do it that very day if Tom didn't keep his promise. She'd get on the bus to a nearby village and turn up on her sister-in-law's doorstep, asking if they could put her up for a few days until she found somewhere to stay. Then, once Rose and her husband, George, had found a home of their own to rent, she would go to live with them, making herself useful by looking after her baby granddaughter while Rose went back to work. Tom would be all alone, and it would serve him right, illness or no illness.

Unable to bear the tense atmosphere in the living room, Liz tore her eyes away from the hypnotic pendulum and returned to the kitchen, trembling as she withdrew dinner plates from the kitchen cabinet. Up until five weeks ago, she had always loved Tom in a peculiar, slightly masochistic way, despite the dark side to his personality. She had always forgiven him and made endless allowances for his dreadful behaviour. Now, the tiny flame of affinity that had persisted and endured throughout the years had been extinguished in her heart by all the tears she had shed recently. She doubted she could ever love him again. She tried to stop herself thinking that it would have been better if Tom had died when he'd tried to take his own life. Tears of guilty despair prickled at the back of her nose. She was a wicked woman to agree with the whispers in her own head and wish her husband dead, but it felt as if everything in her life had been squeezed by a giant hand, compressed into a hard rock of inert substance where her living, beating heart had once been.

Had she done the right thing in giving him a last chance? Was it one last chance too many?

Liz bit her lip hard as her conscience whispered to her. She knew she wouldn't break her marriage vows unless she was pushed to the very limit of her sanity. *For better, or worse. For richer, for poorer. In sickness and in health.* It was her wifely duty to stand by her husband in his time of sickness. She needed to be strong: she had to take charge of his life and make sure he kept his promises to her and his appointments at the psychiatric clinic. He had been diagnosed with a chilling illness and she needed to look after him. It was their only chance. Their last chance. If either of them failed, it would have to be the end, or else she would surely lose her sanity.

24

With a deep sigh she pressed the heels of her hands over her eyes. Once he'd ended his affair with Doris, she would just have to come to terms with everything and try to put it all behind her. Silently, she cursed her marriage vows. She would never have married Tom if she'd known how quickly, and with no conscience whatsoever, he would break every single one of them, tossing them aside like discarded stones in his vegetable patch. In the thirty years of their marriage, she had kept every, single vow and Tom had broken them all.

There were two ways Violet knew when her Uncle Tom was secretly visiting her mother. The first way was when her mother changed the sheets on her bed when it wasn't a Monday, and the second way was when she pulled the curtains in the front room right back, instead of level with the stone mullions of the bay window.

Violet always knew that after the changing of the sheets or the pulling back of the curtains, her mother would proclaim she had an urgent errand that afternoon, and she would be met from school by her mother's best friend, Peggy. She would then have to endure two hours of boring snakes and ladders or Ludo with her spiteful son, Eddie, who smelled of boys and didn't wash his hands when he came in from the lavatory in the yard. At tea time, Eddie's big sister Kathy would walk her home, and when she opened the back door there would be a faint, familiar smell of pipe tobacco and her mam would be singing softly as she made tea for her dad who would not yet be home from work. There would be money on the mantelpiece for her –

sometimes as much as half-a-crown.

When she was very small, her mother used to take her to Wicksteed Park on a Saturday or a Sunday and they would accidentally bump into Uncle Tom. The three of them would sit, hidden away from prying eyes in the rose garden, and she would play while her mother laughed her funny, high laugh and her Uncle Tom smiled his slobbery, wet smile, and they weren't laughing at her, or with her, and she might not really have been there but for the big ice cream she was always given at such times to keep her quiet. Then they would sit very close together on the green park bench, their legs touching as her Uncle Tom lay one hand on her mam's thigh while they shared whispered conversations she couldn't hear. The accidental meetings in the park had stopped a couple of years ago, though. Soon afterwards, she began to realise that perhaps it wasn't the usual thing for someone's Uncle Tom to visit their mother quite so much when their dad wasn't there, and for the visits to be accompanied by changing of bed sheets and pulling back of curtains to a place they didn't belong and for a little girl to have to play with her dolls' house in the front room and be good while her mother and Uncle Tom went upstairs. On such occasions, when they came downstairs again, Uncle Tom would wink at her and give her half-a-crown 'sweet money'.

The half-a-crowns had stopped, too, a few weeks ago when Uncle Tom had been taken to the hospital and nearly died. It had never actually been said that the money was dependent on her silence about Uncle Tom's secret visits, but Violet had always known that the money was compensation for keeping the heavy burden of secrets and lies she carried on her young shoulders.

Without knowing exactly why she felt compelled to save it, Violet instinctively knew that the secret-keeping money would be needed, one day, for something far more significant than sickly treats or childhood fripperies. The money would, at some time in the future, be her saviour.

As Violet sat at the piano in the front room of her Auntie Liz and Uncle Tom's house practising her scales, she kept glancing out of the window. She hoped her mother would come for her before Rose came back home. She wrinkled her nose at the thought.

She didn't like Rose.

The front room door creaked open.

'Did you get bored with the wireless?' Liz asked.

Relieved her aunt had stopped crying and seemed to have recovered, Violet answered. 'There was nothing on. And you told me to switch it off. Remember?'

'Do you want me to sit with you while you play?'

Violet leaned forward and pretended to study her music sheet. 'No, thank you,' she replied. 'I'm just practising while I wait for Mummy to come back from shopping.' She bit her top lip and frowned, sensing her aunt's eyes boring into the back of her head.

'Did you know that flats and sharps that occur outside the key are called accidentals, Auntie Liz?'

Violet waited for a reply but didn't expect one.

Liz glanced at the clock on the mantelpiece. 'I shouldn't think your mother will be much longer. It's nearly dinner time. Rose and George will be back soon. Perhaps baby Margaret will be awake and you can play with her for a little while if you like.'

Violet grimaced. Although she hated Rose, her grown-up cousin, she liked her other cousin, Daisy who was not quite so grown-up, even though she had just had a baby herself. *"In the family way"* they'd said. *"Been knocked up"* and *"got caught out"*. She'd used those words in a poem, but she'd not shown it to anyone yet. Up until Uncle Tom had chucked her out of the house because *"she'd got herself up the way and brought shame on him",* Daisy had always made time for her, and smiled at her or given her a hug, but since Daisy had gone away there were no more hugs and certainly no more happy faces.

Rose never looked at her properly when she spoke to her. She always looked away, or pretended to adjust the buttons on her cardigan. Mostly, Rose just ignored her as if she wasn't there. It was really hurtful, because Rose was always so nice to everyone else. Somehow, she knew that the pulling back of the curtains, and the changing of the sheets and the trips with Uncle Tom and her mam to Wicksteed Park on the edge of the town when she was a little girl were all tangled up with Rose not liking her. Violet fought back the urge to cry as she carried on practising her scales. She pressed her lips together tightly and blinked back tears. She never cried: even though she was only nine years-old and should be allowed to cry about not being loved by anyone.

'Do you want anything? Are you warm enough in here?' Liz asked.

Violet didn't answer the question. She knew that her Auntie was thinking that it was about time her mother came back from shopping and collected her.

'Auntie Liz. Were you upset just now because of Uncle

28

Tom? And what is the matter with Rose?'

Violet spun round on the shiny leather-topped piano stool to face Liz, who stood motionless with one hand on the door knob.

Liz's eyes slid away from meeting her niece's gaze. She let go of the doorknob and looked at her feet. 'Rose is upset because your Uncle Tom has been very poorly and nearly died, just like we all are, Violet. It's been a very worrying time.'

Violet studied her aunt's face with a furrowed brow and narrowed eyes. She meant to get to the bottom of the secret no one was talking about.

'Rose found Uncle Tom on the floor in his allotment shed, didn't she? What happened to him? Why did the ambulance get called out? Why did he have to stay in the hospital?'

Liz changed the difficult subject and bustled over to the polished mahogany writing bureau next to the mantelpiece. She took out a box of matches, but her hands shook as she fumbled to open the box.

'If you're going to stay in here, I think I'll light the fire ...'

'Daddy said Uncle Tom tried to ...'

'Oh dear! Look at the time!' Liz interrupted. 'I'd better put the potatoes on for dinner. Your Uncle Tom will be home soon. I do hope he's all right. It's only the second time he's been out on his own since his illness.'

'... top himself,' Violet finished. 'And I don't know what it means. What does topping yourself mean?'

She watched as her Auntie Liz's eyes brightened again, and heard the slight catch in her throat as if she'd suddenly put her hand on something hot. She spun back round on the seat and placed her hands on the keyboard. She had tried to be nice to Auntie Liz, but Auntie Liz wasn't exactly being nice to her, so it didn't matter if she upset her again. Gritting her teeth in determination, she jabbed her index finger repeatedly on one white key, the single note clanging with the energy of pealing church bells.

'What does it mean to top yourself, Auntie Liz?'

Liz shielded her eyes with a trembling hand, shaking her head. 'Oh Violet,' she whispered. 'What on earth are we going to do with you? You're too young to know such things. Much too young.'

The gated entrance to the alleyway that led to the back door of Violet's house was just visible, on the opposite side of the road. The curtains in the front window hadn't been pulled back and the sheets on her parents' bed hadn't been changed that morning, so Violet knew that her mother wasn't expecting a visit from Uncle Tom.

Violet kept one eye on the street as she rippled her fingers over the piano keys, playing nothing in particular. She was bored waiting for her mother to come back from shopping, and Auntie Liz had gone back into the kitchen without explaining the meaning of *topping yourself*.

Violet turned her attention towards a music sheet and began to play a tune. After a few minutes she stood on tiptoe and looked out of the window over the top of the piano. She was astonished to see her mother walk past – obviously only just going out to the shops. She glanced at the clock on the mantelpiece; it was nearly mid-day. Shouldn't she be coming back from the town now, not just going out? As her mother drew level with the window on the opposite side of the road, her head was down and she had a handkerchief in her hand, covering her nose as she walked along. Another movement made her cast her glance further up the street. The gate had opened again, and her Uncle Tom poked his head out, looking this way and that before he slid around the gate, shut it, and strode off in the opposite direction.

Violet absent-mindedly twizzled one of her blonde plaits around her forefinger.

About three or four minutes later Tom appeared in front of the window. He'd obviously just strolled around the block and was pretending to the neighbours to have just come back from a walk. Violet watched as he stepped off the pavement to cross the road. Why did adults behave like little children? Did they really think no one was watching them act out their silly little secrets?

Tom shut the back door behind him.

'Well?' Liz said, her eyes blinking a little too frequently.

Tom sighed. 'It's done. I promised I'd finish it – now I have. Like I said afore, it didn't mean owt.'

'Jolly good. Sit down, then. The dinner won't be long,' Liz twittered in a strange, high voice. She didn't want to talk about her husband's affair with her younger sister ever again, although she had thought about little else all morning. It was over and done with now. She'd just have to sweep all his adulterous lies and deception under the carpet as if they had never happened and see how things went.

Liz busied herself while Tom sank down at the kitchen table and shook open the morning newspaper with a theatrical flourish. When Liz didn't look round, he shook it again.

Liz's voice was still high. 'Did you go to the bookies, too?'

'Yes,' Tom said, hesitating slightly before he spoke. 'I popped in before I went to see Doris. Just to say hello and get it over with – I didn't stay.'

'Oh dear, what did people say to you?'

'They were all right. Just asked me how I was feeling and then just ignored me mostly. I suppose they were too embarrassed after I lost all Rose's money. No one talked about it.'

Tom coughed, took out his handkerchief and spat into it. He wiped his mouth with his handkerchief and shoved it back into his trouser pocket. 'I just want to put all this trouble behind us now. Get back to normal, old gal, and start puttin' things right, eh?'

Liz didn't answer him. How on earth did he think they could just get back to normal with an exaggerated shake of a newspaper? Did he think he could just brush aside all the shattered dreams and remnants of broken hearts and everything would be just the same as before? Did he not care that he had lost them their daughters because of the terrible things he had done to them both?

'Have Rose and George been back yet?' Tom said.

'No.'

Liz picked up a fork and poked viciously at a saucepan

of boiling potatoes on the stove. A lock of lank hair fell across her eyes. She supposed she had always known that, one day, she would lose her love for Tom. Through all the dreadful rages, the slapped cheeks and even the extra-marital affairs with cheap, clown-faced women she had always been able to maintain the affinity she'd once had for the strange man who was her husband and father to her children. The flickering flame had gone out in her heart, and she had no idea if it could ever be rekindled. And it wasn't easy for a mother to forgive the father of her children for hurting them in such dreadful ways, but a wife just might be able to paint out the imagery of an extra-marital affair or two, even if it was of the worst sort imaginable – with her own sister.

Tom sighed, then gave a little cough.

'I don't know how many times I have to say I'm sorry, Liz. I really am truly sorry for the things I have done.'

Liz shrugged. She really didn't care how many times he said it. It wouldn't make any difference. Saying sorry a million times couldn't make the love come back.

The sound of multiple footsteps and Rose's voice silenced any further conversation between them. The back door opened with a creak.

George Foster walked backwards into the house, lifting the front of the big pram over the threshold while his wife, Rose, manipulated it into the kitchen. Tom stood up, folding his newspaper in half, and moved the tiny kitchen table so that it created a gap for the pram.

No one spoke, but the sound of Violet playing the piano in the front room and the bubbling saucepan on the stove were not enough to drown out the tense hum in the air.

The atmosphere snapped taut, before it cracked and showered Rose and George's sleeping baby daughter with the invisible fragments of her broken future.

Tom coughed again and walked through to the living room, mumbling an incoherent greeting to George, who returned a curt nod. Before he'd been ill, Tom would have filled the house with loud jokes, bawdy idle chat and exaggerated slaps of his son-in-law's shoulder, but now he just slid away, much too embarrassed to speak to his daughter and son-in-law who, because of him, now faced a black and grey future when it should have been ruby red and gold, stretching out before them.

Rose glanced at her mother who was bent over the kitchen sink, concentrating much too hard on straining the potatoes, her shoulders slumped with worry. For the first time in five weeks, a hint of optimism was evident in Rose's pale blue eyes. She took off her hat and unpinned her hair before unbuttoning her coat. George, always the perfect gentleman, took her hat, gently lifted the coat from her shoulders and, without saying a word walked through the living room to the hallway and hung them on a coat hook. Rose smoothed down her pleated skirt and adjusted her cardigan, buttoning it around her as if she was readying herself for a long, arduous walk. She reached over to the pram, lifted up the pink pram blanket and extracted an old, battered tobacco tin. Loose coins rattled slightly as she held it out to her mother.

'We don't need your money, Mam. You can have it back. We really appreciate your thoughtfulness, but ...'

Liz interrupted, picking up a tea cloth and drying her hands. The money she had given to Rose last week was all she had in the world. Rose would need every single penny if she was to rent a home of their own. Also, if Tom reneged on his promise to break off his affair with Doris, she would need somewhere to stay when she left him. Rose and George's future might be *her* future, too.

'Why?'

'Because we have decided we are not going to move out. We are going to stay here with you and Dad. It's all right, Mam. Don't worry anymore. We won't leave you all on your own with him.'

Liz shut her eyes as relief wrapped itself around her as completely as the warm blanket enveloping her baby granddaughter. She spoke in a whisper.

'You can still have it, Rose. I know it's not much, but it will be a start to replacing your savings.'

'No,' Rose mouthed, shaking her head as she stepped over to Liz and put head close to her mother's so she could hear her whispered reply. 'Daisy and I have decided to try and ... well, try to, anyhow ... for your sake. We both love you so much, Mam. We'll stick by you.'

Liz knew Rose couldn't bring herself to say the word *forgive*. She wasn't yet ready to say it; in fact she doubted Rose would ever entirely forgive her father for stealing their money, saved as a deposit for a home of their own. Rose placed the tin on the kitchen table and slid an arm around her shoulders. Liz began to tremble as she felt Rose's strength flood into her. Knowing that she was not going to be alone in the house with Tom felt if she had just stopped spinning and was now regaining her balance after five weeks of being in the middle of a hurricane.

Rose continued, still whispering so that her father

wouldn't hear the conversation. 'Daisy and Bill need the money more than we do. They've got nothing, Mam, not even a proper chair to sit on in the evenings. I know they've got a brand new council house, but it's not a home. It's just like she's camping out in some sort of prison. If you're going to give your bit of secret savings to one of us, then let it be Daisy and Bill, so they can get some proper furniture and a cooker, and some nice things for the baby.'

'Is ... is Daisy all right?' Liz asked, her voice returning to a normal level. She missed her youngest daughter so much it had turned into a physical ache in her heart. She had not seen her for almost a month now, ever since Daisy had vowed she wanted nothing more to do with her father and would never again set foot in his house.

Rose nodded. 'She's a bit down in the dumps, but she's coping with the baby and everything. She's so grown up, Mam. No one would ever believe she's only seventeen.'

'Oh Rose, I'm so relieved. I've been going mad with worry because the pair of you were off hooks with each other. I'm so glad you've made it up.'

'It was hard, Mam. I was so angry that Daisy was given a council house when we had lost everything. With no prospect of us having our own home now, unless we go into rooms or rent a hovel, you can understand why I was so flipping annoyed about it all.'

Liz sighed with relief. 'I'm so glad you're not going to move into one of those dreadful cottages by the gas works. They want pulling down ... no lavatories ... no proper kitchens. Perhaps you'll get a council house soon, like Daisy?'

Rose shook her head. 'No, we won't. When Dad threw

36

Daisy out, it meant they were given priority on the housing list. It won't be easy staying here with him, Mam. I can't pretend it will. I hate him – I just can't help myself. I can't even look at him. I can't imagine I shall ever forgive him for what he's done to us, but Daisy wants us both to try, for your sake. Goodness knows why, after what he did to her.'

'We all have to try,' Liz whispered, meaning every word, but wishing she could find just a scrap of love in her heart to give her hope. 'After all, he does have an illness, even though it's not physical.'

'We can't leave you alone with him, Mam. We just won't. There's no telling what he might do to you. This psychopathic disorder he's been diagnosed with is unpredictable. I know he's being treated, but that's no consolation for us if we abandon you by moving out and then something bad happens.'

Tom steadied himself with a trembling hand on the stair bannister and sank down onto the bottom step of the stairs. With Liz and Rose saying hurtful things about him in the kitchen, George puffing silently on his pipe in the living room and Violet tinkling away on the piano in the front room, there was nowhere for him to go but the hallway.

He bowed his head and covered his face with his hands, overwhelmed by his struggle with perpetual disappointment that he hadn't died in his allotment shed. While he was gravely ill, paralysed, with doctors shaking their heads in wonder at his survival, everyone said he should have died. He'd even heard one doctor say that he had never heard of anyone surviving the ingestion of so much ant paste. It was supposed to be lethal. The warning was written in big red letters on the tin. So why had he been spared? There were plenty of people more worthy than him of being saved – people who hadn't done such terrible things to their families.

It was such rotten luck that he had survived, but somehow, for the first time in his life, he was beginning to feel stirrings of remorse. Having walked to the cliff edge of his own life, and been pulled back by the scruff of his neck, the fear of continuing his miserable existence was still as great as it was when he plunged his fingers into the tin of ant paste poison and sucked on the foul-tasting substance, certain that welcome obliteration of his failed life would quickly follow. But now the fear of living had been partnered by remorse for his past wrongdoings, it just intensified his helplessness even more. He bowed his head into his knees. After a while he looked over his shoulder at the staircase rising above him. Was the first step of the stairs on which he sat symbolic in some way? Subconsciously, he pushed himself up until he was sitting on the second step, but his body still ached and his knees were weak. He grimaced with the pain, but it reminded him that physical discomfort was nothing compared to the obstacles he faced if he was to make it to the top, save his marriage and win back his wife and daughters.

He reached into his jacket pocket and took out his wallet. Carefully, he extracted a photograph from one of the compartments and studied it, running his thumb gently back and forth over the monochrome image. Taken when Violet was a toddler, his hand rested gently on the back of a chair, where Doris sat, smiling at the camera, with his secret daughter on her lap. It was the only photograph ever taken of the three of them. He took out another photograph, professionally taken when Daisy had been May Queen of Kettering in nineteen twenty-six, and felt queasy. Even if Rose and Daisy did eventually forgive him, no one in their right mind would ever again leave him alone with a child. He bowed his head in shame: the terrible thing he had done to Daisy when she was only twelve years-old would haunt him for the rest of his life. At the time, he had cursed Rose for telling Liz. Now, for the first time, he was thankful. If that first aberration hadn't been discovered and nipped in the bud, goodness knows what might have happened to Daisy.

His thoughts returned to Doris and he pursed his lips and blew with relief that the affair was finally over. He should never have allowed it to continue for so many years. He'd had no idea she had actually fallen in love with him.

'Did I *really* live?' he whispered to himself, fleetingly wondering if it was all just an illusion, and the reality was that he had died and was living in a hell every bit as painful as mankind feared, but without the burning flames. He pressed his hands together and locked his fingers under his chin, as if praying. He sensed the warmth of his body; his heart beating in his chest and his lungs, although damaged from pneumonia caused by inhaling his own vomit, still breathing in the air around him. His broken body, with every agonising breath, was being infused with the oxygen to survive and the opportunity to put things right in his life. He looked over his shoulder at the staircase again and pushed himself to his feet. He had overcome the first, huge obstacle by breaking off his affair with Doris. Surely that would make the next one a bit easier?

Silently, he opened the door to the front room where Violet was playing her piano. After overhearing whispered words of hatred in the kitchen, he was grateful for the obliterating sound of piano music. Violet stopped playing and twisted around on the stool, conscious of another person in the room.

'Hello, Uncle Tom.'

Tom forced himself to smile at her. 'Hello, Petal. I'm glad to see you're using your new piano.'

'I love it, Uncle Tom. I really like to play and can't wait to take my next exam. My piano teacher says she thinks I'll be a famous pianist when I'm older if I carry on practising hard.'

Tom pulled himself up with paternal pride. Little Violet was good at playing the piano, but the money-grabbing piano teacher certainly knew how to ensure that her small clients persuaded their families to carry on paying for lessons, which was something he wouldn't be able to continue with now he had to start to pay back Rose and George all the money he owed them.

'Are you feeling better now,' Violet asked politely.

Tom didn't answer, because at that moment the front room door squeaked open again. Rose and George stepped into the room and George shut the door behind him. He leaned back on the door and cleared his throat.

Anxious of what his son-in-law was about to say, Tom's

eyes darted around the room, looking for an escape route. His way out was blocked by George, so instead he bent down and picked up the brass poker and prodded at the glowing coals in the fireplace, wincing at the imminence of yet another awkward conversation.

George Foster wasn't a tall man. His stature was slight and his eyes were kind and benevolent. But his voice was deep, steady and resolute as he spoke. He placed a protective arm around Rose's shoulders.

'Tom. We'd like a word with you, please.'

'What?' Tom said with an uneasy glance at his daughter, who seemed to be inspecting her shoes and wouldn't look at him.

Rose's eyes flickered upwards briefly and then she glanced sideways at George, nudging him in the ribs to silence him before he could speak.

Her voice cut into Tom as painfully as if she had just taken a kitchen knife and plunged it into his heart. 'You know you said the other day that we could have this room and Daisy's old room if we stayed here with you and Mam, instead of renting the cottage by the gas works?'

'Aye ... that's right. I don't want you to go. You know that. I just want to make things right wi' yer both. I'll pay yer back, you know. Every last penny ...'

George cleared his throat again, but it was Rose who continued.

'If we can have this room as our own living room, and our Margaret can have a bedroom of her own, then we'll stay here until we can save up enough money to rent somewhere decent.'

'You didn't like the house by the gas works, then?' Tom

41

said unable to disguise a defensive hint of sarcasm in his voice. 'Decided that this old place ain't so bad, after all, have you?'

'Look, Tom,' George said. 'By rights we should have moved into our own house by now. If you hadn't lost our ... well ....' He glanced at Violet and modified his words. 'If all this business hadn't happened, we would be living in our own home in Exeter Street. You've offered us three rooms, sharing all the household expenses, and we have decided to take you up on your offer. It will be a business arrangement – more like sharing a house with you than living as a family.'

Tom bit his lip and flinched at the word *"family"*, the dreadful things he had done driving hard, painful spikes through his spine and limbs, riveting him to the floor.

He shuddered, cold, even though the warmth of the fire was burning his hand as he held the poker. It was good news that they were going to stay, but the terms of their staying would be difficult for him to accept if his goal was to get family life back to normal.

Violet stared from one grown-up to the other. Had they forgotten she was in the room? She sat on her hands, worried they would take on a life of their own and start playing the piano again when she really ought to be quiet and pretend she was invisible.

She frowned, puzzled by the conversation. This was *her* room. This was where *her* piano was. This was her most favourite place in the whole world. She scowled at Rose and fidgeted on the seat. With Rose and George using the

42

room as a sitting room, she wouldn't be able to practise. She wanted to speak, but the grown-ups had obviously not noticed she was there.

Violet had noticed Rose shut her eyes momentarily at the word *"lost"*. This was interesting – now she knew that her Uncle Tom had lost Rose and George's money, she'd also discovered where the money had come from when *"he'd bet a fortune on the gee-gees",* which was something she'd overheard a few weeks ago. This must be the reason he tried to *"top himself"*, whatever that meant.

More secrets.

'We still want to buy our own house,' Rose continued. 'We are going to save hard again, and eventually we will be moving out into a decent rented house while we do, but in the meantime we want this room for our own private living room. I want some proper armchairs ... and I want *that* monstrous thing out of the way.' She gestured towards the piano with a dismissive toss of her hand, ignoring Violet. 'I'm not having a piano in here, taking up valuable space. I want to keep the table and chairs, though, so that we can eat our meals on our own. We want some privacy so that we can live our own lives.'

'I'm sorry, Rose.' Tom interjected. 'I'd give anything to turn back the clock, you know I would. Just give me a chance to make amends. Please?'

Violet opened her mouth, indignant that her Uncle Tom was apologising to Rose. They should all be saying sorry to her for taking her room and wanting her piano gone. 'What will happen to my piano?' she said in a small voice.

No one replied.

'Privacy?' Tom said. 'Why? And why on earth would you

want to eat your meals in here when I'll be eating mine in the kitchen or living room with your mam? We *are* a family, after all. There's no escaping that fact.'

Rose sighed and looked up at the ceiling. 'See, George? I told you he wouldn't understand and would go back on his word.'

'I'm not going back on my word, it's just that ...'

Rose flashed a bitter look at her father. 'What?'

'Well. It just all seems pointless. Let's just get back to normal, you know, how we were before? We were happy enough then ...'

'Normal!' Rose shouted, interrupting him. 'Get back to normal? How can we ever do that after what you have done to us?'

George patted the air with both his hands, trying to damp down Rose's anger. 'Look, let's all calm down for a bit. Tom – we can't just go back to where we were before you ... er ... your illness, because what has happened has changed things. Just accept it, can't you? It's going to take time to mend things. Let's just take one step at a time, eh?'

'All right, all right!' Tom said, snapping in frustration. 'I'll dip into my savings for some armchairs for you, but I was going to have to use that money to pay for my psychiatric treatment. You can go out and buy two fireside chairs and another wireless set for in here, and I'll pay.'

'You don't need to use your savings, Dad,' Rose said. 'Anyway, you'll need every penny of your money, and probably more, to pay for your treatment. We can easily sell the piano to pay for the chairs.'

Violet felt her head snap back by some unseen force.

She pulled out one of her hands from beneath her bottom and flung it backwards, protectively sliding her fingers over the cool, white keys. She began to tremble. The piano was hers, bought by Uncle Tom at great expense for her birthday last year. The old piano had woodworm and couldn't be tuned properly, so he had bought a brand new shiny one, especially for her. It was her most treasured possession and made up for all the bad feelings about not being wanted or loved.

'Can't we just move it over to my house?' she said in a small voice. But, again, no one answered. 'It's mine ...' she added, a little louder, panicking.

'What a good idea,' Tom said. 'I hadn't thought of that.'

Violet's heart lifted somewhat at his words. But he was smiling at Rose and not looking at her. The good idea wasn't her idea about moving the piano over the road to her house, it was Rose's good idea about selling it to pay for some fireside chairs.

'I didn't think of selling the piano,' Tom said. 'I probably won't get back what I paid for it, but it'll be enough to buy some furniture.'

'But it's mine ...' Violet repeated, a little more loudly, her eyes filling with tears. 'It was a birthday present.'

Rose glanced around the room and absent-mindedly brushed a fleck of dust from the top of the writing bureau. 'I think we'll keep this, too.'

She nodded at the linoleum floor and worn rugs. 'I'd like some new, more modern, lino. And a brightly patterned rug ... and we'll get the room redecorated.'

'Rose. Please? The piano's mine – it was for my birthday. It was a present.' Violet's voice cracked and broke as she began to cry, but no one was watching or listening.

Tom walked over to the piano, but didn't acknowledge Violet, who shot him a beseeching look through her tears. He ran his hand over the polished mahogany top.

'Someone will get a bargain with this. It was brand new when I bought it.'

'Uncle Tom! You and Auntie Liz bought it for my birthday ... so it's mine!'

Violet brushed away her tears with a trembling hand as she realised she wasn't worth anything. No one cared about her. She had no value in the family and might as well be dead. She might not be able to cry because not one single person in the world loved her, but the thought of losing her most treasured possession was just too much to bear.

Chapter Three
Arrogance and Careless Talk

'I'm not a criminal, Doctor. 'Tom paused for a few seconds, aghast at his psychiatrist's comment. 'I'm a law-abiding, upstanding citizen of this town. I feel quite affronted by that remark.'

'Mr Jeffson, I'm not suggesting you are a criminal, far from it. I'm just saying that your condition makes it difficult for you to know when you are acting in an inappropriate way, and there's no escaping the fact that you stole your daughter's money to gamble on a horse, which is a criminal act.

Dr Ernestine Crabtree, Clinical Psychiatrist, reached up and adjusted her glasses so that she was looking straight at Tom over the top of the frames.

Tom sighed, bit his lip and stared back at her, his gaze unwavering. It was only his second appointment with his psychiatrist but he was beginning to wonder just how effective his expensive treatment would be. He was already finding it harder to resist the drink than he had ever imagined. His hands were in a constant state of tremor and the urge to drink alcohol pervaded his every waking moment. He was addicted to it. He knew that now, but he was also determined he wasn't going to renege on his deal

48

with Liz and his family. He was resolute in his promise to turn over a new leaf and become a new man, but all this psychoanalysis was painful and raised issues he had pushed to the back of his mind for years. Although he could see his behaviour and thoughts were not the same as other folks, he firmly believed he wasn't a criminal and he was going to make sure Dr Crabtree understood that.

'I'm in charge of the clicking shop at Webb and Wilkinson's Boot and Shoe Factory – I'm practically *management*. What I don't know about the boot and shoe trade isn't worth knowing. I'm not short of bob or two – well, I wasn't, until ... until.... And, after all, Dr Crabtree, I *am* a voluntary patient. If I was a criminal, I wouldn't want to get better, would I?'

'Mr Jeffson, from the tests we have carried out, you display no evidence of psychosis and suffer no delusions. I've already ascertained that your social values are not far off normal. But you must understand, Mr Jeffson, you *do* have a complex psychopathic disorder and from some of the things you have told me, and from some of the dreadful things you have done, including *stealing* your daughter's life savings, you do need to come to terms with this disorder and modify your behaviour somewhat. The medication will help calm you down, but you have to accept your condition, too, and try to keep it under control. I can help you do that, but it won't happen overnight. It's going to take time.'

'I'm not daft, you know. I'm quite a clever bloke ...'

'Yes, I've no doubt you are, Mr Jeffson,' Dr Crabtree interrupted. 'No doubt at all. Your condition doesn't have any impact on intelligence.'

Tom sighed again, defeated. 'We'd better get on with it then, Doctor.'

'Tell me about your daughters, Mr Jeffson – you have three, I believe?

'Well, strictly speaking, yes. But there's another daughter that no one knows about. My sister-in-law's girl, Violet.'

Dr Crabtree crossed off the number three on her notes, and substituted it with a number four. She leaned forwards. 'Tell me a little about each of them, and then tell me how you feel towards them. What are their names?'

Tom smiled politely, wringing his cap in his hands. 'Lily, Rose, Daisy and Violet.'

Dr Crabtree smiled back, trying to win Tom's confidence. 'What pretty names - all after flowers. I was named after my grandfather, and ended up an Ernestine. I've always hated it.'

Tom smiled politely again and nodded, feigning interest. 'Lily is my eldest daughter. She's married and I don't see her very much. In fact, Lily keeps away from me. She doesn't care for me and makes no secret of it. A cool customer is our Lily.'

Dr Crabtree crossed her legs under the desk and scratched the side of her nose before adjusting her glasses.

'Does she live in Kettering?'

Tom nodded.

'Do you visit her?'

'Sometimes, but I'm not welcome. She hates me. Said so with her own lips, she did, in nineteen twenty-six when our Daisy was May Queen and I ... I ...'

50

Tom cleared his throat and looked away, unable to bring himself to reveal to the psychiatrist the worst thing he had ever done in his life to one of his daughters. 'Let's just say there was a bit of trouble in the family. Lily rarely comes to our house. She's got her own life now. But the wife visits her and she sometimes sees her sisters and her mam when I'm at work. They go on shopping trips and do women's things together. She slipped through my fingers and went and got married when I was pre-occupied with other things, like our Arthur dying of the consumption.'

'Oh. I'm sorry, Mr. Jeffson, interrupted the doctor. 'I completely forgot you had a son.' Dr Crabtree flicked back a few pages in Tom's notes. 'Ah, yes. He died in nineteen twenty-two, didn't he?'

She wrote down *"one son"*.

'That's right. Our Arthur. Actually, I lost two sons in nineteen twenty-two. I tell you doctor, if ever there was a time I nearly ended up in the nuthouse, it was then.'

Dr Crabtree crossed off the number one on Tom's notes and substituted it with a number two. 'The other son – what was his name?'

'Frank. Frank Haywood. He wasn't the wife's. He was the result of a secret affair I had with an older woman when I was sixteen. I discovered, quite by chance, that he was working for me in the factory in nineteen twenty-one. I was thrilled to bits I'd found him again, but it was short lived because he died of the consumption, too. Both my sons died at about the same time.'

'Oh, I see,' Dr Crabtree said, scribbling on Tom's medical notes. 'Did your wife know about Frank?'

Tom grimaced. 'Good Lord, no, Doctor! She never

51

knew, and she can't ever find out. She'd be mortified. It was so hard to lose two sons in one year, and then to not be able to tell a living soul how I was grieving for my secret son, as well as our Arthur – it was absolutely bloody dreadful. Then, to top it all, Violet was born at Christmas that year. I felt like I had been put through Liz's mangle with losing two sons and gaining a daughter in weeks. No wonder I ended up with psychopathic disorder.'

Dr Crabtree wrote a lengthy sentence on Tom's notes. After a while she said: 'now, what about Rose? How do you feel about her?'

Tom scratched his head uneasily. 'Our Rose ain't a pretty gal, but she has a certain something. A refinement and air of composure about her. You won't see our Rose losing her temper, or raising her voice. She's like her mam. Usually keeps it all in here.' He thumped his chest over his heart. 'She's married to George and they've got a baby girl called Margaret. They live with us. She's a good gal, is Rose, but a little bit plain-looking. Unremarkable in every way. It was their money ... I ... er ... borrowed before I ...'

Tom flushed a deep red, his voice lowering to a whisper as he looked at his shoes in embarrassment. 'Before I tried to do myself in.'

Dr Crabtree didn't look up, but kept scribbling on Tom's notes. 'I should imagine she's quite upset now, though, because you *stole* her money.'

Tom's lips quivered. He began to jig his leg up and down as he fought to remain in control.

'And Daisy?'

Tom's face softened into an affectionate smile as he looked up again. 'My Daisy. Did you know she was

Kettering's May Queen in nineteen-twenty-six?'

Tom reached into his jacket pocket, extracted his wallet and took out the photograph of Daisy when she had been crowned May Queen. He handed to the doctor, and stretched his chin with pride. 'Pretty as a picture, ain't she, but she's headstrong. She's got her own mind all right. Cleverer than all the rest of 'em put together is my Daisy. Out of all my gals she's the one who winds me up the most. Completely out of control, she is. Got herself in the family way earlier this year. Had to get married. Completely ruined her life. Got a little baby girl called Eileen, now.'

Dr Crabtree handed him back the photograph, which Tom slid carefully back into his wallet. 'And your fourth daughter? The one that was born out of wedlock the same year you lost your sons?'

'Yes, our Doris's girl, Violet. She's coming up for ten now. To tell the truth, doctor, she's growing up into a right little madam. Spoiled rotten, she is. Snaps her fingers and gets just what she wants.'

Tom lowered his voice, even though there was no one else in the room. 'Her father, Walter, is a queer, you know. Attracted to men, he is – that's why I had to ... ahem ... oblige my sister-in-law. They'd have been childless otherwise.' Tom's voice dropped to a whisper and he gave a low chuckle.

'He has a bit of a job to ... well ... you know ... get it up.' He held up his arm, a limp wrist suspended in the air in front of his smirking face.

Dr Crabtree raised her eyebrows, wondering if Tom's wife and the homosexual husband had co-operated with

53

this bizarre arrangement. She lowered her glasses, holding them on the tip of her nose with her thumb and forefinger.

Tom frowned at the Doctor's lack of reaction and let his arm drop into his lap. 'This *is* confidential, isn't it, Doctor? I'd hate my sister-in-law's husband to be prosecuted for being a poofter.'

Dr Crabtree nodded and replaced her glasses, looking back down at her notes. These appointments with me are entirely confidential, Mr Jeffson. It's imperative you tell me everything. Absolutely vital to the success of your treatment. Did your wife know of this arrangement? And does she know that Violet is really *your* daughter?'

Tom rubbed his chin and sighed. It wouldn't take a blinkin' genius to work out that Violet might have been fathered by someone else, but I don't think Liz knows it was me. It was a private arrangement with my sister-in-law. Nothing to do with the wife. But we carried on seeing each other for a little while – well the last eleven years actually. Liz found out about our affair earlier this year, and made me end it, which I did about three weeks ago, but it's hard, doctor. Bloody hard. I really miss her, and poor Doris – my sister-in-law – has took it really bad. She's living off her nerves, she is. A ditherin' wreck most o' the time and gawd knows how many bottles of the ol' mother's ruin she's getting through. And the wife won't have nowt to do with her anymore, which is a bit of a shame, because they used to be really close.'

Dr Crabtree put down her pencil, took off her glasses, rubbed her eyes and sighed. 'Did you not think it was wrong to have a child with your sister-in-law?'

Tom was bemused. 'No. Why?'

'It was adultery, Mr Jeffson, and with your wife's sister, too! Did you not ever imagine how wretched your wife would feel if she discovered your infidelity with her own sister?'

Tom laughed. 'When it started, back in nineteen twenty-one, it was no more than a bit on the side, only more clinical-like. Doris wanted a baby. It was a private arrangement – nothing more. Then we enjoyed it so much, it just sort of carried on. Just for a bit of 'ows yer father and slap an' tickle, you understand. Anyway – what about when I was sixteen, doctor? Frank's mother only wanted me for that very same reason. It turned out that her husband was impotent, too old to give her another baby, so she chose me to give her one because I was young and fit. I can't see any difference. I really can't. I'd bet a shillin' to a pound o' pig shit it goes on all the time on the quiet. I can't see anything is wrong with such an arrangement. It's only a tiny seed, after all.'

Dr Crabtree wrote on her notes again.

'Are there any more children, Mr Jeffson? And can I just confirm this affair with your sister-in-law is the same extramarital affair you told me about at your first appointment last month, when I recommended you end it right away?'

Tom pursed his lips and looked up philosophically at the ceiling. 'Well, there might be more children, I suppose.' He tossed a leery grin at Dr Crabtree, enjoying revealing evidence of his virility. 'I'm a bit of a lad on the quiet, aren't I, with all these woman wanting me to give them babies? And yes, the affair I told you about last time is the one with Doris – although there have been a few more with other women over the years. I'm a virile man – I can't be expected to be practically celibate while I wait for the missus to ... ahem ... oblige me.'

Dr Crabtree lowered her glasses again, but didn't smile or acknowledge Tom's remark. She scribbled a question mark on Tom's notes.

'What is your relationship with your sister-in-law now?'

'Doctor Crabtree, I am trying really hard to keep my promises for Liz's sake. I haven't spoken to Doris since I ended our affair. The missus is not speaking to her, either, but that's understandable. She'll come round eventually. I shall probably visit Doris now and again when all this business has died down. I can't just drop her like a stone, can I? And after all, little Violet is my daughter. I'll be discreet. Liz won't know about it and there won't be any more slap an' tickle. I give you my word.'

Tom's promise seemed sincere, but when he winked at Dr Crabtree and tapped the side of his nose, there was no doubt that he had little intention of keeping to his word.

Later, when Tom had left the clinic, Dr Crabtree looked back over his medical notes. She puffed out her cheeks and then exhaled, before shaking her head in despair at a cynical note written by a doctor earlier that year when Tom had been admitted to hospital after breaking his hip in a fall down a drain. Drunk, probably, she thought to herself.

"Thomas Jeffson has a complete lack of conscience and wouldn't know right from wrong if it walked in his front door, announced itself and stayed for tea."

It was going to be a long job, curing Tom Jeffson of his psychopathic disorder. A very long job indeed.

Violet sat cross-legged on her bedroom floor, listening to the conversation downstairs in the living room. She had been away from school again, this time by sticking her fingers down her throat and making herself sick in her bed in the middle of the night. She didn't want to go to school. There was just no point. She wasn't really learning anything from her teachers that she couldn't learn for herself from library books, and not only that, she didn't have any friends to play with. No one liked her. No one loved her.

Her mother had made her stay in her bedroom all morning and had hardly spoken to her, apart from bringing her a drink and a sandwich. Violet could hear her snivelling and crying downstairs – she knew her mother was on the bottle again. Now it was early afternoon and her mother's best friend, Peggy, had come round for a cup of tea and a chat. The conversation drifted up the stairs and through Violet's open bedroom door, wrapping itself around her so tightly she felt almost suffocated.

'I was desperate, Peggy,' Doris said. 'There I was at twenty-eight, trapped in a marriage based on a lie. What else could I do? I just had to find someone who could give me a baby. Walter couldn't, and it was nothing to do with his war wounds.'

'So Walter's not really Violet's father?' Peggy said, her eyebrows almost vanishing in surprise.

Doris didn't answer, but lowered her gaze and looked at

the floor.

'I've never told anyone this, Peggy. And you have to promise me you won't repeat a word of it. I didn't know about Walter when we got married. I was young and stupid ...'

'What didn't you know about Walter?' Peggy cut in, raising her eyebrows again in speculation.

'Do you promise never to breathe a word of this?'

'I promise.'

Doris shut her eyes and shuddered, as bad memories surrounded her in shame like a foul-smelling, damp blanket. She almost wished she'd not mentioned it to Peggy, but there was no going back now.

'I'd always assumed that the reason Walter never got fresh when we were courting was because he wanted to do the right thing and wait until we were married,' Doris said. 'I met him at the church youth fellowship. He was quiet and reserved, much like myself, really. He'd suffered from shell shock and dreadful injuries in the Great War and I felt sorry for him.'

'What? He never tried *anything* on? Ever?' Peggy said.

Doris shook her head.

'What about your wedding night?'

Doris shook her head again, embarrassed. Up until she started her affair with Tom she had always blamed herself for Walter's lack of interest in her. Her wedding night had left her bewildered and confused, wondering if it was usual for a newly married twenty year-old woman to still be a virgin the day after her wedding. She'd stumbled through her honeymoon in a cold and windy Clacton-on-Sea imagining that she had something wrong with her, and it was all her fault.

'It was months, Peggy,' she whispered. 'Months and months. It was horrible. Hour after hour he tried and then, when it eventually happened, he was so disgusted with himself he actually threw up in the lavvy ...'

'Oh, Dolly. I don't know what to say. That's dreadful. You poor, poor girl.'

Peggy adjusted her baggy cardigan over her chest and then, almost as an afterthought, delved into the pocket and took out a packet of cigarettes and box of matches. Doris picked up an empty glass tumbler from the floor, inspected it with a sigh of frustration and rose from her chair. She bent down and extracted new bottle of gin from the sideboard, her hand trembling as she poured out two generous measures before passing one to Peggy. Still standing, she gulped hers down, almost emptying the glass. She sank back down in her armchair, accepted an already lit cigarette from Peggy's outstretched hand and took several drags in quick succession.

'I was hanging out washing in the garden one day about twelve years ago. The teenage lads who lived next door were talking about Walter: they couldn't see me behind the sheets on the washing line. They didn't realise I was still there.'

'What were they saying?'

'They had apparently watched Walter go into the men's toilets in the Pleasure Park and do things with other men. I tell you, Peggy, as God is my witness, until then I never suspected Walter was a queer. Some of the things they were saying – well – it turned my stomach inside out. I didn't know such disgusting, dirty things went on in

Kettering. This is supposed to be a nice, decent place to live.'

"Doris! That's dreadful. What did you do?'

'I followed him the next time he went out, and saw him go in for myself. You remember the old tramp who used to camp out under the bushes in the park?'

Peggy's mouth dropped open. 'Oh no, Doris. Not with him. Not that dirty old sod!'

Doris shook her head. 'I don't think he ever did anything with the tramp, but just after he went into the toilets, a shifty, effeminate-looking spiv went up to the tramp, gave him some money and then he was quite obviously keeping watch outside. Walter was in there for a quarter of an hour with the spiv. It doesn't take that long to spend a penny, does it?'

'Oh Doris ... this is awful. I had no idea. You poor little lamb. What did you do then?'

'I was disgusted. Don't ask me how I got home. I went straight to bed and hid under the sheets. I was bilious for nearly two days. It brought on a terrible headache and I just couldn't stop being sick.'

Doris stubbed out her cigarette in an ashtray and then blew her nose, shaking her head. A tearful confrontation had followed when Walter had returned home. He'd confessed to her straight away. He'd cried and cried as if his heart would break and clung to her like a child at its mother's apron.

'Did you have it out with him? Tell him you had seen everything?'

Doris replied with a nod of the head. '*Don't leave me*', he kept saying over and over again. '*I'll stop. I promise I'll*

60

stop.' Doris bowed her head and looked at her slippers.

Peggy took a large gulp of gin and then placed her hand on her friend's arm. 'You should have left him, Doris. You couldn't be expected to carry on in a marriage like that. Why on earth didn't you leave him?'

'I couldn't, could I? It would have been such a dreadful scandal. I just couldn't bear the thought of the whisperings and humiliation. I was so naïve back then. But I did make him promise he would give up seeing men for the rest of his life and try his hardest to give me a baby. Not only that, everyone knows homosexuality is against the law and he would have been prosecuted and sent to prison. I would have lost my home and everything. I'd have been destitute.'

Doris finished her gin, her head beginning to throb. From that day onwards she had blanked out the awful discovery in her mind, and they had both tried to make the best of things. In return Walter had made sure he was a good husband and provider and, materialistically, she'd wanted for nothing. A veneer they both created and nurtured began to form around the marriage, but a hollow wanting had pervaded the sterility, and the inevitable natural yearnings for a child had matured within her until, one day desperation had overwhelmed her rational senses and a butterfly of an idea had fluttered into her head. It had flapped and swirled and whirled around in her mind until it filled every crevice of her brain, blurring distinctions between right and wrong with the beat of its delicate wings. If Walter couldn't manage to provide her with a son or daughter, another man could.

Peggy's voice sliced through Doris's thoughts and she

visibly jolted back into reality.

'So who is it then? Who's Violet's real father?'

'I couldn't help envying my sister,' Doris said with a sigh. 'She managed to have four children with ease. It was obvious that Tom Jeffson was a proper man who could give her babies, whereas my Walter was just a pathetic excuse for one.'

'So you just went out and found a man to give you a baby,' Peggy said, shaking her head. 'Who was it?'

Doris paused and extracted another cigarette from the packet. She lit it and took a long drag before blowing the smoke into the air. She knew she shouldn't tell Peggy that Tom was Violet's real father, but the gin had loosened the words swirling around inside her head and she couldn't stop them slurring from her lips

'Tom Jeffson doesn't love Liz. 'He's a completely different man when he's with me.'

'Oh no, Doris. Please don't tell me Tom Jeffson is Violet's real father!'

Doris nodded, imagining Tom's peaceful, handsome face as he lay beside her after they had made love.

'Eleven years I've loved him, Peggy. Eleven years he has kept me sane. He's so kind and generous. If only Walter could have learned how to be normal, it wouldn't ever have happened. It was all his fault and he knows it. He doesn't care that someone else fills his marital shoes, it helps him to keep up appearances.'

Doris's voice broke and tears spilled out of her eyes as she wailed. 'And on Saturday Tom finished it with me. How am I going to go on without him, Peggy? I love him so much. He's all I have to live for. I thought I was going to

62

lose him forever when he was ill, only for him to pull through and now I've lost him anyway.'

Peggy sat on the arm of Doris's chair and put an arm around her friend. She pulled her head onto her shoulder. Doris shut her eyes thankfully; it felt good to offload her sordid secret.

Violet crept downstairs, Peggy's voice ringing in her head. "Please don't tell me Tom Jeffson is Violet's real father," she'd said. She'd heard it all. Every single word.

Uncle Tom was her father? No, it couldn't possibly be true. Her dad, Walter, was her father and she loved him, even though he was very quiet and studious. Was that the reason why Uncle Tom had been a big feature in her life with his comings and goings and his half-a-crowns on the mantelpiece? She stared through the open living room door at her mother, slumped on Peggy's chest, an empty gin glass in her hand. Peggy looked up, shock giving her face the appearance of a toddler's scribbled picture.

'Violet!' What on earth are you doing here? Aren't you supposed to be at school?'

Violet didn't bother to lower her voice. 'I was sick in the night. I've been upstairs all day, in bed.'

'Oh my giddy aunt,' Peggy breathed, flustered as she shook a slumped Doris by the shoulders and forced her to look up. 'You didn't tell me Violet was here, poorly upstairs.'

Doris frowned, confused.

Violet flicked her hair over her shoulders. 'I've been learning my poetry. I feel better now.'

She watched dispassionately as her tipsy mother

covered her face with trembling hands. She looked up at the ceiling. Speaking without inflection in her voice, she quoted a couple of lines from The Tiger.

'When the stars threw down their spears, and watered heaven with their tears. Did he smile his work to see? Did he who made the Lamb, make thee?'

Her mother began to wail like a yowling cat. 'Tom doesn't want me anymore, Peggy. He's gone back to *her!* What am I going to do without him?

Chapter Four
Worthlessness and Anger

The next morning, when Violet awoke from a restless night's sleep, for a moment she couldn't remember who she was. She drew the bedclothes over her head. The horrible nobody-feeling had been happening to her quite a lot recently, and sometimes it even happened in the daytime. Peculiar thoughts would march like an army of soldiers through her head, and then she would watch life pass her by as if watching a silent film at the cinema, standing outside herself: a nonentity: an invisible being.

There was a loud noise in the room, like someone scraping a fork on a saucepan. Round and round and round it went, with each beat of her heart, until it turned into a continuous, grinding buzz in her head. A few more seconds passed before she remembered that she was Violet Grey and lived in Cornwall Road, Kettering. She sat up, and the noise stopped. It was early and still dark outside, so Violet closed her eyes and wondered how the noise had got there and where it had come from.

She stared into the darkness. There was someone downstairs. She couldn't hear them, but she knew they were there. Sliding out of bed, she pattered barefoot across the cold, linoleum floor and opened her bedroom door. A child giggled – a girl, she thought.

Padding down the stairs, Violet was curious: was there another child in her house? What was she doing there? Was she a burglar?

Opening the door to the living room, Violet shivered and hesitated as a girl's voice somewhere behind her whispered, incoherently at first. She had to concentrate hard to hear the words and make sense of them because some of them were meaningless and others she was sure were made up, as she hadn't heard them before. It was like listening to a whispered foreign language, but one she was on the edge of understanding.

The voice was telling her to open the kitchen door, open the drawer and find some sharp scissors.

'Don't look round,' the voice said, suddenly loud and clear. 'It's a game.'

Violet was scared. She put her hands over her ears. Was the voice really just behind her or was it in her head?

'Do it.'

Violet stepped forwards, frightened.

She did as she was told and padded through to the kitchen. It was very dark and the quarry tiles were icy cold underneath her feet, but she felt her way around the table and chairs and managed to find the kitchen drawer. As she slid it open, the cutlery clinked and she held her breath for a moment, before closing her fingers around the shape of the kitchen scissors.

'Get them.'

Violet withdrew the scissors slowly from the drawer.

'Cut it,' the voice demanded behind her.

Instinctively, Violet knew the voice wanted her to cut off

her hair. She drew in her next breath sharply. She was proud of her hair – it was golden blonde, the same lovely colour as her mother's, but thick and lustrous, like her father's.

But who was her father? It might be Uncle Tom. Was the conversation she had witnessed yesterday really true?

The girl's voice behind her was authoritative and clear. 'Cut it off: all of it.'

Violet slid the scissors onto her fingers and sectioned off a section of her long hair.

'Go on then. Do it.'

Without a moment's hesitation she hacked off a strand of her hair, close to her head. It fell silently onto the cold quarry tiles.

'Faster, faster, faster,' the girl ordered.

Violet thought she might be in the middle of a nightmare, but did as she was told anyway, because she could not ignore the voice.

Before long the kitchen floor was covered in long strands of blonde hair. Violet began to laugh as she danced on the warm, feathery soft carpet beneath her bare feet. The girl was also dancing, giggling, beside her. She felt liberated. Free. New. It was like being reborn into another life where, as a different person, she would be noticed and loved. She whirled and twirled and danced and swirled, giggling in harmony with the girl beside her.

A scream rang out in her head. Was it her? Was it the girl?

Light flooded into the kitchen.

'What the bloody hell ...'

She stopped spinning around and squinted, her eyes

unaccustomed to the light. Violet stared at her father in the open doorway: his chest was heaving and his mouth was opening and closing, but she couldn't hear the words or sounds coming out of it. He grabbed her arm and echoic, distant words flooded into her brain.

'Oh my God, oh my God,' he was saying over and over again. 'What on earth have you done to yourself?'

He took the scissors from her hand and stared at them as if he had never seen scissors before.

Then, her mother appeared behind him with her hands clamped to either side of her head and her mouth open in a silent O.

Violet opened her mouth to speak, but no words came out, even though they were resonating in her head so loudly she thought she would die.

'I cut my hair,' she tried to say. 'The girl told me to do it.'

Across the road, Tom opened his eyes and stared at Liz, still sleeping beside him.

For the first time since his return from hospital, Liz had shared his bed instead of sleeping in Daisy's old bedroom. This incredible woman had stuck resolutely by his side through thirty years of what must have been one of the most difficult marriages ever endured. His eyes watered and filled with tears of admiration. Was it possible she could learn to love him again? He resolved to ask Dr Crabtree if she could give him any advice as to how he could rekindle his relationship with his wife. Surely there was a way for a man to win back his wife's heart if she had willingly climbed into his bed and slept beside him.

Tom Jeffson had always been the type of man who wanted it all. Not only did he want it all, with absolutely no sacrifices, he wanted it there and then. He was impatient, impulsive and his inherent lack of conscience meant that these tendencies were free to carve their deadly path through his life. Before his illness, in his own blinkered mind, he had done no wrong in his marriage, blaming Liz for making him lose his temper, or annoying him by not completing household chores to his exacting standards. Now Dr Crabtree had told explained to him that his behaviour towards his wife had been so diabolical that she wondered why Liz hadn't left him years ago, he seemed to be falling in love with her all over again, marvelling that she had decided to stay and nurse him through his illness. Dr Crabtree had advised him to write down all the wrong things he had done to her in a little notebook with a red cover, just as a reminder to himself, and then work out how he was going to make amends. Finally free from the distraction that was Doris and their deadly affair, he had never been so determined in his life. This lovely woman deserved to be treated like a queen for the rest of her days. He would work hard to give her the type of life she had always wanted. He would stay off the drink and keep well away from the temptation of the Working Men's Club. Soon, he would be fifty-two years old. He set himself a goal. He would make no marital demands on this lovely woman who slept peacefully beside him. Hopefully, if everything went to plan, she would fall willingly into his arms because he had treated her so well and not forced her in any way at all. Tom smiled to himself, feeling proud of the positive start he had made. With supreme confidence he allowed himself another prediction. In one year's time, he would have kept every single one of the promises to himself, to his daughters and to every single person he had wronged in his life, and Liz would have learned to love him all over again.

Tom sighed, contented. Tomorrow, he would write down all his promises in the notebook with the red cover. He would not waste the precious last chance he had been given – even though it did mean sacrificing Doris to achieve his goals. Determination and resolve, the one redeeming trait in his complex character, would guide him to success. He knew that for certain because Dr Crabtree had said so. The red notebook would be his bible – his way through the jungle of tangled creepers and vines that would inevitably block his path. It wouldn't be easy, he knew that. But Dr Crabtree had said that as long as he kept his resolutions, and remained determined, he would stand a good chance of hacking his way through his problems and living a decent life from now on.

'Shave it all off,' Doris screamed at Walter when, later that morning, they tried to figure out what was to be done about Violet and the terrible thing she had done to herself. 'We can tell people she has that ... that condition. What's it called? You know, where people's hair falls out overnight?'

'Alopecia?' Walter said, looking at Doris across the top of Violet's hacked, tufted head as she sat shivering on a chair, having been stripped naked by her mother.

'No!' Violet yelled. 'I don't want to have my head shaved.'

'You'll have to shave her eyebrows off, too,' Doris wailed. 'I knew a woman from *The Hollow* in Stamford Road who had it once. Every single hair on her body fell out overnight.'

'No, Mam ... I'm sorry. I thought it was a dream – I heard a voice tell me to do it. I – I –'

Hysterical tears glistened wet on Doris's cheeks and clogged her eyelashes. 'Shut up! Just shut up.'

Violet put her arms over her head and cowered on the chair as Walter began to swirl a shaving brush round and round a shallow shaving dish.

'Sit still,' Doris screeched. 'You're such a naughty girl. Just sit still and let your father shave off the rest of your hair.'

'BUT HE'S NOT MY FATHER. I heard you say so to Peggy yesterday afternoon when you got drunk on gin.'

Doris stepped back and leaned against the closed kitchen door, her palms flat on the panelled, varnished wood. 'You are an evil little witch, Violet, to tell such terrible lies. What on earth have I ever done to deserve such a wicked daughter as you?'

Violet began to sob as she gave in and let Walter soap her head with his shaving brush. Rivers of tears bubbled out of her nose and eyes and she gripped the edges of the chair seat with both hands, her eyes screwed shut in terror as the cold cut-throat razor scraped its path across her scalp.

She was surely going mad, just like Uncle Tom. Her heart was beating so fast it was as if a dozen hammers

72

were raining blows inside her chest. If Uncle Tom was really her father she knew she would be like him. Everyone said he was mad, especially since he had tried to top himself. Everyone said he should be locked away in a nuthouse. Who would she call *Daddy* now? Should it be Uncle Tom or the man who was shaving her hair off her head?

She heard her mother open the door, shut it behind her and then dreadful, animal-like wailing in the living room. She didn't love her mother. She didn't love Uncle Tom, either, but she did love her father. He was mostly kind and thoughtful, and took interest in her music, what she was reading at school, her poetry and other writing.

Calming down as Walter finished his task and wrapped her head in a warm towel, she remembered the time a few weeks ago when he had helped her with her homework and, together, they had read *The Pied Piper of Hamelin*, discussing the importance of keeping promises, and the dire consequences if promises were broken. It had been a special, rare moment between the two of them. After she had read the story, she had asked her father if he had ever made any promises to anyone and then broken them. Her father had laughed, tweaked her nose and said that grown-ups broke promises all the time. She had loved spending time with her daddy that day, but it had only happened because her mam had forgotten to buy some sugar and had popped out to the corner shop, because usually her mam didn't allow her to be alone with her father. She knew he was a *"queer" because* she had once heard some people say it, but to her he wasn't odd at all. Violet couldn't make sense of her mother's reasoning.

Perhaps her mother thought her father's queerness would make her queer, too.

Walter removed the warm towel from her head, and smoothed her eyebrows with soap from the shaving dish. The cut-throat razor loomed large in her line of sight and she shut her eyes in renewed terror as she realised her father was about to shave off her eyebrows.

'Daddy,' she wailed. 'Don't cut my eyes with the razor, please don't cut me ...'

'I won't, I promise. It will be over in a few seconds. Just hold still and I won't cut you.'

Violet's legs began to twitch involuntarily and she pushed down hard on the chair with her hands. Her father had promised not to cut her, but so many promises had been broken recently she didn't believe him.

'No, Daddy. No ... not my eyebrows ... please?'

Walter hesitated. Violet opened her eyes.

'I'm sorry,' he said. 'I'm so sorry, but I've no choice. Your mother says ...'

Violet screamed, terrified as the razor made contact with her forehead.

'You can wear a headscarf and we'll tell your teacher and everyone else you have alopecia. It wasn't your fault, poppet. Don't worry. It'll grow back in no time,' her father said as he scraped off her eyebrows with the razor.

It was over.

Doris allowed Walter to help Violet get dressed, shutting herself in the living room with only a bottle of gin and her cigarettes for company. She sobbed out loud, rocking herself back and forth in an armchair, desperate to feel Tom's arms around her, making everything better. A sudden flash of heat washed over her as all her problems joined into one big tangled ball of confusion and overwhelmed her. What were people going to say? How could she explain the falling-out with Liz without it all coming out about her affair with Tom? And now Violet had hacked off all her hair, there was something else to worry about.

Her mouth hanging open in a grotesque, gargoyle-like expression, she crumpled the front of her nightdress in her hands as if a small child. How had her life come to this? What was she going to do now?

Eventually, the living room door opened and Violet stepped inside, dressed neatly in a red gingham dress and a white cardigan. Her eyes were red-rimmed and her voice nasal with crying so much, but now she felt clean, liberated and light as air. For the first time in her life her father had helped her to get washed and dressed, gently pulling her underskirt over her head, then her dress, fastening the buttons on the back and then, with the gentlest touch she had ever felt, he had helped her into her best white cardigan, buttoning it up for her. He had even pulled on her socks, eased her shoes onto her feet and then buckled them up. He'd found one of her mother's headscarves and they had laughed together as he tied it up at the front and said she looked like a charlady before tweaking her nose and kissing the top of her head. She didn't know why her mother had never allowed her father to dress her before.

All these years she had believed it to be somehow wrong for a little girl's father to see her naked, but, today, she knew there was nothing wrong about it at all. No matter what anybody said, Walter was her father. It couldn't possibly be Uncle Tom. Her mother had made a mistake when she'd told Peggy that it was him.

'Mummy?'

Doris didn't answer.

'I'm sorry about my hair.'

'Just go away,' Doris spat at her. 'Get out of my sight. I can't bear to look at you.'

Violet backed away and shut the door, the short-lived fresh and new feeling replaced by self-revulsion. No one was going to want to look at her now she had no hair.

A minute or two later, Walter wrapped his arms around his daughter and hugged her close to him for the first time since she had been two years-old and his wife had declared that *"queers shouldn't be allowed to touch children"*.

'Daddy?' Violet said into Walter's chest.

'Yes, my love?' he replied softly, kissing the top of her head again.

'I really want you to be my daddy, not Uncle Tom.'

Walter took her by the shoulders and crouched down so that his face was level with hers.

'Violet. What you have done to yourself this morning has made me realise you deserve to know the truth ... or rather an explanation. If I tell you a secret, can you promise me you will keep it?'

Violet nodded.

'A long time ago, I was a soldier. I fought in the Great

War, as you know. I suffered some terrible injuries.'

'Did it hurt?'

'Yes, Violet, it did hurt. Do you know how babies are made?'

'No.'

'Well, it takes a man's seed and a woman's seed meeting and joining in a woman's tummy to make a baby.'

'Some boys were talking about that at school. It's disgusting.'

Walter laughed. 'That's because you're much too young to understand what it's all about. You will, when you are a bit older. Well, when I was injured in the war my seeds were damaged. Your mother must have asked Uncle Tom if she could use some of his seeds, and so you were made.'

'Did you know they were Uncle Tom's seeds that made me and not yours?'

'I knew another man had used his seeds, but I didn't know who it was,' Walter ran his hands lightly up and down Violet's arms. 'I always wondered about it. But it doesn't matter whose seeds made you. I always did, and still do, love you very much. You are *my* daughter, not Uncle Tom's, because I have brought you up.'

'Why won't mummy let you hug me and read me stories when I'm in bed?'

Walter stood up. 'It's something that makes me very sad, Violet. Your mother doesn't think I am a fit person to be around children.'

'Why?'

Walter smiled and pinched Violet's nose affectionately. 'Because "y" has a long tail and you haven't.'

Although her face maintained his affectionate smile,

Violet was unable to resist a wry, sarcastic comment.

'I haven't got any hair now, either,' she said.

'*You* can take her to school tomorrow,' Doris said to Walter one evening a couple of days later, when most of the fuss over Violet's sudden hair loss had died down. 'It's about time she went back: she's been off school for a week and a half now. You'll have to go in and see the Headmaster and explain that Violet's hair and eyebrows have fallen out overnight on account of alopecia.'

'Fine. I'll be happy to take *my* daughter to school.'

Walter stood up and pulled on his cap. 'I still can't believe you got drunk and told Peggy that Tom Jeffson was Violet's real father. You might have known she'd be listening upstairs. She's sharp as a knacker's knife – doesn't miss a trick just lately.'

'I didn't say a word to Peggy. It's all lies – Violet's just making it up. You know what a vivid imagination she has. And anyway, what has that got to do with cutting off her hair? She's just a naughty girl who is seeking attention. Anyway, I think it was *you* who put ideas into her head.'

Walter shot Doris a look of disgust and shrugged on his jacket. 'How could it have been me when I didn't even know myself?'

Doris frowned. She had been convinced Walter knew that Tom had fathered her daughter, even though nothing had actually been said over the years.

'Where are you going?'

'I'm going to write a note about Violet's alopecia and post it through the office door explaining to my boss that

I'll be a little late into work tomorrow morning because I have to take her to school. And then I might go to the Club for a beer.'

Doris shot him a warning look. 'To the Club? And just who might you be meeting there?'

'I shall go on my own. The same as I always do.'

The Headmaster's office smelled of pipe tobacco and old books.

Violet gripped Walter's hand tightly as Mr Partridge, the Headmaster of Park Road Junior School, shut the door behind them and then smiled at her. She could tell he was sympathetic to her predicament, and that might be useful if anyone bullied her because of her charlady headscarf. She gazed all around her and studied the photographs on the dark, panelled walls while her father talked to Mr Partridge about her sudden hair loss. She could already spell alopecia: she had asked her father to write it down in her new exercise book and then copied it out a few times.

Bored, she suddenly became aware of the ticking clock on the mantelpiece and began to count the ticks. It was strangely comforting to count the ticks while she looked at the photographs on the wall. There were groups of teachers from years ago and another photograph of children dressed in old-fashioned smock dresses holding a shield before them. The school choir, she supposed. There was another photograph of a maypole, with lots of children standing like statues around it. Her eyes fell upon a small photograph of a pretty girl with a crown made of flowers around her head. She recognised the photograph well. It was Daisy, her cousin. Underneath it said *"Daisy Jeffson, aged 12 years, a former pupil of Park Road School, May Queen of Kettering 1926"*.

It was exactly the same photograph as had sat proudly on her piano in her Auntie Liz's front room before it had been wheeled away down the road on Tuesday morning, sold to pay for armchairs and new rugs for Rose so that she could live in the front room and not have to mix with her Uncle Tom.

Overwhelmed, Violet thought she might start to cry. She bit her top lip until she tasted blood. Everything she valued in her life had been taken away from her in the space of a few, turmoil-filled days. First her piano, then her hair and now her daddy, and it was all Uncle Tom's fault.

Violet's attention drifted back to her father talking to Mr Partridge.

'It's something her grandmother suffered from when she was a girl. The doctor thinks it might be hereditary. There's nothing to be done but to wait for it to grow back.'

'Oh, I see. How long is it likely to take?'

'I'm afraid it's a bit of a waiting game. The doctor said that regrowth can take up to a year,' Walter continued.

Violet looked at her shoes. Grown-ups told far bigger, and more, lies than children could ever dream of. She hadn't even seen a doctor, and she knew her parents hadn't either.

Mr Partridge stood up. 'You wait in here, Violet,' he said in a business-like voice. 'I'll find a classroom monitor to come with you into your class so that you don't have to walk in on your own.'

Her father stood up and shook hands with the Headmaster. He turned to look at Violet. 'Will you be all right? Your mam will collect you after school so you don't have to walk home alone.'

Violet took a deep breath, bit her lip and then gave a brave sigh. 'I'll be fine, Daddy. You go to work and don't worry about me.'

For a few minutes Violet sat alone in the Headmaster's office, waiting for a classroom monitor to arrive and escort her into her classroom. She told herself she wasn't nervous: after all, nobody had teased her so far, and everyone had been sorry for her and expressed much sympathy for her sudden hair loss. When the door opened, she was rubbing the tips of her fingers over her forehead underneath the charlady headscarf, feeling the slight stubble of her hair growing back. Perhaps it wouldn't take long, after all?

'Ah, Violet, there you are,' Mr Partridge said as he entered his office. 'Mary will go with you to class when the bell goes. I hope everything goes well for you today. Miss Newton will be telling the class about your alopecia so you won't have to be explaining about the headscarf to all your friends.'

Violet stared at Mary.

Mary Summers, she thought to herself. *She's not a classroom monitor.* Then the awful truth dawned on her. Mr Partridge had fetched Mary Summers instead of a classroom monitor because Mary wore heavy callipers on her legs and walked along like a cranky old man. He had fetched Mary Summers because she had something wrong with her and he thought they might make friends because

81

she now had something wrong with her, too. Well, she was having none of that. There was no way she was going to be seen to be friends with a *cripple*. People would be bound to laugh at her then.

Violet stood up, pulled her charlady headscarf down over her ears and then flounced out of the door, turning her back on Mary.

'It's all right, Sir,' she said with more confidence than she was feeling. 'I can walk to my classroom on my own.'

Chapter Five
Conciliation and Pride

She came to the back door, which Tom thought was a little forward, considering he had only ever met the woman twice in his life. Not only had she come round the back, just after Liz had gone out, but she had also let herself in the unlocked kitchen door, which irked him somewhat, giving him no chance to pretend he wasn't at home.

He was sitting at the kitchen table, reading the daily newspaper, so there was no escape from either the awkward confrontation that he suspected was to follow, or from offering his unwelcome visitor a cup of tea, since the teapot rested, freshly brewed, in the centre of the table.

Tom stood up to greet his visitor.

'Hello, Mr Jeffson,' Peggy said. 'I see you are feeling a little better now after your illness. I hope you don't mind me popping round.'

Tom extended his hand. 'Hello, Mrs ... Mrs ... Peggy, isn't it? I'm sorry, I don't know your last name. How can I help you? I'm afraid my wife isn't here.'

They shook hands.

'Parsons,' Peggy said. 'Peggy Parsons. And it's you I've come to speak to. I'm a friend of Mrs Grey, your sister-in-law.'

'Ah, yes,' Tom said politely through his teeth. 'I think we have met before, haven't we? Please do sit down. Would you care for a cup of tea?'

Peggy sat down and took off her hat. 'That would be very nice Mr Jeffson. I'll get straight to the point if you don't mind. I've come to see you about your sister-in-law and niece.'

Tom's stomach lurched. This was all he needed at a time when he felt almost cheerful. He took his time over extracting a china tea cup and saucer from the kitchen cabinet, and then made a great show of adding the sugar and milk before pouring the tea.

Over the past three weeks he had made great inroads into getting his life back on track. His psychiatrist was pleased with him: his daughters were speaking to him again: even if it was only about the chilly weather and Marlene Dietrich, a film star in which he had less than no interest. To his surprise, he had also been allowed to hold Daisy's baby girl for the first time: even if he had felt three pairs of female eyes boring into him while he cradled her, cooing at her and rocking her gently back and forth. Yesterday, he had received some good news, which had further enhanced his optimism for the future. The treasurer of the working men's club had turned up on the doorstep to tell him that, just before his illness, he had apparently won the monthly tote. Without hesitation, he'd divided the money into three equal sums, and had pressed it into the hands of Liz, Rose and Daisy, telling them to go into town and treat themselves to some nice clothes and a new hat. It had given him great pleasure to do this, and he was proud that he'd not taken a single penny of his winnings for himself.

Tom sighed. He didn't want to speak about Doris. Even though he had heard about Violet's alopecia, he had put it right out of his head, concentrating hard on getting his marriage and his relationship with his daughters back on track.

'I have a letter for you, Mr Jeffson,' Peggy said, opening her handbag. 'It's from Doris.'

Tom shrank back in his chair. He reached into the pocket of his waistcoat, extracted his pocket watch, flicked it open and held it at arm's length. Looking at his watch was far preferable to looking at the envelope in Peggy's hand.

Peggy put the letter on the table. He didn't pick it up.

'Aren't you going to open it?'

'Perhaps later. I'm on a tight schedule today. Got a lot on.'

'I think you should.'

Tom shook his head. While the envelope was still sealed, he was keeping his promise to Liz. Once he opened it, there was no telling what would happen to his resolve. Doris was good with words and he knew they would weave their way around his heart, silently dragging him over the road and into deadly temptation.

'Well, for what it's worth, I think you have treated Doris badly and you at least owe her some support. I know you've been ill, but you can't just abandon her now she is going through the terrible trauma of Violet losing her hair. She has no one now your wife has turned her back on her, too.'

'Excuse me,' Tom said. 'Can I please ask you what

business this is of yours?'

'I'm all she has in the world, Mr Jeffson.'

Tom sneered. 'No you're not. What about Walter?'

'They aren't speaking to each other. From what I can make out, there's been some trouble ...'

'That's no business of mine, Mrs Parsons,' Tom said, tucking his watch back into his waistcoat pocket. 'And can I just say – it's no business of yours, either?'

'But you don't understand, Mr Jeffson. Your niece has lost all her hair ...'

'So I heard.'

'I'm worried about her, too. She's so withdrawn and pale. She's such a poor little thing.'

'Nowt to do with me, I'm afraid.'

'Mr Jeffson. I'll be frank with you here. I know exactly what's been going on between you and Doris and I'm not happy about being taken for a fool all these years. I don't think you realise that it has been me who has been collecting Violet from school and looking after her, just so you could take advantage of poor Doris.'

Tom shrugged. 'I don't know what you mean.'

'Look. I'll get straight to the point, Mr Jeffson. I know about your affair: Doris told me just before poor Violet lost her hair. So it *is* my business. Had I known that Doris only wanted me to look after Violet so that you could carry on your dirty little affair, I would never have agreed to it. I'm both shocked and disgusted, Mr Jeffson. You have taken advantage of a vulnerable, innocent young woman and you should be ashamed of yourself.'

'Well, what do you think I should do about it?'

Peggy finished her tea and stood up.

'For a start you should at least read Doris's letter. And for what it's worth, it wouldn't hurt you to take a bit of interest in little Violet. All this trouble must be having a dreadful effect on her to make all her hair fall out overnight. Doris told me the true nature of your relationship to Violet, and I think it's disgusting the way you have just ignored the poor little girl when she's going through such an awful thing in her life.'

'Have you finished, now?' Tom asked, handing Peggy her hat.

'I think so, Mr Jeffson.'

Tom stepped over to the back door and opened it.

Peggy and Tom glared at each other in mutual antipathy.

'Goodbye then,' he said. 'And I'll thank you for keeping your nose out of my family's business from now on.'

When Peggy had gone, Tom paced up and down in the kitchen, anger building like a stoked steam engine in his chest. Eventually he let out a roar of frustration, banging his head over and over again on the kitchen wall.

He picked up the letter from the kitchen table. He almost opened it, but his hand was shaky, reminding him that there was an unopened secret bottle of scotch, hidden away in his tool shed at the bottom of the garden for emergencies. He needed a drink after the confrontation with Peggy. Just one little tot would do it – barely enough to cover the bottom of the glass. That should be enough to quell the shakes.

He opened the back door and strode purposefully down the garden path, the unopened letter in his hand. With each step, the contents of the whisky bottle took on far

87

more importance than Doris's words, which he knew would cut into his resolve like a hot knife through butter.

Rose's brand new, matching chocolate brown two-piece suit was semi-fitted, which clung to her maternal figure and mirrored her neat, plain and sensible character. Daisy's velvet-collared dark green coat, although bought off the peg in the smallest size available, hung loose on her slender figure.

Violet perched on the arm of a chair, edging her way into Tom's line of sight. She, too, had new clothes. Her daddy had taken her into town and bought her a whole new wardrobe of clothes after she had cut off her hair.

Tom didn't look at her. She bit her lip and stared at her new, shiny shoes and white socks. If Uncle Tom was really her father, surely he would have bought *her* a new outfit, too, just as he had bought Rose and Daisy new clothes and hats. It just proved that her mother had got it all wrong and Walter was her real father, because it was he who had spent a lot of money on her to cheer her up.

Violet was excited. Just a few minutes after Peggy had taken her mother's letter to Uncle Tom, her cousin, Rose, had called in on her way back from the shops and an unexpected outing had been agreed without anyone asking her whether or not she wanted to go to the Monster Fete and Carnival at Wicksteed Park on bonfire night with Rose and Daisy and their families. Uncle Tom and Auntie Liz would join them all later in the day and it would give her mother *"a bit of a break"*. Her mother's letter to Uncle Tom had obviously been a fantastic success.

Violet smiled politely at Daisy, who had just stroked the headscarf covering her shaved head. She liked her big cousin who, despite her new coat and hat, always looked slightly scruffy. Her thick auburn hair was escaping from the hair grips, and wisps framed her face and around her ears in a childish untidiness. Her eyes crinkled into laughter lines at the corners in a way that made it impossible not to smile back. Violet wished she could be more like Daisy because nothing seemed to pull her down: even when Uncle Tom had chucked her out of the house earlier that year, she had bounced right back up, married her husband, Bill, and now they even had their own brand new house, as well as a new baby.

Daisy held out her hand. 'Come on then, Violet. Let's get going. You can push Eileen all the way to the park in her pram if you like.'

Tom helped first Daisy and then Rose out of the back door with their big prams. 'Your mother and I will see you all later,' he said, pride shining bright in his eyes. 'We will meet you by the boathouse for the fireworks.'

Violet fingered the stubble under her headscarf. Yesterday, she was supposed to be visiting the doctor's surgery: she had overheard her mother talking to Miss Newton, her teacher, telling her that she had an appointment in the afternoon and would need to be fetched out of school early. But instead, she had been marched back home in silence and told to get up the stairs and *"be quiet and keep out of my sight"*. It was then she'd known that the appointment with the doctor had been made up for the benefit of her teacher.

Another lie.

As Violet walked ahead, pushing Daisy's baby in her pram, she listened to the conversation between her cousins.

'Dad had a letter yesterday,' Rose said. 'I think it might have been something to do with his psychiatric treatment, but he's so touchy about it, no one dares to ask him. He's hidden the letter somewhere because mam can't find it.'

Violet turned to look at Rose over her shoulder. 'That letter was from my mam. Peggy took it to him for her.'

'Watch where you're going!' Rose yelled. 'Here, you'd better let Daisy take over, you're a complete menace with that pram.'

'What's psychiatric treatment, Daisy?' Violet asked.

Daisy ignored Violet's question as she took the pram handle.

'Get George to look for it. He might be able to find it. Snoop about a bit, go through his pockets and things. Try in his workshop, or in the allotment shed.'

'Daisy!' Rose laughed. 'We can't do that. It's deceitful!'

Violet wrinkled her nose. Her mam's letter to Uncle Tom was private. It wasn't nice for Rose and Daisy to go around the house snooping, hoping to read the words her mother had written to Uncle Tom, even though she herself had sneaked downstairs and peeked at the letter while her mother was looking for an envelope.

Daisy's eyes twinkled wickedly in the late autumn sunlight. 'Why not? The perverted old bugger rifled through your underwear drawers, didn't he, when he stole your money?'

'I couldn't. But I might be able to persuade George to do it.'

'How much does he owe you?' Daisy asked.

'It's still over two hundred pounds,' Rose replied. 'Because he's using his savings to pay for his medical fees.'

'At least you're back at work, though. You're lucky that you can go out to work. It's all right for some – I can't work, can I? Mam won't look after my Eileen as well as your Margaret.'

Violet puffed out her cheeks. It was obvious Daisy was jealous because Rose had a part-time job. Her Auntie Liz looked after baby Margaret while she was out at work at the factory. When she had been taken over the road to Uncle Tom's house that morning, she had peeped into the front room. It was lovely, having been transformed into a place where Rose and George could sit with baby Margaret, away from Uncle Tom. Since she had last sat in the room, playing her piano while Uncle Tom visited her mam, it had been redecorated and there was a new rug on the floor; there were new fireside chairs and new curtains. But there was also great big gap where her piano used to be.

Although Daisy had a big, new house, Violet knew she had no proper furniture and practically no money. Daisy was obviously miffed that she couldn't go out to work, like Rose, and earn some money, because she had overheard her Auntie Liz say: *"I can't be doing with looking after two babies all day long"*.

Violet loved her Auntie Liz. Even more so, now, because yesterday, after Peggy had visited Uncle Tom and taken him the letter from her mam, and Rose had invited her to spend the day with them, Auntie Liz had knocked on the door of her house and had made friends with her mam again after their falling-out. She had crept downstairs and listened at the kitchen door, where her mam and Auntie Liz had been talking. They were only pretending to be friends again, though. It was only because of her. *"For the sake of little Violet"* her Auntie Liz had said. *"And to keep up appearances"*.

Then, today, her mam had not stayed in bed all day with a bilious attack, but had got up early, dressed in her best clothes and had started tidying the house, which was a relief because it had got really messy and dirty just lately. Before she had been fetched by her Auntie Liz, she had watched her mother change the bed sheets, humming a tune to herself while she worked. It was just like the old days, when her mam would change the bed sheets when she was expecting a secret visit from Uncle Tom.

Perhaps, when she got home later, things would be back to normal and she would be allowed to come downstairs instead of staying in her bedroom all the time.

It was lonely upstairs.

Violet skipped on ahead to join George and Bill, who were deep in conversation. Bill smiled at her and she took his hand. Things had got much better since she cut off her hair. People were buying her presents and she was beginning to feel loved and wanted by everyone except her mam. And today she was out with Daisy and Bill, who were the nicest people she knew.

Daisy felt bad for being envious of Rose. She wouldn't want to change places with her older sister for all the

92

money in the world. The thought of living under the same roof as her father didn't bear thinking about. Rose and George were trapped – there was no doubt about it. She couldn't see them ever escaping from the four walls of the family home; at least not until her father had been cured of his dreadful illness. Privately, she doubted her father would ever be cured, and she couldn't see him giving up the drink, despite his promises and good intentions.

'Just snoop about and find his letter when he's out,' Daisy said. 'Go through *his* drawers – after all no would blame you after what he's done to you, Rose.'

'Do you know, I think I just might,' Rose laughed.

As the two families reached the gates to Wicksteed Park, the sound of a brass band playing in the distance filled the air. The sweet smell of candyfloss mingled with that of frying onions, hotdogs, saveloys, faggots and pease pudding and children of all ages whooped, shouted and laughed as they played on swings, roundabouts and slides. Bill and George, by now each pushing their baby daughters in their prams, paused to read a sign posted on a huge hoarding while Daisy, Rose and Violet sauntered on ahead.

Kettering & District Hospital Guild
Hospital Week
Monster Fete and Carnival
Bonfire and Fireworks
In aid of New Operating Theatre, Sunlamps, Massage

'I wonder if Tom could eventually get his treatment through the Hospital Guild?' Bill mused. 'Look, there's going to be a Psychiatric Department.'

George nodded an agreement. 'I don't know how we can broach the subject with him though. He's forbidden anyone to even mention it. If he can get it paid through the Guild – and it looks as if he might be able to – he won't have to pay privately and he can give us some of our money back.'

A deep sound of growling engines filled the air, as a trio of tiger moths from the Northants Aero Club buzzed overhead. George and Bill looked up and watched as they performed a series of acrobatic moves, shielding their eyes with their hands. After a while, they walked towards the playground, where Daisy was pushing Violet on a swing.

'Did you know that Tom's started his treatment?' George said to Bill. 'I reckon he's had two sessions by now, but he gets really uppity if anyone asks him how he's getting on.'

'Not surprising, really,' Bill replied. 'He must be too embarrassed. I don't think I would want to go broadcasting it if I was having to see a psychiatrist, either.'

George nodded in agreement. 'He went back to work last Monday, but finished early on Tuesday. I only know

94

because I can see the bike shed from the finishing shop window at work, and his bike was gone by three o'clock. And he was already home when Rose and I walked in the door, so he must have been somewhere. He could have been out tomcattin' again, but I wouldn't have thought he'd dare after Liz read him the riot act. Apparently, just before he took our money, she'd found out he'd been at it again?'

'Who with? Do we know?'

George scratched his ear. He didn't like lying to Bill, but he wasn't about to open the closet door and release the dancing skeleton when it needed to be kept firmly locked inside.

'Nah. Rose said her mam wouldn't tell her. All she said was that she'd caught him tomcattin' with some red-lipped strumpet and that she was going to read him the riot act and give him an ultimatum. She even packed a suitcase and said if he didn't stop it, she was leaving him for good. Apparently he can't help himself with all this tomcattin' because it's part of his illness.'

Violet trailed behind George and Bill, trying to listen to their conversation. Before last Sunday, when she had cut off her hair, she had always sensed that people in her family didn't really like her, but she hadn't known why. George was obviously hiding the truth about Uncle Tom being her real father from Bill. If someone said nothing, did that mean they were telling a lie? Had Rose known all along, too? Did that explain why Rose had never liked her? It was all very confusing.

95

Now, all of a sudden, when people thought she had suffered from alopecia, even Rose had been sympathetic and concerned about her. She had been taken out by her father and brought new, pretty clothes and headscarves to match, Rose had treated her kindly and her Auntie Liz had hugged her tight and cried real tears into her bald head.

When she had met Uncle Tom in the street when out walking with her father, he had said he was sorry for selling her piano and had asked her father if he could find room for a second-hand, cheaper one in her house. Everyone had rallied round, she had been bought lots of sweets, some new books to read, new shoes, a new winter coat and a brand new wireless set had appeared in the front room of her house, where a space was to be made for her piano when it arrived.

Violet briefly touched her head and adjusted her headscarf. Her head had been shaved again that morning, because it was getting very bristly. Her mam had said it wouldn't do for her hair to grow back just yet because the lady who lived in *The Hollow* in Stamford Road, who had lost all her hair, had to wait nearly a year for it to start to grow back, and then, when it did, it was all soft and tufty. If losing her hair for a while meant that people would keep on taking notice of her, it would be worth it.

That morning, when Rose had knocked on her door and asked her mam if she wanted to go to the Monster Fete and Carnival with them, and then stay on in the evening for the fireworks, she had skipped and hopped around her bedroom all morning, so excited was she. Now she had walked the entire length of Windmill Avenue with them and into the park she realised no one had so much as even acknowledged she was there. No one had asked her if she was all right. Tears prickled in her nose and began to well up in her eyes as she trailed after George and Bill, who were still talking about Uncle Tom. She might have known all the attention was too good to be true. Her mam was only interested in herself and sent her upstairs to bed at every opportunity because she couldn't bear to look at her. Her father was a *"homo"* and a *"queer"*, which this week she had discovered meant that he liked men better than women, and there had been no further mention of her having another piano to take the place of her shiny new one, sold to buy furniture so that Rose didn't have to mix with Uncle Tom.

Violet began to tremble. Yo-yoing between being given lots of attention and then being ignored felt as if she was being repeatedly cut open and stitched up again. Just a few weeks ago, she had always been able to harden herself to the horrible feelings of not being loved, but since the voice in her head had told her to cut off her hair, and she had spent a blissful week of being loved by everyone except her mam on account of her "alopecia", it seemed as if her previously hardened defences had been swept up and thrown into the dustbin, along with her lovely blonde hair.

Even Daisy hadn't yet spoken to her properly that day. It hurt so badly. Daisy had always been nice to her, but obviously didn't want her now she had her own baby to love.

Could she run away? She wondered how she could do it as she trailed forlornly behind her cousins, their husbands and new babies. 'How much did it cost to run away? Was there enough secret-keeping sweet money in her tin? Were there people in, say, London who would let a little girl with no hair stay with them if she had enough money to pay them?

As they reached the huge banners that signified the entrance to the Monster Fete, the smell of food made her feel hungry and she realised her mam had forgotten to make her some breakfast. George turned around to look at her.

'Do you want anything to eat, Violet?' he said with kindness in his voice but not in his eyes.

Violet nodded, glancing up at a large menu at a food stall. The smell of hotdogs, a new type of sausage from America, was making her mouth water.

'I'd like a hotdog, please, George.'

She would need to eat to keep up her strength if she was going to run away.

Tom didn't believe in coincidences, predestination or fate. He had always scorned Liz and Rose, who were superstitious, and had dismissed any concept he didn't understand with a wave of his hand and a cynical sneer, deliberately putting new shoes on the table, spilling salt and strolling nonchalantly under every ladder he came across.

So it was with a certain amount of providence that, the same day Peggy had brought Doris's letter to him, he had that morning received another letter in the post from a solicitor, giving him the good news that he was the sole beneficiary in his great aunt's estate. He had thought the official-looking letter was about his psychiatric treatment and so he had opened the letter in private in his tool shed.

He had almost whooped and jumped into the air with joy, excited about his unexpected inheritance. He hadn't expected to even receive a small bequest after his great aunt had passed away, let alone to be the sole beneficiary. But something had stopped him sharing the news with his family. Instead, he had hidden both letters away in his tool shed. One opened and the other unopened.

Later, he had placed the emergency bottle of scotch beside the unopened letter from Doris and stared at them for a long time. For the first time in his life he had resisted temptation and he was proud of himself for his resolve. But little did he know that the coincidence of one opened letter and one unopened letter received on the same day was to create a series of tremors in the bedrock of his new life which would leave him struggling to keep his balance on the constantly shifting ground beneath his feet.

On the morning of the Monster Fete and Carnival at Wicksteed Park, Tom had bought her some gifts: a dozen red roses; a silk-lined box with six hand-made fancy chocolates in tiny fluted cases and a fancy leather box with a gold clasp, containing an expensive sapphire and diamond necklace.

He had pecked her on the cheek. He had told her that he didn't deserve her and, once again, he had said sorry for the terrible things he had done to her in the past. When he had given her the gifts, bought from the finest shops in the town, he had said she was twenty-four carat gold, just like the necklace, and that words couldn't describe the love he felt for her.

Why, then, did she feel so empty and bereft?

Liz stared at the gifts, lined up like sentries on the sideboard, guarding the sepia photograph of her and Tom on their wedding day. She should feel pleased because he had been honest with her and confessed that, while she had been out shopping, Doris had sent her friend, Peggy, to deliver a letter and he hadn't opened it. He'd also told her there was an unopened bottle of scotch on the bench in his tool shed, and had asked her to fetch it for him.

He'd twisted the top off the bottle, in front of her, and poured the contents down the kitchen sink.

She should be happy.

Happy. Happy. Happy.

Liz rubbed her forehead with a trembling hand, repeating the word over and over in her head, trying to force herself to be cheerful and grateful for Tom's gifts and kept promises.

But it was all much too hard.

Tom and Liz stepped in silence out of their front door, shut it behind them and began to walk along the road. By force of habit, Tom always had to walk a few steps in front of Liz. She long ago stopped running to catch him up, because he always hurried to get ahead of her again. Liz wondered how far they would get before Tom spoke. She reckoned it would be around half way to the park.

She was wrong.

They had taken only a few steps before he had slowed

down to walk beside her instead of in front of her. He had taken her arm, pulled it through his, patted her hand and told her all about his first week back at work after his illness. He'd said how happy she had made him by agreeing to start all over again after the terrible things he'd done over the last thirty years. Most startling of all, he'd talked about his sessions of treatment with the psychiatrist, but had made her promise not to tell the rest of the family, or to give them any details of his sessions.

Tom was beginning to talk to her as an equal for the first time in thirty years of marriage. He had kept his promises. He had bought her lovely gifts. So why, then, did she not feel happy? Why could she not even bear the slightest touch of his hand, or to even be in close proximity to him? Even the sound of his voice grated on her nerves until every part of her felt raw and exposed. He was her husband and she should not be feeling this way.

Several times Liz tried to extract her arm from his. When she'd resolved to try and mend her broken marriage, *"for better or worse, in sickness and in health",* she had not reckoned on Tom becoming so loving and thoughtful. She had somehow believed that it would be she who would do all the running, make all the effort and lead him, like a remorseful child, back into their marriage.

He had made no physical demands on her either, which was something else she didn't understand. Throughout the turbulent years of their marriage he'd not been able to keep his hands off her: why did he not want her anymore? In one way, it was a relief, but his odd behaviour was confusing and strangely unsettling.

Each time Liz withdrew her arm on the pretext of

adjusting her hat as they walked along, Tom just grabbed hold of it and threaded it through his again.

He changed the subject.

'It'll be a clear night for the firework display.'

'Umm, nice for the children,' she agreed.

Then there was silence, the atmosphere between them strained and fragile. Liz withdrew her arm again and stopped, tucking imaginary strands of stray hair into her hat.

Tom glanced over his shoulder and smiled. 'Come on, old gal, or else we'll be late and miss the start of the fireworks.' He waited for her to catch him up.

Tom began to count his steps under his breath. It was twenty-three before he spoke to her again. Some things hadn't changed. It was the little things like his obsessive counting and measuring that would probably be the hardest things for his psychiatrist to cure.

The letter from Doris sat on the work bench in Tom's tool shed, growing in its unopened significance with every hour. The words it contained were carefully crafted, having gone through several stages of metamorphosis since the idea of sending Tom a letter had first been conceived. Doris had been pleased with the final version, her words honed and sharpened until she was satisfied they would fly, as straight as an arrow, right into the centre of Tom's heart.

She had been careful to make sure Peggy took the letter to Tom when her sister would be out. She had then worked out how she was going to win her way back into Tom's affections. By the time she had finished with him, there was no way he would be able to resist her.

It had not occurred to her that Tom might not open it.

"Ask Liz and Rose if they can have Violet for me on Saturday afternoon, and we can be together one last time." The neatly scripted words sat, concealed and unread inside the envelope in Tom's dark tool shed.

It had been pure coincidence that that Liz had visited that morning and, with a reluctant sigh, had held out the metaphorical olive branch, said they should close the door on the past and make a fresh start. Then, after Liz had gone, Rose had turned up suggesting that they could take Violet off her hands for the afternoon and give her a bit of a break.

Liz, although a little bristly and off-hand, had said that they were still sisters and there was no point in being off hooks for the rest of their lives now that *"she had forgiven Tom for his misdemeanours, because after all, they had been caused by his psychopathic disorder, which was a mental illness from which he was now making a good recovery"*.

Doris's spirits had lifted in an instant. Her letter to Tom had obviously worked: he must have persuaded Liz and Rose to take Violet to the bonfire night celebrations at Wicksteed Park so he could spend the afternoon with her. Walter wouldn't put in an appearance until tea time, which gave her lots of time with Tom. She had busied herself all morning, tidying the house, stripping her bed and remaking it with immaculately pressed white bed linen, washing her hair and setting it in rollers and finally dressing in silk underwear under her best clothes. She could hardly believe it had been so easy.

But Doris had waited ... and waited. For over an hour

she had paced from room to room, peeping endlessly around the curtains in the front room. What had happened to prevent Tom from complying with her plan, falling into her arms and rekindling their passion for each other? Finally, feeling abandoned and dejected, she had sank into an armchair, a glass and a bottle of gin to hand, and had sobbed and cried until her heart ached.

Her life was over: her sister was only speaking to her for the sake of keeping up appearances and she knew they could never, ever truly be friends again; her daughter had cut off all her hair, forcing her to make up stories about alopecia; her husband was a homosexual and had drifted away from her so far she hardly recognised him anymore. But above all, Tom's cruel denial of his love for her, and the humiliation of him deliberately standing her up took over her whole being and consumed her in a bitter, overpowering jealousy of her sister's perfect life.

But, by far the worst thing of all had been when she had looked out of the window and watched Tom, with Liz on his arm, walking off in the direction of Wicksteed Park. He hadn't even glanced in the direction of her house. He had been laughing, patting her sister's hand as he strutted, tall and proud, along the street.

Doris had sobbed and cried for an hour before coming to a decision.

She understood that sticking your head in the gas oven was the option of preference to end it all. She'd several times read about various celebrities in the newspaper who had decided to end their lives after a romantic tryst had ended tragically. It was far more desirable than the more painful options of throwing yourself from a great height, leaping in front of a train or jumping from the banisters with a rope around your neck. Poisoning didn't always work, either. After all, look at Tom? It hadn't worked for him, had it? The ant paste hadn't killed him, but merely left him temporarily paralysed and infected his lungs with painful pneumonia when he'd inhaled his own poisoned vomit.

The prospect of a reasonably painless means of exiting her pitiful life made good, solid sense. After all, the alternative option of remaining on the earth until death by natural causes seemed completely pointless. Why carry on when the means of ending it all was right there, in her very own kitchen? Not only that, her cold and distant daughter wouldn't be home until after the fireworks had finished. She doubted there would be a better time.

Walter was somewhere else, with someone she didn't know, probably doing things she didn't want to think about. She had plenty of time to carry out her plan. She was wearing her best clothes and underwear and she had done her hair and make-up, which was another good thing because when her body was discovered, she would look just like the Sleeping Beauty, and Tom would surely be devastated and regret his cruel actions and would immediately want to join her in death.

She needed to make sure the gas couldn't escape, and so she plodded up the stairs and collected all the towels from the linen cupboard, before soaking them in a sink full of cold water. She'd have to stuff them up against the doors, she thought. And she mustn't forget the draughty kitchen window – she'd need to pack wet tea towels in the gap between the sashes.

'George,' Violet said. 'Can I go home now? I don't really want to stay for the fireworks. I'm so tired.'

'Are you sure? There's going to be a really grand display. You'll be sorry if you miss it. Anyway, you'll probably see some of your friends from school down by the lake.'

Violet shook her head. 'I don't have any friends.'

George smiled at her. 'I'm sure you do – every little girl has friends.'

Violet stared straight ahead and shrugged, pouting her lips. What was the point in staying for the fireworks now she had made up her mind to run away? She would go home, go straight up to her bedroom and count the secret-keeping money. Then she would find a small overnight case in the box-room and pack some clothes, while her mam drank gin downstairs and her father sat in the kitchen, staring at the wall. Then tomorrow night she would stay awake all night so she could get up really early on Monday morning, before dawn, creep silently from the house with her case and her money and walk to the train station. She could wait on the platform for the early train to London and if any grown-up asked her where she was going she would put on a sensible voice, show them her bald head, and explain that she was visiting her grandparents in London to recover from her alopecia. She knew there would be an early morning train because her parents had taken her to see Buckingham Palace one Sunday in the summer. She could tell the ticket master that her grandfather was going to meet her at St Pancras Station, which was where they had needed to get off the train before. If she dressed nicely and made sure she washed her face no one would ever suspect she was a runaway.

'Shall I walk you back?' George said.

'I'll be all right on my own. It's not quite dark yet.'

George grimaced, doubtful. 'Are you sure?'

Violet nodded. 'I'm allowed to go anywhere I like on my own now.'

Bill, who had overheard the conversation, shook his head. 'No, Violet, you're not walking back on your own. It'll be dark soon. I'll come with you and we can pick up my bicycle on the way to save time.'

'Good idea,' Daisy said. 'I'll wait here with Rose and George and then, when you get back, we can go down to the lake and meet up with Mam and Dad by the boathouse.'

Chapter Six
Loneliness and Attraction

Quentin Andrews, Alderman of the Borough and President of the local St. John Ambulance Brigade, was also a member of the Kettering Rowing Club, whose headquarters were based at Wicksteed Park lake.

As the late afternoon sun melted into the horizon, Quentin was busy with preparations for the firework display.

He looked up as he heard a vaguely familiar, gruff voice behind him.

'Hello, Mr Andrews. It's going to be a grand night.'

He turned around. Tom stood before him, his hand extended, beaming broadly.

'Mr Jeffson. How are you? It's so good to see you're out and about again. Are you feeling better now?'

'Good to middling', Tom replied. 'The old hip plays up now and again, but apart from that, I can't complain.' He thumped his chest. 'Still get outta puff, but well ... it's me own fault, eh?'

Quentin shook Tom's hand vigorously with both hands. 'Good. I'm really glad to hear it.'

He tipped his cap at Liz. 'Mrs Jeffson – how are you m'dear?'

'I'm very well thank you,' Liz said, completely taken by surprise that someone had actually asked after her husband's state of health and shook his hand. Usually people looked the other way and avoided him.

'Is that a beer tent? Tom asked, nodding towards a dubious canvass structure about twenty-five yards away.

'Yep.'

Tom rubbed his hands together. 'We're supposed to be meeting my daughters and their families for a bit of a get together in a while, but I've just about got time for a swift half. Would you care to join me, Mr Andrews? I'd like to say thank you for saving my life.'

With that, Tom strode off, leaving Liz stranded behind him.

'Tom,' she shouted, as she began to run after him, clutching her hat to her head. 'Remember what the doctor said –'

But Tom didn't hear her over the din of excited children squealing and running around. Panic stricken, Liz turned to Mr Andrews. 'He's not supposed to drink – not after his ... his ... er ... illness.'

'Tom!' she shouted again, and ran after him.

Tom stopped at the entrance to the beer tent, turned around on his heels and shrugged, his palms upturned.

'It's just a quick half. Stop mitherin', woman. It's a special occasion. Do you think I'm going to ruin everything with just one swift half?'

With that he turned his back on her and strode off into the tent, leaving Liz on her own. She went in after him, but the tent was full of men: as far as she could see there were no women around. She hesitated, unwilling to venture further inside.

Tom had disappeared.

She looked over her shoulder. Quentin was standing behind her.

'I'm afraid I don't have time for a beer at the moment,' he said. 'Can you thank your husband for me and tell him I'll join him later, once the firework display has finished?'

'I'll just wait outside for a while. I'm sure my daughters will be here soon. They came this afternoon, you see, to watch the air display and have a bite to eat.'

'I'd best get on, Mrs Jeffson. If you want anything, just shout.'

Quentin walked over to the boathouse to continue his checks on the fireworks in readiness for the display. When he had finished, he peered outside. It troubled him that Tom Jeffson had left his wife alone outside the beer tent, even though she was expecting her family to turn up any minute.

She had gone.

He walked back over to the beer tent and his ears told him what his eyes couldn't make out in the dim light. Tom Jeffson was guffawing loudly. He had obviously found someone he knew with whom to share a pint of ale. He supposed Mrs Jeffson had met up with her daughters and was now mingling with the crowds, but something about her demeanour had made him uneasy. He'd been acquainted with the Jeffson family for a while now and Quentin felt sad for poor Mrs Jeffson, especially when upsetting details about how her husband had tried to poison himself with ant paste and whisky had been reported in the local newspaper, citing himself as a hero for saving Tom's life.

Only a couple of days after the incident, his ambulance had been called out again to Tom's heavily pregnant daughter who, it transpired, had been thrown out of the family home by her father when she'd got herself in the family way at seventeen. His heart had gone out to the waif-like girl and her young husband, who had nothing in life but each other.

He'd pulled a few strings at the Council and made sure that Daisy and Bill Roberts went to the top of the housing list, and just a few weeks ago had been allocated a brand new house in Windmill Avenue. Since then, he'd called on the young couple several times and they'd made him so welcome, even though they had nothing. They had made a pot of tea and given him home-made cake and he'd felt quite at home in their sparsely furnished house, glad of some company to ease his lonely life.

Quentin busied himself with setting up the firework display, suddenly feeling the pain of being surrounded by happy families. Although he had six sons, three had married, two of them moving away from Kettering and two were in the army, which meant he didn't see them often.

After his wife had died in childbirth, he had thrown himself into charitable causes and had stood as a candidate for the local council, which after his election had kept him busy and his mind off things. He couldn't help himself feeling bitter about Tom Jeffson, whose reputation in the town had now taken a serious nosedive. He had it all – a devoted wife (and devoted she most certainly was, to put up with him in the way she did), a trio of smashing daughters and baby grandchildren he could see every day of his life if he wanted to, even though he knew his eldest daughter was already estranged from him and there was much trouble in his family following his attempt to take his own life.

Quentin gazed across to the beer tent, where Tom's loud voice could be heard above the cacophony of excited voices of a group of children as they queued up for hot potatoes. As darkness began to fall, he felt a sudden sense of foreboding. Mrs Jeffson had warned her husband he wasn't supposed to drink, and he quite obviously had ignored her.

The overpowering smells of the newly lit bonfire, hotdogs, roasting chestnuts and onions diminished the further upstream Liz ventured. The river rippled gently along before it flowed out of sight into a thicket of trees, the light from the flickering bonfire dancing in yellow and gold flecks of colour on the water. It was a still, cold evening and there was hardly any breeze. If it had been summer, it would have been warm, but because it was early November there was a sharp nip in the air. Liz shivered as the dampness of the ground rose through her shoes and chilled her to the bone, the rustling of the trees somehow strangely synchronised with the crunch of her feet on the fallen carpet of leaves underfoot. She found a fallen branch and sat down for a while to collect her thoughts.

She wanted to be alone.

She couldn't bear to be near Tom any longer, or hear

the sound of his leery laugh or his bawdy jokes. She'd just had to get away from the vicinity of the beer tent and, as more and more folk gathered at the lakeside for the bonfire and fireworks, she had felt an overwhelming urge to escape.

She slumped forwards on the broken tree branch and hid her face in her hands. She'd had enough. Even though he had kept his promise to end his affair with her sister, and despite the flowers, the chocolates and the beautiful, expensive jewellery and his behaviour having been faultless, she just wanted to get away from him forever.

She had been naïve to think she would be able to sweep all the lies and deceit aside and forgive him. She had turned a blind eye to the occasional flurries of infidelity for thirty years, but his affair with her sister, coupled with the dreadful things he had done to their daughters in the last year had hurt her too deeply.

She hadn't bargained on feeling as wretched as this. She hadn't realised just how hard it would be to forgive him and how dreadful she would feel at the dark thoughts that invaded her inherent decency in wishing that her husband had died when he'd tried to take his own life.

Bill Roberts stood on the edge of the crowd, craning his neck around bobbing heads, holding onto his bicycle with one hand and Violet's hand with the other.

'Are you looking for Tom Jeffson?' Quentin shouted above the noise.

'Have you seen him?' Bill yelled. 'And my mother-in-law?'

'He's in the beer tent,' Quentin shouted in reply.

Bill groaned. 'I might have known. Look mate, I'll never get through this crowd with my bike. Could you tell Tom there's been a bit of trouble? We have to go home and are giving the firework display a miss?'

Quentin nodded and stuck a thumb up in the air. Over the noise, he'd only caught the bit about having to give the firework display a miss. 'All right lad – will do,' he yelled.

Violet felt sick and bewildered, but she hadn't cried.

It was a good job Bill had walked home with her. She knew she would never, ever forget the jammed back door, the faint smell of gas that emanated from the keyhole and then the sight of her mother's feet, encased in silk stockings, as she lay prone on the kitchen floor, dressed in her best clothes, her head in the gas oven.

Bill had told her to go and wait in the living room, but the smell of the gas had been too strong, so she'd gone upstairs into her bedroom, rocking backwards and forwards on her bed, hugging her knees in bewilderment, wanting to cry but finding that the tears were locked away inside her head somewhere, building up pressure like the steam train she would no longer be able to catch on Monday morning because her mam had put her head in the oven.

It was all Uncle Tom's fault.

All the secrets that had been piling up for the last few weeks had resulted in another tragedy, narrowly averted only because she had wanted to go home early from the Monster Fete and Carnival so that she could get ready to run away.

After Bill had dragged her mam out of the oven, opened all the doors and windows, helped her up and sat her in an armchair, he had knocked on a neighbour's door and had somehow found out where her father was. He was now with her mother, wrapping her in blankets and making her a cup of tea, and she had been made to come back to the firework display with Bill. Her legs wouldn't somehow work by themselves, so Bill had let her sit on his bicycle saddle while he pushed her along. Frightened and bewildered, she allowed herself to cry, leaning on him as she ground her knuckles into her eyes.

Bill stopped for a while to comfort her. She heard him mutter to himself, and then heard him say a bad swear word. After a while, he pulled her head onto his chest and stroked her bald head while her tears soaked into his coat.

'Don't worry, Poppet, you can come home with me and Daisy tonight.'

She rested her head on his shoulder, exhausted. It was very, very hard to have to be a grown-up when you weren't even ten years-old.

Quentin zig-zagged his way through the crowd and into the beer tent. Tom was sitting at a trestle table, arm-wrestling with an acquaintance as cigarette and pipe smoke fogged the yellow, flickering lantern lights inside. His peaked cap was twizzled over his left ear, and Quentin could see that he'd already had a few too many.

'Mr Jeffson,' he shouted.

Tom waved his free hand in the air. 'Be with you in a

minute, mate.'

Laughing, having lost the challenge, he beckoned Quentin over.

'Pint?' he said.

Quentin shook his head. 'Got things to do. Better not, but thanks all the same. Your Bill just came to find you. He told me to tell you that they've had to go home, so they won't be meeting you at the lakeside for the fireworks.'

'All right, mate. Thanks.'

Tom went back to his arm-wrestling without another thought.

Quentin spent a few minutes looking around for poor Mrs Jeffson, but there was no sign of her. Had she just slipped off and gone home with the rest of her family?

As Quentin left the area around the bonfire, the first firework exploded in the air above him. The crowd had now spread out around the intensifying heat, sparks drifting high up into the night air, the flames roaring and crackling as the dry, brittle dead wood burnt bright red and amber. His work was done. He'd leave it to the experts to light the complicated firework displays. He sank down onto the edge of the boathouse jetty for a well-earned cigarette. He'd go and find young Theo in a while, he thought. His youngest son had gone off to play with his friends without a backward glance half an hour ago, promising to come back for the display. It was a lonely old life being a widower, but he didn't want to intrude on Theo's life now he was growing up.

There were loud ooohs and aaahs as a particularly complex array lit up the sky, leaving puffs of red, blue and white smoke hanging in the air. Out of the corner of his eye, Quentin spotted a lone female figure, profiled momentarily in the flickering red light of the firework. She was sitting by the river about fifty yards away. Was it Mrs Jeffson? As the remnants of the firework dimmed and then melted into the inky sky, he strained to pick out the woman in the darkness.

It was a minute or two until the next aerial display lit up the surrounding area. Quentin was ready this time. The woman's outline was clear. It most definitely *was* Mrs Jeffson. He stood up, jumped off the jetty and strode through the fallen leaves along the track to the river bank. Following the river in the orange glow of light from the bonfire and with the intermittent crackle of fireworks behind him, he made his way to the spot where Liz was sitting on a fallen tree branch.

'Hello,' Quentin said. 'I saw you sitting on your own and wondered if you were all right.'

Liz looked up. She'd seen, and heard, him walking towards her. She knew it was Quentin Andrews, the ambulance driver who had saved Tom's life.

'Yes. Thank you, Mr Andrews. I'm fine ... just waiting for ...' She shielded her eyes from his gaze as her voice faded. 'Have you seen my daughters?'

'They haven't stayed for the fireworks. Bill asked me to tell you and Mr Jeffson. They've gone home with the babies – but I don't think it's anything to worry about.'

'Oh. I wondered if that might happen. I said to Rose only this morning that little Margaret would never keep going for the fireworks. She's only five months old. Too little for fireworks, really, don't you think? And Eileen, my other granddaughter, is only three months old. They really shouldn't be out on a chilly night like this.'

'Mr Jeffson is just having a ...'

Liz buried her head in her hands, shaking it slowly, interrupting him. She spoke quietly, her voice brittle. 'I don't want to know what my husband is up to. I've had enough, Mr Andrews. I just can't stand it anymore. '

Quentin shifted his weight. Liz could tell he was embarrassed.

'Right.' he said, with a nervous grimace. He sat down next to her. 'Would you like me to walk back with you?'

Liz shook her head. 'I don't know. I can't ... I don't want to ... you know ... deal with Tom if he's ... he's ...'

Liz took a handkerchief out of her coat pocket and held it to her nose. She squeezed her eyes shut. She wouldn't cry – not here. Not now. Not in front of the nice Mr Andrews.

'Shall we just sit here quietly for a while and watch the firework display from here, then?' Quentin said. 'There's no rush to get back, is there?'

Liz nodded. 'Yes, I'd like that.'

They sat in silence for a few minutes.

'It must be very exciting, being an ambulance driver,' Liz said eventually, making conversation.

'Not really. It can be quite upsetting at times, although it keeps me busy. I'm a widower, you see. Other than that I've got my council work and my youngest son and I are both in the rowing club here at the park.'

Liz smiled at him, keen to take her mind off Tom. 'Tell me about the council. I've always wondered what it's like to be a councillor.'

Quentin sighed and shook his head. 'It's a thankless task really. People think councillors are such important people, but all we do is sit in smoke-filled chambers on our General Purposes Committee, or our Street Lighting Sub-Committee, arguing over motions, amendments and resolutions, while the long-suffering Committee Clerk scribbles in his notebook for dear life, trying to keep up with all the self-important ramblings, and all the time the public are banging on the door – metaphorically speaking, of course – trying to get their opinions heard when we might just as well have our fingers stuffed in our ears. They really ought to let the public listen to our meetings – and have their say, too. Well, that's what I think, anyhow, but it'll never happen, not in my lifetime.'

Liz laughed. 'It sounds like something out of a Charles Dickens novel.'

'I suppose it is, really.' Quentin chuckled. 'The Town Clerk, poor chap, tries his hardest to keep everyone in order and to play by the rules, whilst the Chairman waits for the chance to bang his gavel when someone says something they shouldn't and someone else stands up and shouts: *point of order, Mr Chairman, point of order.*'

Liz laughed out loud at Quentin as he pulled back his shoulders and stuck out his chest in the manner of an indignant, offended councillor.

'It sounds like the town council in the Pied Piper of Hamelin: do you know it? It's a poem by Robert Browning.' Liz cast her eyes up into the dark night sky, trying to remember the verses. After a few seconds she spoke, quietly, hesitating in places as she recalled the part of the poem about the council and mayor.

> *"At last the people in a body*
> *To the Town Hall came flocking:*
> *"Tis clear," cried they, 'our Mayor's a noddy;*
> *And as for our Corporation – shocking*
> *To think we buy gowns lined with ermine*
> *For dolts that can't or won't determine*
> *What's best to rid us of our vermin!"*

Quentin clapped. 'Well done, Mrs Jeffson. Do you know it all the way through? I'd love to quote that part at a council meeting – just think of people's faces if I did?'

Liz chuckled. 'I used to know great big chunks of it when I was a girl. My niece has been learning it recently at school; that's why it came to mind. And please ... do call me Liz.'

She bit her lip at her recklessness. It wasn't the done thing for a male acquaintance to call a married woman by her first name. It was considered to be forward – a little too familiar.'

'Only if you call me Quentin.'

Liz hesitated, and then shrugged off the cloak of caution and etiquette, which irritated her and weighed her down. 'It's just that sitting here in the dark with all the fireworks going off, I don't really feel like a Mrs Jeffson whose husband has cleared off to get drunk in a beer tent and left her on her own. I feel like a Liz.'

Quentin laughed. Who would have ever thought that hidden in the depths of this quiet, timid lady was a vibrant, intelligent woman with a sense of humour that had been buried for so long beneath layers of self-deprecation that it was a wonder it had survived.

'How old are you, Quentin?'

Quentin was taken aback. It was a strange question and out of context.'

'Fifty. Why?'

'I just wondered. I'm fifty too.'

'Mrs Jeffson! A lady is not supposed to tell a gentleman her age. It's not the done thing.'

'I don't care who knows how old I am. I can assure you, Mr Andrews, that I don't imagine I shall ever be bothered about revealing it. I've been sitting here for a while now, thinking about my life and wondering if it's all been a waste. Fifty is a bit of a milestone, don't you think? I'm not old, but I'm past being middle-aged. It feels like I'm wandering around in no-man's land, with bullets whizzing past my ears and bombs going off all around me.'

'You've been through a lot just lately. It's perfectly understandable for you to feel that way.'

Impulsively Liz pulled off her hat and sat with it in her lap. She shook her head and ran her fingers through her salt-and-pepper hair. Breathing in the smell of the bonfire and the earthy aroma of decaying fallen leaves, she wondered why it was that she did not recoil at the closeness of Quentin Andrews. He was looking straight at her face and she didn't feel embarrassed, or frightened, or full of revulsion, and she didn't know why. She inhaled and breathed in again. He didn't smell of stale pipe tobacco, or reek of whisky, or - worst of all - vomit. She fancied she caught a whiff of Brylcreem and soap. He was smartly dressed, like Tom, but unlike Tom he was clean and fresh. She hardly dared admit it to herself, but she could have easily pecked him on the cheek for lifting her spirits and taking her mind off Tom getting drunk in the beer tent.

Quentin didn't notice Liz's sunken eye sockets, or the worry lines that surrounded them. He saw only the tiny sparkles of the light of fireworks exploding in her eyes and they were bright, twinkling like a young girl's. He studied her lips and didn't notice the deep lines that ran from her nose to the corners of her mouth. He marvelled at the contours of the smile, and the way it reached right up to her eyes. Her greying hair was lost in the inky blackness of the sky: the bonfire flickering yellow and burnt orange in the distance lighting up her hair in shades of golden brown and auburn. He had to fight down the urge to put up his hand and run his fingers through the softness of it. And then as briefly as the young, carefree look had brushed across her face, it disappeared to be replaced by something Quentin recognised as a deep unhappiness beneath the surface that had repressed her spirit, and beaten her to the ground. It was something dark and terrible, and he knew that Tom Jeffson had done it to her. He wanted to brush away the darkness and make her smile again.

Liz stared at the Adam's apple that sat just above the open neck of Quentin's shirt: it bobbed twice as he swallowed and she heard him breathe in sharply. Her eyes fell to his hands, and she was moved to see that on the little finger of his right hand he wore what was, quite obviously, his dead wife's wedding band. She couldn't stop herself lightly touching the ring.

'Did this belong to your wife?'

Quentin didn't pull his hand away. 'Yes,' he whispered. 'My Betsy. She was a wonderful wife and mother. She gave me six sons, bless her, and lost her own life giving birth to the youngest.'

Liz looked up from the wedding ring into his eyes. Although it was dark, she could sense he was staring straight into hers. Another firework exploded and, in the light of its aftermath, Liz studied the worry lines on his forehead, the slight stubble appearing on his clean shaven upper lip and chin and knew without any doubt that Quentin still suffered terribly from the loss of his wife. She could have almost reached out and touched the loneliness and grief, even though many years had passed by.

'It must have been absolutely dreadful for you to be left all alone to bring up six children, one of them a tiny baby, when you were grieving for your poor Betsy.'

'I coped. I managed. Had a lot of help from my sister and her husband, you see. My boys are good lads – all of them. Just got young Theo left at home, now. He'll be eleven next year ... growing up fast.'

His words tailed off as he moved his hand away from hers.

'I'm so sorry – ' Liz began, but she didn't know what else to say. Quentin had clearly loved his wife very much. She felt envious of Betsy Andrews and then immediately felt guilty. After all, the poor woman had lost her life.

She stood up and replaced her hat on her head, embarrassed at her uncharacteristic and inappropriate behaviour with a man she hardly knew. What on earth was happening to her? Quentin stood up and hurried after her as she walked off in the direction of the bonfire.

'Don't feel sorry for me,' he said falling in step beside her. It's just life. I manage. 'Here – take my arm – we don't want you tripping over all these tree roots in the dark.'

Chapter Seven
Despair and Kindness

Walter Grey shut the bedroom door, running a trembling hand through his thinning hair. A tall, bespectacled, stooped individual, dressed in a smart black suit, his clean shaven face froze into a mask which hid his true feelings as he pressed his lips together.

'She's settled,' he said to George. 'But what the hell are we going to do now?'

'We'll have to keep all this quiet,' George said. 'It's just one thing after another in this family. First Tom, and now Doris ...'

Walter tutted, annoyed. 'What a bloody mess ...'

George nodded in agreement. 'Gawd knows what it will do to little Violet. Bill said she saw everything.'

Walter clamped his hand to his forehead. 'Our Violet's seen and heard things no little girl should ever know about just lately. I'm so worried about her. Where's it all going to end up, George? What damage has Doris done to her?'

George scratched his head, thinking out loud. 'If Violet's staying overnight with Bill and Daisy, it'll give you a bit of a chance to talk things through with Doris.'

'All right,' Walter replied. 'I'll try. But don't you breathe a word of all this to Tom and Liz. After all, there's no real harm done. We'll keep it a secret, eh? But there's something you should really know about our Violet.'

George frowned. 'What?'

'She didn't lose her hair through alopecia – she cut it all off herself.'

'Bloody hell. No!'

'Doris had a pink fit, as you can imagine. We shaved it all off last Sunday morning just after it happened; I had no choice but to go along with it because Doris came up with this story about alopecia to save folks knowing that Violet had cut off all her hair. I must admit, though, I thought it was a good idea at first, but now Doris says we'll have to keep shaving it off for the next few months because alopecia doesn't cure itself overnight.'

'You can't do that!' George said, horrified. Poor little lass, she must be going through absolute hell to cut off her own hair. Is it because Tom has sold her piano, do you think? She was right upset about that.'

Walter shook his head. 'If only you knew what went on with our Doris and Violet, it would make *you* tear your hair out by the roots. It's no wonder the pair of them are permanently off hooks. All Doris wants is a little girl who doesn't ask endless questions, plays quietly with her dolls' house and who she can dress in pretty clothes so that she can show her off like a prize poodle. She just doesn't want to accept that Violet is growing up. She's sharp as a razor – a right clever child. She wants no more than to be left alone with her poetry, her music and her books. To tell the truth, George, it worries me half to death because she's become so withdrawn.'

George sighed. As well as all the trouble in his family, it

126

was obvious Doris and Walter were having problems, too.
Once George had gone home, Walter crept back into the
bedroom. Doris was awake, staring at the ceiling.

'Oh, the embarrassment!' she wailed. 'How on earth can
I face folks now, with everyone knowing I stuck my head in
the gas oven?'

'Don't fret, Doris. We can keep it quiet. I've just had a
chat with George. Only the family knows the truth. We'll
tell all the neighbours you fainted with one of your bilious
attacks. You really must try not to get so worked up about
things ...'

'It's all Violet's fault,' Doris retaliated. 'I just can't
endure having a daughter with alopecia on top of
everything else I am expected to put up with. If only Bill
had been just twenty minutes later, it would have all been
over.'

'But she hasn't got alopecia, has she? She's disturbed
and needs to see the doctor if you ask me my opinion.
Look, you haven't inhaled too much gas and George and
Rose won't tell Tom and Liz. There's no real harm done.
Bill's going to have a word with Violet and explain that she
mustn't tell anyone what happened, and that you've been
poorly with your nerves.'

Doris dabbed at her mouth with a handkerchief. It
looked as if she was going to be spared the embarrassment
of folk knowing she had tried to gas herself. But she would
tell Tom. Oh yes, she would definitely tell him what she
had done. She'd make him feel guilty and blame himself
for causing her to feel so wretched because he had ignored
her letter. He would be bound to feel sorry for her and
everything would be fine again.

Doris turned over in bed and shut her eyes in despair. All she wanted was to curl up in Tom's arms and to hear him say that he loved her.

Liz was in bed, dozing, when Tom arrived home from the firework display. She heard the back door open and Tom muttering to himself as he took off his coat and cap and hung them up in the hallway. She heard him stumble back through the kitchen and then shuffle noisily out of the back door to the outside toilet.

When Quentin had offered her his arm, and she'd had no choice but to take it as the track beside the lake at Wicksteed Park was so uneven. His arm had felt warm and secure. The unfamiliar closeness of him had lingered and had nestled somewhere in the centre of her abdomen and even though she tried to put the thoughts out of her head, she couldn't help reliving the experience over and over again as she lay in bed, waiting for Tom to return.

They had found Tom slumped over a trestle table in the beer tent, snoring, his head resting on his arm with a whisky glass clutched in his hand. After trying, to no avail, to rouse Tom, Quentin had offered to walk her home, and she'd accepted without a second thought. *"He'll find his own way back,"* she'd said to Quentin. *"When he's sobered up a bit."*

It had been nice to stroll along Windmill Avenue with a man who wasn't drunk, who walked with her and not in front of her, and who actually talked to her instead of at her and didn't count his steps all the time. He had offered her his arm along the Avenue, but she hadn't taken it this time because someone may have seen and jumped to the wrong conclusions even though his son, Theo, was walking alongside them. When they'd arrived back at Cornwall Road, she'd asked him and his son in for a nightcap and some supper and it had been lovely to sit with Rose and George in front of a crackling fire, toasting crumpets and chatting about the Hospital Guild Monster Fete that afternoon, the annual rowing competition on the lake, in which Quentin and Theo had taken part, the air display by the Tiger Moths and the lovely fireworks at the end of the day

Rose had asked where Tom was, and Liz hadn't answered. Twice Rose had asked, and twice she had ignored her questioning. Eventually Quentin had to explain to Rose that her father had stayed to chat to some friends.

It had been a strange evening and had not gone to plan, but she had enjoyed herself chatting to Quentin and didn't want to spoil it by talking about Tom, or wondering how he'd get home. Quentin had eventually left, worried about the late hour and Theo needing his sleep. Now, as she lay in bed on her own, she felt excited. Although it had been unintentional and unplanned, she had, for the first time in their marriage, enjoyed a social occasion without Tom. Not so very long ago she would have been worried about him getting drunk in a beer tent, but now all she felt was indifference.

The bedroom door creaked open.

'Liz?'

She didn't answer, keeping her eyes tightly shut.

'You awake?'

Liz lay very still, hoping that Tom would think she was asleep.

'I know you're awake, Liz.'

Liz braced herself, waiting for the inevitable. She wasn't sure if she could endure it. Not tonight when the delicious feeling of being walked home by a real gentleman was still so alive in her.

'I'm so sorry, Liz,' Tom slurred as he sank down on the bed to take off his boots. 'I don't know what happened. I was so full of good intentions. What is it they say? *The road to hell is paved with good intentions.* That's right, isn't it old gal? Don't know who said it though. Do you?'

Liz heard Tom sigh. She didn't answer. She waited for him to roll into bed towards her and for the inevitable rough hand to part her legs, and for him to heave himself on top of her. She hoped it would be quick. She just couldn't stand it, not tonight.

She heard him hiccup, and there was a catch in his breath that sounded like a sob. Surely he wasn't *crying*. She opened her eyes and looked at his back and heaving, troubled shoulders. He was sitting on the edge of the bed with his head in his hands, great racking sobs shaking his body.

Then she felt guilty. Guilty because she'd abandoned him in the beer tent. Guilty because she knew, deep down, that he couldn't help his psychopathic disorder. But more than anything, she felt guilty because she didn't feel one little bit remorseful about being walked home by someone other than her husband.

'I love you, Liz.'

She still didn't move. This must surely be the end. She

felt nothing for Tom anymore. He could cry and sob all he liked, but it was too late. Much too late to turn back the clock and love him again.

Walter was unable to sleep: each time he nodded off in the fireside chair in the cold living room, he jolted awake again as the events of the last few hours stabbed at his consciousness. He despised himself for being unable to provide fulfilment and normality to his domestic life. Since Doris had forbidden him to be alone with Violet when she had been two years old, he spent his spare time wandering around the town, frequenting various places where he knew there were men such as himself – trapped in marriages but wandering around in the no-man's land between domestic normality and the forbidden and illegal life that always beckoned. There was a teashop in town where he and several of his friends in the same predicament would meet up to talk, the sympathetic owner turning a blind eye to the conversations he must surely overhear.

Walter rarely looked in the mirror. Staring at his reflection always forced him to face up to the type of man he really was – a complete failure to masculinity. Wallowing in self-punishment was the only way he could find equilibrium between burying the shame and loathing and acting out the role of a devoted husband and father.

However much Walter despised himself, he could not help loving his daughter. Even though he had always known Violet was another man's biological child, he always felt she was his. He had been dealt a devastating blow when Doris had declared that *"queers shouldn't be allowed to be alone with children"*, but had half-agreed with her. Perhaps the love he felt for a child that wasn't biologically his was unnatural, just as his feelings for men were unnatural.

Walter shook his head in the darkness. Over the last week, as Doris had fallen over the crumbling edge of depression, he had risen to the challenge and slipped effortlessly into fatherhood, soothing and comforting his daughter through her torment. He had grieved for the lost years of her childhood, agonised with the guilt because he had let her down, and suppressed the anger he felt towards his wife, who really should be pulling herself together and making the best of things. After all, he really *had* been injured in the Great War, and yes, it had affected him in more ways than he had ever admitted, even to himself. Was she not grateful he had turned a blind eye to her affair with another man? Did she not realise that he had accepted how dreadful if must be for her to be married to a man who could not satisfy her? But how could she have chosen Tom Jeffson? He could not think of a worse candidate for biological fatherhood. It had been a dreadful shock, finding out that Tom was Violet's real father and he was having a terrible time coming to terms with it.

Doris had talked recently about wanting another baby – a brother or sister for Violet. As the mechanics of conceiving a baby would most likely have to be carried out by another man, and without actually saying the words, Walter had, with a nod of his head, given her his blessing to go out and find one who would oblige. But God forbid it would be Tom Jeffson again.

Walter levered himself up from the armchair and crept upstairs to check on Doris, who was asleep. Inhaling gas had given her a dreadful headache and made her vomit, over and over again, and she had taken some pills which had made her sleep heavily.

On the way back downstairs, surrounded by an eerie half-light, Walter glanced into Violet's bedroom. It was just as she had left it a few hours ago, before she had hurriedly been despatched off to spend the night with Daisy and Bill.

He switched on the electric light by the door and gazed around the room. He picked up discarded clothes from the floor, put them on hangers and replaced them in the wardrobe. He reached under the bed for stray socks and his fingers brushed against a cardboard box of old toys. Pulling it out he recognised a ragdoll he had bought for his daughter when she was small. He clutched it to his chest, smiling at happy memories of his baby daughter's first few months of life when he was allowed to cradle her in his arms and be a proper daddy to her. As he replaced the ragdoll back in the box, he spotted an old tin, nestling in the corner of the box. He lifted it out: it was obvious Violet had been saving some pennies.

He gasped in surprise when he opened the tin. It was full of half-crowns. He tipped them onto the bed and counted them into piles of eight. His daughter had nearly twelve pounds beneath her bed – a fortune for a little girl not yet ten years-old.

His heart gave an alarming thud in his chest. Who had given it to her? What had she been doing to warrant being given this huge amount of money?

What on earth had been going on?

Violet awoke in a strange house, in a strange bedroom. She slid out of the ancient, creaky truckle bed, her legs rubbing across a ridge in the sheet where it had been cut in half and stitched up again down the middle, to get a couple of years' additional use out of the worn bed linen Daisy had been given. Old, faded curtains were drawn across the window, and in one of the drawers of the dressing table she knew she would find some clean clothes and underwear, hastily grabbed by her father the night before when she had been unceremoniously plucked from her home by her cousin Daisy and her husband Bill after her mam had tried to gas herself.

She drew back the frilled curtain fixed to the underside of the top of the dressing table. It seemed like months ago that Daisy had borrowed Rose's sewing machine, which was kept in the front room of her Uncle Tom's house beside her piano. She had practised her scales while Daisy had cut and sewed the old material to make the spare bedroom curtains and a matching frill for the battered dressing table, its spindly legs covered with dents, scratches and chips in the old wood.

Violet remembered that day because Daisy had crept furtively into the house to use the sewing machine. Uncle Tom had still been in hospital and her mam had been secretly visiting him. Auntie Liz had been asked to watch her, but had gone out shopping, leaving her alone for an hour or so, and the front room hadn't yet been turned into a living room for Rose and George. Just a few weeks had passed since that day, but it seemed like a lifetime ago that Daisy had crept into the house, treadled the sewing

134

machine faster than she had ever seen anyone use it before, and expertly made the curtains and the frill that covered the legs of the dressing table. Daisy had made her swear on the Bible not to tell anyone she had been there.

Another secret.

Violet ran her hand over the surface of the dressing table. It had been sanded smooth and then varnished by Bill, and she could still smell the varnish. She cast her eyes out of the window over the newly dug back garden, where Bill had sectioned off a little vegetable patch and had already planted some vegetables. Daisy and Bill had lived in this new house for only a few weeks, but already it felt more like a home than her own house ever had. She heard her cousin singing downstairs as she made up the fire in the living room, then the gurgling and cooing of baby Eileen in the room next door to the spare room. She smiled. Her cousin Daisy's home was really nice. In fact, she could easily stay here, couldn't she? If she didn't cause any trouble and minded her Ps and Qs, she might be able to stay with Daisy, Bill and baby Eileen while her mam recovered from her nervous breakdown. It would be a much better alternative than to run away to London.

She pulled on her cardigan over her nightdress and crept, barefoot, to the top of the stairs. There was no carpet or stair rods, but the wood was new and clean beneath the soles of her feet. As she descended the stairs, the front door opened and Bill stepped over the threshold.

'Hello, Flower,' he said. 'Did you have a good night's sleep?'

'Yes, thank you. I like the new bedroom.'

Bill held out his hand to her, and she ran down the

stairs and took it.

The newly-lit fire crackled and spat in the grate, and as Bill and Violet joined her in the living room, Daisy set a heavy old fireguard on the hearth to protect the threadbare rug. On either side of the fire were two, huge armchairs. The material was old and frayed, and the stuffing was coming out of a hole in one of the arms, but Violet jumped into it, feeling happy and loved.

'Would you like some toast,' Daisy said, handing her a toasting fork. 'Once the fire gets going you can help me make it.'

'Oh, goody,' Violet said, her eyes wide with excitement. Her mam never made toast on an open fire. She said it was common. Toast in Violet's house was made under a grill on the new gas cooker – the one her mam stuck her head into and tried to gas herself.

Later that morning she helped Bill tend to the front garden, where he sectioned off an area with wooden pegs and some string, indicating where the new lawn was to be sown. She had skipped and hopped along Beech Crescent, talking to Daisy and Bill's new neighbours while they had planted daffodil, tulip and crocus bulbs in the areas which were to be the borders of the new lawn, and then she had helped them sow the grass seed, plunging her hand into the waxy brown paper bag and then carefully sprinkling the seeds evenly over the sectioned off area. Bill explained to her that it probably wouldn't grow very much until next year, but then it would burst into life with the warmth of the sun and by the summer she should be able to play on the lawn.

She had pushed the toddler son of one of Daisy and

Bill's new neighbours on his wooden, home-made trolley up and down the street while the neighbours chatted as they worked on making their own front garden nice for springtime next year.

She had been out in the fresh air all morning and, when Daisy called her in for her Sunday dinner, she was hungry, dirty and happy. She had fallen over, more than once, and skinned both knees, but they didn't hurt.

At lunchtime, Violet washed her face in the kitchen sink and glanced, shocked, at her reflection in Bill's shaving mirror on the kitchen window sill, suddenly realising that she had completely forgotten to tie on her charlady headscarf to hide her bald head.

Not one, single person in Beech Crescent had mentioned her baldness that morning. No one had said she should wear her headscarf to hide it, and above all, the word *alopecia* hadn't even been mentioned.

She had bolted down her boiled potatoes, cabbage and heated-up left over stewed beef and cleaned her plate of gravy with a chunk of bread. Then, in the afternoon, they had all gone out for a walk, but she still hadn't worn her headscarf. Instead she had put on one of Bill's tweed caps to keep her head warm in the chilly air, tied on by one of Daisy's scarves. She had pushed baby Eileen in her big pram, and then, when her arms ached from all the pushing, she had held Bill's hand and walked by his side. When her legs ached from all the walking, she had ridden, piggy-back style, on his back, telling him to giddy-up as he ran along the street, jigging her up and down until her sides ached from laughing and squealing.

After a tea of bread and dripping, Violet curled up with

Bill in one of the big armchairs by the fire as he cradled baby Eileen in his arms. She lay her head on his shoulder, laughing out loud at the comedy play on the Black Cat wireless set. The fire crackled comfortingly in the grate making her feel warm on the inside as well as on the outside.

If only she could live with Daisy and Bill, everything would be all right again.

Just when she thought they had forgotten about her, and she would be able to stay with Daisy and Bill for another night, the front door knocker was rapped three times. Violet buried her head in Bill's shoulder.

'I don't want to go,' she wailed. 'Please don't make me go. Please can I stay here?'

Chapter Eight
Desire and Guilt

'Come in, come in,' Quentin said with an enthusiastic shake of her hand. 'How lovely to see you, Mrs Jeffson.'

Liz stepped over the threshold into the hallway of Quentin's house. She felt a flush spread up her neck to her face, but it was a pleasant feeling. It complemented the nice sensation inside her that made her arms feel weak and her heart beat faster. Deeply committed to her marriage vows, for the last thirty years she had not really known where Tom ended and she began. But now she felt as if she had found her end of the thread on a reel of cotton on Bonfire Night, and now she'd pulled it out, she wanted to carry on pulling.

'I wanted to show my appreciation for your kindness in walking me home last Saturday, so I baked you a fruit cake.'

'What a lovely surprise. That's ever so kind of you Mrs Jeffson.' He gestured with his hand. 'Won't you come through? Perhaps stay for a cup of tea?'

Liz knew she shouldn't. She knew it would be quite improper of her to take afternoon tea with Quentin

Andrews, with him being a widower and her a married woman. She knew she was unravelling; the reel spinning so fast it was almost out of control.

There was a bicycle in the narrow hallway and she had to squeeze past it. Quentin held out his hand in apology. 'Sorry about this. I shouldn't keep it in here really, but it's so handy.'

'That's all right, Mr Andrews,' she said as she grasped his outstretched hand and squeezed past the bicycle. This feeling really was quite delicious, she thought to herself, as a little tingle started in the palm of her hand and snaked its way up her arm.

Liz stepped through into the tiny living room. It was evident that Quentin lived alone with his young son, as his home lacked a woman's touch. He moved a boys' comic for her to sit down and took the fruitcake, wrapped in brown greaseproof paper, from her hand.

As she sat down, her hands began to shake and so she clasped them together in her lap.

'Did your husband arrive home safely?' Quentin said from the kitchen.

Liz bit her lip. The word *husband* was one she didn't really care for at the moment.

'Yes, he did – eventually. It really was very kind of you to walk me home.'

Soon, Liz had a cup of tea in one hand and a plate, holding a slice of fruit cake in the other. She put the cake on her lap. The cup rattled on the saucer and she had to make a conscious effort to stop her hand shaking so that the tea wouldn't spill.

'You have two lovely daughters, Mrs Jeffson. Your Daisy

has grown up so much since the first day I met her when Mr Jeffson had his first unfortunate accident. It's hard to believe it was only a year ago that he broke his leg when he fell down the drain.'

For a few moments, neither of them spoke.

Quentin finished his tea and put his cup and saucer on the floor. Liz bit her lip. She knew she was behaving like one of Tom's loose women, but she couldn't help herself. If Tom had torn her heart in shreds and scattered it far and wide during their difficult marriage, Quentin was unwittingly picking up the pieces and putting it back together. The process had started at the firework display, when for the first time since she had married Tom, she felt like a proper woman. Over the past week she had felt anger instead of indifference when something Tom said grated on her nerves; enthusiasm instead of apathy when she'd been arranging cut flowers in a vase and had actually laughed out loud several times over the past few days.

'I know,' she said, staring into her tea cup. 'I do know I'm not myself and I am maybe a little forward with you, but I just can't take anymore. I think I need someone to help me through ...'

Her voice trailed off, and her throat tightened, strangling her voice in mid-sentence. Then the tears came. Great, fat tears that rolled from her dark eyes down her cheeks and dripped off her chin into her lap. Motionless, she cradled her cup and saucer, slumped in her chair, letting the tears flow, trying not to make too much noise.

Quentin reached into his trouser pocket, pulled out his handkerchief and let her cry without saying a single word.

She cried for a long time.

Quentin didn't know what to do. Everyone knew what a difficult time Liz Jeffson was going through since her husband's suicide attempt. Of course, he'd heard rumours about Tom and the family's dirty washing had been hung out all over the front page of the Kettering Evening Telegraph a few weeks ago. He'd never much cared for the man, but there must be something more that made an intelligent, respectable woman like Liz Jeffson crumble in such an embarrassing manner in front of a mere acquaintance.

'I'm sorry. So sorry, Mr Andrews,' she mumbled into his handkerchief. 'I don't know what came over me. It's so embarrassing –'

'Call me Quentin.'

'Quentin,' she repeated without looking at him.

'Quentin leaned over and plucked Liz's cup and saucer from her hand. She sat back in the chair, her cheeks flushed. She tried to pat down her hair with her fingertips.

'I really must apologise ...'

Quentin smiled. 'No need. We can talk for a while if it will make you feel better.'

Liz nodded and smiled back at him, her eyes bright and red-rimmed.

'So how old were you when you took up with Mr Jeffson, then?'

'Eighteen.'

'How did you meet him?'

'At the church in Broughton.'

142

Quentin nodded. 'Aahh. I know it. Did you live in Broughton?'

Liz nodded. 'So did Tom. He was such a nice young chap. Very clever, clean and he worked hard. He lived with his great aunt and uncle. We stepped out together a couple of times. It was all very proper. Then – then – it all began to go wrong.'

Quentin leaned forwards, interested. 'What happened?'

'One Sunday afternoon we were out walking just outside the village. He had been drinking at lunchtime and I think he must have been a little drunk. That was the one thing I didn't like about him. The drink. I wasn't used to it, you see. I didn't understand what it did to a man. He ... he ... forced himself on me.'

Quentin's eyes widened as he briefly wondered if he had heard her correctly, as the words had been spoken with no inflection.

'Forced himself?'

'Yes. It was the drink. I wasn't willing. I wasn't that type of girl. I struggled and protested but he put his hand over my mouth so I couldn't scream out. It was so silly of me to go out walking alone with him when he had been drinking.'

Quentin took her hand between both of his. 'It wasn't your fault. You shouldn't blame yourself.'

'It resulted our Arthur who died in nineteen-twenty-two of the consumption. I tried to get rid of the baby with boiling hot water in a tin bath and drank some castor oil. I've still got the scars on the tops of my legs where the water scalded me. My mother caught me and there was an awful argument with my father. He made me marry Tom,

143

even though I told him, over and over again that he had forced himself on me while he was drunk. They didn't want any scandal in those days and just brushed things like that under the carpet.'

Quentin dropped his head and shook it slightly in shock, unable to speak.

'But that's all in the past. I know it is my duty as a wife to stand by my husband in his time of sickness. And Tom is ill, even if the illness can't be seen and is in his own head. I have always respected my marriage vows.'

Liz twizzled her wedding ring around on her finger. Alarmed, Quentin wondered if she was about to take it off

'I don't know why am I telling you all this. I've never spoken about it to anyone else.'

Quentin shook his head. 'I think you perhaps need to get it all off your chest after what you've been through just lately. But I'd never have guessed. You always seemed like such a respectable family. It just goes to show, you never know what goes on behind closed doors, do you?'

'He used to treat me roughly sometimes, too,' Liz went on. 'But it was usually my own fault. I'm so clumsy and forgetful. The thing is, since he came home from the hospital, when our Rose swore at him that if he ever touched me again she would hang for him, he's been a perfect husband.'

Liz withdrew her hand from his. 'Tom can be such a delightful man when he stays off the drink. Please don't repeat this to anyone, but he has been diagnosed with a psychopathic disorder. Since he tried to end it all, he's having treatment with a psychiatrist. When he's on the wagon, he really is quite a nice, generous man. He's polite and attentive and only a couple of weeks ago he bought me red roses, hand-made chocolates and a gold necklace. He can be quite normal for a while, until something, or someone, annoys him. He'll reach for the scotch bottle, which then triggers a rage, and then he loses all control of his senses. But there's always a reason, so I suppose he can be excused for his past behaviour, given his psychopathic disorder.'

Liz stopped to draw breath. She lowered her eyes, and there was a moment's silence.

'It's a real illness, you see. Only it's an invisible one. I'm his wife and I have to help him recover. I really must be getting back to him now. I've wasted far too much of your time.'

There was another silence.

Liz cleared her throat in embarrassment. 'I'm so sorry to have been such a nuisance.'

Quentin held out his hand to help her out of the chair.

She looked down at her feet as she stood up. She was still holding his hand and he knew that neither of them wanted to let go. He pulled her towards him and it was inevitable they would hug. Quentin felt the warmth of her body and breathed in sharply. It had been such a long time since he had held a woman in his arms. He felt his heat flood into her and give her strength. The warm feeling curled around his heart and made it beat faster. It stretched its fingers up into his hair and made his scalp tingle. She leaned into him, and he almost heard her whisper his name, but wasn't sure if it was in his head or was real.

His voice was croaky; his words somehow inadequate.

'Liz. I'll always be here for you –'

'I know. I ... I ... yes ... oh, I wish things were different.'

'Sshhh,' he said, stroking her hair.

With a conscious effort, he pushed away from her, embarrassed as he came to his senses. What on earth was he thinking of, embracing a married woman? But his heart was racing and desire for her was beginning to cloud his usual careful judgement.

She picked up her hat and set it on her head with a purpose; ready to face the world again.

'Goodbye, Quentin. And thank you for being so understanding. I'm so sorry for being such a nuisance.'

'You weren't. You're not,' he said with a sympathetic smile.

It was almost dark when Liz left Quentin's house. Everyone would wonder where she'd been. She could not lie: she would tell Tom she had called on Mr Andrews to take him a cake on account of his kindness in walking her home on bonfire night. What she wouldn't tell Tom, though, was how long she had stayed in his house, or that, just as she was leaving, he had mentioned he was visiting Daisy and Bill for tea the following Saturday and would be there at three o'clock on the dot.

JUNE 1933

ᘒᙄ

Chapter Nine
Humility and Spite

One Saturday morning the following summer, Tom was in Cobley's grocery shop in Kettering town centre. Proud of his progress, he had only one more entry to tick off in his red notebook. The promise to make amends with Billy Potter, a neighbour, had been added to the list after he had explained to his psychiatrist that he had treated the lad badly in the past.

'That will be one shilling and sixpence ha'penny, Mr Jeffson, sir,' Billy said, holding out his hand after he had served Tom.

Tom thrust his hand into his pocket and drew out some loose change.

'Here, lad. Take it outta that.'

Billy Potter raked through sixpences, three-penny pieces, pennies and halfpennies in Tom's big palm, extracting various coins, counting carefully out loud.

'Billy, lad ...'

'Yes, sir?' Billy Potter said, unable to disguise the nervousness in his voice.

'I'm sorry for all the nasty things I've done and said to you over the years. You're a credit to your mam. It can't have been easy for her, bringing you up on her own after your old man died in the Great War.'

Billy Potter fumbled with the money in his hand and glanced over his shoulder, looking for his boss.

'Don't worry, I won't ever call you names again, Billy. I know you're trying hard to make something of yourself. You're doing really well, holding down a decent job like this.'

'I ... I ... I'll just pack your groceries for you, Mr Jeffson ... sir. If you'll just let me have your bag.'

Tom passed Billy his string bag.

'Do you like working in here?'

'Er ... yes, it's all right, sir. Mr Cobley is very good to me.'

Tom smiled and stroked his moustache thoughtfully as Billy carefully packed his bag for him.

'You're good with your hands, lad. That little wooden birdie-house you made for our Daisy's garden when she moved into her new house last year was smashing. And my missus tells me that the kitchen cabinet you made for your mam was really well crafted.'

Billy Potter hung his head, embarrassed. He blushed a deep red as he handed Tom his bag.

'What I was going to say, lad, is that I want to make amends for how badly I've treated you over the years. I've called you some horrible names and made fun of you because of ... well ...I shouldn't have, should I? After what happened to me last year I was in no position to make fun of you. Pot calling the kettle black, if you know what I mean.

'Your mam was talking to the wife the other day about you having nowhere to make up your bits and pieces of woodwork. I was wondering if you'd like the use of my workshop at the bottom of my garden. I only keep a few garden tools in there and I can easily make space for your woodworking equipment.'

Billy Potter's flabby lower lip fell open in surprise as he struggled to understand Tom's uncharacteristically kind gesture. Usually Tom Jeffson's visits to the grocers were accompanied by nasty comments such as *"half sharp"* and *"a shillin' short of a pound"*.

Tom shrugged his shoulders, holding his hands up in the air. 'There's no ulterior motive, lad. I just want to make it up to you and your mam.'

Billy mumbled, struggling to find the right words. 'Thank you, Mr Jeffson. That's right kind of you.'

When he arrived home after shopping at Cobley's, Tom extracted his red notebook and a pencil from his jacket inside pocket.

'That's the last one ticked off, Liz,' he said as he marked the page with an exaggerated flourish and showed the book to her. 'I've made amends with young Billy Potter and told him he can use my workshop for his woodwork.'

'Good,' Liz said. 'You've done well. Billy Potter is so gifted with his hands. I'm sure you won't regret it.'

'Dr Crabtree is delighted with my progress,' Tom said, grabbing Liz around the waist, whirling her around and planting a kiss on her cheek. 'And now I've made amends with everyone I've wronged in the past, I want to take you away for a little holiday, just the two of us.'

Liz's heart sank. She didn't want to go away on holiday. Not with Tom anyway.

'There's no need, Tom. We shouldn't waste money on a holiday, not when you still owe Rose and George money.'

'Don't talk rubbish, woman. I reckon we've deserved a little break after all we've been through. And anyway, I want to take you away to say thank you for sticking by me through all this trouble.'

Tom drew Liz into him and kissed her on the lips. She recoiled away from him, feeling pressured.

'We could go to Clacton-on-Sea, or Great Yarmouth, or even Cleethorpes. You like it at Cleethorpes.'

'I ... I don't know, Tom. We'll have to see.' She pushed him away and turned, clutching at a dish cloth and rubbing hard at the already spotlessly clean kitchen table.

'Leave that, woman. It's all right. I'm cured now. Don't mind a bit o' muck here 'n' there. Come here and give us a kiss, ol' gal. A proper one, just to let you know how much I love you.'

Doris smoothed her tight skirt over her hips, whispering excitedly to herself in the hall mirror. She then hastily fluffed up her hair and rubbed some rouge into her cheeks and lightly stroked some lipstick on her lips. She was wearing her best clothes – a new, brown tweed skirt with a matching jacket, a cream, silky blouse and shoes and handbag to match.

Violet frowned. There was something afoot. Her mam

seemed almost happy, and her mam was never happy. In fact, Violet couldn't remember the last time there wasn't someone out to make trouble for her, fictitious or otherwise, or she hadn't been ill with some ailment or another.

As her mother carefully placed her hat on her head, pinning it into place with a long hat pin, Violet ran her fingers over the front of her head, under her headscarf, the bristles of regrowth reminding her that she still wasn't allowed to have any hair.

'Mam, can I let my hair grow back? After all, I've been bald for eight months now.'

'No. Not yet. We need to wait a year, Violet. I've told you before, the lady I knew with alopecia was bald for a very long time before her hair grew back.'

Violet screwed her eyes shut against familiar tears of frustration and despair. 'But Mam, I'm fed up with not having any hair and wearing a headscarf all the time. It makes my head hot.'

'Well, you should have thought of that when you cut it all off,' Doris retorted. 'Anyway, I can't stand here all day talking about your bald head, I'm meeting Peggy and we are going shopping in town.'

'Why can't I come?'

Doris replied quickly. 'Because you can't. Peggy has an important appointment and I have to go with her.'

'Well, I can go to the Library and read some books, or to the Art Gallery and look at the paintings.'

'No. You are not coming with me and that's final. You are ten years-old, Violet. Old enough to stay here by yourself now. Your father will probably be back soon anyway – that's if he can tear himself away from that damned Solicitors' practice or whatever else it is he gets up to on a Saturday afternoon.'

Violet unpicked the knot from her headscarf, dragged it over her bristly scalp and stepped into the living room, trailing it behind her, suddenly scared of being left alone in the house. Since she had cut off her hair last year she had lost her confidence. She didn't quite know whether cutting her hair off had been because of the voice in her head or whether it was the secrets that had made her do it, but she did know that she was probably going mad, just like Uncle Tom.

She heard voices in her head talking to her all the time, now, although she mainly ignored them. But when she was alone in her bedroom, or doing her homework quietly in the front room, the voices made her do things to herself, like hitting her shins with a heavy iron bar she had found in the shed at the bottom of the garden. The voices had almost made her set fire to her bedroom, too, when they had instructed her to steal a box of matches from the kitchen drawer, hide them in her bedroom and then carry out a little challenge to see how close a flame could get to a scrap of paper before it caught fire. The voices had also made her cut her arm, just a little bit, with the vegetable knife and watch in wonder as the blood ran in a thin, red rivulet down her arm and dripped into the kitchen sink.

All the time people told her she was a very brave girl, on account of her alopecia. She didn't feel brave. She just wanted to curl up in corners most of the time and rock backwards and forwards while she tried to clear her naked, bald head of everything swirling around inside it

152

and concentrate on nothing.

'I have to go to the allotments after dinner,' Tom said to Liz. 'There was a note in the door last night – someone's been stealing vegetables and a few of the chaps are having a get together this afternoon to see what we can do about it.'

Liz shut her eyes, relieved she would have some peace if Tom was going to the allotments. His behaviour had been impeccable and he had changed into a loving and gentle husband, just like he had promised. Since his mild aberration on Bonfire Night, she had almost willed him to fall off the wagon again and give her an excuse to escape her marital duties. It was ironic that, over the years, she had yearned for the time when Tom would turn over a new leaf and be the type of husband she had always wished for. Now it had actually happened, she felt nothing. The love had died and disintegrated as completely as the dried-up, brittle red petals of the roses he frequently brought home for her as a token of his enduring love.

Liz didn't know how much longer she was going to be able to tolerate being married to Tom. Since meeting Quentin, she was completely unable to detach herself from thoughts of him, and concentrate on something else, like what she was going to cook for dinner, or whether the sun would shine the next day so that she could get her washing dry. All she thought about was Quentin. All she looked forward to was meeting up with him at Daisy's house on Saturday afternoons, when they would eat cake, drink tea and chat.

'What have you got planned this afternoon, old gal?'

'Baking,' Liz replied. 'And then I'll go to see Daisy and take her a cake.'

'Do you mind if I go to the allotment, then?'

'Of course I don't.'

After lunch, limping slightly as he hurried along the street towards his allotment, Tom felt content and pleased with himself. His estranged eldest daughter, Lily, was back in his life, even if she did keep him at arm's length; Rose was being civil to him again and Daisy was always popping in to see her mam, giving him the chance to see baby Eileen. Yes, he thought to himself. He'd made good progress over the last year. Dr Crabtree had been so pleased with him at his last appointment, she had said he was a model patient.

He had been resolute about Doris, too. He had felt sorry for her when she had leapt out on him in the street when he was coming back from work one day a month ago. In a flood of tears, she had confessed to him about Violet returning home with Bill on bonfire night the previous year and finding her with her head in the gas oven because she was so upset about him deliberately standing her up.

"I don't know what you mean," Tom had said to her. *"I've never given you false hopes. I've stayed away and kept my promise to Liz."*

She had rambled on about a letter, and how he had arranged for Violet to go to the Monster Fete and Carnival at the park on bonfire night so they could be alone for the afternoon, and then deliberately stood her up

"What letter?" He had scratched his head: he had

154

completely forgotten about the unopened letter from Doris that still gathered dust in his tool shed. He had felt bad, then, and had taken her in his arms and comforted her, realising that it was all his fault for how desolate she obviously felt. Ending the affair had been too abrupt – and he should have seen that. He knew that he should have been gentler with Doris and let her down gradually instead of going in like a wild boar and delivering his mercenary speech about not loving her on the day he had ended their affair.

He doubted she had *really* stuck her head in the gas oven on bonfire night. After all, no one else in the family had mentioned it. She was probably making it up to make him feel sorry for her.

As resolute as an executioner wielding a razor sharp axe, ready to swing it over her shoulder and kill Tom's marriage, she sat on a grassy knoll by the riverbank, throwing small pieces of bread to a few squawking ducks. She had placed herself strategically so that he would have to pass her on his way to the fictitious meeting with his fellow allotment holders.

As he approached she smiled at him.

'Hello, Tom. How are you?'

He stared at her, the look on his face telling her that he was spellbound by her smart, new clothes and porcelain smooth skin. She might now be forty years old, but she knew she was still as pretty as a picture with her immaculately made-up face, her fine, blonde hair swept back into an elegant chignon and her fashionable two piece suit. If anything, her maturing beauty suited her much better than the innocent charm of twelve years ago when they had first started their affair.

'I'm fine,' Tom said. 'Now if you'll excuse me I have a meeting ...'

Doris picked up a wicker basket. 'I brought us a picnic,' she said, peeling back the green gingham tablecloth that covered neat packages of brown greaseproof paper, tied up with string. 'We could go for a little walk if you like.'

Suspicious, Tom shifted his weight uneasily.

'You don't have a meeting,' she said softly. 'The note was from me. It was the only way I could think of to arrange to speak to you, alone.'

Tom rolled his eyes and sighed. 'No, Doris. It's over. You know how it is, I have kept every single one of my promises and I'm a changed man now ...'

Doris gave a wide, red-lipped smile and gestured towards the basket. 'But I've made us a delicious picnic.'

Tom threw her a wary smile. 'It looks lovely, Doris. But Liz would go absolutely mad if I had a picnic with you.'

'I know. But I have something important to tell you. We can stroll along the river bank with some lettuces and spring onions in my basket. If anyone sees us we can say I've been down here for some fresh salad. It's not a crime is it? After all, we *are* related by marriage.'

Doris knew she had him hooked. He was curious, itching to find out what she had to say.

He scratched his chin. 'I suppose it wouldn't hurt ... just for a few minutes. I'll just go and dig up some spring onions and cut you a lettuce.'

They walked, together, towards his allotment shed,

where Tom opened the door to fetch a garden fork. Doris shot in behind him and shut the door.

'What are you doing?' Tom said with a frown, squinting at her in the dull light. 'I thought I was just going to get you some salad stuff and then we were going for a walk?'

Doris spread the gingham tablecloth over the dirty chaise longue and sat down, patting the seat next to her. 'Come here, Tom. I've got something exciting to tell you.'

He frowned as he sat on the edge of the seat. 'What?'

'I'm going to have another baby.'

Tom gave a cynical laugh. 'You must be mad. Whose is it? It can't be Walter's. For gawd's sake, woman, I can't believe you'd be so stupid.'

'It's yours, Tom,' Doris said with arched eyebrows and a scornful smile.

Tom threw back his head, laughed out loud and stood up again. 'Now I know you've gone completely round the bend, woman. It can't possibly be mine. We haven't even spoken properly to each other since before Christmas.'

Doris raised her eyebrows.

'Well, I can easily tell Liz and everyone else it's yours. I wonder who Liz will believe?'

Tom's face fell. 'You can't do that.'

'Can't I?'

'What about Walter? Is it *his* baby? Did he manage to ... to ...'

'No, it's not Walter's, but he's really pleased. It will help us to keep up appearances. No one will ever suspect anything is wrong with our marriage if I am going to have another baby. But you owe me, Tom Jeffson, and it would do you well to remember that. Just one word from me, and

Liz will pack her bags and leave you. That's all it will take
– just one word. Unless, of course, we can start to see each
other again, now and then.'

Doris smiled in triumph at Tom's horrified face. She
knew there was no way for him to prove to Liz her baby
wasn't his. He'd have no choice but to rekindle their affair.

She stood up and snaked her arms around his neck.
'You will be gentle won't you? We have to be very careful
because of the baby.'

Chapter Ten
Neglect and Infidelity

It was a hot afternoon and the sun blazed into Violet's bedroom window. She was lonely, with no one to visit, no one to play with and no one to care about what she did or where she went.

She ran her hands over the bristly regrowth on her scalp. Tomorrow morning, they would force her to have her head and eyebrows shaved again. It was now routine: every Sunday morning she would watch her dad swish and swirl the shaving brush around in the dish of soap, her mam would lift her nightdress over her head so that she was naked, and she would be made to sit on a kitchen chair while her dad shaved off the bristles on her head and eyebrows. Every week she pleaded to be allowed to let her hair grow back: every week her mam would stare at her with frozen, hard eyes and tell her that alopecia didn't grow back for at least a year, and that she should have thought of that when she hacked off all her lovely, blonde hair with the kitchen scissors.

She sat on her bed with a book. She would read and wait for her dad to return from work, when hopefully they could go to the park or for a nice walk somewhere. Sometimes, he didn't come home on a Saturday afternoon, though. Sometimes, he would come in at teatime, say the office was absolutely bogged-down with work and that he couldn't get away. But she would know he was lying. She always knew when her parents were lying. Her mam had been lying, earlier, when she had got herself dolled up to the nines, smothered her lips in red lipstick, put on her best hat and said she was going to an appointment in town with Peggy.

After a few minutes Violet sighed, unable to concentrate. She slid off her bed and padded over to her dressing table, where she placed her book, face down on the surface so that she didn't lose her place. She slid open the top drawer and extracted a magnifying glass she had been given for Christmas. She played with it for a few minutes, inspecting the grain of the wood, the whirls and swirls on the tips of her fingers and a solitary ant that crawled over the linoleum floor in her bedroom. She placed the magnifying glass on the top of her dressing table. There were some hairy caterpillars in the garden. Perhaps she could take the sharp knife out of the kitchen and cut one up to see what was inside a hairy caterpillar using her magnifying glass. Anything would be better than having nothing to do and nowhere to go.

It was nice and sunny in the garden as Violet searched for hairy caterpillars and other insects she might dissect with the vegetable knife. She lay, face down, lazily burrowing her fingers into the newly mown grass, enjoying the warmth of the sun on her bald head. She could do anything she liked when there were no grown-ups around to tell her what to do. What she would find inside a real, live animal to inspect with her magnifying glass? She could kill it, slit open its belly and then look at its little heart, its lungs and its liver. She could even cut open its head and look at its brain. She sat up, suddenly excited. Now, what could she find to kill and dissect?

Liz dried her hands on a towel and glanced at the clock in the living room. Her baking finished, she quickly pulled on a colourful summer dress and washed her hands and face. She hung the towel on the front of the oven door to dry and hurried into the hallway, where she placed a light hat on her head and collected her handbag, ready to visit Daisy.

Occasionally, she would visit Quentin on a Saturday afternoon. She would cover his favourite fruit cake in brown greaseproof paper, tie it with string, wrap it in a clean tea-towel and take it round to his house. His neighbours would smile and nod their heads as she walked down his road, remarking that it was so good of her to bake a cake for Quentin and Theo when they had no wife and mother to bake one for them, poor souls. She would reply that it was the least she could do, seeing as Quentin had saved Tom's life when he had been found, collapsed, in his allotment shed last year.

The neighbours would be pleasant to her as she passed the time of day with them; they would doff their hats and Liz would feel wonderful, knowing that in just a few minutes' time she would be with Quentin and she could finally feel like a real woman.

She wasn't visiting Quentin at his home today, though. She was visiting him at Daisy's house. Although she cared for him, and lived for the Saturday afternoons when they could spend some time together, Liz had never felt the need to dress up for Quentin, slather lipstick over her lips or brush her cheeks with rouge. He made no demands on her, but she knew he fully understood her unhappiness and inability to love Tom again after the dreadful things he had done to her and her daughters. He was someone to whom she turned for genuine advice and their friendship had steadily deepened. However, despite the platonic nature of their friendship, Liz knew she loved him, and when they were apart she could think only of him, and the life they could have shared if only Tom had died last summer. She was never quite sure if the strength of her love was reciprocated, though. He always kissed her lightly on the cheek in a greeting when she arrived and sometimes they would occasionally hold hands while they talked. Frequently, he told her how fond of her he was, but had never said he loved her.

If he had done, Liz knew she would have told him she loved him, too.

Although the doctor had confirmed her pregnancy and the morning sickness had started, Doris could still hardly believe her luck. The man she had so easily lured into her bed was young and virile, and it hadn't taken long for her to become pregnant. Once she had achieved her aim, she had sent him packing.

'The doctor has calculated that my baby is due in

162

December,' Doris said as they sat by the riverbank.

Tom squinted in the sunlight. His reply was clipped and stilted. 'Same as Violet, then'.

Doris was disappointed he wouldn't look at her, but she knew that once they got back into the swing of things, he would get over being blackmailed into rekindling their relationship.

Tom stared straight ahead. 'How is she? I haven't seen her out playing in the street.'

'She's being really difficult. Spends nearly all her time in her bedroom and never speaks to me, unless I speak to her. Sometimes she speaks to Walter, but she's gone right into her shell since she lost her hair.'

'Oh dear,' Tom said, with no emotion in his voice. 'Do you think it might be because you allegedly stuck your head in the ...'

'Tom! Stop it. My nervous breakdown has nothing to do with it. It is because of her alopecia, for certain.'

'I was only saying'. After all, it can't do a lassie much good if you reckon she saw her mam's legs sticking out of the ...'

Doris was quick to interrupt, with a theatrical massage of her temples with perfectly manicured fingertips. 'Please don't. I can't bear to talk about it. It upsets me.'

'All right. Keep yer 'at on. I was just trying to help. Anyway, what does the doctor say? Is her hair showing any signs of growing back, yet?'

Tom was still staring straight ahead. He hadn't looked at her once since they'd left the shed. 'No,' Doris lied. 'It takes about a year, apparently. Do you remember that woman who lived in The Hollow in Stamford Road? She

163

lost all her hair and it was a year before it started to grow back.'

'Aye, I remember her,' Tom replied. 'It happened just after her old man was found hanging from the stair banisters.'

Violet was bored with cutting up hairy caterpillars. She had also cut up a wood louse and a beetle, but there was nothing interesting to see inside them with her magnifying glass. She screwed up a sheet of old newspaper around the grizzly remains and put it in the dustbin.

She had enjoyed cutting open the caterpillars. It made her feel in control, and she hadn't felt in control of anything since she had cut off all her hair and her mam had tried to gas herself.

Bored, Violet wandered from room to room. She looked at the clock in the living room. Would Auntie Liz be at home? Auntie Liz was nice and she was also normal, like Rose and Daisy. Auntie Liz wouldn't have shaved her head and made up stories about alopecia. She would have let it grow back straight away and not forced her into enduring months of ridicule and teasing at school about her charlady headscarf and her bald eyebrows.

Violet made up her mind. She was fed up with being bald and wanted to let her hair grow back. She would go over the road to Auntie Liz's house and tell her the truth about cutting off all her hair with the kitchen scissors, and her mam and dad making her have her head shaved every Sunday morning, because alopecia took a year to grow back. She would tell Auntie Liz everything that was bad

164

about her parents, and hopefully, although she would get in dreadful trouble about it all, they would let her hair grow and she wouldn't be bald anymore.

She let herself out of the back door and ran down the alleyway, completely forgetting to put on her headscarf. It would be nice to go and see Auntie Liz. Her mam rarely allowed her to see any of her family since she had cut off her hair and she really missed them, especially Auntie Liz and Daisy.

The back door was locked. Violet peered in the kitchen window, disappointed that no one was at home. By now, she felt a desperate need to talk to someone about her hair. She just couldn't bear the thought of hearing the cut-throat razor scraping its way over her scalp tomorrow morning, or to have to smell the distinctive aroma of shaving soap, or feel the wetness of cold water running down her naked back. But the worst bit was her eyebrows. The soap inevitably got into her eyes and made her cry out as the stinging, gritty liquid seeped through her eyelashes and made her eyes smart so badly she couldn't see properly for the rest of the morning. No, Violet thought. Tomorrow morning things would be different. Tomorrow, everyone would know what a terrible thing she had done in cutting off all her hair with the kitchen scissors, but they would also know what a wicked thing her mother had done in telling lies about alopecia and making her father shave her head.

She would wait. Auntie Liz wouldn't be long; she had probably popped to the grocer's or the butcher's. Violet wandered down the garden path and sat on the lawn for a while, picking daisies to make a daisy chain.

After a few minutes, she stood up again; the hot sun was burning her head because there was no shade in the garden. She walked over to the outside lavatory door and opened it. She knew where the back door key would be – everyone she knew kept it hanging on a piece of string. She stood on tiptoe, only just able to reach to hook it off.

It was nice and cool in Auntie Liz's house and she could smell that someone had been baking. It made her feel hungry and she realised that she hadn't eaten anything since breakfast-time. She wandered into the pantry, where a cake was cooling on a wire rack before being filled with jam and buttercream. She opened the adjacent cake tin – it was full of rock buns, her favourite.

After eating two buns, her eyes fell onto a row of keys hanging on hooks behind the pantry door. One of them belonged to the workshop at the bottom of the garden, where Uncle Tom kept his ferrets. She knew which one it was because there was an old, brown label hanging from it that said *"workshop"*.

Uncle Tom's ferrets were tame, as he handled them every day. Sometimes, before her mam had tried to gas herself, Violet had been allowed to play with them. Remembering the feeling of cutting open the hairy caterpillars, she wondered how it would feel to plunge a vegetable knife into a ferret. The insides of a ferret were bound to be more interesting than the insides of a hairy caterpillar.

Violet opened the kitchen drawer and took out a sharp knife. She would just take it up to Uncle Tom's workshop. She probably wouldn't kill a ferret, though, because someone might come back at any time. But she loved the feel of the knife in her hand. It made her feel strong and powerful instead of weak and frightened, especially if she cut herself just a little bit until the hurting in her arm took away the hurt inside.

Billy Potter had taken off his jacket, rolled up his shirt sleeves and slung his jacket over his shoulder and whistled all the way home from work that sunny Saturday afternoon. He could hardly believe his good fortune. There would be plenty of room in Mr Jeffson's large workshop for him to store his woodworking tools and materials and practise his craft. The offer had come at just the right time, too. After making his mam's new kitchen cabinet, he had received an order from one of her friends and he couldn't wait to get started.

He had heard people talking about Tom Jeffson. Folks were saying that he was mad and was having to see a special doctor. If that were true, then he ought to make allowances for him and accept the hand of friendship and apology that had been offered. After all, if Mr Jeffson couldn't help his nasty nature, then who was he to criticise? Especially as he, himself, was a *"retard"*.

He fingered the key in his trouser pocket. *"Here, take this key,"* Tom had said as he had handed it over that morning. *"Use my shed as a workshop whenever you like, I don't mind."*

On the spur of the moment, Billy Potter turned into the entrance passageway of Mr Jeffson's house. He'd just have a little look around before going home and work out whether he needed to put up some more shelves on which to store his tools. After knocking on the back door and ascertaining no one was at home, he sauntered down the garden path, still whistling.

He was surprised to find the door was already unlocked. He opened it slightly and peered into the dim light.

'Hello? Is anyone there?'

He opened the door wider, to let in some more light and gasped in horror. Sitting on the dirty floor of the workshop was Violet Grey, Mr Jeffson's little niece who lived over the road. She was holding a knife. Her pretty dress, her forearms, her bare legs and white socks were soaked in blood and her eyes were staring at him, hypnotised like the wild eyes of the ferrets locked in the cage behind her.

Chapter Eleven
Truthfulness and Cruelty

'He did it to me!' screamed Violet as Evelyn Potter wrapped her in a blanket. 'It was that *retard* who did it. He cut my arms and legs with the knife.'

'I never, Mam. I just found her like it.'

'And what were you doing in Tom Jeffson's workshop, Billy Potter. Don't lie to me now – I want the truth!'

'He gave me the key this morning when he came into the shop – said I could use it for my woodwork.'

Billy Potter dropped the knife he held in his hand.

'There's no one in, Mam. They have all gone out. I knocked on the back door.'

'I'll take her home,' Evelyn said, dabbing at Violet's wounds with a clean tea towel. 'Run over the road to tell her mam and dad she's with me. Quickly now.'

Billy shot off.

Can you walk?' she said, putting an arm round Violet's thin shoulders.

Violet nodded. 'He did it to me, she wailed. It wasn't me.'

After a frantic search for Violet's parents, it was evident everyone was out, and she had been left on her own in the house. Evelyn Potter took her back into her own home.

She gently bathed her wounds, which luckily were superfluous and not too deep. Shocked, she began to question Violet, who still insisted Billy Potter had cut her with the kitchen knife.

Before long, the family began to drift back home from their various secret liaisons. Liz was first to return from Daisy's house, where she had spent an enjoyable afternoon with Quentin, followed by Walter, who had been out walking in the countryside with a male friend and then Tom and Doris within minutes of each other.

In Evelyn Potter's living room they all crowded round the pitiful figure of Violet, who, cowered beneath a blanket and shivering with shock, had just had her arms and legs dressed with white bandages.

'So, are you all telling me this poor little mite was left alone, all day?' said Evelyn to the gathered family.

'She's ten years-old, Mrs Potter. She's old enough to be left for a couple of hours,' Doris said, the tone of her voice cold and defensive.

'Well, that's a matter of opinion,' Evelyn Potter retorted. 'It's not my Billy, you know. He wouldn't harm a fly, would you Billy. And in any case, what sort of mother would leave her daughter on her own all day long when she was ill with alopecia? Look at the poor little soul. Goodness knows what this will do to her on top of everything else she is having to endure.'

'But *who* has cut her?' Liz cried out. 'If it wasn't your Billy, who was it?'

'Yes,' Walter said. 'We should fetch the Police.'

'No,' Evelyn said, close to tears. 'Please? It can't be Billy. He's not capable ...'

'Yes,' everyone agreed, interrupting her. 'We need to report this to the Police.'

Violet shook and shivered under her blanket, unable to speak. It had been the voice in her head had told her to cut her arms and legs, and it had felt so good she couldn't stop. She had only been playing when it happened. She wouldn't have killed a ferret, even though she was curious to know what a heart looked like.

She began to cry. She had been hurting so much inside, all she had wanted to do was to tell Auntie Liz the truth about her hair. Now somehow she had ended up slashing her arms and legs to let the hurt out, which was not normal.

She was surely going completely mad, just like Uncle Tom.

'Every child goes through a difficult period,' Dr Norman said, looking at Walter and Doris over the top of Violet's head. 'Some children go through phases of temper tantrums, others bite and hit their peers and others are sly, causing trouble for other people by telling lies about them. But I am very surprised you didn't bring her to see me about her alopecia. Even though you say her grandmother suffered from the same condition, I should still have liked to have been consulted, because there may be some emotional disturbance going on in her mind that needs medical help.'

'Doctor Norman,' Violet began, her voice almost a whisper. 'Please can I talk to you on my own?'

'Is she aggressive, at all?' Dr Norman went on, ignoring

Violet, raising his bushy, white eyebrows at Walter.

'No, never,' Walter replied. 'In fact, she is a very quiet, timid little girl. She is a bit of a loner – prefers her books and music to going out to play with other children. She is very clever, though. She is way in front at school, academically-speaking. '

Violet was trying very hard to be brave. Even though she had eventually told the truth to the policeman, and had been made to apologise to Billy Potter for making up the story that *he* had cut her arms and legs, she was still very frightened about telling the truth about her hair to the doctor. Telling the truth was something that Billy Potter had said she must do. He had been very kind to her when she had been made to go out into the garden, where he was sitting on the back lawn, his head bowed. She had cried when, in front of the policeman, she had said sorry for accusing him. He had stood up, told her not to worry about it and then said she must be sure to tell someone from the authorities about why she had wanted to cut her own arms and legs. The policeman had nodded, agreeing with Billy, and had told her mam and dad they had to make an appointment with a doctor, right away, or else he was going to arrest them for child neglect.

Now, even though she felt very nearly brave enough to tell the doctor about cutting her own hair and hurting herself, he was ignoring her. Billy Potter was a really kind man to forgive her for lying about him, even though he was *"a shillin' short"*.

'Has she ever had temper tantrums at all?' the doctor asked.

'No,' Doris said emphatically. 'She has not. My Violet is

172

a sweet little girl who has always done as she was told.'

'Or tried to harm another child or a pet?'

'No,' Walter said quickly.

The doctor smiled at Violet. 'You won't do anything like this again, will you? You could have hurt yourself really badly, and if the cuts had been deeper they would have needed to be stitched at the hospital. Now you don't want to have to go to the hospital, do you?'

'No,' Violet said in a small voice. It was obvious no one was going to listen to her, even the doctor.

'Anyway, Mrs Grey,' Dr Norman said to Doris as he put the envelope containing Violet's notes to one side. 'You must try not to worry about all this. It won't do you any good at all. You need to look after yourself now you are going to have a baby, especially at your age,'

A baby!

Violet's head snapped up in alarm. Her mother was not the type of lady who should be allowed to have babies. After all, look at what she had done to her.

'Come along, Violet,' her father said kindly, putting a hand on her shoulder. 'Let's get home and we can tell you all about the new baby.'

'Doesn't she know?' the doctor said. 'I'm sorry, I shouldn't have mentioned it.' He turned to look at Doris. 'You are at a very delicate stage of your pregnancy, and should be avoiding any trouble like this.'

Doris gave a false smile and put her hand on Violet's shoulder. 'Never mind, it's a nice surprise for you, isn't it Violet? You've always wanted a little brother or sister to play with.'

Violet stood up, her heart pounding painfully in her

chest. The unexpected news that her mam was going to have a baby changed things. Billy Potter's voice rang out in her head. *"You must tell the doctor the truth"*. The words swirled round and round in her head like the shaving brush on her scalp – *the truth, the truth, the truth*. But the truth somehow stuck in her throat and she couldn't tell it. She bowed her head and let her father lead her out of the door by her hand. Her mam shut the door to the doctor's surgery behind them. It was too late. She couldn't tell the truth now.

'Does she need another appointment?' the doctor's receptionist enquired.

Walter let go of her hand and scratched his nose. 'I don't think so,' he said. 'But you had better just check with Dr Norman.'

Her mam opened the door to the street and gestured Violet to go through it.

'Come along, Violet,' she said. 'Hurry up. We've wasted enough of Dr Norman's time already.'

Something in Violet's bald head snapped. She was *not* a waste of time. She was a little girl who had learned terrible secrets and suffered the dreadful indignity of having to have her head and eyebrows shaved off. But most of all, the baby growing in her mam's belly was not a waste of time, either. If she said nothing now, then the baby would end up being a waste of time, too, just like she was, because her mam had time for nothing and no one, except herself and her secrets. Her mam might put on her posh voice, dress in fancy clothes and smear lipstick all over her lips and pretend to be a perfect mother, but inside she was cold and nasty and shouldn't be allowed to have babies.

She remembered back to a time when she was seven and had been locked in the cupboard under the stairs all day in the dark. Proper mothers didn't do that, and if she said nothing now, while she had the chance, then the baby growing in her mam's belly would be shut under the stairs in the dark, too.

'Come on, Violet. Hurry up.'

The truth. The truth. The truth. The words repeated themselves over and over in her head. Hyperventilating with fear, her breaths were coming in short, sharp gasps as she hesitated in the doorway. *The truth. The truth.*

'I AM NOT BALD,' she suddenly shouted at the top of her voice to everyone in the doctor's waiting room. 'SHE MAKES ME HAVE MY HAIR SHAVED OFF.'

Six days later, Tom summoned everyone to his house for a family conference. The entire family was crammed into the front room to consider the doctor's advice about what should be done about Violet, who sat sulkily in chair in a corner, chewing the collar of her dress.

Daisy looked at Bill, who gave a slight nod of his head. 'She can stay with us,' he said quietly, placing his hand on Violet's shoulder. 'We will look after her, but we can't do it for nothing. Having another mouth to feed will be a big strain on us, money-wise.'

Tom gave a sigh of relief. Doris had been in bed for nearly a week with a terrible bilious attack after Violet's shocking accusations. Of course, the doctor hadn't believed the child. He hadn't believed her when Violet told him about her mam sticking her head in the gas oven on bonfire night, either, or about the time she had been listening on the stairs and had heard her mother telling her friend, Peggy, that Walter was not her real dad. It was a good job the doctor hadn't believed a single word Violet had said, or else it would have caused no end of problems.

The doctor had shaken his head in disbelief at Violet's revelations about her family. 'Shocking,' he had said to her just before he had given her a lecture about telling the truth. 'If you were mine, I'd have you wash your mouth out with soap for telling all these lies.'

'Is that all right with you, Walter?' Tom said, raising his eyebrows. 'Can you give them something towards Violet's keep?'

'Aye,' Walter replied, looking uncomfortably at his shoes. 'We need to keep her away from Doris while she is at such a delicate stage of pregnancy'.

'I think it will be for the best,' Tom said, smiling at Violet. 'It will be like a little holiday, to stay with your cousin for a few months. And then, when you come back home, your hair might have grown and you won't need to wear a headscarf all the time. You can use the time you are away from your parents to think about what a naughty girl you have been.'

'We will need another stove, too,' Daisy said, quick to realise that the family would do, and pay for, anything to get rid of Violet and the dirty secrets that were now being swept under the carpet. 'I am really struggling to cook proper meals on the rickety old thing we have been given. It doesn't light half the time.'

Walter sighed. 'I'll buy you a new one, then.'

Daisy sat on the arm of the chair beside Violet and slid

her arm around the little girl's shoulders. Bill winked at her, trying his hardest not to laugh at Daisy's audacity.

George took Rose by the arm, and motioned with his head for them to step outside in the hallway.

'I can't stand by and see her blamed,' he hissed into Rose's ear. 'We should speak up and go and tell the doctor what we know.'

'We *can't* say anything, George,' Rose whispered back at him. 'It will only upset the apple cart. It's best all round to just let Daisy and Bill look after her for a while and then the four of us can try and make her happy again. At least we know she is going to be properly cared for.'

George nodded. He could see the sense of it. If he came clean to the doctor about Walter and Doris's abuse of Violet, she would most likely be taken away from her parents, and everyone knew that would be a bad option. It was probably for the best that the family resolve the problems themselves.'

Tom peered through the door uneasily. 'What are you two whispering about?'

'Nothing,' Rose said.

'Don't you dare say anything ...'

'Don't worry, we're not going to.'

Violet's wishes finally came true as she packed her bags, ready to go and live with Daisy and Bill. She didn't care that the doctor hadn't believed her. She didn't care about leaving her comfortable bedroom and nicely furnished home for a room with only a rickety old bed and second-hand dressing table and nothing on the floor but wooden boards. Although Daisy's house in Windmill Avenue was only a short walk from her house, it might have been on the other side of the world, so glad was she to be finally getting away.

'Take your headscarves with you,' her mother said. 'You don't want people looking at your horrible bald head.'

Violet glared at her mother. 'I don't care about people looking at my head,' she said. 'I shall be proud of my hair now it's being allowed to grow back. I'm never going to wear a headscarf again. I hate them.'

Doris looked up at Walter for moral support. 'Tell her, Walter, please?'

Walter shook his head. 'It will be up to Daisy and Bill now. Let them decide what's best for Violet.'

'You'll pop back sometimes, won't you?'

Violet stared coldly at her mother. 'I don't care if I never see you again in all my life,' she said. 'I hate you for what you have done to me.'

With each fraction of an inch her hair grew that summer, Violet gradually regained her confidence. The scars on her arms and legs healed and she thrived in the care of Daisy and Bill. Some people tutted and made comments about the Jeffson family, palming off the difficult and strange ten year-old onto the hard-up young couple with a baby, who had only just begun their married life, but the truth was, after the shocking emotional neglect that had occurred under their noses without anyone realising or even caring, each and every member of the Jeffson family shouldered some of the guilt and went out of their way to make sure

Violet was happy.

For Daisy and Bill though, the summer of nineteen thirty-three marked the turning point in their fortunes, which curiously seemed to go hand in hand with the love and care they poured into Violet. Not only did Walter buy them a new gas stove in appreciation for all they were doing for his daughter, but he gave them a generous allowance each week for her keep, which boosted the family's finances and lifted them out of the poverty in which they were living.

Gradually, that summer, the additional money bought Daisy and Bill some new rugs, a carpet for the stairs, an iron bedstead on which they could place their mattress and some good quality second-hand wardrobes for their bedroom. They were given a bone china tea-set, some nearly-new linoleum, a new rug and a second-hand table and chairs for the living room. Daisy bought a few yards of upholstery material at a knock-down price and, with Rose and Liz's help, made some bright loose covers for the old armchairs. Their baby daughter, Eileen, was treated to a whole new wardrobe of clothes and a brand new cot in which to sleep, which replaced the old wooden drawer Daisy had been using since her birth.

At school, Violet's academic ability began to suffer, but her teachers were not concerned because it meant she was finally behaving like a little girl instead of burying herself in an adult world of inappropriate books and dark poetry. She skipped and played her way through the summer, learning how to be ravenously hungry and so tired she couldn't even climb the stairs, happy for Bill to carry her up to bed over his shoulder in a fireman's lift, where she

179

would fall into a deep sleep, exhausted from playing in the fields or down by the river with her new friends from the council estate.

Autumn came and went, and as her hair grew longer the days grew shorter. One day, Daisy came home from shopping with some new, pretty slides for her hair. Violet couldn't stop giggling with happiness when the lady next door came round with some hairdressing scissors and trimmed her hair into a neat and tidy style, her short fringe clipped back with the new slides so that she didn't look like a boy. Finally, she looked normal again.

The arrangement was that, once her baby sister or brother had been born, Violet would return home to her parents, but it was something the family didn't speak about because, privately, each and every one of them doubted that Doris was going to be able to cope with the new baby when it came, let alone a new baby and a demanding ten year-old daughter.

As for Violet, she couldn't think about going home. She wanted to stay with Daisy, Bill and baby Eileen forever.

Having confined herself to bed for the previous six weeks on the pretext of having the flu (for the fourth time since she had become pregnant), Doris was huge, far bigger than when she had been close to giving birth to Violet.

Dr Norman had been listening to the baby's heartbeat with an ear trumpet, a concerned look on his face. He put it down on the bed and took his stethoscope out of his bag, placing it on his ears, trying to locate the baby's heartbeat.

'Ahh,' he said. 'There it is. I can hear it clearly now.'

With the stethoscope hanging around his neck, he palpated Doris's abdomen, feeling for tiny arms and legs. 'I can't be fully sure whether this baby is breech or not,' he said. 'I think it's in an unusual position.'

'Could it be twins, doctor, do you think? I'm so big, I keep thinking I might be having twins.'

The doctor shook his head. 'I don't know, Mrs Grey. I'm fairly sure there is only one baby, but it is in an odd position. I think it might be best if we admit you to hospital for the birth, instead of you having it here, at home. Sometimes when babies are in an odd position, like this little lass or lassie, there can be some difficulties at the birth.'

'Oh,' Doris said with a tingle of fear. She most definitely didn't want to have to go to the hospital to give birth. She hoped it wasn't going to be a long and painful affair. She had thought she was going to die when she was having Violet, but the midwife had said the birth had been easy.

'I see from your notes that your daughter's birth was without complications,' said Dr Norman. 'By the way, how is little Violet getting on?'

'To be quite honest with you, Doctor, I am despairing of the way she is being dragged up while she is staying with my niece and her husband. They are both only nineteen, you know. Little more than mere children themselves. I dread to think what terrible manners she will have picked up when she comes home.'

Doris gave a conspiratorial, high-pitched chuckle as she continued. 'Between you and me, Doctor, she's a headstrong, feisty piece, my niece. She had to get married, you know. Got herself in the family way when she was only seventeen. Of course, my brother-in-law threw her out. He was mortified at the shame she had brought on the family. He has such high morals, my brother-in-law. My niece and her husband are common as muck – they live in one of those new council houses on Windmill Avenue, but goodness knows how they got that. There's folk wait years to get a council house. They are not *my* type of people really, but Violet seems happy with them for the time being.'

'Oh dear,' the doctor said. 'I fear you are going to have your work cut out with that young lady when she returns home, she'll be as wild as a feral cat. Still, I'm sure with some proper parenting, she can learn to grow out of her childish lies and silly accusations and she will soon learn some manners. Some children have absolutely no idea of which side their bread is buttered, Mrs Grey, do they?'

'Quite,' Doris replied. 'Still, perhaps she will be sorry for what she's done when she comes home. Roughing it with my niece and her husband will have made her realise what a lovely home she has here. Do you know, doctor, my husband even had to buy them a gas stove before we could send her to live there? And up until a few months ago, they were sleeping on a mattress on the floor because they couldn't even afford a proper bed. Living like gypsies, they were, camping out in a house with just a Primus stove and a couple of old crates for a table.'

'What about her alopecia?' Dr Norman asked, while prodding Doris's abdomen again, trying to find the baby's head.

'Her hair's growing back now. I can hardly believe she

182

made up that dreadful story about her father shaving her head.'

'Good,' the doctor said. 'That's good. At least her hair loss wasn't permanent.'

Doris's waters broke the next evening, three weeks before her estimated due date. Following another visit from Dr Norman, who had declared that her waters had broken because she was carrying too much fluid, but that labour was progressing nicely, she was spared having to be carried off to hospital in an ambulance. The reason he had been unable to feel the baby's position in the womb, he had said, was because he hadn't realised the birth had been so imminent when he had examined her yesterday, and the baby's head had descended into the birth canal, ready for the birth. The baby was now in an optimum position for delivery, and therefore the risk of needing medical intervention had decreased. Did it matter that the waters had been stained pink with blood, a worried Walter had asked him. *"No,"* he had replied. *"I don't think so"*. The doctor had then gone on to explain that sometimes there was a small show of blood at the same time as the waters ruptured.

Mrs Mutton, a midwife, was to be called out to deliver the baby.

Rose and Liz were summoned to assist Doris in her labour, and, once all the fuss had died down, George was ordered to go and deliver the news to Bill, Daisy and Violet.

'So will the baby be all right, being born three weeks

early?' Daisy said to George as he took off his cap and stepped into the hallway.

'Aye, I think so. It will just be a bit small, the doctor thinks.'

'Hello George,' Violet said, appearing at the top of the stairs in her nightdress, having heard him come in.

'Oh, Violet, come on down, Poppet,' Bill said. 'Did you hear what George just said? Your little brother or sister is going to be born soon.'

Violet ran down the stairs and flung her arms around George's waist, pleased at his unscheduled visit, but George could tell she didn't want to listen as he told Daisy and Bill what the doctor had said. It was just too bad that her mam's baby was coming early because it meant that she would have to go back home earlier.

George sat down in one of the two armchairs. Violet sat on his lap and he stroked her shiny, clean hair.

'You smell lovely – have you been stealing some of Daisy's bath salts?'

Violet giggled. 'I've just had a bath. I always have one on a Sunday night, ready for school, and then we toast crumpets in front of the fire, and I give baby Eileen her crumpet and the butter runs all down her chin.'

Daisy laughed. 'Since her ladyship came to live here, we get loads of little treats from people, including fancy bath cubes. Everyone has been so kind to us, haven't they Violet?'

'I don't want to go home, George,' Violet said. 'Please don't make me go back. I'm so frightened of my mam. She really did make me have my head shaved after I cut it all off, but the doctor didn't believe me. Just like he didn't

184

believe me about mam sticking her head in the gas oven and all the hurt inside me making me want to hurt on the outside. That's why I cut myself. It was because of all the hurt inside.'

George looked up at Bill, alarmed. This was the first time Violet had mentioned cutting her own hair, and he knew she had never once talked about the traumatic experience of witnessing her mother's suicide attempt, or the terrible day in June when she had been found in Tom's workshop, covered in blood, clutching a knife after slashing at her arms and legs.

George made up his mind. If Violet was now beginning to talk about these things, then it was time he gave her some validation.

'Violet. I have a confession to make to you.' George said. 'On bonfire night last year, your father mentioned to me that you had cut off all your hair with the kitchen scissors. He told me that he had shaved it all off because it looked so tatty and uneven. Then, with all the mention of alopecia, I forgot about how you had cut off your hair yourself and really thought that it had all fallen out from alopecia. I was so busy at that time, caught up in working hard at the factory, helping Rose to look after baby Margaret and decorating the front room and Daisy's old room. Had I known how unhappy you were, I would have done something, for sure. But I didn't think about you enough, and I am really sorry for not sticking up for you about your hair when you told the doctor what you had done.'

Violet smiled at him. 'It's all right, George. It wasn't your fault that Dr Norman didn't believe me. And I know you and Rose had enough on your minds because of Uncle Tom stealing all your money.'

Daisy, sitting on the opposite side of the fire in an armchair, put her hands over her eyes as all the old memories came flooding back.

'I'm sorry, too, Violet,' she said. 'None of us paid enough attention to the terrible things you were having to endure, we were all so wrapped up in our own problems, we didn't realise you were so unhappy. But there was a good reason we didn't say anything to the doctor. We wanted you to come and live with us so that you could get better. If we had told the truth, you would have been taken away and sent to live in a children's home. It's the same reason why the family kept it quiet when your mam tried to gas herself. We were afraid the authorities would send you away because of her nervous breakdown.'

Violet slid off George's lap and knelt on the floor in front of the fire.

'And another thing. I'm sorry about your new piano,' George went on. 'It was our fault it had to be sold because we wanted to have some privacy and live in the front room. We should have made your Uncle Tom keep his promise to look for a second-hand one to put in your front room so that you could keep on practising.'

'It doesn't matter,' Violet said, uncomfortable because the most important grown-ups in her life felt guilty about her. 'It was just a piano, not something really important, like – like –'

'Being loved,' Daisy finished with a smile, drying her eyes. 'And Violet, we all love you. It has been a pleasure having you to live with us and we will miss you when you

186

go home. You have been such a good girl.'

Whatever terrible things had happened to Violet in the past, the last few months had made up for it. She had been happy for the first time in her life. She would soon be eleven years-old, which was much older than being nearly ten, which was when things had first gone horribly wrong. Being eleven would mean that she would be nearly grown-up and could look after herself, if she needed to.

'I don't want to go home,' she said in a wobbly voice.

'Look, Violet,' George said. 'Just remember when you have to go back home that we are only over the road. If you feel unhappy or anything happens to you to make you feel bad, you can come and tell us. You mustn't bottle everything up inside you again. Promise?'

'I promise, George.'

Chapter Twelve
Dogmatism and Vengeance

Doris declared for the umpteenth time that she was surely dying. During the night her screams could be heard outside in the street, and her neighbours on either side hadn't had a wink of sleep.

Mrs Mutton, the midwife, wasn't too concerned. She came across fussy women like Doris Grey all the time – "the screamers", she called them. There were no complications with the birth as far as she could tell: she estimated that Doris's baby would be born around six o'clock that morning.

'Now come on, Mrs Grey,' she said. 'Just try to calm down, sweetie, and think of your neighbours, trying to sleep. The more you try to fight the pains, the more they will hurt you.'

'Nooooo,' Doris yelled. 'I can't stand it anymore. Just get it out of me, please? I can't bear the pain.'

Mrs Mutton rolled her eyes at Rose, who, ashen-faced, was clutching Liz's arm at Doris's bedside.

'I hope I wasn't like this when I had our Margaret,' Rose muttered. 'I wasn't, was I, Mrs Mutton?'

Mrs Mutton winked at her. 'No, Rose, you weren't.'

After another hour of screaming, Doris let out a

terrifying high-pitched yowl. Mrs Mutton went over to the wash-stand and washed her hands thoroughly before examining Doris again. The birth was imminent.

'Doris, can you hear me? It's nearly here. In a few minutes it will be over and your baby will be born.'

The baby's head crowned briefly between Doris's legs before disappearing again. Mrs Mutton gently probed inside the birth canal, her heart beating so fast she thought it was going to leap into her throat. She waited for the next contraction to push the baby forward. As it built in intensity, and the baby progressed further down the birth canal, her fingers felt the baby's nose and mouth, and she swept them expertly around the baby's head.

'Rose, Liz, can you go and fetch me a clean sheet, please?'

Both Rose and Liz bolted for the door simultaneously. 'I'll go,' said Rose, who was beginning to feel squeamish.

'Is everything all right?' Liz asked Mrs Mutton as she sat down again.

Mrs Mutton smiled with false confidence, hoping the horror on her face was not evident. If what she suspected was wrong, she needed to act quickly when this baby was born. 'Just fine, Mrs Jeffson. Just fine,' she said.

Rose appeared with the sheet. 'Where would you like me to put it,' she said.

'Just here, right beside me,' Mrs Mutton said, swiping a clean towel from her side and shoving it under Doris's bottom as bright pink amniotic fluid seeped out from her birth canal. 'When her waters broke, can you remember if they were stained in any way?' she asked Liz.

'I don't know,' Liz replied. 'We will have to ask Walter –

190

he was here when they went.'

'I'll go,' Rose said as she slid around the door.

When she came back, Rose confirmed that Doris's waters had been stained pink, but that Dr Norman had told Walter that it was just because she had experienced a show of blood at the same time as they ruptured.

Mrs Mutton tutted under her breath. Had the doctor mentioned this to her earlier she would have recommended a hospital birth. When would these doctors learn to take childbirth seriously?

'Can you sit either side of Doris?' Mrs Mutton said. 'Each of you needs to take a hand and give her something to hold onto as the baby comes. Just concentrate on Doris and don't worry about what's going on at this end.'

Mrs Mutton gathered up two more clean towels and laid them across Doris's stomach, folding them to fashion a makeshift barrier. On top she placed the unfolded clean sheet, ready to grab quickly as soon as the baby was born. She needed to make sure Liz and Rose couldn't see what was going on. Liz caught her eye and in a brief, shared, glance Mrs Mutton knew that Liz Jeffson had somehow picked up on her concern and suspected that something was wrong with the baby.

Liz dropped her eyes from the midwife's glance. She had an inkling of what was happening. Years ago, her mother had been present at the birth of her aunt's baby, which had been badly deformed, and afterwards had recounted a similar tale of being told not to look as the baby had been born, and towels being piled up on the mother's abdomen to spare the mother at the moment of birth.

She gripped Doris's hand tightly, wishing she could tell Rose not to look.

Doris began to bear down, growling with each effort. Briefly, Liz wondered if the baby had been fathered by Tom, but then she brushed the thought away. Tom's behaviour had been impeccable since he had broken off his affair with Doris. He had ticked off every single thing in his red book. Next to Doris's name had been a huge tick, completed with a flourish as if underlining the fact that he was no longer having an affair with her sister. In fact, Tom's new leaf was fast becoming her thorn in the side. She couldn't fault his attentiveness or behaviour, which made her feel all the more guilty about her secret friendship with Quentin Andrews. She still didn't love him, though. All her love for him had died inside her when she had discovered that he had been having an affair with her sister and had hurt their daughters so badly. She stared at Doris's screwed-up face and perspiration-soaked hair, glad she was suffering. She might have reconciled with her sister, up to a point, just to keep up appearances, but she could never feel sisterly affection for her again. Quentin Andrews was her saviour and her best friend and without him she could not have endured life as Tom's wife and Doris's sister, of that she was sure.

Rose half stood up, wanting to see the baby being born.

'Rose,' Liz hissed. 'You mustn't look.'

Rose frowned. 'Why?' she mouthed.

Liz shook her head. 'It's not the done thing,' she said quietly.

'Why? Rose repeated in a loud voice. 'You and our Daisy

were gawping at me when Margaret was born. In fact, it felt as if the entire street was looking at *my* private parts. Why should she be any different? Who does she think she is? Ruddy Queen Mary?'

Doris gave a high-pitched scream. 'Push Doris. Push. Harder. Come on, another push. Harder. Harder,' said Mrs Mutton, working her hands busily as she tried to manipulate the baby's head as it finally popped out.

Liz looked at the midwife's face. Every pore, every cell in her body was pumping out trepidation. She didn't know how the midwife was managing to keep calm.

Rose stood up, craning her neck to see around the barrier of towels and the clean sheet piled up on Doris's swollen abdomen.

'Sit down!' Liz hissed and let go of Doris's arm as she gestured with her hand for Rose to sit back down.

Doris began to scream again, and Rose bumped back down on her seat, her face ashen with shock.

'Oh my word! 'What on earth ...?'

'Keep quiet, Rose,' Liz hissed through her teeth. 'Just be quiet and keep still.'

Rose took hold of Doris's hand again, and put her free hand up to her mouth.

'Rose! Just go,' Liz said gesturing towards the door with her head, panicking as Doris bore down again and Mrs Mutton looked up at her in mutual understanding.

The baby's body was born and Doris gave a low, rumbling growl of relief.

Mrs Mutton grabbed the sheet and quickly wrapped it around the flaccid baby so that no one could see its terrible deformity. She tied and cut the cord quickly and deftly, severing the child from its mother.

No one spoke. Doris's panting was the only sound in the room as the three women stared at each other in shock.

Then, from the bloody, crumpled up sheet that surrounded the baby came a high-pitched, unnatural cry.

'My baby,' Doris said. 'Oh, my precious, darling baby. What is it?'

'Here,' Mrs. Mutton said to Liz. 'Take the baby out, quickly, and don't look at it.'

Liz grabbed the bundle and shot out of the room, closely followed by Rose.

'What's the matter?' Doris said, trying to sit up. 'Why have they taken my baby?'

Mrs Mutton took Doris's hand.

'I'm afraid your little boy was stillborn, Doris.'

'Noooo,' Doris screamed. 'I just heard him cry ...'

Walter burst into the room. 'What's going on?' he said. 'Why have Liz and Rose taken the baby downstairs, wrapped up in a sheet?'

'It was stillborn,' Mrs Mutton said, as she hastily covered up Doris's lower regions to preserve her modesty. 'I'm so sorry Mr Grey – it was a little boy.'

Walter sank down onto the bed as Tom appeared, hovering at the bedroom door. Mrs. Mutton turned her head towards him to explain.

'It was stillborn, Mr Jeffson, I'm afraid. A little boy –'

'It bloody well isn't stillborn – it's screaming its head off downstairs.'

Mrs Mutton leapt up and ran downstairs to the kitchen, where Liz and Rose had unwrapped the sheet from around the baby. Its little lungs were straining with every breath, emanating a pitiful high-pitched cry every time it exhaled.

'Oh no,' Mrs Mutton cried, her face white with shock. 'Anencephalic babies are not supposed to be born alive.'

'But this one has been,' Rose said, regaining her composure. 'We have to fetch the doctor out, quickly, to see what can be done for him.'

'I'm afraid nothing can be done, Rose. Anencephaly is incompatible with life. I'm not sure we can do anything but wait for ...'

Tom burst into the kitchen, his voice bellowing in panic. 'What's goin' on?'

He stopped, dead in his tracks as his eyes fell on the squirming baby, with its bulging, frog-like eyes, squashed nose and huge, open congenital defect where the top and back of his head should have been.

He stared at Liz, hyperventilating. 'What's happened to it?' he shouted as he crumpled onto a kitchen chair in shock. 'Did they drop it on its head or summat?'

Violet was in her bedroom, getting ready for school when the knock came on the door.

She finished putting her books into her leather satchel and then ran to the top of the stairs to see who it was. It was Mrs Bellamy from next door, who was talking in hushed tones to Daisy.

'Ah, Violet,' she said, looking up the stairs. 'Would you and little Eileen like to come next door with me for some breakfast? Then you can walk to school.'

'Is Mam's baby here?'

'Umm, no, not quite,' Mrs Bellamy said. 'But Daisy needs to fetch Margaret from Cornwall Road, so I hope you don't mind coming to my house for a bite of breakfast.'

Daisy's mouth quivered as she spoke. 'Will that be all right? You don't mind going next door for half an hour until it's time to go to school?'

Violet ran down the stairs. 'What's happened? Is Mam all right?'

'Everything is fine. Don't worry, it's just a little complication.'

'All right,' Violet said. 'I'll get Eileen's pram. Mrs Bellamy might need it.'

With Violet and Eileen dispatched next door, Daisy shut the front door and leaned on it. Mr Bellamy had been cycling to work when he had met George, running along Windmill Avenue to give Daisy and Bill the sad news that Doris's baby had been stillborn. He had turned back to give Daisy the message that she needed to collect baby Margaret right away.

When Daisy arrived at Cornwall Road, she found Rose, dishevelled and white-faced, sitting at the kitchen table, drinking a cup of tea while eighteen month-old Margaret sat on a cushion on a chair opposite, playing with a ragdoll.

Rose shook her head and closed her tearful eyes with a shudder.

'Oh Daisy, it was awful. The baby had a horrible deformity – the back of its head was missing and there was just an open wound where its skull should have been.

It was shocking. I thought it must surely be dead, but it was alive and squealed for about ten minutes before it died in my arms. It was a little boy.'

'Oh my word,' Daisy said, slumping down at the table beside Rose. 'Is our mam with her now?'

'Yes,' Rose said. 'Dad and George have had to go to work. Uncle Walter and Mam are over the road with Auntie Doris and the midwife, waiting for the doctor to arrive.'

'What could have caused it to have such an awful deformity?' Daisy said. Rose shook her head as Daisy lifted Margaret onto her knee. 'Who's got Eileen?'

'Mrs Bellamy next door. She gave Eileen and Violet their breakfast and now Violet's gone to school.'

'So you don't have to rush back, then?'

'Not really,' Daisy replied. 'Not if I can do anything here.'

'I thought something was amiss when I examined you the other day,' Dr Norman said to Doris, who held a handkerchief to her red-rimmed eyes. 'Still, the outcome would have been the same, even if you had been in hospital for the birth. I'm afraid your baby boy had a condition that is incompatible with life.'

Mrs Mutton sank down onto Doris's bed and took her hand in hers, patting it comfortingly. 'I'm so, so sorry, Mrs Grey. It's just one of those things. You mustn't blame yourself in any way. It wasn't your fault.'

The doctor scratched his bald head before stroking his white moustache thoughtfully. 'These dreadful deformities are usually due to some sort of trauma at a crucial time in a pregnancy, or the mother seeing something terrible in the early days. Monster births, they are called. They are rare, but well-documented.'

Doris visibly flinched and screwed her eyes shut, upset by the doctor's comment.

Mrs Mutton stared coldly at Dr Norman. He was out of touch and should have retired years ago. His funny opinions and dogged adherence to old-fashioned wives' tales annoyed her. Before today, she had never delivered an anencephalic child herself, but she had studied the midwives' advisory notes carefully in readiness for the unusual occurrence. Although it had been a shock to her when she first suspected the baby had such a terrible defect, her training had stood her in good stead to cope with the birth. The advisory notes said that under no circumstances should the infant be referred to as *"a monster birth"*, which was an old-fashioned term and tended to cause the mother unnecessary distress. What she hadn't realised, though, was that such babies could be born alive. She frowned slightly. Surely the advisory notes had made reference to live anencephalic births, hadn't they? Thinking clearly for the first time since the birth she recalled reading that these poor babies were *almost* always stillborn. It saddened her to think that she hadn't known what to do to make the child's brief few minutes of life as comfortable as possible.

'Your baby wasn't a monster,' she said kindly to Doris before glaring at Dr Norman. 'It was just one of those things that couldn't be prevented – no one is to blame. It's what is called a congenital deformity.'

Liz stood up. 'I think I'd better go home. I'll leave you all

in privacy, if you don't mind. That's unless you want me to
– to –'

'No, it's all right. I'll see to the baby,' Mrs. Mutton said.
'But before you go, didn't I overhear you mention to your
daughter that an aunt of Doris's had a baby with a similar
condition? Is that right Mrs. Jeffson?'

Liz sat down again. 'Yes,' she said, looking at Dr
Norman. 'And also a cousin of mine had a baby girl with
the same defect.'

'There!' Mrs Mutton said to Dr. Norman. 'It will be
something hereditary in Mrs Grey's family that has caused
her little boy's deformity.'

Dr Norman shook his head. 'No,' he said with
unwarranted conviction. 'It will be all that upset with her
daughter back in the summer. It was a crucial time for the
baby's development, and it is well documented that a big
shock or traumatic experience can damage a baby in its
mother's womb. It will be Mrs Grey's daughter who is to
blame, because of the terrible thing she did to herself
when she cut her arms and legs. It was dreadful shock for
poor Mrs Grey to see her daughter covered in blood like
that and then hear all those terrible lies she told about her
father shaving her head and her mother trying to gas
herself.'

Mrs Mutton glared at Dr Norman again as Liz put her
head down and walked silently from the bedroom. If the
poor child got the blame for this, it would scar her for life.
She knew Liz Jeffson wouldn't ever mention it to the little
girl, but she couldn't be so sure the child's own mother
wouldn't. She would have to have a word with Liz Jeffson
and warn her that Doris's daughter must not be blamed at

any cost.

ఛౙ

Chapter Thirteen
Duplicity and Euphoria

Tom sighed, his shoulders slumped forwards as he screwed his eyes shut in despair. Liz had just left the house for her fortnightly Saturday afternoon visit to Daisy and it was almost three o'clock – his own, personal witching hour when demons and ghosts of the past would dance around in his head, reminding him that the predicament in which he now found himself was entirely of his own making.

Soon, it would be two years since Doris had given birth to her tragic baby boy. He had thought, after the event, that the horrific experience would put her off wanting another child and he would be let off the hook, but now he was drowning in deep, dark water and had no idea how to extricate him from the situation.

Each time he tried to break away from Doris, she tightened her grip, reminding him that she would have no hesitation in telling Liz that he had been the father of her baby. She refused to accept Tom's argument that she was now too old to have another child and, for the past two years, had been blackmailing him.

Reluctantly, he pushed himself up from his armchair. Earlier, he had suggested to Liz that he accompany her to Daisy's house that afternoon. Sitting politely with a cup of tea and a slice of home-made cake, making small talk with a brood of clucking women, was now becoming far preferable to his usual Saturday afternoon romp with Doris, which had now become nothing more than a tedious chore.

He had been shocked when Liz had been quick to deliver an emphatic *"no!"* She had been quite annoyed that he wanted to go with her to Daisy's, saying that her Saturday afternoons with her daughter were sacrosanct, with absolutely no men allowed.

A few minutes later, Tom sneaked into Doris's house via the alleyway that ran along by her back garden to perform his duties as reluctant baby-maker.

She opened the door as he arrived: she had obviously been waiting for him. He averted his eyes, unable to look at her frizzy blonde hair, bright red lips and clown-like cheeks. She grabbed his arm, pulling him inside, almost making him trip over the back doorstep.

'You're late,' she said.

Tom looked at his pocket watch. 'Only a couple of minutes. How's Violet?' he said, changing the subject before she could deliver her usual lecture about him making sure he was always on time for their Saturday liaisons. 'I haven't seen her for a couple of months.'

'She's turning into right little madam now she's getting the body of a woman and don't I know it. She used to be such a quiet little thing and keep herself to herself, but just lately I can't even speak to her without her snapping my head off.'

'Oh,' Tom said, only mildly interested, even though he was fond of Violet. 'She'll be thirteen soon. It's a difficult age for a girl.'

Violet looked at Tom with disdain. 'Your wife is beginning to grate on my nerves just lately. I wish you'd do something about her. She struts over here looking down her nose at me, constantly trying to tell me how to bring up my own daughter. She's turning into a proper sanctimonious old woman. Anyone would think Violet was *her* daughter.'

'Come off it, Doris. What do you expect? The poor child hasn't exactly had an easy time of it over the last few years, and we are all trying to do our best by her. And don't start calling my Liz behind her back. Salt of the earth, she is. Look at how she sat by your side all night when you lost the baby?'

Doris shuddered. 'No one knows what I went through. No one. And I'm still suffering now. I bet you didn't know that your precious wife had the brass neck to threaten to go to the authorities and tell them about Walter's inclinations if I ever blamed Violet for my baby's deformity.'

Tom raised his eyebrows. He hadn't known about that. There had been a time when Liz wouldn't have dared threaten to go to the authorities about anything. There was no doubt, Liz had changed and grown in confidence since his illness, but somehow it only made him love her all the more.

'She's right, though, Doris. It wasn't Violet's fault. It

204

was a hereditary defect in your family and nobody's to blame for it. God rest his soul, the poor little chap.'

'I can't believe how you swallow all Liz's lies, Tom,' Doris said as anger flushed up into her neck and face. 'Dr Norman quite clearly said to me, in front of your wife, that my baby boy's deformity was down to the shock of discovering Violet covered in blood that day she broke into your workshop and cut her arms and legs. One day, I shall tell her – you see if I won't! She's not getting away scot-free with murdering my baby. I only promised Liz not to accuse the *child.* I said nothing about keeping quiet when the child is a *woman.'*

Agitated, Tom turned away, unable to bear to look at Doris. He could hardly believe the highly-strung, self-centred, nagging woman before him was the same innocent young girl he had first taken gently into his arms fourteen years ago; the lovely woman who, looking up at him with huge, innocent eyes had begged him to help her have a baby.

'Look Doris. Don't you think it's about time you called it a day and stopped trying to have another child? You're the wrong side of forty and it's not good for you to spend your entire life hankering after something that, quite frankly, just ain't going to happen.'

Doris caught his arm and forced him to look at her. She pressed her lips into a thin, mean line and her eyes narrowed in contempt.

'If you were a proper man, Tom Jeffson, getting me pregnant with a *normal* child would be easy. Look at you – all you can manage is a wicked, murderous daughter whose sole aim in life is to give me another nervous breakdown. Then, on your second pathetic attempt, you give me a monster baby, and the less said about that, the better.'

Tom sighed. 'Doris – you're obviously suffering from delusions. It wasn't mine. It was some other bloke's.'

'Oh no it wasn't,' Doris screamed. 'Where did you get that idea from?'

'Because ... because it couldn't have been mine, Doris. Have you forgotten? We hadn't even seen each other for months until you lured me into my allotment shed to blackmail me. That was when you told me you were pregnant.'

'I don't know what you're talking about. If you walk out on me now, Tom Jeffson, I'll see to it that your precious Liz walks out on you. I'll tell her everything – yes EVERYTHING.'

Tom opened the back door and tried to walk away. 'It was some hapless young lad who got you pregnant. You told me so with your own lips. I know damned well it wasn't mine.'

Doris caught his arm.

'Don't you dare turn your back on me, Tom Jeffson!'

'There's no reasoning with you when you're like this ... I'm off if you can't even be civil to me.'

Doris pulled him back inside the door, slamming it shut behind him.

'You just can't wait to get away, can you Tom? You can't wait to get back to HER.'

'Look,' Tom said, patting the air in front of him. 'Just leave my Liz out of all this. It's bad enough that I promised to give up seeing you three years ago, and yet we have still carried on. I'm only here because I've got no other option. You know I'm only doing this to stop you ruining my marriage. There's nothing else in it. I have no feelings for you.'

'Shut up!' Doris yelled as she turned the key and locked him in. 'Don't you ever say that. I know it's not true.'

Tom scratched his neck. When Doris was in one of these moods there was no alternative but to let her rant and rave until, exhausted, she fell into his arms and cried herself calm again.

There was no doubt about it. Doris was slowly losing her mind.

The following Monday, Violet had an English lesson at school. Her mother had been sobbing and crying all weekend and so Violet had kept out of the way, learning Tennyson's poem, The Lady of Shallot, for her English homework.

"Out flew the web and floated wide."

Violet cast her eyes around a class full of dropped jaws and spellbound stares. She continued reciting from memory, without looking at her poetry book. *"The mirror crack'd from side to side. The curse is come upon me, cried The Lady of Shalott."*

When Violet had finished, there was a dumbfounded silence in the classroom. Violet grinned and then rolled her eyes before dropping back down on her chair.

'Well, Violet. That was a pretty impressive performance,' the teacher said.

Violet pouted her lips and her glance slid to one side.

207

She was watching Theo Andrews, subconsciously picking at a spot on his chin as he cradled the side of his head in his hand, elbow on the desk. He yawned. He hadn't been impressed.

'I didn't expect you to learn it off by heart, Violet.' the teacher said, her voice tinged with annoyance at Violet taking over her English class barely cloaking her obvious admiration of the child's capacity to learn poetry.

Violet shrugged. *The Lady of Shallot* was her Auntie Liz's favourite and it hadn't taken her long to work out why. Her Auntie Liz felt as if she was imprisoned, just like the Lady of Shallot, looking at the world going by in a reflection in a mirror. And it was all because of Uncle Tom.

'Have you anything to add, Violet?'

'No, Miss.'

Violet smirked at Theo Andrews, who was now looking out of the window, obviously indifferent to her ability to recite a poem completely from memory.

Violet glanced around the classroom and noticed that all the boys, except Theo, were staring at her. The girls, though, were picking at their nails and glancing at each other under their eyelashes in a conspiratorial mocking of her ability. Violet hated girls. She could not have endured school life at either Kettering High School or Rockingham Road Secondary School for Girls. Boys were much easier to get along with.

Theo Andrews was different to other boys, though. He was like her – encased in a hard shell of self-protecting armour, with a few close male friends but completely indifferent to girls. She was intrigued and determined to break through the brick wall he had built around himself.

As she sat back down in her seat, the bell sounded for home-time. She bent down and picked up her brown leather satchel, her loose, shoulder-length blonde hair falling forwards. Through the curtain of hair she gave a small self-satisfied smirk. Theo was staring at her at long last. With her other hand she deftly pushed back her hair and tucked it behind her ear; she wouldn't look at him for a second or two, but would then shoot him a coy look under her eyelashes. Boys couldn't resist that. And it drove grown-up men wild, too. She knew. She might not yet be thirteen years-old but she was learning fast how to fill the vast emptiness inside her with fleeting moments of being desired. It made her feel good – just for a short time – before the loneliness in her life descended again and she had to return home to her hysterical, nervy mother and a father who was very rarely at home. Now she was learning to play the trumpet in music lessons it was such good fun to annoy her mother and make the neighbours complain about her practising.

Theo Andrews caught up with her as she walked home from school.

'You're a right little clever clogs, aren't you?' he said grinning at her. 'Fancy learning that poem off by heart and then standing up and reciting it in front of everyone like that.'

Violet flashed him a cheeky smile. 'Got to liven things up somehow. English lessons are getting rather boring, aren't they?'

'They're all right,' Theo replied, kicking a tiny stone

along the pavement as they walked along the road. 'Have you read, *Brave New World* yet? It's a great book, set in the future. It's written by Aldous Huxley. Much better than stupid poetry.'

'No, I haven't' Violet said. 'But I've read about it in the newspaper – it's caused a bit of hoo-ha, hasn't it? My mother would have a pink fit if I left *that* lying around the house. Can I borrow it when you've finished?'

Theo grinned, he had overheard his father and his lady friend, Mrs Jeffson, talking about her niece, Violet, and what a difficult young lady she was, and it intrigued him.

'You're Mrs Jeffson's niece, aren't you?'

Violet scowled at him. 'How do you know that?'

'The old man. She bakes us cakes. Sometimes she stays for a bit and is still there when I come home from school. Then at other times, my dad visits your cousin, Mrs Roberts who lives in Beech Crescent along Windmill Avenue. Mrs Jeffson is sometimes there, too, when he visits.'

'I used to live with Daisy and Bill,' Violet said. 'I didn't realise Mr Andrews was your dad.'

Theo shrugged. 'She bakes great cakes. She's a nice lady, your aunt.'

'Why doesn't your mam bake cakes, then? Is she ill or something?'

'No,' Theo laughed, but then a sadness drifted across his face and he was suddenly serious. 'I never knew my mam – she died giving birth to me.'

Violet stopped walking. Theo paused, feeling embarrassed. He had told no one at school that he didn't have a mother, apart from his best friends who he had

210

known since infant school.

Violet touched his arm. 'That is awful, Theo. I didn't know. I'm sorry –'

Theo smiled. Violet's devil-may-care attitude had changed in an instant. 'I've never known any different. I have five brothers, older than me, but they've all left home. It's been just me and my dad for years now,' he said.

'My mam nearly died giving birth to my brother two years ago,' Violet said. 'That's why I was sent to live with Daisy and Bill for a few months. She didn't want me around her when she was pregnant because I was too much trouble.'

'She sent you away? Why were you too much trouble? I didn't know you had a brother.'

'I don't,' Violet said. 'He was born dead. If I tell you what happened to me, will you promise to keep it a secret?'

Theo raised his eyebrows. Violet Grey was about to tell him a secret? That was a turn-up – Violet Grey didn't tell anyone anything unless she had to. She must quite like him. He pulled himself up out of his usual slouch to his full height and hitched his heavy satchel up on his shoulder. Perhaps she liked him enough to kiss him, if he was lucky. She was the prettiest girl in the school. With her blonde hair, steely-blue eyes and developing breasts, she looked much older. She could easily pass for sixteen, or even more.

'Only if you don't tell anyone at school that my mother died giving birth to me,' he replied 'It's just that I like to keep it to myself. I don't want everyone blaming me because my mother died.'

211

Violet smiled. 'All right then. I'll keep your secret if you keep mine.'

Theo suddenly realised that he hadn't offered to carry Violet's satchel for her. Damn! How many times had his father drilled into him that he must always show the utmost respect for girls and carry their bags for them, open doors and give up his seat on buses for them? He was so stupid. She would think he was rude.

'Can I carry your satchel for you?' he said.

Violet hesitated and laughed. 'I can carry my own satchel, thanks very much', she said, and then seeing the hurt look on his face she slid it from her shoulder. 'Only joking – thanks.'

Passing her satchel to Theo, Violet continued. 'When I was nine, my Uncle Tom – my Auntie Liz's husband – tried to kill himself. That was when everything started to go badly wrong. Then I overheard my mother telling her friend that my dad wasn't really my dad and I think that is probably why I cut all my hair off.'

'You cut your hair off? Why?'

I don't know. It's all a blur – I thought I was in a dream and heard a voice telling me to cut it. When I woke up, there I was standing in the kitchen with the scissors in my hand and my hair all hacked off on the floor. My mother went absolutely crackers – screaming and wailing like a scalded cat.'

Theo laughed and punched her arm playfully. 'What a nitwit you are. Still, I suppose it beats sleep-walking. It's not everyone who can say they've been sleep-haircutting!'

'Then my lunatic of a mother only went and made it up that I had alopecia – you know, where your hair all falls

212

out overnight – and made my dad shave it all off.'

'No,' Theo said, shocked. 'Did they make you go to school like it?'

'Oh yes. And the Headmaster tried to force me to make friends with Mary Summers, the cripple. I wasn't having any of that. Imagine it, being friends with a cripple? I don't think so. Mam made me wear a headscarf to cover it up but I used to take it off whenever I could. I hated it. I'd rather have walked around with a bald head than look like a bloody charlady!'

Theo stopped walking, bent over nearly double with laughing. Violet carried on talking, recounting several occasions where her baldness had shocked people. After a while he clamped his head in both hands, declaring that his ears were ringing with laughing so much.

'You are such a girl, Vi. I love your spirit,' he said.

Violet giggled with him, but Theo couldn't fail to notice a certain sadness in her eyes. Still, perhaps she would tell him everything, once she was his girlfriend.

"I love your spirit," Theo Andrews said to her when she had told him how she had loved to shock people when she was bald by pulling off her headscarf on special occasions, like when she had been about to have her photograph taken at a family wedding. The words gave Violet a warm glow inside her as she stopped at the corner of Cornwall Road, holding back, not wanting to go home. *" I love your hair,"* he said after she told him about the time she had cut it off. *"I love your laugh,"* he commented after she had giggled her head off when he had told her about how he had made his

213

father fall in Wicksteed Park lake one day when they had been in a rowing competition. *"I love it when you make the teachers look stupid in class"*. Love, love, love, love: Violet just couldn't get enough of it. Each time Theo mentioned the word it filled in a little bit of emptiness inside her and gave her a thrill.

Violet grinned at him. 'Can I have my satchel back now, please?'

Theo shook his head. 'No way – I said I'd walk you home, and so you can't have it back until we reach your front door.'

Violet grinned at him. He was really quite a polite boy. Much too nice to be falling in love with such a weird person as her.

As they walked towards the tiny alleyway that ran behind her house, Violet's high spirits began to desert her as a familiar feeling of desolation descended around her like a cold fog.

'You can leave me here,' she said to Theo. 'I always use the back door.'

'All right then,' Theo said handing back her satchel. 'I've really enjoyed walking you home. Do you think we might do it again tomorrow?'

Violet nodded slowly, looking straight into his eyes. Was this going to be the very first time she would be kissed? She flicked back her hair and looked at Theo under her eyelashes.

'Bye then,' he said, and turned and walked away.

Violet turned around, elated and yet disappointed. She had wanted to know what it felt like to kiss a boy. Still, perhaps it would happen tomorrow, when he walked her home from school again.

The back door was locked. Violet frowned. This was strange – nobody locked their back doors unless they were going into town or away on holiday. Everyone just walked straight in. Puzzled, she stood still for a few minutes; she could hear her mam's voice inside, talking to someone, so she knew she was at home. She tapped on the window, but there was no response.

Sighing, she opened the lavatory door and extracted the spare front door key. She would just have to walk all the way round to the front of the house and let herself in the front door.

Seconds later she stepped into the hallway. Her mother's voice drifted from the living room as she shut the door behind her. Then she heard her Uncle Tom's low voice murmur in the background. As she hung her satchel on a coat hook, her mother's voice was raised, loud enough for her to hear what she was saying.

'I hate Violet for what she did to my baby. The day she cut her arms and legs in your workshop was the day she murdered my baby boy and I'll never forgive her for that. NEVER!'

ᘒᘓ

Chapter Fourteen
Love and Loss

Eileen sat in Tom's armchair, her bottom lip quivering in a sulky pout, her arms crossed in anger.

'I want to go too.'

'Well, you will,' Tom said. 'You'll go when you're six.' He gestured for her to get out of his chair. 'You're three months younger than Margaret. It's a shame you're not going, too, but it can't be helped.'

Eileen jumped down and sat on the hearth rug, her knees tucked under her chin.

'It's just not fair,' she wailed to Daisy.

Margaret sat on a dining chair, swinging her legs. She cast her eyes upwards in a look of superiority. 'It's because *I* shall be six next month. *You* won't be six until September, Eileen. You have to wait until you're six to go to country dancing lessons.'

Tom patted Eileen's head. 'It's the rules. They can't make an exception just for you.'

'You can come with me and Grandma to look round if you like,' Margaret said to Eileen. 'Then you'll know all about it in September when you learn how to dance.'

Tom laughed at the look of pure horror on Eileen's face at Margaret's suggestion. There was no way she was going to be seen just watching her cousin at her first try-out dancing lesson when she had another whole three months to wait before she was allowed to go.

The last three years had seen Tom happier than he'd ever been in the whole of his life. It was a struggle at times and he'd suffered relapses, but these were now few and far between. There was still one problem, though, and it was the reason his psychiatrist had not discharged him following his appointment that afternoon. His need to control his family remained strong and it was something he now had to work on. Tom had been disappointed at Dr Crabtree's verdict and was upset that he hadn't made such good progress as he had thought, even though he'd managed to persuade Doris that she should give up trying to have another baby because the obsession was driving her insane.

'Rose will get the tea when she gets in from work,' Liz said. 'I shall pop into the Council to have a word with Quentin Andrews about the arrangements for his mayoral dinner before I go back to collect Margaret from her dancing lesson.'

'Righty-ho,' Tom said, as he sank into his chair, determined to demonstrate that he had no intention of controlling anyone. 'I don't mind, I can sit and read the paper until Rose and George get home from work.' He shook the newspaper open. 'Eileen, come and choose your grampy a horse. I'll read out the names and you can tell me which one to pick.'

217

Eileen jumped onto her grandfather's lap.

'I'll make a cup of tea, Dad. And then we'll have to be getting back for Bill.'

'It's so exciting, isn't it, Kettering becoming a borough and Mr Andrews being elected as the Charter Mayor,' Liz said to Tom as she pulled on her hat. 'I feel so honoured that he's asked me to help plan the mayoral dinner.'

'Umm,' Tom said, concentrating on the racing pages in the newspaper. 'Who knows, he might even find himself a nice young wife now he's going to be Mayor. I should think his grand fur-trimmed frock and lacy thing around his neck will be quite fetching.'

Liz's stomach flipped. The thought of Quentin marrying someone else was horrifying. 'It's called a jabot,' she said.

'A what?' Tom said, screwing up his face.

'A jabot. The lacy thing. That's the proper name for it.'

'Oh.' He shrugged his shoulders. 'If you ask me it's all a big waste of money. Wouldn't catch me wearing a fancy red frock, a three-pointed hat, chains round my neck and a lacy bib ...'

Tom stopped speaking, his attention drawn to the list of runners. He began to read out the names of the horses to Eileen.

'Yes, well, I'm not asking you, am I?' Liz interrupted, annoyed, as she stood in front of the mirror over the mantelpiece, adjusting her hat. 'And anyway, you have to be on the council to get elected as Mayor, so there's a fat chance of you having to wear a frock and bib.'

Daisy bit her lip. Her mother was conducting a friendship with Quentin Andrews right under her father's nose. For the last five years, Quentin had visited her house for tea every other Saturday afternoon. He would arrive at three o'clock on the dot, followed five minutes or so later by Liz, who would have baked a cake. Bill and Eileen would make themselves scarce in the garden, or would take themselves off to the corner shop to buy something that Daisy had forgotten. Then she would busy herself in the kitchen and shut the door between the living room and the kitchen and give her mother some private time to chat with Quentin. Then, when Bill and Eileen came in from the garden, she would knock tentatively on her own living room door and would take in a tray, on which would sit her best china teapot, matching cups and saucers, a sugar bowl and jug of milk. She knew both she and Rose would always turn a blind eye to their mother's friendship with Quentin because her mother needed the regular injection of happiness that he brought to her life.

'Where are you going while I'm at my dancing lesson, Grandma?' Margaret asked as they set off.

'I'm just popping into the town hall to see Mr Andrews about the menu for his mayoral dinner. It's very exciting, isn't it?'

'Oh. You won't be late picking me up will you? Promise?'

Liz looked down and smiled at her granddaughter. 'No, of course not,' she said. 'I might even come back a little early and watch you dancing.'

'You look nice today, Grandma. Really, really pretty.'

The newly decorated mayor's parlour was very grand. Paintings from the town's Alfred East art gallery adorned the walls, and the new gilded Mace, bought by the town's Co-operative Society, sat regally in a glass case on the huge shiny walnut desk.

The officious newly-appointed Mayor's Secretary showed Liz into the Parlour.

'Alderman Andrews? Mrs Elizabeth Jeffson for your appointment.' She shut the door behind Liz.

Quentin was unpacking the new chains of office, which had arrived only that morning. He rolled up his shirt sleeves as Liz stepped over the brown paper discarded on the floor. He held them up to show her.

'Liz! How lovely to see you. Look at these,' he said. 'Aren't they absolutely magnificent?'

Liz felt a pang of yearning what might have been. The mayoress's chain of office was sitting on the desk in an open, velvet-lined box. Quentin carefully replaced the new mayor's chain in an identical box beside it.

Liz lightly brushed her fingertips over the mayoress's chain of office. 'Oh, Quentin. These are lovely. Who is going to be your Mayoress and wear these beautiful chains?'

Quentin straightened up and put one of his arms around her waist from behind and with the other plucked out her hat pin and pulled the hat from her head. He set it down on the desk and then buried his head in her hair.

'Quentin! Someone might come in,' Liz admonished as she pulled away slightly. 'Behave yourself,' she added, laughing.

'If I could have just one wish, Liz, it would be that that you could be my Mayoress, as my wife.'

Liz turned around and snaked her arms around his

neck. They kissed. The kiss skipped lightly across the waves of adultery, a gentle, delicate kiss that underlined their deep friendship but tasted of their desire for each other.

They broke away. Quentin took Liz's hand. 'But as that is an impossibility, my sister is going to be my Mayoress.'

Liz stepped over to a new gold brocade-covered sofa, ornately embellished with dark, polished walnut arms and feet. She ran her hand over the expensive material as she sat down. 'This is lovely,' she said. 'It must have cost a fortune.'

Quentin sat down next to her.

'I was thinking the other day,' Liz said. 'One small action can change the whole of your future. In my case, everything hinged on me picking up my alarm clock at five o'clock in the morning.'

Quentin laughed. 'That seems a bit of an extreme statement. How did you arrive at that conclusion?'

'I know that all we share is friendship, Quentin, and so I feel that we haven't really done anything wrong, but we *are* aware of our feelings for each other, and we do speak of the affection between us. Things would have been quite different for us if Tom had lost his life six years ago, instead of pulling through, and everything is down to that alarm clock.'

'Go on,' Quentin said, bemused at Liz's logic.

'When I woke up that dreadful day, and Tom was missing ... well, I say woke up, but I hadn't really slept ... I picked up the alarm clock and held it up to a chink of light so that I could see the time.'

'How could that have changed things?'

'Because when I set it down again on my bedside table, the alarm bells tinkled and the noise brought Rose into my room. If Rose and George hadn't gone out to look for him so early, he'd have died for sure. The doctors told us that if Tom had remained undiscovered for just one more hour, probably less than that, he would have lost his life because of the effects of the poison and alcohol.'

Quentin rubbed his chin. 'I see. So you think you would have been widowed, too, and we could have been man and wife. Is that what you're trying to say?'

Liz nodded. 'Yes.'

'Aahh! But if Tom had died, you wouldn't have been at the fireworks display because you would have still been in mourning. Don't forget, Liz, it's not the done thing for a widow to go out gallivanting at firework displays when her husband has just passed away. And there's another thing you haven't thought of – Tom would have been dead so he wouldn't have been in the beer tent getting drunk, even if you *had* been at the firework display.'

Quentin wagged his forefinger at her, and gave a philosophical shake of his head. 'It doesn't do to think like this, Liz. Everyone can say *what if*?'

Liz clasped his wagging finger in her hand and shook her head. 'We *would* have met eventually, because of how you helped our Daisy to get a council house.'

Quentin nodded. 'I suppose so. I'm really fond of Daisy and Bill – like my own flesh and blood they are now.'

'So that's why I think just one tiny action can affect the future in such big ways. Without realising, you arrive a crossroads in your life and one little thing you do – or don't do – is of a huge significance. No, Quentin, if I could have just one wish, it wouldn't be to be your Mayoress, it would be to turn back time and lay quietly in bed on that morning, not pick up the alarm clock, and not wake Rose. Who would think that a simple thing like looking at the time could affect the whole direction of my life?'

Quentin's face fell and he sighed and shook his head. 'Liz. You really mustn't say things like this. It's like saying you wish Tom was dead.'

'I feel guilty about it all the time,' Liz replied truthfully. 'I can't help it. But I don't feel guilty about our friendship and I am not being dishonest. Tom knows I am helping you out with the mayoral dinner and I even told him I was coming here today. He's tried so hard to keep all his promises, and there's no doubt he's a changed man. Ironically, Tom's behaviour towards me is the kindest it's ever been throughout our married life, and yet I just can't make myself love him anymore. It's too late. He might not have died in that allotment shed, but my love for him did, for certain.'

'But Tom *is* alive, and you're still married to him. Whatever we share, Liz, Tom is still your husband. It's what we agreed. No adultery. Friendship is all we can share while you're a married woman. It's enough for me though, I'd rather have your friendship than nothing at all.'

Quentin and Liz chatted for a while, choosing the menu and flowers for his forthcoming mayoral dinner.

When they had finished, Liz stood up and walked over to the polished desk. She picked up her hat and pin from the surface, hesitated and then put it down again, as if changing her mind about something.

'Quentin, you're a good man and I'm so proud of you.' She placed her palms on the cool surface and leaned on the solid desk with her back to him. She took a deep breath and then exhaled slowly before her voice faded away to a whisper. She almost didn't say it. She very nearly remained silent. She stared at her reflection in the lacquered walnut surface and the eyes that stared back at her were haunted with a hunger for something that, if this golden opportunity were not grasped now, would be lost forever. She made up her mind – she was going to put her reckless proposition to him.

'I want to know, Quentin. I *have* to know,' she whispered. She stared at the lips of the woman in the reflection as they moved and said the words that had been swirling around in her mind ever since she had learned that Tom had to go to London with his boss and stay in a hotel overnight. The woman in the reflection was young, her face unlined and her complexion clear, temporarily free of the torment of an unhappy marriage.

Quentin felt a rush of blood in his ears. He stared at Liz, leaning on the table with her back to him. Was she actually suggesting they slept together after almost six years of self-enforced abstinence? She had always been so steadfast and resolute about their relationship, quoting her marriage vows and reminding him about the sanctity of marriage, especially the promise she had made to *"love, honour and obey, forsaking all others?"* He loved her; there was no doubt about that. They'd talked about their feelings and decided exactly what constituted adultery and

224

what didn't. They'd decided that sharing afternoon tea and the occasional private hug or kiss could not possibly constitute adultery.

'But Liz – we agreed.'

'I know.' Liz's voice was still a whisper. Quentin turned her round by her shoulders and hugged her to him.

'Are you absolutely sure? It will only have to be the once. Just once. No more.'

Liz nodded her head against his chest.

'I just want one time, Quentin, before I'm too old. I want to know what it's like to be loved.'

Quentin shook his head. 'I don't know – you're such a lovely, honest woman, I don't want you to feel guilty afterwards. I couldn't bear to think you would have it on your conscience. Oh, God knows, Liz, I want it just as much as you do – but I really don't think it would be a good idea.' Quentin closed his eyes and ran his fingers through her hair. She felt like a young woman in his arms: the wife she would have been if Tom had died in his allotment shed and she had been free to remarry.

Liz looked up, her eyes meeting his. 'It's a golden opportunity. Tom and his boss are staying in London overnight – they are meeting a big new customer over a grand dinner to talk about supplying boots for the armed forces. He's coming back the next day. I ... I could stay with you that night, provided we were careful not to arouse any suspicion, and your Theo could go to stay with your sister. We'll have to be very discreet, though, especially with you becoming Mayor.'

Quentin pulled away from her and looked straight into her eyes, holding her at arm's length by the shoulders. He still wasn't sure. 'What about Rose and George? They'll wonder where you are.'

Liz bit her lip. A half smile reached her eyes and they twinkled with a secret conspiracy.

'It was Rose who suggested it.'

'What!'

'Well, not in so many words, but she said to me yesterday that, with her father away in London, no one would know if I had a little break, too, and stayed overnight with a friend. She said it would be lovely for her and George to have the house to themselves for a change. She winked at me, and I know that she was suggesting we spent the night together.'

Quentin was shocked, but then relaxed as he realised that Liz's daughters knew exactly what a miserable life she'd led with Tom, and it would be naïve of him to think that Daisy wouldn't tell Rose about their twice-monthly Saturday afternoons at her house. He supposed it was a kind of perverse loyalty to their mother. Well, whatever it was, it was obvious that neither Rose nor Daisy would say anything.

He shut his eyes and as his lips met hers he knew he could finally show Liz just how deep his feelings were for her, but he was still worried.

'Why won't your father let you stay in the house on your own?' Violet said to Theo. 'After all, it's not as if you are a child anymore. You're sixteen with a job for goodness sake.'

Theo rolled his eyes. 'It's probably because he doesn't

trust us.'

Violet sighed. It was ironic that her parents probably wouldn't even have noticed if she wasn't at home, and she could have easily slipped out of the house and spent a night with Theo, but it was his hoity-toity father who was pouring cold water over their secret plans by sending Theo to his auntie's house for the night while he went to a stuffy council conference.

'Look, I'll see what I can do,' Theo said. 'Perhaps we can both say we have band practice or something. Dad's got a spare front door key somewhere. I'll have a look for it and we might be able to snatch a few hours while he's away, but my auntie definitely won't let me stay out all night.'

Violet hugged her knees in excitement. Only that day, she had been practising writing *Violet Andrews* on a scrap of paper. She knew without doubt she would marry Theo. They had been inseparable ever since the first day he had walked her home from school. Against all the odds she had come through the ordeals of her childhood unscathed. She had done well at the Central School and was set to pass her School Certificate with ease. A talented musician, she was the only female in the Munn and Felton Works Band, playing the trumpet alongside Theo, the pair of them the youngest members of the prestigious band.

Although Violet knew Theo's family thought she was a bad influence on him, she was determined to be a good wife. She would have to somehow persuade him not to want children, though, reasoning that, being Doris's daughter, it was inevitable she would be a bad mother herself.

When the hot, sultry day of Tom's visit to London arrived, Liz was jittery with reckless anticipation. It was as if she was two completely different people – on the one hand a respectable married woman and a devoted mother and grandmother; but on the other she was a woman craving for fulfilment, and although she'd had four children they'd not been conceived in love. It was pure temptation, she thought to herself. Temptation was something not to be led into. She had tried so hard to love her husband again, even though her friendship with Quentin had got in the way and muddled her good intentions. She hardly dared admit it to herself, but she was practically counting the minutes until she could lie in Quentin's arms and feel the warmth of his skin on hers. She knew it was adultery, but she pushed it to the back of her mind, more than ready to scatter her wedding vows with just a mere whisper of breath on the dandelion clock of her marriage.

But would she have the courage to go through with it?

She picked up a shopping bag containing a change of clothes and some toiletries and stepped out of the front door. It was best to go while Rose and George were out for an early evening walk with Margaret. It would avoid having to say an embarrassing goodbye when both of them would know where she was going and who she was going to spend the night with.

Tom had bought her flowers that morning. He hadn't wanted to go to London with his boss, and he had tried to make excuses at work as to why he could not go. Part of her had wanted him to stay, because then the temptation of adultery would have been taken out of her hands.

"I love you, Liz," he had said as he pecked her on the cheek when he had left. *"I wish I didn't have to go, but I'll be back tomorrow afternoon. I'll bring you something nice from London."*

She'd shut the front door behind him, closing her eyes momentarily. She wished he hadn't said that he loved her. It just made everything harder.

Quentin's house was situated in Princes Street only a few minutes' walk away from Cornwall Road. She set off, trying to look purposeful, as if she was just popping out on an errand. Although she consciously held her head high, it felt like a heavy, wobbling weight on her shoulders and Liz imagined people's eyes were boring into her back, certain they knew what she was about to do. It had been a close, warm day and Liz perspired as she hurried along the road.

When Tom returned tomorrow, would he somehow guess that she had committed adultery? It wasn't too late to turn back, was it? She could easily just walk around the block and return home, her morals intact and untarnished. But something urged her on. The precious gift of womanhood given to all young women had been hidden away and buried deep beneath her feet after she had met Tom over thirty years ago. He had damaged her, and so was not worthy of sharing her gift. When she had met Quentin on bonfire night six years ago, she had resurrected her gift of womanhood out of the earth, examined it and gazed at it in wonder, because despite being buried for so long, it had remained untarnished over the years. As their friendship had deepened and turned to love, it had grown and become embellished with bright jewels in her heart. She had just one chance to know what it felt like to finally set it free and know what it was like to be a proper woman. Tom had committed adultery so many times in their marriage, surely it couldn't be wrong for her to take this one precious opportunity?

By the time Liz turned the corner into Princes Street, all the guilt had disappeared from her conscience and she felt light and bouncy, despite the heat. Quentin had said he would be watching out for her, so she needn't stand on the front doorstep for too long. As she approached his front door, it opened with perfect timing. He stood before her, newly shaved, wearing a clean, white open-necked shirt. She stepped into his hallway, her eyes as wide as a frightened rabbit's.

'Are you certain you still want to go through with it?' he said as he shut the door.

Liz felt her legs wobble beneath her. 'Of course I do. I've thought about nothing else all week. Are you sure, too?'

Quentin rubbed his forehead, hesitating before answering. 'It must only be the once, Liz, and I need to know you are completely sure.' He stepped aside and gestured towards the stairs.

A few streets away, Violet and Theo sat on the grass in the Pleasure Park in the evening sunlight.

'I couldn't find the key,' Theo said. 'We can't get in, so there's no point.'

'Can't we just break in,' Violet replied. 'It's a golden opportunity. Come on, Theo, where's your sense of adventure?'

Theo bowed his head. He had searched for his father's spare key for hours before he had gone off to his council conference, but to no avail. 'I don't know, Violet. I've been thinking. You're still only fifteen ...'

'So,' Violet said. 'What's that got to do with anything?'

'I'd rather wait until you're sixteen at Christmas. And you might get pregnant. And the neighbours might be suspicious if they see us trying to get in while my father's away.'

Violet punched him playfully on the shoulder. 'We'll be engaged to be married next year. And anyway, we are practically related already, with your father being such good friends with my cousin, Daisy, and my Auntie Liz. Everyone knows I am your girlfriend and it's not as if I don't come round your house all the time when your dad's there. No one will even take a second glance.'

Theo sighed. 'All right then,' he said. 'I'll see if I can open a sash or something and we can get in, but I'll have to be back at my auntie's house before ten o'clock or else she'll be worried about me.'

Liz shook out her nightdress and lay it on Quentin's bed. Made of the palest pink silk, edged with white lace and with straps as thin as a shoelace, it was a nightdress made for love.

'Just give me a shout when you're ready,' Quentin said from the spare bedroom.

Liz smiled. He was such a gentleman, giving her the time to compose herself.

She pulled out her hatpin and placed her hat on the

231

dressing table. Unbuttoning her coat she looked around for somewhere to hang it, and tentatively opened Quentin's wardrobe, extracting two wooden hangers. She shrugged her dress from her shoulders, letting it fall to the floor, before picking it up and hanging it on the coat hanger. When she was naked, she slipped the silky, cool nightdress over her head.

She was standing in front of the dressing table mirror, pulling a comb through her hair when the bedroom door opened. Nervously, she smiled at Quentin's reflection.

'It's not too late to back out, Liz. I need to know you are one hundred percent sure about this ...'

'I'm sure.'

He shut the door behind him and leaned on it. He chuckled and thumped his chest with his fist. 'You're so beautiful, Liz, I can actually feel my heart beating in my chest.'

He sat down on the bed. Liz knelt before him and unbuttoned his shirt before running her hands over his bare chest.

'I love you so much,' he whispered.

'I love you too.'

'I've ... I've something for you.' Quentin reached over to his bedside drawer and extracted a folded sheet of paper and a single red rosebud. 'I cut this rosebud this evening, and wrote this poem out for you to keep. Don't feel ashamed. Don't feel guilt. Trust in destiny and, once tomorrow morning comes, seal tonight in your heart and don't look back on it with a guilty conscience. Before we go any further, I need to know that you won't feel guilt, because I just couldn't bear for you to think of tonight as

232

something to be ashamed of.'

Liz sat back on her heels, unfolding the sheet of paper, reading the words of a poem. 'This is so lovely, Quentin. Thank you.'

'Carpe diem,' Quentin whispered. 'But you must promise me – no regrets tomorrow.'

Liz touched his face with her fingertips. He kissed the palm of her hand and then helped her up. Before she climbed into Quentin's bed, she carefully tucked the rosebud and poem into her bag.

Theo thumped the kitchen window sash three times with the heel of his hand.

'It's no good, Vi, it won't budge.'

Violet sighed. It was just one thin pane of glass. Surely it wouldn't make too much noise if it accidentally got broken.

'Try again,' she said. 'I saw my Uncle Tom do this once when Mam lost her front door key. If you hit it hard enough, the catch jumps off and you can push on the sash and open it.'

Theo thumped again on the window frame. 'It won't shift, Vi. The catch is too stiff.'

Violet picked up a large stone from the rockery.

'What are you doing?' Theo said, alarmed.

'This, Violet replied, and whacked the window with it.

'You stupid idiot! My dad will go absolutely mad. He'll think someone's broken in and burgled the house while he was at the conference.'

'Exactly,' Violet said with a grin as she replaced the stone. 'That's the idea.'

Worried that someone would have heard the breaking

glass, Theo glanced over his shoulder towards the neighbour's back door.

'Hurry up, then,' she said. 'Stop gawking. Stick your hand in and open the sash.'

Theo unlocked the sash and then clambered through the open window. He unlocked the back door from the inside.

'I can't believe you,' he said, grinning as he grabbed Violet's arm and pulled her inside. 'No wonder my family think you are a bad influence on me.'

Violet began to giggle.

The door between the kitchen and the living room flew open.

'Oh it's you! What the hell are you doing?' Quentin roared, brandishing a black umbrella he had grabbed from the hallway as protection. 'I thought someone was breaking in.'

'I ... I ... we ... I forgot my ... er ... anyway, what are *you* doing here? I thought you were supposed to be at a conference?'

'I felt ill, so I didn't go.'

Violet giggled again. Theo's father was dressed only in a pair of long johns, and beads of perspiration were glistening on his forehead.

Quentin struggled to catch his breath. 'Which one of you broke the window? It scared me half to death, I thought it was a burglar.'

'It was me,' Theo said quickly. 'I tried to jump the catch on the sash, and put my hand through it by mistake.'

'Huh,' Quentin said with a cynical glance at his son's hand, which was unblemished, with no traces of blood.

234

'I'm not as green as I'm cabbage-looking.'

Theo mumbled, embarrassed at his father's remark. He tried to squeeze past Quentin. 'I'll just go upstairs, and fetch my ... er ...'

'Oh no you won't,' Quentin said, grabbing him by the scruff of his neck and hauling him back.

'Why?' Violet said, still giggling. 'Have you got a lady friend hidden up there?'

'You, my girl, are too forward for your own good. No I most certainly haven't. And even if I had it wouldn't be any of your business.'

Quentin clutched at his chest and gasped. 'Oh my word. I really don't feel too well, Theo. I think it's the shock of thinking someone was breaking in.'

Violet watched as Quentin stumbled forwards, his hand outstretched as if trying to find something on which to steady himself. She stepped back as he crumpled to the floor. She had to hand it to him. It was a pretty impressive way to stop Theo going up the stairs and finding a strange lady, naked in his father's bed.

Theo fell to his knees. 'Dad!' he screamed in horror. 'What's up?'

Violet's smile slid from her face as she realised Quentin was not feigning illness to stop Theo going upstairs. She stopped giggling, sinking down to the floor beside him. Theo shook his father's shoulders. There was no response.

'Check if he's breathing,' Violet yelled. 'You might need to give him mouth to mouth resuscitation.'

'I can't tell. I can't bloody well tell.'

Violet put her hand on Quentin's chest. 'I don't think he is.'

Theo bent forwards and began to breathe into his father's mouth, pinching his nose shut.

'Quentin!' a woman's voice screamed out from the stairs.

Violet looked up, shocked, as footsteps thudded on the staircase. She obviously hadn't been wrong about Theo's father entertaining a lady friend while he should have been at the conference.

As the door burst open, Violet only just managed to stop herself squealing out her aunt's name in surprise as she stood in the doorway, dressed only in an expensive pink silk and white lace nightdress. Was it really her Auntie Liz? Violet squinted. She looked completely different.

Theo sat up. 'Is he breathing, Vi? Check and see if it's working.'

Violet turned her attention to Quentin.

'I think it might be working, but carry on until he coughs or something. I'll run and get some help.'

Liz stood still in the doorway, her hand clamped over her mouth, her eyes wide with shock.

Violet sprang to her feet, roughly pushing her aunt out of the doorway into the hallway. She pulled the door shut behind her.

'Go and get dressed, we've got to get you out of here quick,' she hissed in her aunt's ear. 'I think he's had a heart attack or something.'

'No, I can't. I have to get to him.' Liz grasped the doorknob, but Violet knocked her hand away, grabbed her arm and propelled her towards the stairs. 'Believe me, Auntie Liz, you need to get out of here. Trust me.'

'Is ... is he breathing?' Liz whispered.

'Yes. Just go, Auntie Liz. It's probably this heat and he's just fainted or something.'

'You'll go and get help for him?'

'Yes, but I can't do it while I'm standing here arguing with you, can I? Get your things and just go. I'll come round tomorrow and let you know how he is.'

Chapter Fifteen
Grief and Bravery

Daisy was hanging out washing in her back garden when she heard the front gate open, and then slam back on the latch. She picked up her wicker laundry basket and peered around the side of her house, wondering who was calling on her.

'Hello,' she said, recognising the man who was walking down the garden path with his cap in his hand. He was one of Quentin's sons.

'Mrs Roberts?'

Daisy nodded. 'Yes – how can I help you?'

'I'm John Andrews, Quentin's son. I'm afraid I have some bad news. It's my father ... he ...'

The man bowed his head and rubbed his forehead with the back of his hand before continuing.

'I'm afraid my father had a heart attack last night. My nephew was there with your cousin, Violet. They tried hard to save him – managed to bring him round, raise the alarm and get him straight to the hospital – but it was no good. They couldn't do anything for him. He passed away in the early hours this morning.'

Daisy dropped her washing basket in shock. Quentin? Dead? She gulped and a shiver went down her spine. Was her mother there when it happened? She picked up her basket.

'Does ... does my mother know?'

The man shook his head. 'No. Not yet. I know how fond my father was of Mrs Jeffson. He was such a good friend to so many people. He'll be sorely missed.'

'He was such a lovely man.' Daisy shook her head, blinking back tears. 'Would you like to come in? Can I make you a cup of tea?'

The man shook his head. 'No, that's kind of you, but I've still got some people to tell.'

'If there's anything we can do ...'

'If you could just let Mr and Mrs Jeffson know ...'

John Andrews and Daisy stared at each other in a strange moment of connectivity. It was as if they'd one day met briefly as strangers, and then the next day passed each other in a crowded street, their eyes locking in recognition but without acknowledging each other. It was an intense and private moment of perfect understanding. Daisy had only met John Andrews a couple of times, but at that moment they both knew that his father and her mother had shared something very special, and the knowledge fused in the air between them and pulled them towards each other.

'I'm so, so sorry.' Daisy said, tears spilling over her eyelids.

'If things had been different ...' Quentin's son said with a shrug of his shoulders, before offering Daisy his hand.

Daisy nodded in agreement and shook his hand. 'Please let me know when the funeral is, Mr Andrews.'

'Yes, of course.' He pulled his cap on tightly, and then

240

turned and left. Daisy watched him close the gate and walk along the road. Her mouth and throat felt dry and tears filled the back of her nose. Lovely, gentle Quentin – the man who had given her mother a few, snatched moments of shelter from years of a stormy marriage; the saviour who had given them this lovely home. How on earth were they going to break the news to her? And what had happened last night? Had her mother been there when he had his heart attack?

Rose and George always walked home together from the factory, while Tom used his bicycle. They didn't hurry home: it was the only time they found themselves alone and Daisy knew that they looked forward all day to the twenty minutes or so it would take them to walk from the factory to Cornwall Road. She waited just around the corner from the factory entrance, scanning the bubbling sea of faces for her sister. She zig-zagged through the crowd of factory workers walking in the opposite direction. Rose was waiting by the factory gates for George to join her.

'Daisy! What on earth are you doing here?'

'Oh Rose, I've had some dreadful news ...'

'What? Oh my God. It's not Mam is it? Where's Eileen?'

'No, it's Quentin. I've left a note for Bill on the kitchen table and Eileen's with the neighbours.'

'What about Quentin?' George said, hearing the tail end of the conversation as he joined his wife.

Agitated, Daisy looked at her sister. 'Did Mam go to him last night? Was she back home this morning?'

'No, for some reason she didn't go,' Rose said. 'Something must have happened. She went to bed early.'

Daisy shut her eyes in relief. 'Thank goodness. He had a heart attack last night and passed away in the early hours this morning.'

'Oh no!' Rose reeled in shock. 'Does she know?'

'No, not yet. We can't tell her with Dad around, can we? He'll be back home from London by now. What are we going to do, Rose? We've got to tell her, but we can't just come out with it with Dad lurking in the background.'

'No, you're right,' Rose said. 'Mam will be devastated. Come on, George, what can we do? How can we get Mam on her own?'

George shook his head. 'Poor Liz. I'll take Tom into the garden as soon as we get home. I'll tell him I spotted some blackfly on his roses or something, and then we'll have a smoke outside while I keep him talking. I'll keep him out there as long as I can.'

Daisy nodded. 'All right,' she sighed. 'I'm not looking forward to this. Which one of us is going to tell her?'

'I will,' Rose said. 'Then you can fill her in on the details.'

'We should all go to the funeral,' George said. 'And hope that your father doesn't, because your mam is going to be inconsolable.'

Rose shook her head. 'He will. He loves a good funeral.'

Liz's face was pale and a bead of sweat broke out on her upper lip as her hand flew to her chest. The air was heavy, making her gasp and thunderclouds were building

242

outside. A sudden intense flush of prickly warmth rose up her legs, into her torso and then flowed down her arms and up into her face and then, as quickly as it had come, it disappeared and left her shivery and trembling.

Last night, after hastily pulling on her dress, hat and coat and grabbing her bag, she'd bolted out of Quentin's front door, panicking, her heavy legs somehow propelling her forwards until she arrived home well before Rose, George and Margaret had returned from their walk. She'd gone straight to bed, pulling the bedclothes right over her head, but she hadn't slept, tossing and turning, worried about Quentin. She had hoped Violet would knock on the door and let her know how he was, but she hadn't. Early that morning, she'd ran over the road to her sister's house, fraught with worry and desperate to speak to Violet, but all she found was Doris, pacing up and down the kitchen smoking a cigarette, furious because Violet had stayed out all night. Then, as she left Doris's house and ran back across the road, a black car had almost knocked her over. She had only caught the briefest glimpse of the occupants, but a man, who looked just like Quentin, had looked over his shoulder and appeared to blow a kiss at her as the car drove away. The man had been sitting in the back with a woman, a chauffeur driving the expensive, shiny black car. She couldn't be completely sure it had been Quentin, but the sight of the man had reassured her somewhat. If Quentin had been passing in the Mayor's car early that morning, then he must have just fainted with the heat last night and was now fully recovered.

But now, reality filled her heart with dread. As Rose and Daisy stood before her in the front room, she knew it was not good news.

'No, he's not,' she cried out after Rose gently broke the news to her. 'There's been a mistake. It's not Quentin. I saw him early this morning. He waved to me from the road when I came out of Doris's. He was in the new Mayor's car.'

Rose took her mother's hand and led her to an armchair in the front room.

Daisy began to explain as she shut the door behind them. 'It happened last night, Mam. He had a heart attack at home, and then passed away in the early hours of this morning in hospital. Violet was apparently there with Theo when it happened and they managed to bring him round, but there was nothing anyone could do.'

Rose touched her mother's arm. 'Why didn't you go to Quentin's last night? Did you have second thoughts?' She grimaced as her mother put both hands over her face and shook her head from side to side in anguish.

Liz's voice was muffled as she cried into her hands. 'No. No. You've got it all wrong. I saw him! He was in his car; there was a woman beside him. They both gave me a smile, waved to me, and ... and ... and then he ...'

'What, Mam?' Rose said, puzzled.

Liz took her face out of her hands and looked up. 'It looked as if he blew me a kiss out of the window.'

'He couldn't have, Mam. Not this morning. It couldn't possibly have been Quentin in the car.'

'He did! It *was* him. Someone's made a mistake. I know what I saw.'

Liz didn't cry. Not then. Her voice faded away and collapsed in on itself, leaving her face alabaster white and

244

her eyes glazed as she stared at the wall. There was a bright flash of lightning outside, followed moments later by an ear-splitting crash of thunder. A few moments later she stood up, went into the kitchen and started to peel potatoes. She peeled until there was a huge bowlful – far too many for the family tea. Rose and Daisy fussed around her, sharing worried glances. This was not the reaction they'd expected.

The sisters sat at the kitchen table in silence, as lightning flickered and thunder rumbled around them. Daisy began to cry and Rose pulled a handkerchief out from her sleeve and offered it to her.

'He was such a lovely man,' Daisy said in a shaky voice. 'I liked him right from that first day, when we had to fetch the ambulance out to Dad when he broke his hip by falling down that drain.'

'I remember,' Rose. 'And then he pulled strings at the Council and got you a house ...'

'Stop it!' Liz shouted in a strange voice, without looking up. 'Stop talking about him in the past tense. He's not a *was* he's an *is*.'

Rose and Daisy looked at their mother and then at each other as their father and George appeared outside the kitchen window.

Blood dripped from Liz's forefinger into the sink. The cut had been a deliberate act on Liz's part. She wanted the sharp pain of it to travel up her arm and ease her thumping, heavy heart, which was giving her a dull ache in her throat, but it didn't work. The pain in her chest was so intense she could hardly breathe.

'You've cut your finger, Mam,' Rose said,' her chair

scraping on the floor as she stood up to fetch a clean rag from a drawer.

'Leave it! Don't touch me!'

Liz leaned on the kitchen sink, the red blood dripping and curling around in the potato peelings. Rose sat down again, and Daisy dabbed her eyes.

The back door opened.

'I'll put the kettle on,' Liz said, wrapping the rag around her finger, her voice high with forced composure. 'We need a cup of tea after hearing such bad news.'

'What bad news?' Tom said, hearing the tail end of Liz's comment.

'Didn't George tell you? Quentin Andrews died this morning. He had a heart attack,' Rose said. 'His son called on Daisy this morning and asked her to let us know.'

'Bloody hell,' Tom said, rubbing his chin as, outside, the rain came. Huge, fat drops began to patter on the kitchen window in a haunting, sad melody.

He picked up the empty teapot from the kitchen table. 'I'm spittin' feathers, 'ere, I could do with a brew.'

He took the kettle from Liz's hand, filled it up and banged it down on the stove to boil. He glanced in the saucepan on the wooden draining board. 'How many are you expecting for tea, woman? There's enough taters here to feed a hundred Irish navvies!'

Liz flinched as a loud crack of thunder shook the kitchen window.

'What's up, Liz? You're not scared of a little storm, are you?' Tom said with a laugh.

Liz shrugged her shoulders and turned away.

'What's the matter with your mam?' Tom said to Rose

as he sat down at the kitchen table, shaking out the evening newspaper. 'Deathly pale she is. I reckon she's coming down with the flu.'

Liz, hearing Tom's comment, made a decision. That was exactly what she would do. The sky was shedding the tears she couldn't, and the thunder was drowning out the pounding grief in her heart so that Tom could neither see nor hear it. She would come down with the flu and then she could lie in bed all day and not have to face life without Quentin.

Just over a week later, the Jeffson family attended Quentin's funeral. Liz had hidden away in bed under the false cloak of illness for almost a week, but had composed herself and made enough of a recovery to attend the funeral, her nostrils tinged red with rawness and her eyes bloodshot. The family had sent flowers to the Andrews family and Tom had written out the card in his perfect copperplate script. He couldn't possibly go into work, he'd told his boss, not when it was the funeral of such an important, close family friend who would have been the Mayor of Kettering, had he lived. Now the inaugural Mayor was going to be a Gotch, whose family were very eminent in the town, which was something Tom agreed with wholeheartedly, and the First Substitute Mayor was to be a woman, which was something Tom didn't agree with at all.

Rose and Daisy were worried that their mother's grief would manifest itself in the church, and their father would suspect her affair. Neither of the girls had witnessed Liz shedding even a solitary tear since she'd heard the news, yet they both saw the evidence of the days spent in self-enforced solitary confinement. They had made hasty arrangements for Margaret to play with Eileen each day after school to give their mother time off from looking after her granddaughter, so that she could have some privacy to grieve for Quentin. But they both knew that the sorrow was still knotted up inside her, just waiting to uncoil itself at any moment. They just hoped it wouldn't be at the funeral, or at any time in front of their father, because he would then surely know about the real nature of her friendship with Quentin.

The sisters didn't realise, though, that because of Tom's psychological disorder, he found it difficult to read others' reactions to stressful situations. If Liz had broken down in a disproportionate display of grief for a family friend, he'd not really have noticed or questioned it. He certainly wouldn't have suspected that his wife had been having an affair with the deceased man. He would merely have said: *give over and pull yourself together, old gal. It's not as if it's the end of the world. Everybody has to kick the bucket someday.*

Liz walked into the church on Tom's arm. It felt as hard as steel beneath her hand, and not warm, soft and safe like Quentin's. She was perfectly composed and had chosen her outfit with care, declaring that she was not going to wear black. Instead she wore a dark, midnight blue lightweight coat and matching hat, decorated with tiny red rosebuds. Pinned to her coat was a brooch of exploding sparkling gemstones in red and blue interspersed with tiny diamonds. Underneath her coat she

248

wore a pale blue summer dress: it had been Quentin's favourite. Around her neck was a delicate gold filigree necklace, studded with tiny diamonds, sapphires and rubies to match the brooch. Tom had complimented her jewellery, which he hadn't known she possessed, frowning slightly when she said that he must have forgotten she had it. Tom had been puzzled. The jewellery looked expensive and he wondered just how much he had spent as he must have surely been three sheets to the wind when he'd bought it, as he was damned if he could remember. He'd then noticed a diamond ring on her finger. Liz had never been much of a one for rings, saying that they irritated her. He'd not seen that before either, but accepted Liz's explanation that it had once belonged to an old friend of her mother's. It was just that she'd never worn it before because it only fitted on her little finger.

He asked her why she was not wearing her usual, black funeral coat but she'd not answered him straight away, setting her jaw in a defiant, determined stare before turning her back on him. *"Tom,"* she'd said to him. *"I'll wear what I like, if you don't mind."* He'd seen a determined, independent look in her eyes as she turned away. He couldn't understand it because he'd been kind to her and hadn't laid a finger on her for nearly six years. The disconnected look in her sincere, brown eyes saddened him. Up until his illness, he'd grown used to the doleful, puppy-dog devotion of Liz, which had endured no matter what awful things he had done to her, and now it was gone and he couldn't understand why. Almost six years he had been kind to her and had tried his hardest to be a good husband, father and grandfather. As for the drink, he'd hardly touched a drop since bonfire night in nineteen thirty-two. If it wasn't for the irritating problem of Doris, he would have kept every single promise he'd made after his suicide attempt.

Why could Liz not love him again when he had been so good, for so long?

Liz knew Rose and Daisy were just a few feet behind her, and she drew strength from their presence as she walked into the church on one of the saddest days of her life and sat down in the pew, with Tom by her side. Daisy slid along the polished wooden bench on the other side of her and discreetly squeezed her hand.

Was there an afterlife she wondered? Was Quentin hovering somewhere above her head, watching his own funeral? Did he know how much she was grieving for him, whilst in public she was having to act as if he was merely an acquaintance – a family friend on the periphery of her life, and not the love of it? Was he with his deceased wife now, and if he was, what would happen to her when she died? She couldn't be with him if he was now with his wife. He couldn't wait for her if Betsy Andrews had reclaimed him for her own. It seemed to Liz that they were destined never to be together, neither in this life nor the next. Their souls would forever orbit each other in a magnetism that would both attract and repel, and they would never, ever, be together.

It was during the hymn that Liz cried, but she gulped down the tears that rose into her eyes and nose, unable to see the words in the hymn book. Daisy had snaked her fingers around her hand and given it a comforting squeeze, a welcome warmth against her icy cold skin. Tom sang at the top of his voice with inappropriate gusto. His tuneless voice grated – intruding on her private pain. He turned his head while he was singing and slipped his arm through hers, noticing her tears and the trembling pages of her hymn book. He stopped singing, delved into his trouser pocket for his handkerchief and handed it to her. She could grieve properly for Quentin, she thought, when there was a graveside to visit. As the hymn concluded, she drew a strange comfort from the thought of sitting alone in the cemetery with her private thoughts. She could then place red rosebuds on his grave and whisper her goodbyes properly.

One week later, Violet tapped on Liz's back door and let herself into the kitchen.

She had lied to Theo for the first time in their relationship, when, on the day of his father's funeral he had suddenly recalled hearing a woman's voice calling his father's name when he had been trying to save his life as he lay dying on the floor.

"I didn't hear anything," Violet had said, hastily rearranging her expression from one of sympathy to one of exaggerated puzzlement. *"You must have been mistaken."*

"No I wasn't. I've only just remembered it, but I clearly heard a woman's voice say Dad's name."

Theo had dwelt on it, had cried into her hair and said it wasn't fair that he was an orphan at only sixteen. She had hardly left his side, supporting him through his grief and had been a constant visitor at his aunt's house, where he was staying, winning her way into the family's good books. But his aunt, who had been there when Theo had made the comment, hadn't let it go. She had mentioned it to the vicar after the funeral, who had said that Theo hearing a woman say his father's name was surely a sign that his poor mother had reached out to him from beyond the grave. Violet had bit her lip, remaining silent. She hadn't liked lying to Theo, especially now he firmly believed that he had heard his dead mother saying his father's name when he was close to death on the living room floor.

Violet closed the back door behind her.

'Are you on your own?' she said to Liz.

Liz nodded.

'You look awful.'

Liz bowed her head. 'It's not what you think, Violet. I … I … we hadn't done anything wrong.'

'Don't worry, Auntie Liz. I haven't told a soul. Your secret's safe with me. But I have to say I was really surprised. I knew you were friends with Theo's father, but …'

Liz put up her hand to stop her talking. 'It didn't happen, Violet. It was meant to, but you and Theo coming home when you did … well, it was just like the alarm clock.'

'Alarm clock?' Violet said, puzzled.

'Sit down,' Liz said, pulling out a kitchen chair for Violet. 'I need to tell you about the alarm clock on the day your Uncle Tom tried to take his own life. I was talking to Theo's father about it about it only a few weeks ago. Quentin and I were only ever meant to share friendship – I

252

know that now.'

After Liz had told Violet the story of how she had picked up her alarm clock to look at the time on the morning Tom had tried to end his own life, Violet sat in quiet reflection. Despite her awful childhood, she had come through it unscathed and now she had an unbreakable bond with her Auntie Liz through the secret they shared. She was her own person, soon to be an adult. She would care for Theo, marry him and they would live happily ever after in his house in Princes Street and who, knew, she might even reconsider her decision not to have children.

Theo was like his father: solid, reliable and a perfect gentleman and she loved him completely. She knew there would never be any other man in her life.

Nothing and no one could ever take away her bright future as Violet Andrews.

Chapter Sixteen
Vulnerability and Fear

Liz's Bible wasn't hidden away and Tom could have discovered the sheet of paper inside it at any time, had he been searching for it, but it was almost a year after Quentin Andrews' death that, completely by accident, Tom found the poem.

Liz had carelessly left her Bible lying on the bed, and Tom had picked it up to put it back in its rightful place. Just a tiny corner of a folded sheet of paper had been visible. At first he gave it only a cursory glance, thinking it was merely a bookmark, but when the pages fell open at the place where the sheet had been inserted, Tom saw that, folded carefully in white tissue paper, was a dried and pressed perfectly formed crimson red rosebud.

He unfolded the sheet of notepaper and read the words of the poem Quentin had written out for Liz.

Gather ye rosebuds while ye may,
Old time is still a-flying;
And this same flower that smiles today
Tomorrow will be dying.
The glorious lamp of heaven the sun,
The higher he's a-getting,

The sooner will his race be run,
And nearer he's to setting.
That age is best which is the first,
When youth and blood are warmer;
But being spent, the worse, and worst
Times still succeed the former.
Then be not coy, but use your time,
And, while ye may, go marry;
For, having lost but once your prime,
You may forever tarry.

Tom became obsessed with the poem. At every opportunity he would slip silently into the bedroom, slide open the drawer in his wife's bedside cabinet and withdraw her Bible. Soon, he came to realise the place marked was within the pages of the book of Corinthians, at the verses that referred to love. He would unfold the sheet of paper on which the poem was written and study the words until they had imprinted themselves indelibly into his troubled mind. Every time he thought about the poem, or took the rosebud out of the tissue paper, all he wanted to do was cry. He would scratch his head, the words repeating themselves over and over in his head. He would clutch the poem to his heart and the tears would roll over his cheeks until they disappeared into his moustache. Instinctively he knew they held a deep, secret meaning. A meaning that was testimony to the reason why Liz could not love him again.

Several times he thought about confronting Liz with the discovery, part of him wanting to hear her laugh, and say that the rosebud was pressed by one of his granddaughters, and the poem was written out years ago when she was just a girl, but he just couldn't bring himself to do it.

Instead he would sink down onto the bed and put his head in his hands in despair because his lovely Liz had in her possession a poem that was not written in her handwriting, treasured a pressed red rosebud and hidden it amongst words of love in her Bible.

It could only mean that, once, she had loved someone other than himself.

One day, just after Tom's discovery of the poem, Liz pulled out a hat she hadn't worn for months. It was midnight blue and the brim was decorated with tiny red rosebuds. As she placed it on her head in the hallway, declaring that she was going with Daisy and Rose to place some flowers on the grave of Quentin Andrews, he remembered that she had worn the hat for Quentin's funeral.

And then he knew.

Liz had been in love with Quentin.

On Sunday, 3rd September 1939, war was declared over the airwaves to a hushed nation. Within only a few days, children began to arrive in Kettering from London and other areas at high risk of bombing, with name tags pinned to their coats and their belongings stuffed into rucksacks and battered old cardboard suitcases.

In the days that followed, seven-year old cousins, Margaret Foster and Eileen Roberts were excited as they met new evacuee friends and exchanged stories about their different lives. The start of the new school term was delayed because of the war, and children milled around the streets looking for mischief right up until the beginning of November. It had been exciting at first, before boredom set in, and by the time the schools finally opened their gates most children were disappointed that they had seen no German aeroplanes nor heard any distant exploding bombs. But the adults were constantly fearful, waiting for the air raids that never came. People began speaking about the 'phoney' war and homesick evacuee children began drifting back to the city, collected by their relatives.

Kettering, located in the heart of England, was surrounded by countryside. Despite its relatively safe location and lack of bombings, local people were still frightened. The presence of a steelworks in the town of Corby, only eight miles away, meant that the area could be bombed at any time, should the Germans discover its location. Additionally, there were RAF air bases only a few miles away at Molesworth and Alconbury and the town's railway station was always busy, it being on one of the country's main railway lines.

One Friday afternoon a few weeks after war had been declared but before they went back to school, Margaret and Eileen sat squashed together on the front doorstep of Bill and Daisy's house in Windmill Avenue. They were sharing an apple, cut exactly in half, as they watched men cutting down railings.

'We won't get sweets anymore,' Margaret said.

'Why?'

'Because Gramp says they'll be rationed.'

258

'Why?'

Margaret took another bite of apple and, with her mouth full, gave a seven-year-old's view of what they would and wouldn't be able to eat during the war. 'And Gramp says they'll be fighting in the shops and people will be filling their pockets with things like butter and sugar on the black market.'

'Where's the black market?' Eileen wrinkled her nose. 'Is it dirty place?'

Margaret shrugged. 'I dunno, but it sounds *horrible*. It must be where grown-ups go, so don't worry, I don't think they'll make us go with them.'

Eileen, impressed by Margaret's seemingly vast knowledge of rationing and dirty markets, said, 'My dad's 'scripted now.'

'What's 'scripted?'

Eileen giggled. 'I dunno, but it sounds *horrible*.'

The two girls fell about laughing.

Daisy appeared in the doorway. 'What on earth are you two giggling about?'

'Dad being 'scripted.'

Daisy sighed. She was worried about Bill's imminent conscription to the armed forces. The letter had arrived soon after war had been declared, he had duly attended his medical and all that was left now was for him to leave for military training before being posted. One of the ironic things about the war though, was the way the children were so excited about it, whilst the adults were so fearful. Daisy felt like scolding the girls for laughing about Bill's conscription, but it was obvious they had no idea what it meant – in any case, what was the point of worrying them with the details? They would find out soon enough.

Margaret and Eileen sat on the front doorstep all morning, watching the workmen remove the railings, and then they stared with huge, wide eyes as heavy trucks arrived, delivering Anderson air-raid shelters to every family along the street. They also saw their Uncle Walter walk past Daisy's house.

'Hello, Uncle Walter!' the girls shouted in unison, jumping up and waving. 'Where are you going?' added Margaret, curious because he was carrying a suitcase.

Walter tipped his cap and waved back.

'Hello, girls,' he said, with a smile on his face.

'Where are you going, Uncle Walter? Can we come?' they shouted.

Walter turned and tapped his nose. 'Not today, I'm afraid. Be good girls, won't you.'

Two hours after Margaret and Eileen had spoken to Walter as he walked along Windmill Avenue, Violet slipped on her shoes and checked her lipstick in the hall mirror. At sixteen, she looked much older, her blonde hair set in a neat bob around her heart-shaped face. With her difficult childhood now well behind her, she now had a job as an assistant at a chemist's shop, where she was highly regarded for her hard-working nature and meticulous attention to detail.

A year after the death of his father, Theo Andrews had moved back into the house in Princes Street, his aunt declaring that he could fend for himself now he was seventeen and almost old enough to fight for King and country.

Studying the slip of paper she had just been secretly given by her father, Violet memorised the address in the highlands of Scotland before tucking it into her purse. She would dispose of it later, once she was safely at Theo's house.

Her suitcase was packed, ready for moving out. Theo could be called up for active service at any time once he reached eighteen, and they both wanted to make the most of the time they had together before he went away. They had talked about marriage, but Theo's brothers had said they were far too young, so they had agreed to wait until the war was over.

Before he had left the house that morning, her father had given her his blessing. They had talked way into the night just a week ago and her father had said that she should ignore the gossips, as being at war changed things and people couldn't be expected to play by the rules anymore. Violet had been excited: no longer would she be trapped in the same house as her mother. No more would she have to constantly, day-in, day-out, be reminded that it had been her fault that her mother had given birth to a monster baby. Today would be the last time she would have to make excuses to the neighbours for her mother's nasty accusations about something she had lost, which had been "stolen", the petty arguments about the noise of children playing in the street, the imagined gossiping behind her back or complaints about the neighbours' cats that yowled and fought in the night. She would move into Theo's house in Princes Street and, if he was called-up next year, she would work hard on creating a comfortable home for them both, ready for the war to be over. Then, they would get married. No one would be able to say they were far too young.

She crept upstairs to fetch her suitcase, hoping that her mother wouldn't hear her. She shut the front door gently behind her and exhaled in relief.

She made her way to the end of the road where Theo was waiting for her on his motorcycle. He gave her a brief kiss before hauling her suitcase into the sidecar. She clambered on the back, holding onto his waist tightly as they roared off.

Back inside the house, Doris sat in the untidy living room with a glass of sherry. She rubbed her forehead with a shaky hand. Something was afoot: both Walter and Violet had been acting strangely and the house had seemed to be buzzing with activity for days, with much slamming and banging about upstairs. There had been very few words spoken, but when she had ventured up the stairs to investigate, she couldn't fail to hear the whispering and then notice the knowing glances between Walter and Violet as they went about various household chores.

After Walter's solemn promise to Doris to keep away from men, to her knowledge, he had kept to his word. Now she wasn't so sure. Things were changing and Walter had a male friend. He had always kept his distance from friendship, but this time it was different. Doris sensed, but had no proof whatsoever, that he was closer to a colleague at the solicitor's practice where he worked than was appropriate.

Outwardly, Walter seemed the same as always. Although their marriage lacked physical closeness, he had always treated her with respect and courtesy and they rubbed along adequately in their own way. He had gone to work that morning, as usual, returning at lunchtime for his dinner, which wasn't quite so usual. Doris knew something was wrong. Perhaps it was the war, she wondered? Perhaps Walter was worried about being called up for service, but he shouldn't be: he was too old.

Doris realised that Violet had left the house when she heard the front door close: she hadn't even said goodbye and had left no clues about where she was going or what time she would be back. Sighing, she downed her glass of sherry, stubbed out her cigarette in an ashtray and then trudged upstairs to try and find out what all the recent activity had been about. Violet had left clothes strewn on her unmade bed. It took Doris a few minutes to put everything away and make the bed. Throwing the dirty washing on the landing to collect later, Doris stepped into the main bedroom.

On the pillow on her side of the bed was an unaddressed, unsealed envelope. With a feeling of dread, she picked it up and drew out the single sheet of paper inside.

Dear Doris,

I don't quite know how to tell you, and I hope you will forgive me for being a coward and not speaking to you directly about this.

For all the years of our marriage I have suppressed

my true nature. I don't regret my decision, because I made a promise to you and I wanted to keep that promise. But Violet is now almost a grown woman, she will be seventeen at Christmas, has a mind of her own and I know she will go her own way regardless.

It is time for me to leave my artificial life as a married man behind me and start a new life. The war makes it much easier to disappear. Please don't try to find me. You can just tell folks I have been called up for war work. It will spare you any embarrassment.

I'm sorry to do this to you, Doris – but I just cannot live as a married man any longer. If you go to Jarvis's Solicitors you will find that I have signed the house over to you. Mr Jarvis will also deal with the divorce, if you want one, so that you, too, can begin a new life.

I have left a separate letter for Violet. I hope you will both forgive me.

Love Walter

xx

Doris sat on the bed, surprised at her lack of emotion. She supposed she should be having hysterics and weeping and wailing because her husband had left her, but the truth was, she felt nothing. But what would happen if the authorities realised Walter had disappeared? Would they track him down and would he be prosecuted for being a homosexual? After all, homosexuality *was* against the law, war or no war. And what was she going to do for money? With only Violet's wage coming into the house, it wouldn't be long before they were in trouble and she couldn't bear

264

the thought of having to go out to work herself.

She tucked the letter back in the envelope and went downstairs. She pulled on her coat and shut the front door behind her.

She needed to tell Tom – right away.

Tom stood in Theo Andrews' living room, eyes blazing and fists clenched as he glared at Violet.

'You *knew*?'

Violet gave a loud exaggerated sigh, and cast her eyes up in the air. She crossed her arms defiantly.

'I knew.'

'You knew your father was planning to run off with that … that … queer and you said nothing? Gawd knows what this is going to do to your mother. I can't believe you, Violet. Are you insane? Why didn't you tell me, for goodness sake?'

'Why should I have told you?'

'And you are sure you don't know where he's gone?'

'No I don't,' Violet lied. 'He wouldn't tell me.'

Tom couldn't continue, flabbergasted that Violet had known about Walter's plans to elope with his lover and didn't seem to care that he was breaking the law and could go to prison.

'Do *you* know where they are?' he asked Theo, who stood, leaning casually on the kitchen door frame, a bottle of beer in his hand.

'No,' he said truthfully, shrugging his shoulders.

Tom sprayed spittle into air as he lost his temper with Violet. 'You're a bloody little liar – I can't believe your father would just take off without telling you where he was going.' His gaze slipped from Violet to Theo and then back again. The anger was building and he needed release. He wanted to take her by the shoulders and shake the truth from her, but he couldn't do it. After all, biologically she was his daughter and he'd never been rough with any of his children.

He slammed his fist on the table instead and the sound resonated around the room. He took a deep, shuddering breath as he struggled to regain control.

'Will you please come back with me now, Violet? Your mother needs you. She's very upset. She's been crying and sobbing on your Auntie Liz's shoulder all afternoon. Inconsolable she is. Completely distraught. Goodness knows what she is going to do for money.'

'I'm not coming back, Uncle Tom. Ever. I can't live in that house with Mam. You know what she's done to me in the past. Now my father's gone, I'm not going to risk being alone with her. I'm going to live here, with Theo, and you can't stop me. In any case, we will be getting married soon, once the war's over.'

Tom opened his mouth to speak, but nothing came out. This was far, far worse than Daisy getting herself pregnant. At least she had the decency to get married and make herself respectable. Violet obviously didn't know the meaning of the word.

Eventually, Tom managed to get his words out. 'Do I take it, then, that you are going to be *living in sin*?'

'You've got it in one,' Violet replied. 'I don't care about getting married straight away and I don't care what people think. Anyway, we are too young to just go off and get married. We need our parents' permission, and my father's buggered off, Mam wouldn't give it and Theo hasn't got any

266

parents, has he?'

'You're just a couple of whippersnappers, you don't stand a chance.'

Theo slung his arm around Violet's shoulders. 'You needn't worry, Mr Jeffson. We do have a plan. If I get called-up next year when I'm eighteen, Violet will carry on living here and make a home for us. I should think I'll get regular spells of leave because they don't send eighteen year-olds overseas to start with. As soon as the war's ended, we will get married. I don't see a problem with that, do you?'

'And just how are you proposing to support my niece?' Tom said. 'I presume you have the means to keep her in the manner to which she has been accustomed?'

Theo shrugged. 'I've got a job. I earn decent money – probably more than you, Mr Jeffson.'

Tom's voice rose in exasperation. 'Do you not care at all about your father, Violet? Doesn't it bother you that you may never see him again?'

'Well, he's nothing to do with me, is he *Uncle* Tom!'

Tom flinched as Violet stressed the word *uncle*, rendered speechless as the irony of the situation suddenly hit him. The son of his wife's secret lover was going to be supporting his secret daughter. It was unbelievable. He turned, and without another word left the house, slamming the front door behind him. What the hell was he going to do now? The thought of Doris with neither Walter nor Violet in the house to keep her under control filled him with terror.

Tom went straight to Doris's house.

'She's not coming back, Doris. I've just been to see her. She's going to live with that boyfriend of hers. I'm sorry, there's nothing I could do.'

The news made Doris tremble and her heart beat wildly. She was silent, still numb with the news of Walter's disappearance, but now Violet had gone, too, she couldn't tell where she fitted into the family. It felt like she had been pulled this way and that by Walter, Violet and Tom for so many years that she had been stretched to a point where she didn't know who she was, where she had come from or where she was going. What was worse? The thought of living alone, with no husband, or dying alone under her kitchen table, killed by a German bomb? When she looked down all she could see was a bottomless abyss, and when she looked up it was just an empty space.

She stared at Tom, bewildered, but she wasn't really listening to him. Tom wasn't hers, and never had been. Violet wasn't hers either, even less so over this past year, when somehow her daughter had seemed to have grown closer to her sister, spending more and more time over the road with Tom and Liz.

This morning, she had a husband and daughter; now she had no one.

'I'm going to tell Liz,' she hissed at Tom. 'I am going to tell her that you haven't kept your promise to her, and have been seeing me behind her back. I shall tell her you were the father of my poor baby son and are really Violet's father.'

She put her face close to Tom's. 'I am going to tell her EVERYTHING. Then you'll have no choice but to come and

268

live with me and we can be together at long last.'

Tom caught her arm. 'That's not true and you know it. I was NOT the father of your baby son. It was that young lad you told me about. And I think you'll find that Liz will stand by me, no matter what lies you tell her. It's your word against mine, and anyway, something has happened to change things. Liz and I are equal, now.'

Doris's face fell in an instant. 'What do you mean – equal?'

'I'm not sayin' owt, especially to you, Doris. But something has happened and I know Liz won't leave me, no matter what lies you tell her. Now, just you think on … you can either keep your mouth shut, keep your head down and we can ride out this bad patch, or you can cut yourself off from everyone.'

Doris's eyes filled with tears and she sank down into an armchair, defeated, isolated and broken.

Early the next morning, with the emerging scandal of Walter's sudden departure playing on her mind, Daisy was in her living room, busy clearing away the breakfast dishes. She looked up at the sound of her front gate opening. It was the postman. The brown envelope plopped through the letterbox with hardly a sound. Daisy thought that was strange, considering the weight of its contents. She stared at it for a few moments before picking it up.

She knew what it was.

Bill appeared beside her, combing his hair ready for work. Neither of them spoke.

Daisy shoved the envelope in his hand and ran

upstairs. Sitting on their bed, the news sank in and quickened her pulse. Tears filled her eyes and she brushed them back with an angry hand. She wouldn't cry. Not now anyway.

Bill opened the bedroom door and sat on the bed next to her, holding the opened envelope and its contents.

Daisy looked up at him. 'When?'

'Five days.'

'Not much notice is it?'

'No.'

'Better start getting you sorted out then.' Daisy jumped up and yanked a dressing table drawer open, flinging underwear savagely onto the bed.

Bill rose and went over to her. He put his hands on her shoulders. She stood still but didn't turn around.

'I love you Daisy,' he said.

She didn't reply. She didn't want him to know that tears were rolling down her cheeks. She bit her lip, hard, until she tasted the salty taste of blood.

'I love you Daisy,' he said again, and gently turned her around.

She roughly brushed away her tears.

'It's not fair.'

'It is.'

'George failed his medical for some stupid reason. Why couldn't you fail yours?'

'I've got to go, Daisy. I've got to fight for Eileen's future, and her children's, and her children's children. Anyway, George's lungs aren't strong enough: it's a good job they found out about his weak chest and his heart murmur.'

Daisy was silent. She knew he was right. But it wasn't

fair that George didn't have to go to war, too. Rose had never had to struggle like she had: she had a built-in babysitter for Margaret and was able to go out to work, which meant she always had plenty of money. Not only that, she didn't have to do any housework, either, because their mam did it all. And now she even had a husband who would be spared having to risk his life fighting the Germans.

Bill looked at his watch. 'Right now, I've got to go into work and sort things out there.'

Five days later Daisy did the hardest thing she had ever done in all of her twenty-five years. It was harder than telling her father she was pregnant. Harder than the agony of giving birth to Eileen. Harder than living in a depressing back room in filth and gloom. Harder even than having to beg the butcher for tick, so that she could feed her husband and daughter. Her legs were heavy with lack of sleep, and she hardly knew how to drag herself out of bed, but she accompanied Bill to the station and waved him off with a beaming smile and a long, lingering kiss. After all, if he was going to die, she didn't want his last memory of her to be one of weeping, wailing and hysteria.

After another difficult confrontation with Doris, and knowing that his life was spiralling and whirling around in a tangled mess, Tom had made an urgent, unscheduled appointment with his psychiatrist. Three things had occurred to knock Tom out of equilibrium, and he had been powerless to stop any of them happening. Walter leaving Doris was probably the one event in his life that he

271

hadn't controlled or manipulated in some way and Liz's affair with Quentin Andrews was another. He could have kicked himself hard for not realising what was going on under his nose in either of the situations. He supposed he could have somehow persuaded Violet to stay at home and look after her mother, who now appeared to be having another nervous breakdown, but the poor girl was obviously happy for the first time in her life now she was living with Theo Andrews and he hadn't the heart to interfere.

'Calm down, Mr Jeffson. Just take a deep breath and tell me what's happened.'

'I can feel myself getting out of control again, Doctor. I've been a fool. A bloody fool.'

'Well, I'm glad you've come to see me rather than slip back into your old ways. Just tell me what's happened and then we'll go from there.'

'I've lied to you Doctor, about ending my affair with my sister-in-law.'

'I knew you were lying about that, so it's no surprise to me, Mr Jeffson.'

'Did you?' Tom was visibly shocked. He'd have put money on Dr Crabtree not guessing he had been lying about Doris.

'Mr Jeffson. Part of your psychopathic disorder is your inability to control your sexual urges – it's well documented. I knew that would be the hardest part of your rehabilitation. But don't worry, we can work on it now you have told me the truth and we can try and channel that energy in different ways.'

'It's not just that, Doctor. Because things have been

going wrong I am beginning to feel the old anger and rages creep up on me. It's getting harder and harder for me to control myself,' Tom admitted.

'Go on.'

Tom put his head in his hands, his elbows on the table. 'It's a mess. A bloody mess. Honest to God, I didn't mean to continue my affair with Doris, but she threatened to tell my wife and stick her head in the gas oven again, and I just sort of drifted into it to keep her quiet. You remember I told you about her baby? The monster birth? Well, she has only gone and convinced herself the baby was mine, even though it couldn't possibly have been. At the time, she told me with her own lips that some young lad had fathered the poor soul. What she's been doing to me is nothing short of blackmail and I don't know how to stop it.'

'Oh, that was the child born with anencephaly, wasn't it?' Dr Crabtree flicked back through Tom's notes. 'I recall we talked about that.'

'Well, whatever it's called, it was a terrible shock. Doris has become a thorn in my side over the years, but I just can't stop, Doctor. She's got a grip on me so tight I feel like I am suffocating. I reckon Walter has always known about us, although no words were ever spoken. I suppose it suited him: I took care of the marital side of things where Doris is concerned and it enabled him to keep up appearances and play the doting father and loving husband – until now that is.'

'A nice, cosy state of affairs, then,' Dr Crabtree said, showing no emotion on her face.

'Well, I suppose it is if you put it like that. Since Doris

tricked me into rekindling our affair, Liz has never known. She thinks I've kept my promise. Anyway, it doesn't matter anymore, because Walter's gone and found himself a lover boy and buggered off with him. Noel, his name is. This boyfriend of his worked in the solicitor's office as a clerk and he found out about a little inheritance I came into just after I started my treatment with you. I had this letter, you see, completely out of the blue. My great aunt died and she left all her money to me. A nice tidy sum, it was, but I didn't tell anyone in the family about the money, doctor, because I knew Rose and George would want me to hand it over to pay off my debt.

'Walter's friend found out about my windfall and knew I hadn't told anyone about it. Then the day after war was declared he caught me up as I was leaving the factory and threatened to spill the beans to Liz unless I paid him fifty pounds.

'I've been using that inheritance money to pay for my medical fees, doctor. I haven't wasted it – honestly – I couldn't have paid for treatment, otherwise.'

'So are you saying you have been blackmailed by this Noel, too, as well as by Doris?'

'Yes, I suppose I have, Doctor. I couldn't let him go blabbing to Rose and George about the money, could I? I've made so much progress with everyone, there's too much at stake now.'

'Did you pay up, then?'

Tom groaned. 'Yes – eventually. The thing is, I still haven't paid Rose and George everything I owe them. I can only afford ten shillings a week and it's going to take another four years before I've paid them back.'

'So what happened?' said Dr Crabtree, leaning forwards with interest.

'I wasn't going to be blackmailed by a queer, or anyone else for that matter, so I punched him on the nose. I thought that was the end of it, but he turned up outside the factory gates when I left off one day. He apologised and told me he was in some financial trouble – that was what had spurred him on to try and blackmail me. He insisted he buy me a drink in the Club on the way home to explain, but then he started dropping hints in front of George and a few other blokes about how it was easy to find out about folks' personal affairs, being a Solicitor's Clerk, and that someone he knew had received a large amount of money in a bequest years ago and not told his family or paid off his debts to them. I don't really remember much after that, other than I panicked. To shut him up, I promised to lend him some money to get him out of trouble. I lent him fifty pounds the next day, and last week, he used it to run away with Walter.'

'Oh dear, do you have an address? Can't you write to him and ask him when he is going to pay you back?' asked Dr Crabtree.

Tom shook his head. 'I wish I did have an address, but no one knows where they've gone. Now, I've just found out that Doris's daughter, Violet, knew about their plans. She reckons she doesn't know where they are, but I think she's lying. She was pretty close to Walter and I can't see him just buggering off and not telling her where he was going.'

'I can see that all this has upset you, Mr Jeffson, but when you made your appointment you said there were three things that had happened to you. What else is there?'

'Our Violet's left home and gone to live with her young man. She's living in sin and doesn't care two hoots about what folks think. But it's not only that, Doctor, Walter and Violet buggering off has left poor Doris destitute. She's got no money coming in now, and it's me who is having to pick up the bill. I haven't got the money to run two households. It's crippling me.

'If all this trouble wasn't bad enough, I've had an awful shock about my wife, too. A few weeks ago I discovered that she had been having an affair with that chap at the council who was going to be Mayor, Quentin Andrews. I had no idea at the time – I even went to his funeral. I was devastated when I found the evidence, but I haven't said anything to her. Liz's indiscretion has upset me so much, doctor, I feel as if I am constantly living in a dark cloud. I've always thought we were making fantastic progress and she was happy. I've learned from my therapy, Doctor. I've completely stopped being rough with Liz, and I've never lost my temper with her since starting my treatment seven years ago. I've learned self-control and I've stayed off the drink, just having the odd shandy in the working men's club to be sociable. I've been loving and attentive, I buy her flowers, chocolates and jewellery and I've done everything in my power to make her happy.'

Dr Crabtree leaned back in her chair. 'You've done very well, Mr Jeffson, on the whole. I can't take that away from you, but surely you must see that what's good for the goose is good for the gander. Now you know just how wretched your wife must have felt when she discovered your affair with her sister.'

276

Tom began to cry, cradling his head in his arms on the doctor's desk. He pulled his handkerchief out of his pocket and blew his nose loudly. He cried for the rest of the allotted time for his appointment as the bottled-up helplessness of being unable to control what was going on around him released itself, rendering him weak and fragile.

With Walter and Violet no longer around to keep Doris in line, and Liz still in love with a dead man, he was completely done for and the last seven years of effort to turn over a new leaf a total waste of time.

Fate has a curious way of repeating itself and, once again, it was Violet returning home unexpectedly that saved her mother from certain death after she had, for the second time in her life, knelt before the hissing gas oven, pushed her head inside and waited for death to rescue her. By coincidence, Theo had also received call-up papers that week and, as his brothers were co-owners of the house in which he lived and had been opposed to Violet taking up permanent residence while he was away, he had gently told Violet that she wouldn't be able to stay, after all.

Violet had no option but to return home to Cornwall Road, where she was greeted by the same sight she had witnessed as a little girl back in nineteen thirty-two. However, this time, Doris had lost consciousness and had almost lost her life.

Again, it was Daisy who came to Violet's rescue that day, but this time it was Violet, alone, who picked up the pieces of her mother's shattered life, stood her back on her feet and nursed her back to health, telling acquaintances and neighbours that she had made herself ill with worry about Walter, who had been called up to help with a top secret war project and no one had any idea when he would be back.

DECEMBER 1943

ဗ Ø

Chapter Seventeen
Authority and Dispassion

The horrors of World War II were to largely sidestep
Kettering and the surrounding area despite the presence of
the steelworks in Corby only eight or so miles away.
Despite the constant fear that Corby would be discovered
by the Germans, and bombed, people made the best of
wartime restrictions and, in true Kettering spirit, marched
through their daily lives with their heads held high in
defiance of the threat. Three RAF air bases were located
within fifteen miles, and although the enemy planes with
their lethal bombs didn't materialise, people lived in a
state of permanent uneasiness that the Germans would
discover the strategically-placed market town in
Northamptonshire which buzzed with wartime activity as
troops passed through or arrived at the town's railway
station, destined for the air bases.

The private face of Kettering was a different matter
altogether. Behind closed front doors families mourned the
loss of fathers, sons and brothers. Young women wailed in
grief as their young men were struck down in the

battlefields and in the air, or drowned at sea in the name of King and country. Names of local men were immortalised in gold leaf inscriptions and obituaries in the local newspaper. The dreaded telegram was the dark shadow that ruined birthdays, anniversaries and wedding days, destroying lives with just a few, short words printed on a flimsy sheet of paper. Fear of the telegram lurked in every wistful dream of happy-ever-after, private prayers for loved ones' safety and hopes for a future that might not exist.

Theo Andrews was just one victim among many, his young life snuffed out on British soil by a stray German bomb two years after he had been conscripted.

Violet was inconsolable. Since she had been thirteen years-old, she had never seen her future as anything other than Theo's wife. With the last threads of optimism hacked away as finally as the kitchen scissors had cut off her hair when she was a child, there was nothing for her to live for.

'I saw her the other night. She was standing outside the Andrews' old house in Princes Street. Stock still. As dark as the midnight sky, dressed from head to toe in black. I spoke to her but she didn't respond.'

Liz held out her hand for her ration book and change. The shop assistant shook her head as she continued. 'She'd do well to remember she's not the only young lady around here to lose her man. There's plenty of others. Kettering's young chaps are dropping like flies, God rest their souls. She needs to snap out of it and not drift around the town like some sort of tragic heroine from a romantic novel. Life goes on. We are all suffering from loss, one way or another.'

Liz snapped her handbag shut, quick to defend Violet. 'She took Theo's death really badly, but I think you're right, she isn't getting any better. The poor girl hasn't had much luck in her life, and now this has happened to her just when she was so happy. I don't know how she's going to get over it, but she can't mourn him forever. She's a young woman with her whole life in front of her.'

After the conversation with the shop assistant, and unnerved about the conversation about Violet, Liz made her way home from shopping. On approaching Doris's house, on impulse she turned into the passageway and tapped on the back door before letting herself in. She would speak to her sister and see if, between them, they could work out a plan to help Violet come to terms with the death of Theo.

'Are you there, Doris?'

Liz was surprised when Violet answered. 'I'm in here, Auntie Liz. Mam's upstairs having a nap.'

Liz stepped through to the living room. 'Aren't you at work today?'

Violet shook her head.

'Are you ill?'

Violet shook her head again. 'There's just no point. I don't spend any of the money I earn anyway. I never go anywhere or do anything.'

'You're going to lose your job ...'

Violet shrugged her shoulders. Liz sank down onto the arm of her chair and put an arm around her. Violet didn't react.

Liz lowered her voice, mindful of Doris, asleep upstairs. 'Look, Violet. I do understand. Remember, I've lost someone I loved, too.'

Violet rubbed her abdomen. 'No one understands, Auntie Liz. It actually hurts, in here, all the time. It's more painful than anything I've ever experienced, even more than having to have my hair shaved off week after week when I was nine. I can't imagine I shall ever be free from this horrible feeling. I'm stuck, going round and round in circles, with nothing I do being of any importance – to myself or anyone else. I can't be enthusiastic about anything, and nothing makes me laugh or smile anymore.'

Since Quentin's death, true to her word, Violet had kept Liz's secret, and in return, Liz had stepped into her sister's shoes and provided the motherly advice and guidance every young woman needs. But the death of Theo had changed Violet and killed her spirit. Whereas Liz had managed to channel her own grief into other things, Violet was caught in the dark recesses of depression.

'I *do* understand, Violet. I had to make a big effort to pull myself through the grief after Theo's father died. I was convinced I'd never get over losing him, and having to keep it all a secret just made things worse, but now I feel ready to face the future without him. I can laugh again; I feel joy in being out in the sunshine and I can sit and immerse myself in a good book. I know I'm making progress, and you can, too. We can make progress together.'

Violet looked up at Liz, doubtful. 'I'm not sure anyone can help me. But I know you loved Quentin just the same as I loved Theo, so if you can get over it, then I suppose I shall – eventually.'

Liz nodded. 'Now, Violet, you need to make a big effort. There's a Christmas dance at the Central Hall on Saturday. Why don't you call on one of your old friends and see if they are going? It will do you good to dress up and have a night out. You're a young woman with your whole life in front of you. Just trust me – the first effort is the hardest and then it gets easier. '

On the stairs, Doris had been listening to the conversation. She gave a small, self-satisfied smile.

So her sister wasn't perfect, after all.

It was still dark, although the clear winter sky had begun to brighten, turning inky blackness into a deep royal blue edged with gold in the east. The air was still and cold, and white mist hung in the valley over frost-covered distant countryside. In a country lane on the edge of town, a young red-haired American GI leaned over from the driver's seat of the army jeep and drew the fair-haired English woman to him in a crushing embrace. Violet giggled and eagerly returned his kiss.

She broke away from the American and looked around her, pulling her fur coat around her neck.

'I know where we can go,' she said. 'It'll be cold, but we'll soon warm ourselves up.' She pulled up her coat and skirt and pretended to scratch her thigh, throwing a sideways look at the American under her eyelashes.

'Show me the way,' he said, not quite believing his luck. He'd been seeing Violet Grey for a few weeks, ever since he'd met her at a dance in Kettering, but up until now had been unable to fathom her complex personality. On the one hand she could be lively, flirty and fun, and then the next time they saw each other, she would be cool and distant and keep him at arm's length. This was the first time he'd brought her back home, though, and tonight she was blowing red hot, rather than frosty cold, despite the chilly weather.

Since the Americans had arrived at a newly constructed air base at Grafton Underwood, only four miles away from Kettering, the area was teeming with hordes of rapacious small-town Americans from places such as Iowa, Arkansas or Virginia, eager to live their lives to the full, not knowing if and when it would be cut short. They were also keen to take the place of the local lads, away from their homes, fighting for their country. With a propensity towards spoiling their women back home, English girls lapped up the Americans' attention, lured by their constant supply of nylon stockings, chewing gum, coffee, cigarettes and sometimes even a bar of American chocolate.

An hour later, Violet tiptoed up to her front door, muddy high-heeled shoes hanging from one hand and a pair of nylon stockings spilling over the top of her handbag in the other. She had taken them off at the end of the street so that she wouldn't make any noise as she crept home.

She had learned through practising that if she put pressure on the key to the left, turned it half way until it met resistance and then put pressure on the key to the right, the lock would yield silently and easily with an almost imperceptible click.

Opening the door without it creaking was another hurdle to overcome. Again, through practice, she knew that it would open about six inches before you had to slide your hand through the crack and grasp the knob on the other side, lifting the door as it opened to avoid a squeak. This she did with accomplished ease before sliding silently into the quiet hallway just before the clock on the wall began to chime seven o'clock.

Violet almost laughed out loud at her luck and quickly shut the door before taking the stairs two at a time whilst the clock was chiming, drowning out her footsteps. Just after the clock gave its final chime Violet shut her bedroom door. She had made it, once again, without her mother realising that she had been out all night, partying with the Americans.

Violet sank into bed without taking off her underclothes and make-up. She had just three hours to get some sleep before she had to be at work for the ten o'clock shift.

Three months later, Violet, Doris, Tom and Liz sat gathered around the dining table. Having called a family conference, Tom had taken charge.

'Well, that's settled then,' he said with his most solemn face. 'As I see it, there's no other choice.'

No one replied, but all eyes turned to Violet, who crossed her legs elegantly whilst looking down to inspect her stockings for ladders. She glanced up at her mother and gave a nonchalant shrug, before taking a powder compact out of her bag and snapping it open to check her lipstick.

'I really don't care, as long as I get rid of it one way or another.'

Tom leaned forward to grasp her wrist, trying to change her mind one last time. 'It doesn't have to be this way, Violet. You could go away and have the baby adopted. We could arrange it. No one would ever know.'

'I've told you once, and I'll say it again until I'm blue in the face if I have to,' Violet reiterated. 'I don't want to have a baby. I'll go to Mrs Whatsername and let her do whatever it is she does. I really don't care, Uncle Tom.'

Doris covered her eyes with her hands. 'Have it adopted. At least give the poor little soul a chance. You can go away ...'

'Oh, mother. For goodness sake!' Violet stood up and snapped her powder compact shut with a flourish. 'I've already made up my mind. Oh, what's the use ... I'm going home!'

She snatched her fur coat from the back of a dining chair and shot a defiant stare at her family as she pulled it on and grabbed her handbag.

Liz kept her eyes on Violet, barely disguising her disgust at her niece's arrogance and complete lack of compassion for her unborn baby. It was hard to believe that Violet could have changed so dramatically in just a few weeks. It was as if she had intentionally set herself on the road to self-destruction, and she hated to admit it, even to herself, but Violet was fast turning into what everyone called a *"loose woman"*. She folded her arms, trying to compose herself as she appealed to Violet's better side, which she knew was there, somewhere.

'Vi – please don't do it. It's dangerous and against the law. You're not the first and I'm sure you won't be the last to get caught out by these damned Yankees. Liz threw a sympathetic glance at Doris, who sat looking at her feet, nervously plucking imaginary specks and threads from her skirt.

'No!' Violet retorted. 'It's my body and my baby. A baby I don't want and the sooner it's gone ...'

'... the better.' Tom finished Violet's sentence for her. 'Let her decide for herself, can't you!' He threw an angry look at Liz and took another swig of scotch.

The family fell silent, staring at each other. Tom slammed the glass down and then topped it up from the half-empty bottle on the table. 'I know it's not ideal –'

Liz stood up, interrupting him, swiping the bottle from under his nose. The chair scraped against the floor with a squeak as she shoved it back. She felt that she was the only one defending the poor defenceless unborn baby against these monsters. Did not one of them think that it was a human being they were going to kill just as easily as if they swatted a fly? Not only that, Violet could lose her life, too. Liz had heard terrible stories of women who'd had illegal abortions and had died awful, agonising deaths as a result.

Liz clutched the bottle of scotch to her chest. 'That's enough, Tom,' she said. 'You don't want to get back into your old ways. I'll have this, if you don't mind.'

'I'll pay,' Tom said, dismissing Liz with a wave of his hand. 'Money's no object.'

Liz tutted, threw an irritated glance at the ceiling and stomped into the kitchen, muttering under her breath

Violet, tight lipped and defiant, pulled the belt tight on her coat, as if trying to squeeze the life out of the tiny life inside her.

'I want it done and I want it done today, if it can be arranged,' she said flouncing out of the room into the hallway.

That evening, Tom approached an Irish woman a few streets away, who was well-known for *seeing to things* in women's matters. Bridget O'Reilly assured total discretion in return for one hundred American cigarettes, two bars of chocolate, two pairs of nylon stockings and ten shillings in expenses. She told an impressed Tom that she had been taught the procedure by a surgeon, who couldn't perform the operations himself on account of the shakes caused by shell-shock from the battlefields of the Great War. She was one of the best there was, she boasted, and always used clean, boiled instruments to minimise the risk to the woman.

When Tom arrived home later that night, Liz was unconvinced by the story. 'Oh come on, Tom – shakes on account of shell-shock in the Great War?' she said to him when he attempted to reassure her about the procedure, the scepticism evident in her voice. 'More like as a result of seeing the bottom of a whisky bottle a bit too often; that's if this *surgeon* really exists at all.'

It wasn't the pain that bothered Violet. Nor the indignity of having to climb on a huge wooden table with her silk slip shoved up around her waist and her bottom propped up in the air on a rolled up pillow whilst unimaginable implements were thrust inside her. The pain would have been agonising, but the American had given her some pills which had not only taken the edge off it, but had given her quite a nice, pleasant, floaty feeling afterwards too; and then she'd had to take some more, new-fangled pills that the American had said she absolutely must take for a while to prevent infection. The pills were those used on the battlefields when soldiers had their legs blown off, or shrapnel embedded in them.

It wasn't even the bright red blood that followed the termination that caused her too much concern – or the tiny mouse-like embryo that eventually her body gave up and expelled with an unceremonious plop into the lavatory pan, its minute fingers and toes tugging briefly on flimsy threads of conscience. There was a total absence of guilt or regret for the life of her unborn baby. However, in the weeks that followed, a kernel of decency battled with her vanity and arrogance. Whispers, real or imagined, made her feel like a criminal every time she walked into a shop or the factory where she now worked with her Uncle Tom and her cousin, Rose, after losing her job at the chemist's shop. Even just walking down the street caused the hairs on the back of her neck to prickle with the feeling that all eyes were on her.

Violet's logic nagged to her that no one could possibly know she'd just undergone an illegal termination of an unwanted pregnancy, but in her heart she sensed that something was not right and every so often a wave of nausea would ripple over her and she'd glance all around, searching for the invisible eyes she thought were staring at her with contempt. She was tearful and emotional and didn't feel much like resuming her wild lifestyle. She couldn't even enjoy her friend's twenty-first birthday party, going home at ten o'clock because she was so tired.

One day, six weeks after the termination, Violet was undressing in her room, alone in the house.

'Well, gal,' she said out loud to her reflection in the mirror. 'You've got a right belly on yer.' She breathed in and tightened her stomach muscles, turning sideways as she contemplated the contours of her usually slim figure in the mirror.

With a sudden feeling of alarm she realised that since she stopped bleeding, she had not even had so much as a show. She had not really been too worried about it until then, as Mrs Whatsername had said things might not be regular for a while. She exhaled slowly, running her hands over her swollen stomach.

Was it possible she could still be pregnant?

'It could only happen to you!'

Tom took a swig of whisky straight from the bottle and focused his eyes on Violet, who sat opposite him at Doris's kitchen table.

'Oh, Uncle Tom, what on earth am I going to do now? I'm so scared! I really don't want to have this baby. Help me, please?'

Tom looked down into his whisky glass, swirling it around as if seeking mystical guidance. After a few seconds he looked up, the world fuzzy and blurred as alcohol began to affect his judgement.

'What about that ginger Yank – will he support you?'

'I don't love him; I don't even see him now ... I don't

know where he is. I think he might have gone back to the States. Oh, Uncle Tom! My life will be ruined. Please? Tell me what to do!'

'Are you absolutely sure you're still pregnant? It might be fluid ... summat like that. I don't know much about women's matters. What did Bridget O'Reilly say? After all, didn't you say you saw it come away? If you *saw* it ... and fingers and toes and everything ... then it can't still be in there, can it?' Tom gestured in the direction of Violet's abdomen.

'Bridget examined me and confirmed it. She said there must have been two babies in there and only one of them came away. I still *feel* pregnant, too.'

Violet began to tremble. She reached across the table and gulped back the remainder of the whisky in Tom's glass.

After a minute or two she rootled in her handbag and took out a packet of cigarettes and pushed them towards Tom. With a shaking hand, he lit one for her and then took another for himself. They looked at each other across the table, both taking long drags on their cigarettes as the nicotine took effect and Violet calmed down.

'You'll have to go through with it,' Tom said. 'It's much too late to do anything about it now. Please, Vi, don't do anything silly. It's too dangerous and you could die. These things have to be performed early on – even I know that.'

'I know I'll have to have it – I'm not stupid,' Violet snapped back. 'I'm not keeping it though. It'll have to be adopted.'

'Oh, Lord.' Tom sighed and poured another glass of whisky. 'I don't know what this'll do to your mam. She tried for years to have you; then there was all that upset over her poor baby boy. All she's ever wanted was another child. She has been really upset about all this business. It's set her back months, and she's been trying so hard to get her life back on track.'

'Well, let *her* have it then!' Violet yelled, losing her temper. She really didn't want to talk about her mother and her problems. She pursed her lips and glared at Tom. 'I think we all know how I came about, anyway, don't we, *Uncle* Tom'.

Tom drew the tip of his tongue across his top teeth and stroked his chin, deep in thought, Violet's innuendo as to her true parentage remaining unnoticed as a hint of an idea swayed around in his brain like a cobra waiting to strike.

'That might be a solution, what you just said about your mam. Yes …yes …we could –'

Violet recoiled in horror. 'Oh, no! You can't be serious. Everyone would know, Uncle Tom. I can't have everyone knowing.'

'Wait. Let's think about this. Your mam's wanted another baby for years, right up until your father took off at the start of the war with his nancy boy. She said to Liz the other day that she'd love to get married again and have another baby, even though she was getting on a bit.'

'How on earth would we get away with it? I can't see how it could work. Mam would be horrified if the neighbours thought she'd gone and got herself in the family way. My dad hasn't been around for months and folks think he's away on active service.'

Tom put up his hand, silencing her as he formulated a

crazy, risky plan. 'Don't dismiss the idea just yet. Just let me think ...'

'Mam's much too old to have another baby. In any case I don't want to be looking at the little bastard for the rest of my life knowing it was really mine ...'

'Just shut up a minute, Vi.'

Violet tutted, stubbed out her cigarette on the bottom of her shoe and threw it into the metal waste bin. Her elegant, long-fingered manicured hands fumbled and shook as she opened the packet to extract another cigarette. Tom covered her hands with his.

'Right. How about this?'

He took a deep breath.

'Your mam might be pushing fifty, but it's not unheard of for a woman to have a ... whatsit called ... baby-on-the-change. Years ago I knew of a woman who had a baby at fifty. All we have to do is to tell folks your dad came home on leave, and she went away to spend the weekend with him in a top secret location. It's bound to happen all the time – there's folk teeming all over the place on secret war missions. Surely they get some leave.'

Violet gave a sarcastic chuckle and shook her head. 'That's ridiculous. We'd never pull it off.' A look of incredulity and a hint of a dry smirk played on her alabaster face and she pursed her bright red lips, taking a drag on her newly-lit cigarette and blew the smoke into Tom's face. 'Would we?'

'You'd have to go away somewhere, have the baby and then Bob's your uncle. We can pass it off as your Mam's.'

'Of course, why didn't I think of it?' Violet said with a facetious twang in her voice as she shrugged her shoulders, her palms upturned, her eyes rolling upwards at the ceiling.

'We'd have to get all the paperwork done secretly, in your mam and dad's name. We'll just perpetuate the story about him being away on a top secret mission. No one will question it.'

Tom raised his eyebrows. 'Is there any way we can contact Walter?'

Violet sneered. 'It's a stupid idea, Uncle Tom. It would blow his cover, anyway.'

Tom continued. 'It's such a simple solution. All Doris has to do is tell folks she spent a secret weekend with Walter a couple of months ago. But it would be better if Walter was in on it. After all, Violet, think about it ... he'll have to sign the papers ...'

Violet narrowed her eyes in thought. 'We could forge his signature. He needn't know ...'

'No,' Tom said, leaning forward, taking charge. 'Walter must be in on it, but this has got to be a big, big secret, we mustn't even tell Rose and Daisy.'

'Well,' Violet said, unconvinced, 'what if he doesn't agree? The whole plan will go down the pan if he doesn't agree to adopt the baby.'

'Oh, he will. Don't worry. I'll see to it. That Noel's a chancer, if ever I saw one. He can be bought.'

Tom scratched his chin, excited. It gave him a thrill to think he was a secret father to Violet and would now be a secret grandfather to her baby. He shivered with glee at the neatness of the solution. He knew he could easily persuade Doris to co-operate. After all, she did owe him a big favour for even giving her a child in the first place. If it hadn't been for him, she would have been childless. It wasn't too much to ask, surely? And it would give her another child to satisfy her incessant maternal cravings, which had always been strong. And the whole thing could be kept in the family, with no scandal for Violet.

The solution was just perfect.

To an onlooker, it might seem bizarre that Tom truly believed he could manipulate his family in such a manner without any thought for the potential risks of such a ludicrous plan. However, his distorted sense of family loyalty appealed to a very precise kind of evil that lurked on the periphery of the Jeffson family, merely biding its time as Violet's pregnancy progressed. The evil was deceptive, irresistible and appealing – almost resembling something divine as Tom's neat package of ideal solutions snaked its way around the family's outward face of respectability.

The evil nestled, concealed amongst secrets and lies, its grotesque truth well disguised behind benevolent eyes of loyalty and understanding, mesmerising every member of the family into the belief that the baby at the centre of the biggest lie of all would, once and for all, satisfy its grandmother's longing for another child.

Chapter Eighteen
Cynicism and Anguish

'She's on the change, she's not *pregnant!*' Rose laughed. 'At nearly fifty?'

'She is,' Daisy replied. 'Violet told me yesterday.'

The sisters were sitting at their parents' kitchen table one sunny April Saturday afternoon in 1943. They were drinking weak tea and dunking tasteless broken pieces of arrowroot biscuits whilst ten-year-olds, Margaret and Eileen, played two-ball against the kitchen wall. The clunk, clunk and chanting of silly rhymes rebounded through stunned disbelief and Rose gave a cynical laugh. 'I can't get my head round it. And with Violet being called up to go to Birmingham to work in munitions, she'll never cope, not with her nerves. She reckons she's fallen for a baby at her age after just one weekend with Walter? Come off it, Daisy. It can't possibly be true. When is it supposed to be due?'

'She doesn't know yet,' Daisy said, taking another biscuit out of the paper bag. 'She says she has got to see the doctor again next week. With a menopause baby you've got no dates to go by.'

Rose giggled as she helped herself to one more piece of biscuit before carefully placing the rest in a biscuit tin.

She flattened the greaseproof paper bag and folded it in four, saving it for another purpose. 'You've got to admit, it is a bit of a hoot. Folks will die laughing when they hear about her getting pregnant. When does Violet go to Birmingham?'

'At the end of the week, apparently. She says she's got no choice as a single woman – it was either munitions or the land army. Could you imagine *Violet* in the land army?'

The sisters stared at each other and roared with laughter at the thought of Violet in the land army.

'It'll be hers; I'd bet money on it.' Rose said. 'It won't be Aunt Doris's.'

'Do you think so?'

Rose nodded. 'They can't fool me. It's such a cock-and-bull story, no one will ever believe it. And I bet Walter wasn't even called up for his so-called war work. I bet he just buggered off, fed up with Doris and her nervous breakdowns. Think about it, Daisy. We've said for weeks that Violet's bound to get caught out. She's out with those randy Yanks nearly every night. She's got a right reputation. She'll never find a decent man now. It's a wonder she's not caught the clap or something, the way she plays fast and loose. Who would have ever thought she could change so much? It's like she's set herself on the road to self-destruction.'

Daisy shook her head, thinking about what Rose had said. 'In any other circumstances, I'd say you were probably right, but Violet's still as slim as ever. When I saw her yesterday, she'd got no sign of a belly. Flat as a pancake it was, and her waist was pulled in with a tight belt.'

'Nah,' Rose said with a knowing shake of her head. 'It's just a careful choice of clothes: dresses with full skirts hide a podgy belly really well, and believe me, I should know.' She patted her stomach and laughed. 'I'll never be slim, like you. I'm just not built the same way.'

Daisy lifted the lid of the biscuit tin. 'Dare we have another?'

'Go on, then,' Rose said, smacking her lips.' You've twisted my arm. When's Bill coming home next?'

'I don't know,' Daisy said, sighing. 'I hate not knowing. *We* want another baby ourselves, but not till the war's over. He's due some leave soon. It's been nearly six months since he came home for a weekend.'

'At least you get letters though. Some women don't get loads of letters like you do.'

'I write him something every single day,' Daisy said, pulling herself up with pride. 'It's a type of journal. I tell him exactly what I've been doing, even if it's only the washing and cooking dinner. Mind you, I'll have something juicy to tell him tomorrow, won't I? It's not every day I have news as interesting as this. He can't tell me what he's up to though because of letters getting into the wrong hands. I don't even know precisely where he is.'

Later that afternoon, when Daisy and Eileen had returned home after their visit to Cornwall Road and were in their own kitchen, preparing sandwiches for their tea, someone knocked on the door.

'Who on earth is that on a Saturday teatime? Get it, can you love?' said Daisy.

Eileen ran off to answer the door.

'Mam!' she should. 'Oh, Mam! Its … its … a telegram.'

Daisy's heart flipped and then thumped in her chest at hearing the word. The fear of the dreaded knock on the door was with her always, but at that moment, making sandwiches for tea and thinking about her Auntie being pregnant at nearly fifty it had been furthest thing from her mind. She found herself in the hallway staring at the envelope that had manifested itself in her hand. It was stamped *priority* and she knew what that meant. Her legs buckled and she sank down onto the bottom stair, the envelope making the skin on her hand tingle and burn. The telegram dropped to the floor.

'Mam?' Eileen said, the panic turning her voice into a squeak. 'Oh, Mam. Do you want me to open it?'

Daisy's breath was coming in gasps. She picked up the envelope and tore it open with fumbling fingers. Her eyes scanned the words but she didn't read them.

'Mam!' Eileen cried. 'Say something, please?'

Daisy's head was almost touching her knees as she sat on the bottom stair, her head bowed low. Despair flowed from her eyes and her nose dripped on her flowery apron. She couldn't speak.

Eileen took the telegram from her mother's hand and read the contents.

'He's not dead, Mam! He's just missing in action.' She wiped her nose with the back of her and thrust the telegram at her mother. Daisy looked up.

'Missing?'

'Yes'

'He's probably been taken prisoner, like Cissie Wilson's

father.'

Daisy exhaled and her whole body shuddered. She'd only read the first few words of the telegram. 'Can you run along the Avenue and get Auntie Rose?'

Eileen opened the front door and jumped down the step. The front gate banged shut as she flew up the road.

When Eileen returned with Rose and George, Daisy was upstairs.

'Mam?' she called.

Sitting on the edge of her bed, clutching Bill's dressing gown to her face, inhaling the familiar smell of him for comfort, Daisy rocked back and forth, her voice a mere croak. 'Here,' she said.

Rose sank down onto the bed next to her and put an arm around her shoulder. 'Oh God, Daisy, I'm so sorry. Are you all right?'

'All right?' Daisy replied. 'My husband is missing in action; how can I be all right? He might be dead. How do you think I bloody well feel?'

Eileen shrank back against the wall. Her mother had said a swear word, and she never swore. She felt a hand on her shoulder, drawing her back from the bedroom. It was her Uncle George, who gestured with a flick of his head that they should leave her mother alone with Auntie Rose for a while and go downstairs.

She sat down at the kitchen table while her Uncle George filled the kettle and lit the gas on the stove.

'Where is it?' he said. 'Where's the telegram?'

'Behind the clock on the mantelpiece.'

George walked through to the living room and found the telegram.

302

'Look,' he said returning to the kitchen holding the telegram out to Eileen. 'There's a letter to follow. We might find out a little bit more when it arrives.'

Eileen nodded. 'I know ... I read it.'

The conversation was broken by a sound like wolves baying for blood. Daisy had collapsed in a heap on the bed, her knees drawn up to her chest and was howling into Bill's dressing gown.

It was almost an hour before Rose came down, her face tear-streaked and puffy. 'She's asleep,' she said. 'I'd better stay here tonight, George.'

Dated 22nd April 1943

Dear Mrs. Roberts,

May I be permitted to express my own and the regiment's sincere sympathy with you in the bad news concerning your husband Corp. William Roberts.

Last week his regiment was deployed to northern France where they were parachuted in to join troops already at the front and since then we have been unable to ascertain his whereabouts. You may be aware that in a percentage of cases soldiers reported missing in such circumstances are eventually reported prisoner of war, and I hope that this may give you some comfort in your time of anxiety.

Your husband was a most proficient Soldier and his loss is deeply regretted by us all.

Your husband's effects have been collected and will be forwarded to you in due course.

303

Once again please accept my deep sympathy, and let us hope and pray that we may soon have some good news as to the safety of your husband.

I would ask that you do not reveal the circumstances of this letter to anyone who may convey this information to the Enemy.

Yours very sincerely,
C-Sgt Major Ronald E Smith

The letter arrived five days after the telegram, but it was to be almost six, long months before Daisy knew what had happened to Bill.

Chapter Nineteen
Elation and Intuition

Daisy endured an agonising summer, waiting to hear news of Bill's fate. One Saturday morning in early September she received a visit from the coal merchant.

'Mrs Roberts?' he said.

'Yes, how can I help you?'

The man took off his cap and wrung it nervously in his coal-stained hands.

'The missus ... she works in the office like ... picked up our telephone when it rang half-an-hour ago and received a message 'bout your 'usband.'

Daisy's heart sank and began to pound in her ears. If she was about to be told Bill was dead, the news shouldn't come from a coal merchant.

'Bill?' she said. 'About my Bill?'

The man had nodded. 'May I come in?'

Daisy had stepped aside, looking at his coal-dust covered boots and not wanting them on her hall floor, but then realising that a bit of coal on the floor was nothing compared to the prospect of news about Bill.

'Of course, come through.'

She shut the door.

'A man telephoned who asked if we could get a message

to you because you are a customer of ours. That's why I'm here.'

'A message about Bill? Are you sure? He's missing in action.'

The man nodded. 'I know: the man told the missus.'

Breathless, because in receiving the news, she had forgotten to breathe, Daisy gasped, 'where is he?'

'He's in Belgium. He's been trying to get a message through to you for weeks. The man who rang said it was too risky for him to send a letter. Then the line cut off. I'm afraid I don't have any more news.' The coal merchant laughed. 'Of all the telephone numbers he could remember, fancy it being mine!'

Daisy sank down onto the bottom step of the stairs, tears of joy running down her face. 'It must be because it's painted on the wall of your yard in such huge numbers – he used to pass it every day on his way to work at the factory before he was called up. He must have remembered it.'

'Well I never!' the coal merchant chuckled. 'Who'd have thought?'

Two days later Daisy eagerly tore open a letter with familiar handwriting, the weeks of torture melting away. Bill had been captured and had been in a prisoner-of-war camp. He had written to her from the camp, but none of the letters from the prisoners had got through. Eventually a group of prisoners, including Bill, had escaped whilst they were being transferred to another camp and Bill had been fortunate in finding a safe haven with a Belgian family. He'd not dared risk sending a letter because the family was putting themselves in grave danger by hiding him until the resistance could make arrangements to get him home. Once he was back on British soil, it wouldn't be long before he was granted an extended period of leave after his ordeal and he could come home.

A few days later, an elated Daisy thought she might be extravagant and light the first fire of the autumn. The morning of had dawned bright and clear, although there was a chill in the air. She moved the fire-guard to one side before picking up the coal scuttle to fetch some slack from the coal bunker outside. The jubilant coal merchant had been generous in his delivery of good news and the free advertising of his business in the form of a newspaper article, and had called by the house on the following Monday with a complimentary sack of coal. Dreading another winter of war she hoped that Bill wouldn't be sent back out to the front after his leave. How she had got through the summer, not knowing whether Bill was alive or dead, she didn't know.

As she slid the bolt on the back door, a face appeared at the kitchen window. It was her father.

'Daisy?' he enquired, peering into the dark kitchen. 'Is that you?'

Daisy opened the door. 'What on earth are you doing here at this time of the morning Dad? Is everything all right?'

'Your Auntie Doris isn't well. She's had a bad night, with the air raid sirens and everything. Your mam's with her now. I was up early so I thought I'd cadge a cup of tea.'

'Oh,' Daisy said. 'Still ... not long to go now is it. Put the kettle on while I fetch some coal.' She was utterly fed up with all the fuss over her Aunt Doris's pregnancy. She'd not left the house much in the last four weeks and had sat in her armchair as if she was royalty, with everyone running rings around her.

At first, there had been a hushed conspiracy with Liz tight-lipped, refusing to discuss Doris's pregnancy. Keeping up the façade of a single woman called up for military service, Violet made sure she sent a steady stream of bright, chatty letters. Still Rose and Daisy remained cynical, knowing instinctively that something was going on, but having no proof that Doris's baby really belonged to Violet.

Daisy slammed the coal shed door shut and locked it, straightening up as she put the key in her apron pocket.

As Tom watched Daisy set the fire, Eileen appeared in her nightie, rubbing her eyes.

'Gramp?' she yawned. 'You're early.'

Tom hugged his grand-daughter and ruffled her hair playfully.

'I'm tired,' she groaned. 'The sirens kept waking me up and we had to go in the shelter twice in the night. I bet you were walking up and down the garden path smoking your pipe, and I bet Grandma and Margaret were shouting at you to get in the shelter in case the Germans saw the light of your tobacco and bombed you.'

'Yep. You're not wrong there. You won't get me going in no blinkin' tin can in the garden. Fat lot of good a flimsy old air raid shelter would be when a thundering great German bomb falls on top of you. When your number's up, it's up, my girl,'

Daisy straightened up and went into the kitchen to find some matches. Tom rubbed his hands together and followed her.

He placed his hands on the edges of the kitchen table and leaned forwards to look at Daisy, taking a deep breath. 'Guess who turned up yesterday looking as glamorous as ever and asking after her favourite cousin.'

Daisy raised her eyebrows in surprise. 'Vi?

That afternoon, while Eileen was playing with a friend from school, Daisy forced herself to pay Violet a visit. The good news about Bill had lifted her spirits and she had pulled on a decent dress and coat, pinned a hat on her head and brushed a hint of make-up over her face. The sun was shining in a cloudless sky, and it matched the sunshine she felt inside at the prospect of Bill coming home soon. The route took her past her parents' house and, on impulse, Daisy called in to see if her mother was at home before walking a little further on to her Auntie Doris's house.

'It's only me,' she called out as she let herself in the back door.

She took off her coat and gas mask box and opened the door to the living room.

'Daisy!'

Violet, visiting her Uncle Tom and Auntie Liz, jumped up from the armchair and threw her arms around her cousin. 'How are you? You look great. I hear you've heard from Bill at long last. That must have been a worry to you, with him being missing for months on end.'

'It was awful. We were at our wit's end, I can tell you. Enough about me, how are *you*? I was just on my way round to see you.'

'Oh, so-so. I'm glad to be home. I'm really pleased to see all the family again. To tell you the truth, I'm just relieved to be out of that munitions factory. Everyone's on edge all the time thinking we'll be bombed. It's okay living in Birmingham, but the bombs have been much worse than here in sleepy old Kettering. It's been fine for the last few months, though. I can't remember the last time the air raid siren sounded.'

Violet expertly changed the subject. 'Hey, is there any of Uncle Tom's scotch in the cupboard?'

'Violet!' Liz remonstrated. 'Not in the middle of the day.'

'Worth a try,' Violet giggled. 'I do love winding you up Auntie Liz.'

She hugged Daisy and kissed the air in the general direction of her cheek, being careful not to ruin her make-up.

Daisy sat down and took off her shoes. 'How's your mam? Dad called in at the crack of dawn this morning and told me she'd been poorly in the night.'

Liz stood up abruptly and with a glance at Violet, stalked off into the kitchen to make tea.

'Oh, all right ... I suppose. She does make a fuss at times. I think it's the strain of me coming home on top of the baby and everything else.'

'Your mother does *not* make a fuss, Violet,' Liz said from the kitchen. 'You should be grateful she cares about you so much.'

There was a loud clattering as Liz rattled the dishes in

the sink. 'Especially with everything she's got to think about.'

'Oh, Auntie Liz. I was only joking! Lighten up, for goodness sake!'

Daisy frowned. Her mother was not happy.

Liz shut the kitchen door, leaving Violet to give a skilfully embroidered account of her fictitious war service.

Half an hour later Daisy and Violet left together and walked along the road to Doris's house.

'I'll just nip and do some errands,' Violet said, undoing the clasp on her handbag and taking out a packet of cigarettes and a lighter. 'Might as well take the opportunity since the old gal's about to drop any moment – might not get the chance for much longer.'

Violet swayed along the pavement on high heels, her blonde hair blowing slightly in the breeze. Daisy felt old and dowdy in comparison, even though she wasn't yet thirty herself.

She let herself in the back door.

'Only me,' she called out as she shut the door behind her.

Doris waddled into the kitchen.

'Hello. Oh ... it's really nice of you to come, Daisy. What with Bill an' all.'

'Sorry I haven't been in,' Daisy said. 'I've been busy getting ready for Bill to come home.'

'When's he coming?'

'About two weeks, we think. He's had a rough time, but he's not injured or anything, thank God. I think the delay is because he has to speak to some important war people about information he gained while he was on the run in

312

Belgium, and they won't let him come home until his debriefing has ended.

Daisy eyed her aunt up and down, thinking how well she looked considering she'd just turned fifty and was in the later stages of pregnancy.

'Have you heard anything from Uncle Walter?'

Doris shook her head. 'He's abroad, apparently, but his work is top secret, so I don't suppose I shall hear anything until he gets some more leave.'

'It must be nice to have Violet back.'

'Oh, yes. She's got a month's leave, so hopefully she will be able to help me with the new baby when it comes. I still can't quite believe I fell for a baby at my age. I know it's not unheard of, but to tell you the truth I feel a bit embarrassed at what people think.'

'Don't feel embarrassed. You shouldn't worry so much. Tell them to mind their own business. Anyhow, everyone has much more on their plate with this war than gossiping about us.'

Daisy stared at her aunt, who was still rubbing her stomach. A hint of suspicion crawled over her skin. She felt uncomfortable and shivered slightly.

Doris, becoming aware of her hands, readjusted her smock carefully before turning away. 'Do you want a cup of tea? The tea leaves are a bit weak now but it's still drinkable.'

'Just had one round Mam's, thanks.' Daisy furrowed her brow and looked at Doris's ankles. *Not swollen*, she thought. She glanced at her fingers. *Still slim. Manicured nails.*

Doris dropped a teaspoon onto the floor and bent down

awkwardly to pick it up.

Daisy thought back to her pregnancy with Eileen. In the final weeks she would have struggled to pick up a teaspoon from the floor, but although Doris had been awkward, she had not rubbed her back afterwards, or made any grunting sounds at the effort.

'Can I do anything for you while I'm here?'

'Just the washing on the line, love. That will be a great help. It must be dry by now. Could you get it in and fold it for me?'

'Of course I will.' Daisy was grateful to have something to do. It would give her a few minutes to collect her thoughts.

She unpegged the washing, folding it and placing it into a wicker basket as she edged her way along the washing line. Deep in thought, she tried to piece together the puzzle. She folded the last piece of washing and picked up the laundry basket. *No,* she thought. *It's too ridiculous for words.*

She thought back over the last few months. There was no denying it. She and Rose had constantly suspected that Violet was pregnant. She had been mixing with the Americans for months and then it all abruptly stopped just weeks before she went away.

Were they really conspiring to pass Violet's baby off as Doris's?

She dismissed the thought. Violet was home now and obviously not pregnant. But, if her suspicions were true, where was the baby?

Daisy let herself in the back door. Her aunt had gone back into the living room and was sitting in an armchair,

314

queen-like, dressed in a bright flowery smocked blouse and skirt. She shot a regal smile towards her niece. 'Thank you ever so much Daisy.'

Daisy felt edgy and uncomfortable. 'I can't stay long. I have to get back for Eileen. She'll be back from her friend's house soon.'

As the two women chatted, discussing baby care and the arrangements for the birth, Daisy took the opportunity to study her aunt carefully. There really was no logical reason to doubt the pregnancy, but Daisy knew that all was not as it seemed. The only thing that didn't add up was the baby. Where was it? *Also,* Daisy thought, *Vi's so slim she can't possibly have just given birth. And what about Walter. Does he know? He must know, surely. Or was it just a smokescreen story about him being on leave?* Daisy carried on chatting without a hint of the thoughts that were running concurrently through her brain.

What about the doctor? She's been seeing a doctor. With this thought Daisy recalled the colourful accounts of Doris's visits to the doctor and the argument they had supposedly had about her being allowed to give birth in a hospital. She had reported to the family that, as she had no complications, she had to give birth at home, despite her age. *Surely that's not right – a fifty year old woman would surely have to give birth in hospital?*

After a while Daisy looked at the clock.

'Oh ... look at the time! I really do have to be making tracks. Eileen will be home soon.' She jumped up and grabbed her coat. 'Don't get up, Auntie Doris, I'll see myself out.'

Daisy buttoned up her coat, grabbed her bag and

315

stepped over to her aunt's armchair to give her a kiss.

Doris levered herself up. 'It's all right, Daisy, I'll see you out.'

As Daisy grasped the knob on the back door, there was a piercing cry and a loud clatter behind her. She turned around, alarmed, as in the living room Doris crashed heavily to the floor, her arm awkwardly twisted under her, having tripped on the hearth rug.

Daisy let go of the door and rushed over to her. 'Oh my word! What on earth happened? Let's get you up.'

With Daisy's help, Doris tried to haul herself up on the mantelpiece, groaning in pain.

Daisy looked on, riveted to the spot as her gaze became transfixed on her aunt's abdomen which protruded grotesquely from her hip; the carefully arranged padding having been knocked to one side with the fall. They looked at each other for a few seconds before Doris burst into tears and Daisy turned and fled.

Later the same day, at supper-time, as daylight was beginning to fade, Daisy heard a knock at the front door. She rose from her chair, where she had been silently contemplating her shocking discovery earlier that day, Eileen yelled excitedly from upstairs, where she had been getting ready for bed.

'It's Auntie Rose and Margaret!'

Eileen thudded down the stairs and flung open the front door to greet her cousin and aunt, who were standing with gas mask boxes slung around their shoulders. Her Auntie Rose was solemn and grave, whereas her cousin, Margaret, was bouncy and bubbly, pleased at the unscheduled visit.

'Have you finished your summer holiday homework, yet?' Margaret grinned. 'I'm stuck. I absolutely *hate* long division. Can you help me?'

'Why don't you both go upstairs then, and do your long division?' Rose gestured up the stairs. 'We haven't got long, though. We must get home before dark.'

As the two girls fell onto Eileen's bed, Margaret hissed in Eileen's ear. 'Hey, there's something going on – let's see if we can listen on the floor.'

Both girls lay on the bedroom floor, their ears pressed to the linoleum trying to catch snippets of the conversation between their mothers.

'I've been sent round,' Rose said in a serious voice, 'to talk to you about Doris.'

Daisy flashed an angry look at her sister. 'Did *you* know? What the hell are they playing at? I just can't believe it.'

Rose stroked her sister's shoulder. 'Let's sit down and I'll tell you everything.'

Daisy drew the blackouts as the last vestiges of a red and gold sun slid below the horizon. 'I've been trying to fathom it out, Rose. I can't for the life of me work out what's going on, other than it can only be about Violet. Why on earth would Auntie Doris fake a pregnancy otherwise?'

'It was all Dad's idea. He's besotted with Violet.'

Daisy turned round to face Rose, tight lipped and angry. 'You know why that is, don't you?'

Rose and Daisy locked eyes in a knowing stare. 'Are you

saying what I think you're saying?' Rose said.

Daisy nodded her head slowly. 'You think I don't remember Easter Saturday in nineteen twenty-two, don't you?'

Rose took off her headscarf and patted her hair into place with a nervous hand. 'After you told me what you had witnessed with Dad and Auntie Doris when you were just a little girl, you never, ever spoke about it again. I've never mentioned it to you, or anyone else, because I thought you'd forgotten about it.'

Daisy bit her lip. 'Well, I didn't forget. The memory is as vivid today as it was then.'

Rose shifted her weight nervously. 'Well, I thought you'd forgotten about it, and I wasn't about to drag it all up was I? After all you were only a little girl – you were only eight years old. I never told a living soul, Daisy, apart from George.'

Daisy looked at her feet. 'I've had nightmares for years.'

Rose stroked Daisy's arm. 'You should have said something.'

'What could I say? Something like: *by the way Rose, I remember playing with Billy Potter in that empty house and our dad shagging Auntie Doris on the bed right over the top of my head and don't you agree that it was a bit of a coincidence that our baby cousin was born a few months later?'*

'SShhhhh,' Rose hissed. 'Remember the girls are upstairs ...'

Daisy lowered her voice to a whisper. 'Forgotten?' she said. 'How could I forget something like that? I've suffered from bad dreams and cold sweats ever since. And another thing, I can't bear a squeak of bed springs or hear the sound of someone kissing without the awful memories flooding back. It's like having a chronic disease.'

Rose sighed. Was there going to be no end to this miserable mess? With a sudden clarity she realised that the roots of whole fiasco now unfolding before her eyes probably went back as far as Easter Saturday in nineteen twenty-two, when her father had, in all probability, impregnated his sister-in-law, resulting in the enigmatic and complicated Violet – their half-sister and not their cousin.

'Look, can we talk about this later, Daisy? Right now I need to fill you in on what has happened with Auntie Doris.'

Daisy crossed her arms in annoyance. 'Am I the last to know?'

'If you hadn't found out today when Auntie Doris fell over, you would never have known.'

Daisy shot an accusing look at Rose. 'You would have told me eventually, wouldn't you?'

'It's all madness,' Rose said, taking off her coat. She didn't honestly know whether she would have told her sister about the deception, to which she was a reluctant conspirator. She glanced at the ceiling. 'We'll have to keep our voices down. Apparently, according to our mam, Auntie Doris has wanted another child for years, but Uncle Walter ... well, we all know about him now, don't we. Preferring men and all that.'

'Was Doris *ever* really pregnant?' Daisy interrupted.

Rose shook her head. 'Come on, Daisy, be realistic. At fifty? Remember that day we first found out? Neither of us

319

could really believe it, could we?'

'So where's the baby then? Violet looks as slim as she ever did. *Is* it her baby?'

'I'll have to start at the beginning,' Rose said. 'It'll all make sense then.'

Rose told Daisy in hushed tones how the secret had been contrived. She explained that she had walked in on a heated conversation one day a month previously when Tom and Liz had been arguing about the conspiracy, and Tom had reluctantly been forced to let her and George in on the secret.

'Violet apparently got pregnant by a Yank and had an illegal abortion, but she was having twins and only one of the babies came away. When she realised she was still pregnant it was too late to do anything about it. The baby was born a couple of weeks ago in a nursing home in Birmingham. Violet is just lucky that she's got her figure back so quickly.'

Daisy couldn't speak. The horror of the scandalous revelations surrounding Doris and Violet made her just want to run away with Eileen as far away from Kettering as she could get. She didn't want her own little family tainted with the dirtiness of it all.

'I really want no part of it,' Rose said, waving her hand in dismissal. 'It's such a bad idea. It's complete and utter madness.'

Daisy suddenly drew a sharp breath as reality hit her.

'Rose, oh my God. What about ...?'

Rose interrupted. 'I know, the doctor, the birth, everything. They'll never pull it off. We'll be the laughing stock of the town. You can't tell me, Daisy. I think the same. Doris has a huge swollen ankle and I think her wrist could have broken in the fall. How are they going to explain *that* away? She's going to have to see a doctor sooner or later if her wrist is broken ...'

'Rose! I couldn't care less about Auntie Doris, but what about the poor baby!' Daisy clamped her hand over her mouth in horror as she visualised the lonely and deserted newborn baby. 'The poor little soul; what is it? Where is it? How could they leave a tiny baby in cold blood, with no mam to care for it?'

'It's all planned for Wednesday night. They've already had a practice run...' Rose continued.

Daisy became visibly agitated as she imagined the child at the centre of the conspiracy, all alone in the world with no family, and no one to love it. 'No, Rose! You just don't understand. The baby ...where is it? We've got to find it.'

Rose didn't reply, just nodded slowly before taking a deep breath.

'It's still in a nursing home in Birmingham. It's coming on the train on Wednesday.'

Daisy felt sick. 'They've left it in a *nursing home* all alone?' They are going to transport it on a train as if it was just a cow or a sheep? The poor little mite. How could they? Is it a boy or a girl?'

'A boy, with bright red hair apparently.'

Daisy's eyes filled with tears at the thought of Violet's little boy, left all alone in a nursing home whilst his family dreamt up a cock-and-bull story about his birth and conspired to make his entire life a lie.

'How could she just walk away from her baby and come back to Kettering without him? That poor little boy will grow up thinking that she's his sister and his grandmother is his mother. His whole life will be artificial and a lie. How could she, Rose – she's not human!'

Daisy was breathing hard, breathless with concern for the baby. 'Faking a birth is just ludicrous. They'll never pull this off – not in a million years.'

Upstairs Margaret and Eileen clearly heard the last part of the whispered conversation as Daisy's voice had risen unconsciously in her disgust. They whispered to each other with glee at having discovered such a juicy piece of gossip about the wayward Violet Grey and their batty Aunt Doris.

Rose let herself into the house to the sound of a hushed discussion in the living room. Margaret ran straight upstairs to get ready for bed, not wanting to push her luck, especially as she already knew what was happening, having heard it through the floor of Eileen's bedroom. Rose took off her coat and opened the living room door.

'I've filled her in,' she said to Tom in a flat, disgusted voice.

All eyes were on her. She stared at everyone in turn, an antipathetic gaze lingering on Violet. She was completely unable to hide the repulsion that seeped from every pore in her body. The extent to which Daisy had demonstrated her disapproval of the plot only emphasised her own fears for the plight of the poor little boy at the centre of the absurdity. She could hardly bear to look at her family.

Violet looked away from Rose's angry glare and fidgeted. She shot a pleading look at her. 'We think Mam's broken her wrist.'

Rose's voice was curt and short. 'She'll have to see a doctor, then. Or go to the hospital.'

'We can't do that, Rose,' Violet said in a cold voice. 'They'd know she's not really having a baby.'

Rose shrugged her shoulders and picked her way through the living room, into the kitchen, where George sat at the kitchen table, smoking his pipe.

'I'm keeping out of it,' he said. 'Half-baked and daft. It'll never work now. They might just as well call it a day and come clean.'

'I wish I *could* keep out of it, too,' Rose replied. 'But I can't, can I? Not with us living here in the middle of it all.'

Over the road, Doris sat in the dark, all her dreams about adopting Violet's baby boy as her own as shattered as the wrist she cradled to her chest. She knew the family were discussing what to do, but they had left her alone – as discarded and unwanted as the poor baby in Birmingham. She tried to move her fingers but the pain was unbearable. She looked down at her misshapen right arm and knew it was broken.

'Oh, Walter,' she whispered to herself. 'Where are you when I need you? What on earth have I let myself in for, and how has it all come to this?'

Although Tom was good to her in an artificial sort of way, she missed Walter's gentleness. She sighed. *He was not bad, just different*, she thought to herself. *So kind ... such a thoughtful, caring man.*

Doris no longer blamed herself for the failure of her

marriage. Once she had recovered from the second nervous breakdown in her life she could see that it had been doomed from the start. She felt tired and old and wondered how she would manage the baby with a broken wrist, when it came on Wednesday. *If it came on Wednesday.*

She looked up with a start as the back door opened and Violet returned, accompanied by Tom.

'How are you, love? Why are you sitting in the dark?'

'Because I blinking well can't get up and put the light on with this ankle, let alone do the black-outs.'

'Sorry, Mam. We didn't realise.'

'I've been thinking,' Doris said as she looked over to Tom. 'Could you strap my wrist and ankle up for me? I can't give up on all this now, just because of a little fall. What did people do before there were doctors and hospitals? You'll both have to help me out a bit more. I'm sure I'll be right as rain by Wednesday – after all we've got five days to get something sorted out.'

Violet's eyes lit up. 'Of course we can, Mam. Rose has just come back from Daisy's. She won't spill the beans. Says she doesn't want to be a laughing stock and just wants to keep out of it.'

Tom inspected her arm. 'It's well and truly broken, Dolly. Just strapping it up isn't going to work. We'll have to straighten it out and set it in splints. It's going to hurt – a lot – but a tot or two of brandy should dull the pain.'

'Go on then,' she said, in a voice that sounded braver than she was feeling. 'Just get it over with.'

After two large glasses of brandy, Doris buried her face in a pillow, biting down on the downy feathers through the dense material of the pillow ticking, trying not to cry out loud as Tom straightened her crooked wrist by pulling on it as Violet placed two stout pieces of cardboard between the layers of a bandage and tied it in place with pieces of string. Doris almost passed out, the intensity of pain ironically surpassing any labour pains she might have felt had she genuinely been giving birth.

The pain was so intense, they had to stop while Doris was given another large glass of brandy to knock her out before they could continue. Tom sat on the arm of Doris's chair and put an arm around her shoulders while the alcohol took effect.

'Just keep your chin up, love. It's just a little setback, that's all. We'll get this arm set and then you'll be fine.'

Doris looked up at Tom, slurring. 'Do you still care for me, Tom?'

Tom took her hand. 'Of course I do,' he replied. 'But you have to understand, Dolly, my life is with Liz. Now you will have a chance to make a fresh start in *your* life with Violet's little boy. Don't throw it away – you know you've always wanted a little boy to love, ever since you had that poor, deformed little chap – God rest his soul. It will work out, I'm sure, and you are doing the best thing you possibly can for Violet. She can make a fresh start, too, without the burden of a Yank's baby to put chaps off from marrying her.'

'So ... new starts all round, then?' Doris murmured.

Tom nodded. 'I reckon it is.'

Doris tried to speak through the fuzziness that blurred the edges of pain. She mumbled incoherently as second thoughts rose in nagging bubbles of doubt through her drowned sorrows.

Doris, in a medicinal, alcoholic stupor after having her arm set in a crude cast, had nodded off into a welcome sleep, although Tom hadn't noticed.

'It'll turn out all right,' he muttered to Violet. 'We'll just have to help her with the baby a bit more while her arm heals and she rests that sprained ankle.'

Behind closed doors, the final plans were analysed: Doris would noisily fake the labour and birth during the night on Tuesday ready for the baby to arrive on the nine o'clock train on Wednesday morning.

'Have you paid Bridget O'Reilly to rendezvous with the nurse?' Violet asked.

'Yes. That woman's a bloody witch if ever there was one. Money-grabbing cow screwed me for two quid.'

'It was nice to see Dad,' Violet said. 'I didn't think he would risk making the journey to sign the adoption papers, but I think that chap he's living with persuaded him to go along with it. After all, if folks think he fathered a baby with Mam, it's an insurance policy against being prosecuted if they were ever found out.'

'It was only because that shyster, Noel, screwed me for another seventy quid,' Tom said as he carefully wound a bandage around the home-made cast on Doris's arm. 'It's cost me damn near all my life savings to sort out this mess and keep this little lad in the family, so I hope you bloody well appreciate all I've done for you.'

'I do, but are you absolutely sure nothing can go wrong, Uncle Tom?'

Tom straightened up as he smoothed the last piece of tape around Doris's arm. 'As sure as I can be. Black market adoptions are rife, apparently, and that nursing home has arranged plenty of them. The battle-axe of a matron assured me of absolute discretion, but it's cost me, our Violet. It's cost me more than you would believe.'

'It all rests on Liz, Rose and Daisy, though,' Violet said. 'I hope they bloody well keep their traps shut.'

'They won't say owt. Don't worry, they don't want any scandal in the family any more than we do. Just you make sure you get out and about in the next few days. Let all the nosey buggers around here see you looking nice, slim and baby-free. Make sure you go in the butchers, the greengrocers and visit as many people as you can, telling them stories about being in munitions. That'll put paid to any rumours you might be the baby's real mother.'

Bridget O'Reilly and Tom had agreed that the baby would be taken to her home and given a small amount of sherry in its bottle to send it to sleep so that he could collect it later in a large kit bag lined out with baby blankets. He was to go round to the house at eleven o'clock and wait until the baby was suitably settled. Bridget declared she was an expert in such things and that the five minute walk would be a doddle as the baby would sleep well in the kit bag and wouldn't cry.

Liz had made a last-ditch effort to persuade her husband to see sense. 'That Bridget O'Reilly will gossip, Tom. The whole family is going to end up being ridiculed.'

Tom, however, knew she wouldn't.

'She's been arranging illegal adoptions for years and since the Yanks arrived, she's been receiving black market medical supplies from them – expensive medicine that prevents infections after an abortion. I told her – I'll report her to the authorities if she doesn't keep her mouth firmly shut about our Violet. And anyhow, she owes us. If she had done her job properly in the first place, we wouldn't be in this mess now.'

Defeated, Liz had had reluctantly gone through the motions, playing along with the charade, dutifully and mechanically spending the entire night with a non-existent midwife, assisting as her sister "gave birth" to Violet's baby boy.

Chapter Twenty
Exhaustion and Conscience

As dawn broke on the morning of Wednesday, 8th September 1943, its watery light revealed silhouetted image of roofs, chimney tops and the odd tall tree. Tom strode up and down the garden path, anxiously puffing on his pipe. It has been a busy night in the skies over the area and the air raid siren had sounded twice, annoyingly drowning out the distant, contrived sounds of a woman in labour. Tom, as usual, had ignored the siren and had spent most of the night in the garden, unable to sleep, pacing up and down the path as the sound of planes buzzed overhead, no doubt on their way to more important targets than insignificant Kettering.

Tom smiled as he heard the distant sound of a woman's screams drifting through the morning air, sending the message to the neighbours that Doris was in the process of giving birth. He took his pocket watch out of his pocket. The birth was to be at five past seven on the dot – only forty-five minutes to go.

Two hours later, Bridget O'Reilly was impatient. She stood on the station platform, her elbow cupped in her hand, smoking a cigarette, exhaling thin streams of smoke into the air. Her faded gabardine raincoat was slightly too big for her, pulled in tightly with a belt buckled around her waist, and on her head, a grubby headscarf was tied up at the front to cover her straggly, uncombed hair. She stretched her scrawny neck, blew the last of the smoke high into the air and then threw the cigarette onto the platform and stepped on it. She looked up at the clock and grabbed at the handle of the tatty pram with an air of annoyance.

Ten past nine, she thought. *I'm not hanging around all morning if this bloody train's much later.*

At half-past nine Bridget was about to give up and go home. The station master strode out of his office looking at his watch and announced through a loudspeaker that the train would be arriving in ten minutes, having been held up due to debris on the line.

'Bleedin' well time an' all,' Bridget said in a loud voice to no one in particular as she reached into her coat pocket and drew out a grubby piece of paper. She scrutinised the instructions carefully, word by word as she didn't read well. She reaffirmed to herself that she was to wait under the clock for the nurse to approach her, and give her name when asked. Satisfied, she refolded the piece of paper carefully and stuffed it back into the grubby pocket of her raincoat, glancing up at the station clock impatiently.

She walked along the platform a few yards, dragging the pram behind her with one hand, pausing to take out another cigarette and light it. *Bloody hell,* she thought. *I*

330

forgot to borrow some nappies for the little brat. Perhaps that Tom Jeffson will bring some with him when he fetches the little bastard.

The train chugged into the station and belched out a cloud of grey and white steam. It drew to a grinding halt and passengers started to open the doors.

Bridget watched intently, looking for a woman with a baby. The passengers on the platform began to get on the train, mingling with the passengers who had alighted and Bridget stood on tiptoes, her eyes darting back and forth. It soon became obvious there was no nurse on the train and definitely no baby.

'Excuse me.'

Bridget looked round. A guard was walking towards her with an envelope in his hand.

'Are you Mrs Bridget O'Reilly?'

Bridget was suspicious.

'Yes. What's up? I'm supposed to be meeting my sister and her baby. That's what this pram's for.'

The guard handed her the envelope.

'There's been a delay. I was asked to give you this.' With that he turned and strode away, pulling the whistle out of his pocket as he walked to his place at the front of the train.

Bridget sighed with annoyance and opened the envelope. It was a long letter and she couldn't be bothered to try to read it. She stuffed it into her coat pocket.

'Jaysus, give me faith!' she muttered under her breath as she pushed the pram angrily off the platform.

'What? I don't believe it!' Tom stood in Bridget's dingy hallway and ran his fingers through his grey hair as Bridget told him what had happened.

'You'd better come in, anyhow.' Bridget grabbed his arm and roughly ushered him into the dreary living room, where dirty plates and cups littered every available surface. 'Ye wanna a cuppa tea?'

Tom puffed out his cheeks and exhaled, glancing at Bridget's nicotine-stained hands and grimy fingernails holding an envelope.

'I think I need something a bit stronger than tea, Bridget.'

The rickety old pram stood in the centre of the room, triumphant in its emptiness.

Tom glared at Bridget, grimacing at her rough appearance and the filthy house and threw her a look of contempt and disgust as he snatched the letter from her hand. 'Give us the letter then, woman!'

He read the letter quickly and threw it into the pram.

'Bloody hell. What are we going to do now! Doris has well and truly given birth back there – whole ruddy neighbourhood's heard it I should think, the row she made.'

Bridget threw back her head and laughed, cackling out loud at the audacity of the baby, so determined was it to make things difficult, right from the very start when it had escaped the termination.

'Look,' she said, 'we'll sort something out. But it'll cost. I ain't doin' anything else unless I'm paid.'

Tom extracted his wallet and took out a pound note. 'Will that be enough for you? Just to keep you on standby, you understand. I'll be in touch.'

Bridget snatched his wallet out of his hand and extracted another pound note, before tucking the money into her apron pocket.

'That should do it,' she said.

Tom glared at her, turned and let himself out of the front door, leaving his kit-bag behind.

Tom was tired. It had been a long night and he just wanted the whole episode concluded so that he could resume his life. He was sixty-two years old and, although in good health, his knees and hips hurt where arthritis was beginning to set in. He sank thankfully into his armchair and lit his pipe. He needed to think, but thinking was something that eluded him, so tired was he. He thumped his forehead with the heel of his hand in an attempt to clear his head.

Liz had gone up to bed, having been up all night pretending to assist at the birth. Rose and George had got out of bed in silence, tight-lipped and hardly saying a word as they got ready for work and left the house with an inquisitive Margaret, who was packed off to stay with a neighbour before she went to school, annoyingly wanting to know all about the new baby boy that had been born in the night.

He took out his pocket watch. It was almost five to ten and Liz had been asleep since seven-thirty. He shifted his aching bones and sighed, exhaustion washing over him in waves. He knew he couldn't sleep until his carefully laid plans were back on track and the baby had arrived in

Kettering.

He levered himself out of his chair, grimacing with pain.

'Liz!' he shouted. 'Liz, get up.'

He hauled himself upstairs, stepped into the bedroom and shook Liz's shoulder. 'You'll have to get up again – it's all gone wrong.'

'Why? What's happened?'

Tom paced up and down the room, rubbing his grey stubbly chin with an anxious hand. 'The nurse who was supposed to have transported the baby was killed yesterday when a bomb flattened her house. The nursing home couldn't spare anyone else at such short notice, so they sent a letter with the guard on the train telling Doris that the family would have to make their own arrangements to collect him. What are we going to do, Liz? We have a woman just given birth and no baby to show for it.'

'Have you told Doris?'

'Bloody hells bells! No, I haven't. I'm so tired, Liz. Can you go over and tell her?'

Liz sighed and dragged herself out of bed.

Half an hour later, having told Doris the news, Liz walked into the living room carrying a tray with a teapot, two cups and saucers and a small jug of milk. 'She seems all right. Took the news quite well actually. Said it would give her arm a bit of a rest and she could just stay in bed all day.'

Tom raised his eyebrows and ran his fingers nervously through his hair with shaking hands. 'What are we going to do, Liz?'

'We need to telephone the nursing home.' Liz banged his cup onto the saucer, knocking the spoon off as she took charge of the situation. She handed Tom his tea, sighing with frustration. 'I'll have to go and ask if I can use the telephone in the ambulance station.'

Tom slammed his cup and saucer on the table and hauled himself up.

'I'll go. Look. Let's just think about this. We can't afford to lose our heads. Why don't we both go round to speak to Bridget and work through another plan? Perhaps she will go to Birmingham and fetch the baby for us?'

Liz, seeing the sense in the suggestion, said: 'You're right – things won't hurt here for a while and people will just think Doris is resting up after the birth ...'

'And you've told Vi just to stay put for a while?'

Liz nodded. 'Yes.'

'Good. She'd better bloody well do as she's told.' Tom checked his wallet before leaving for the ambulance station. 'That Bridget O'Reilly – she'll want more money. All this bloody money its costing me, it had better be worth it'

Later on that day, a contingency plan had been hastily hatched. The baby was to arrive, on the train as originally planned, the following day. In a whispered telephone conversation on the St. John Ambulance telephone, the nursing home had agreed a further fee and arranged with Tom for someone to deliver the baby, the payment being made directly to the baby's escort.

There was, however, a snag.

The escort had insisted she had to be back in Birmingham by nine o'clock. The baby would be arriving on the early morning mail train and would arrive at Kettering Station at four-thirty am.

'You're having a larf!' Bridget O'Reilly put her hands on her hips and thrust out her chest in defiance. 'I ain't getting up that time in the mornin' – creeping around in the pitch black. I 'ate the dark, 'specially with bombs dropping left, right and centre.'

Tom would have found the exaggerated remark funny in any other situation. The only bombs dropped around Kettering in the last four years had been two off-loaded in the fields around the town as the German bombers returned from raids on Coventry and Birmingham, and a stray crashed doodlebug a few miles away.

Bridget was insistent. She'd collect the baby in daylight or not at all.

Tom and Liz left, angry that Bridget had let them down. They stood on the corner, wondering who they could ask to collect the baby for them.

'No good me going,' Tom said. 'A bloke on his own with a pram at that time in the morning will look mightily suspicious. I'd get stopped by the nosey Home Guard, or the Police.'

'What about Rose and George?' Liz suggested. 'Or I could come with you?'

'Nah. Rose and George have got to go to work and they've turned all sniffy with me. And two old people out with a pram in the dead of night would still look suspicious. Our Daisy just might do it for us though, she's a soft touch where babies are concerned, and no one would look at her twice, as she's a young woman.'

Despite Tom's outwardly optimistic confidence in his youngest daughter's co-operation, a tinge of doubt nagged that she might refuse. Since Daisy had discovered the truth, she had not called round or contacted either him or Liz. Rose had reported to him that Daisy was too disgusted to speak to any of them. Tom just couldn't understand her hoity-toity attitude. After all, he was only masterminding this plan for the best of reasons and to keep an unwanted little boy where he belonged, at the heart of his family.

Tom ran his thumb and forefinger along his watch chain. 'Come on, Liz, old girl, you go and get some sleep. I'll go to see Daisy and talk her round. Time is of the essence, so they say.'

When Tom arrived, alone, at Daisy's house, it was lunchtime and Eileen and Margaret were sitting on the front doorstep in their school uniforms, eating sandwiches, deep in conversation. They looked up when Tom opened the gate.

'Hello Gramp,' they both said in unison.

Tom acknowledged them with a weary wave of his hand. Feeling more exhausted with every step, he just wanted to go home and sleep. He jingled the change in his trouser pocket and pulled out a sixpence.

'Go and get yourselves summat from the shop. He reached into his jacket pocket for his ration book – here you can have my sugar ration.'

'Ooooh.' The girls jumped up, hardly believing their luck. To them, sixpence was an absolute fortune.

'He must want us out the way,' Eileen whispered to Margaret and they both giggled. They'd worked out what was going on but didn't know that the baby had not arrived that morning as planned.

Daisy was at the kitchen sink, washing up. A tightly wound ball of anger thumped in her chest at the sight of her father as he smiled at her through the window and she had difficulty forcing even a polite smile as he let himself in the back door.

'What can I do for *you* then Dad?' Her tone was formal and accusing.

'Daisy, love ...'

'What?'

'*Don't say what – say pardon.*' Tom tried to tease his way back into her good books by repeating a phrase Daisy often said to Eileen. Daisy still didn't smile at him, her wooden expression unchanging as Tom explained what had gone wrong.

'So,' he concluded, 'we really need your help, Daisy. 'Will you go to the station and fetch him for us?'

Daisy stared at him, unblinking, her heart skipping. She wanted to shout and scream and shove him out of her front door, yelling that she never wanted to see him again. She fought down an urge to kneel on the floor and bang her head so hard that the knowledge of the grotesque plot spinning in her head smashed into a thousand pieces and she could shake it out of her ears, getting rid of it forever. She swallowed the rising anger, with an audible gulp. *Think of the baby... think of the baby ... think of the baby.*

338

The words went round and round in her head.

She heard herself speaking, as if she was standing by and listening to a stranger say the words. 'You'll have to take Eileen this evening, then. She'll have to sleep with Margaret. I can't leave her alone in the middle of the night. And I want the new pram round here. And some baby clothes; and a bottle to feed him with. I'll bring him back here. I'm not traipsing round to Doris's at five in the morning. And what if the air raid siren sounds while I'm out?'

Tom banged the flat of his hand against his tired head, trying to wake up his befuddled brain.

'No. You'll have to take it round to Doris's. Straight away. The bloody racket she was making at six o'clock this morning – I should think the whole blasted town has been duped into thinking she's just given birth. Otherwise the neighbours will start to suspect ...'

Daisy gave a sardonic laugh and shook her head, interrupting him. 'This whole thing is half-baked if you ask me. Folks are not as green as they're cabbage-looking, Dad. If I get seen pushing a pram round to Doris's at five in the morning, folk will know something's afoot.'

'No they won't,' Tom retorted. 'I mentioned to the nosey old buggers next door that Doris had fallen out of the bed in a dizzy turn just after the birth, had hurt her arm and I was taking her to the hospital tomorrow to get it checked over. They won't suspect anything. They'll just think we're up and about early.'

'Why the four-thirty mail train? Why not send him later in the day? I just can't see the point ...'

Daisy was cut short by Tom patting the air in front of

him, frustrated with having to explain the situation again.

'Like I said afore, they can't send it later. The lass who's bringing it is doing a spot of moonlighting, earning a bit of cash on the side. She has to be at work by nine.'

'What's his name?'

'What? Who?'

'The baby!' Daisy said, exasperated. It irritated her intensely to hear her father referring to the little boy as "it" instead of "he". Did they have no regard at all for the little chap, whose future was as artificial as his birth?

'And I wish you'd stop calling him an "it". He's a human being.'

Tom placed a forefinger in the centre of his forehead as he tried to remember the baby's name. 'Yeah. I remember. It's Oliver.'

Oliver. Oliver. Daisy repeated the name in her head. She heard herself speak.

'That's nice. Is it after Uncle Todge? That was his middle name, wasn't it? Tony Oliver Jeffson, as I recall.'

Tom shrugged his shoulders.

Daisy thought fondly of her favourite aunt and uncle, who had rescued her and Bill from the hell-hole of a grubby back room after Tom had thrown her out when she had told him she was pregnant with Eileen. Her father's estranged brother and sister-in-law had given her and Bill such a fun-filled colourful start to their marriage while they waited to be allocated a council house. Flo had died quite suddenly at the beginning of the war, no one realising until her death that she was actually almost twenty years older than Tom's estranged brother, Todge. After her death, heartbroken, Todge's own life had drained away until he was a grey flickering shadow of himself, joining his wife in death a year later. Daisy was glad the baby would be named after Todge, but she shook her head: had he still been alive he would have been horrified at the duplicity that was going on in the family.

The girls returned from the corner shop, each clutching a paper bag of boiled sweets, having used up Tom's entire sugar ration for the next fortnight. Daisy was in the process of scribbling a list of the items she needed. She shoved it in her father's jacket pocket, just as the girls let themselves in the back door.

'Here, take this' she said, whispering. 'I'll give the girls their tea when they come out of school while you fetch the pram and things. Then when you come back go straight round the back and put it in the shed so the little minxes don't suspect anything. I'll tell Eileen she can go back with you and stay overnight with Margaret tonight for a treat.'

Margaret and Eileen appeared in the doorway, staring at Daisy, their cheeks bulging with sweets.

'It's time you two got back to school – you'll be late for the afternoon registration at this rate,' Daisy said.

Chapter Twenty-one
Dependability and Compassion

Daisy rolled over in bed and switched off the alarm clock before it went off. She had not slept well, thinking of baby Oliver and worrying if he was being properly looked after on the journey.

Once downstairs, she poked at the embers in the fireplace and put some more coal on the fire, so that the room would be warm when she returned with the baby. In the kitchen, she put the kettle on the hob and then filled a rubber hot water bottle to put under the pram mattress.

Rain pattered hard on the window and Daisy frowned as she parted the blackout curtains whilst sipping her tea. Sheets of driving rain were blowing in waves across the road, tapping on the window like hundreds of long fingernails playing out a dramatic melody.

The melody hummed in her head, like a drumroll signifying the start of a little boy's life that would forever be a lie. He'd grow up with an elderly mother, who was really his grandmother. What would become of him? Would Doris give him a secure, loving home – something which every child deserved no matter how rich or poor its parents were? Or would his innocent life continue in the same vein as it had started, with people manipulating and controlling his future like some sort of grotesque saga being featured in instalments in a magazine?

She stared at the neatly made up pram in the centre of the living room as she finished her tea. As an afterthought, she fetched Bill's thick raincoat from the cupboard under the stairs as an extra cover for the pram.

She looked at the clock. It was two minutes to four. The station was about fifteen minutes' walk away and she calculated that she should leave by five past four to allow a few minutes' grace in case the mail train was early.

She put her cup in the sink and unlocked the back door. Blackness engulfed her. She couldn't see anything. She couldn't hope to make her way to the station without some sort of light. She reached under the kitchen sink for a lamp, but she knew she would have to be careful in its use. Using a lamp during the blackout was illegal and risky.

The journey to the station was horrendous. Not only was the rain persistent and heavy but there was also a cold, stinging wind that drove it into her eyes and blinded her as she forced her way through the inky blackness. Periodically she switched on her lamp for a second or two to see where she was. She didn't know whether to be relieved at the bad weather, which meant no air raid sirens, or curse it because it turned the short walk into a recurrent nightmare to be sporadically repeated during long restless nights for the rest of her life.

Twenty minutes later she pushed the pram onto the platform, the station master acknowledging her with an inquisitive frown.

'Good morning, miss.'

'I'm meeting my sister and her baby off the Leicester mail train. She has to be back in Birmingham by nine, so I hope it's not late.'

'Oh.' The station master looked at his watch. 'She should be all right. The connecting mail train from London's not due till five-thirty, so she'll have a bit of a wait. She should make it back to Birmingham in time.'

Inquisitive, the station master tried to make conversation.

'Not the weather to bring a baby out, miss, if you don't mind me saying.'

Daisy smiled at him uneasily, wondering what he was going to say next. 'No choice, I'm afraid. With the war and everything, common sense goes out the window. The baby is my nephew.'

The sound of a chugging train gradually overwhelmed the noise of the rain on the station's tin roof, which sounded like a crescendo of cymbals in a clashing disapproval of little Oliver's life where nothing would ever be as it seemed.

'Here it is.' The station master turned and walked down to the end of the platform so that he could have a quick chat and a cigarette with the driver as the mail and other goods were unloaded.

As the train pulled in the station, hissing out steam, Daisy searched for a woman with a baby, just as Bridget O'Reilly had done less than twenty-four hours earlier. Her heart was thumping and she felt slightly light-headed with anticipation. *Oliver. Oliver. Poor baby Oliver.* The name rolled round in her head.

A door opened and an elderly guard alighted from the

train's goods carriage.

'Are you waiting for a baby, Miss?'

'Yes.'

'Er ... Got it 'ere.' He reached back into the wagon and pulled out a cardboard box. He looked at Daisy accusingly.

'Never in all my born days have I had to transport a live *baby!* I know it's the war an' all that ... but honestly ... I don't know if that young gal was a relative of yours but she had no intention of accompanying it – twisted me arm, she did – twisted me arm. Said you'd have some money for me.'

Daisy was speechless with shock. Animals weren't treated as badly as this, she thought, as the anger inside her tightened and raised her voice into a squeak. She shoved her hand in her coat pocket and pulled out a pound note.

'Here,' she said, thrusting it into the guard's hand.

'Can you bring him into the waiting room for me?' Daisy's voice sounded distant in her ears.

The guard gave a grunt. 'I suppose so.'

In the waiting room Daisy was left alone with the baby, who was in an uncomfortable fitful sleep. There was a faint odour emanating from the cardboard box – a mustiness mingled with faeces. With a shuddering sigh and profound sense of guilt Daisy shut her eyes for a moment. This was by far the most upsetting sight she had ever witnessed in her life.

Covering the baby was a rough grey blanket folded into four layers with a grubby white sheet folded down over it. An off-white knitted hat with a stiff peak was almost covering his eyelids, which were crusted with yellow matter at the corners of his eyes. The baby's mouth sucked reflexively and he frowned as he slept.

Daisy gently folded back the blanket and sheet. She covered her nose and mouth with her hand as the stench wafted up and the pungent smell of ammonia hit the back of her throat. The baby's nappy was fashioned from rags and was soaked through with urine mixed with dark brown loose faeces, which had penetrated right through the lower sheet to old scraps of blanket that lined the cardboard box.

The baby let out a thin wail and opened his eyes, squinting and turning his head against the dim light of the waiting room.

Daisy unclipped the nappy pin. She took a flask of hot water from under the pram and poured it into a shallow dish she had brought with her. She had also brought some muslin swabs, along with a clean towelling nappy she had set to warm under the pram mattress, next to the hot water bottle, but the plain water and few scraps were clearly insufficient for the huge task in hand. Oliver was dressed in a cotton vest, which was also soaked through. Inadequately, he wore an old blue knitted cardigan that was too large, having been rolled up at the sleeves several times. His arms and hands were cold, and as Daisy held them momentarily in her hands to warm them, she burst into tears.

After a minute or two, Daisy unwound the disgusting nappy from his legs, crying out loud in shock. The tops of the baby's legs, his genitals and buttocks were bright red, spots of blood seeping through the raw, weeping broken skin. He screamed – a pitiful animal sound as his sore skin was exposed to the cold.

After she had cleaned him up as best she could and put the warm, soft nappy on him, she picked him up. Tears ran down her cheeks and dripped off her chin when her hand contacted with his tiny, freezing cold feet. She opened her coat and cradled him to the warmth of her body inside, soothing him, rocking his frantic cries away, saying his name over and over again, singing to him, comforting him, her own tears soaking into his little woollen hat.

As his crying subsided a little and he began to relax, Daisy realised the hat was stuck to his head. Dreading what she would find, she shifted him onto her hip and gently explored with her fingers under the hat's peak. At first, all she could feel was downy baby hair but as she pushed her fingers back further, they hit a crusty substance, mixed with tangled hair. Her fingers could delve no further – the substance had welded his hat to his little head. She felt sick. Never before had she seen such neglect of a newborn baby.

The baby gave a high-pitched cry, which Daisy instinctively knew was hunger. Having set the bottle into the warm water, she retrieved it. It was not very warm but, she concluded, he probably wouldn't care about that if he was so hungry. She sank down onto a hard chair and wrapped the naked infant, save for his nappy, in the soft, warm blanket. The baby drank noisily, giving a little satisfied squeak with every swallow of the milk.

When he had finished his bottle, Daisy shuddered as the station master's face peered into the waiting room window.

348

'You all right in there, m'duck?'

Daisy stood up, and drew Oliver closely and protectively into her.

'Yes, thank you, I'll be getting him home soon. He needed changing and he was hungry.'

Oliver's dark grey eyes were open. Daisy felt drawn into them, sensing the beautiful soul that nestled behind them. This was not just a baby. Any baby. This was poor unwanted Oliver who deserved so much better than the contrived, nefarious lie that was being perpetuated on his behalf. His tiny fist reflexively clenched repeatedly against her arm, and Daisy's heartstrings tightened as a sudden primal urge to unbutton her dress and draw him to her naked breasts overwhelmed her. Oliver's eyelids grew heavy and he gave a contented sigh before his body relaxed into sleep, satiated by the milk and comforted by the warmth of Daisy's body.

Intuition tingled down her spine and she trembled with an instinctive, certain knowledge that something bigger than her, and bigger than poor little Oliver, was conspiring to keep the little boy alive and safe. Fate had delivered her to the station to collect him. Fate had delivered him into her arms to care for, nurture and love.

She placed Oliver, still unclothed, on the warmed pram mattress and swaddled him tightly inside a cosy brushed cotton sheet and covered him with four woollen blankets. His eyes flickered open briefly. Sensing safety and security he gave another little sigh and settled quickly into a deep sleep.

Daisy wrapped the offensive rags in a brown paper bag and dropped them into the waste paper basket. As an afterthought she bundled the rough blanket and soiled sheets and discarded woollen cardigan back into the box and left it by the bin. She pulled her wet coat around her, grimacing and shivering at the thought of braving the rain again.

The station master returned, opening the door with a loud creak. He wrinkled his nose. The smell of wet clothes had mingled with the odour of the dirty nappy, made worse by the fumes from the small paraffin heater in the corner.

'You done, now, miss?'

'Yes, I'll be away now. Thanks for your help. Could you get rid of that for me, please?' Daisy nodded to the cardboard box as she arranged Bill's coat over the pram to shield the baby from the rain.

The station master touched his cap. 'My pleasure, miss. My pleasure. Never in all my born days have I seen anything like it, but the poor little soul will be all right, now it's with you.'

He watched as he held the door open for the young woman. He wanted to say something else, but couldn't think of the right words. Something about the look on the woman's face as she manipulated the pram through the door made him shudder. Her chin was set in a rigid determination, her lips were tight, set in a furious thin line as if she was about to vent her anger on the nearest unsuspecting victim. But the look in her eyes was one of undisguised maternal love.

'Thank you,' she said.

'You're welcome,' he replied. But for the rest of his life he would always remember the look in the young woman's eyes and the bizarre arrival of the war baby on the early morning mail train.

It was still raining, although not so hard. Dawn was just beginning to tinge the sky into a murky grey and Daisy had a much better sense of direction as she hurried home. She decided she was not going to take Oliver straight to Doris's house, despite her father's insistence. There would be plenty of time for that later in the day, and, anyway, it would add at least fifteen minutes each way to her journey.

Daisy walked briskly, breaking out into a run periodically with the large coach-built pram. Her tears mixed with the rain on her cheeks until they escaped noisily as loud sobs. She didn't care if anyone heard. She didn't care if anyone saw her. All that mattered was getting Oliver home.

Daisy opened her back door and clumsily manoeuvred the soaked pram into the kitchen. She glanced through to the living room clock, which indicated that it was now almost six o'clock.

Setting quickly to work, she boiled a kettle of water and found some mild soap. She didn't have a proper baby bath, so instead utilised an old-fashioned ceramic washing basin that stood in the spare bedroom.

While the kettle was boiling Daisy sorted through the baby clothes that her father had brought round the night before. She arranged them, together with two clean nappies and a soft, fluffy towel, on the fireguard to warm. She found some antiseptic ointment to put on Oliver's sore bottom and a tin of Johnson's talcum powder to smooth his skin. As Daisy worked, getting ready for when Oliver awoke, she began humming gently.

Oliver stirred and whimpered. She peeled back the covers on the pram and was pleased to find he was warm as toast. She wrinkled her nose. He still smelled bad, though.

He hardly awoke as she lifted him from the pram and cradled him in her arms, tears prickling at the back of her eyelids. She held him, cradled in one arm as she picked up the kettle and added some hot water to the basin in front of the fire. She then filled a jug with some of the hot water and stood a bottle of milk in it to warm before peeling away the blankets and removing his nappy. He was frightened ... she could tell ... but he must have felt secure in some small way as he didn't cry, his bottom lip quivering and his eyes anxious as he gazed at her face. It was obvious that he had not yet learned the experience of being bathed, as, startled by the unfamiliarity of warm water on his skin, he threw his arms upwards and drew in his breath sharply before wailing in fear. However, the water soothed him and he gradually relaxed as he enjoyed the experience. As the sodden woollen hat gradually separated from his head. Daisy smiled when she saw the colour of his hair – it was a beautiful, deep golden-red. The negligible amount of basic care he had received in the nursing home had caused thick cradle cap to develop on his scalp and she knew it would take weeks to eradicate.

Oliver's expression softened as he enjoyed his bath and tentatively kicked his sturdy little legs. After a minute or two Daisy lifted him out. He cried when she patted dry the stinging soreness around his bottom with a soft muslin square and rubbed in a generous amount of antiseptic ointment, but his cries dissipated once he was dressed.

As Daisy fed him they gazed into each other's eyes, the bonding between woman and child almost complete. Instinctively she unbuttoned her cardigan and blouse and held him close to her, rocking him back and forth gently. She shut her eyes, contented, enjoying holding a baby in her arms again.

By the time the chiming clock in the hallway struck seven, she knew she could never give him up.

Chapter Twenty-two
Realisation and Misunderstanding

Tom sat at the kitchen table, dressed in pyjamas and an old jacket for warmth. Although the rain had eased, it still pattered intermittently on the kitchen window, playing a depressing tune as he extracted his watch from the pocket of his jacket. It was just after seven o'clock. He put his head in his hands and spread his fingers over his face. He needed a drink, badly, but he wasn't going to give in and reach for the whisky. Just lately he had been falling into his bad old ways and he was determined to clamber back on the wagon.

Although he was near to exhaustion, completely without warning he experienced a moment of pure mental clarity. All his life he had been of the opinion that a baby was merely a woman's possession to pet and preen and take out in a fancy pram, dressed in lacy baby clothes and wrapped in delicate filigree woollen shawls. All Doris had ever wanted was a baby, but babies weren't *possessions* to be stored on shelves, like the jars of pickles in his pantry, ready to be taken out for Sunday tea and then put back again. Now, with a leaden lump in his throat, he realised that babies were people with future lives and parents were merely temporary custodians. He had given Doris the gift of a baby, but the little girl that resulted from their adulterous act wasn't to her taste, so she had discarded her, pushing her to the side of the plate of life, wanting to sample another. Now, over twenty years later, he had contrived to give her Violet's unwanted baby as some kind of consolation prize for her disappointment in her daughter. In Doris's view, babies were created to be held up like trophies: to be used, moulded and manipulated for her own means.

Tom dropped his head wearily onto his chest, ashamed that it had taken an entire generation of fatherhood on his part to know that babies should only be made to be loved, cherished and guided into adulthood. He no more owned this poor child than he owned the blue sky above his head or the earth beneath his feet.

Tom knew he should have abandoned his reckless plans long before Doris had her fall and the truth of Violet's continuing pregnancy seeped out of the closet. The poor little lad just didn't stand a chance, not in *his* family, anyway, but it was too late to do anything about it. The arrangements were made, the plot had been hatched and there was no going back.

The door opened, almost silently. Liz slid into the chair opposite Tom at the kitchen table.

'Mornin' old gal,' Tom said as he looked up at her, trying to force a smile.

'You didn't sleep, did you?' Liz said. 'I heard you get up hours ago. The rain woke me up. I wonder how poor Daisy got on. I bet she was soaked through to the skin walking to the station and back.'

Tom's face contorted in anguish. 'Oh, Liz. What on

356

earth have I done? Your Doris really shouldn't be having this baby. I realise that now – not after the mess she has made bringing up Violet. I've completely ruined things for this poor little lad.'

'I've been telling you that for months,' Liz began, but Tom put up his hand to stop her.

'I've been such a fool, Liz. I wish to God I had listened to you. You know when I went on the train with Doris to meet Walter to sign the adoption papers, just two days after the little lad's birth?

'It's unusual for such a speedy adoption, but everyone recognises we are at war and the last thing the authorities worry about is a respectable family adopting a wayward daughter's baby as their own. It happens all the time nowadays ... what with all these damned Yankees on the rampage all over the place with our innocent young women'.

Liz pressed her lips together and shook her head slightly. 'Violet is not innocent, though, is she?'

'Aye,' Tom agreed. 'You're not wrong there. When we sat in the gardens at the nursing home, waiting to sign the papers, Walter told me that he had misgivings from the start and I could tell Doris was beginning to wish she'd never agreed to take on the baby – and this was before her fall, too. *Just hang in there*, I said to her. *Soon you will have your little baby to dress in nice clothes and walk out with in his new pram. It'll all be over and no one will ever know your daughter has had a Yank's baby.*

'When we got to the nursing home there was a nosey old bag who interviewed Doris and Walter to make sure they knew what they were doing in adopting Violet's baby.

Obviously, she didn't know about the planned birth – she'd have had a pink fit if she'd known about that.'

'Really? You didn't tell her that?' Liz interjected with sarcasm.

'Well, this old witch told me that a surgeon and his wife had apparently expressed interest in adopting little Oliver just after his birth. They had been visiting the wife's sister in the nursing home and had heard about Violet planning to have her baby adopted. They went to see Violet and were besotted with him, especially his red hair, because the wife had red hair. They thought he was just perfect. They couldn't have any children, you see, and were desperate to adopt. Well, the old hag who was interviewing Doris and Walter sent me out of the room then – the cheeky old biddy said it wasn't anything to do with me. She spoke privately to Doris and Walter about it and said it might be a better solution all round as the couple were much younger and the surgeon could give the baby a very good life. Violet agreed too, apparently.

'They all broached the subject with me before they made a final decision. I flew into a rage in the nursing home gardens when we were discussing it. I panicked. There was no way I was going to give the baby up after all the money it had cost me. It was as if he were an object, not a living, breathing human baby. Doris was inconsolable, too, so they went back in and said that they wanted to keep him in the family.'

Liz sighed. 'You should have persuaded them to let the doctor and his wife adopt him. He would have a much better life than with my sister.'

The story of procreation in which mother and child are locked in a gaze of eternal adoration is not the story of the red-haired baby boy who was conceived of parents from different continents who cared only for their own gratification.

From the moment of conception, the evil, dark hand of Fate had reached inside the womb and waited for its chance to tear one of the perfect twins away for itself, leaving the other to gestate to finally burst forth into a world bereft of parents and devoid of a mother's love.

Destiny, awakened from a deep hibernation by the first stirrings of love and concern for the red-haired baby boy, sighed in relief and smiled as it delivered the baby into the arms of the Jeffson family's earth mother. Cradled, secure and warm in Daisy's arms, the baby boy began to thrive for the first time in his short life. Instinctively, he knew that the arms that encircled him and the soft breasts on which he rested his head belonged to the one person in the world who loved him. He slept easily, the discomfort of his deprived first few days of his life forgotten.

'Daisy! Daisy ... for God's sake ... open the door.' Tom banged on the kitchen door for the second time. His worried face appeared at the kitchen window, framed by his hands shielding out the light. Daisy stood in the doorway, holding Oliver close and glaring at her father through the window.

'Go away, Dad!'

'Daisieeeeee – please? Your Auntie Doris is nearly going mad back there.'

'No, Dad. Not now. I'll call in later this afternoon when Eileen's home from school?'

'Think of her, Daisy, think of how Doris is feeling. What's up? Why won't you open the door?'

Daisy kissed Oliver on top of the head and stepped forward to reluctantly unlock the back door. Tom burst in and quickly shut the door behind him. His agitated mood changed abruptly to excitement as he strained to get his first look at the child who was biologically his first grandson.

'Let's see the little chap then.'

Daisy held on to Oliver tightly, eyeing her father with suspicion as he tried to peep at the baby's face. 'Dad, we've got to talk. He's a human being, not some sort of doll. I just can't bring myself to hand him over to Doris who is going to make just as much of a mess of his life as she has made of Violet's. I just can't do it.'

Tom's mind flashed back to the first time he'd ever held a baby as a sixteen year-old father of a married woman's illegitimate child and he shuddered. It was just as well no one knew about that.

'I just want to hold him. Please, Daisy, I won't take him away... please ... I do understand you know.'

Tom felt a sudden huge surge of pride for his youngest daughter. She had always been headstrong; he knew that. He long ago realised he had made many mistakes with Daisy and had spent the past ten years or so trying to make it up to her. But there could have been no prouder father that morning. His Daisy was the best homemaker and mother he had ever come across.

Daisy capitulated with a reluctant sigh. Oliver was probably his first grandson – although that was just speculation on her and Rose's part. But she still didn't trust him, and she would *never* leave Eileen alone with him. There was no denying, though, that whenever Tom's grandchildren were in the house, a warmer, caring Tom seemed to rise to the surface in spite of himself. He would play for hours with his granddaughters, not turning a hair at the inevitable messiness, and was generous to the point of spoiling them.

Tom cradled Oliver, cooing and rocking him as Daisy put the kettle on to make tea.

'Why didn't you take him straight to Doris's this morning, then? Didn't everything go as planned? To tell you the truth Daisy – I was worried to death about you being out all on your own. The rain was dreadful; throwing it down wasn't it? I nearly got up and came with you but I was shattered after the day we had yesterday.'

Daisy looked straight at Tom. 'There was no one with him, Dad. They just threw him into a cardboard box and put him in the goods carriage as if he was just a parcel. He's in an awful state – look. Daisy took a deep breath and gently peeled back the white shawl. She unpinned his nappy. Oliver slept contentedly and didn't stir.

Tom was visibly shocked at Oliver's soreness. 'The poor little sod. The bastards. How could they let him get in that state?'

Daisy set her jaw in a determined stare. 'I'm the only person in the world who loves him. I want to keep him. No

... there's no *want* about it ... I'm *going* to keep him.'

Tom stared at her. 'Daisy, you can't. He's Doris's baby. They have already adopted him. It's all official and not only that, she's gone and given birth back there. The bloody racket she made the other night, it's a wonder half of Kettering didn't hear her.'

Daisy pinned up Oliver's nappy as he slept in Tom's arms.

'When Bill gets home, I'm sure he will agree with me. *We* could adopt him. It would be a good solution all round. Nobody really wants him, do they? After all, Violet tried to get rid of him. We could say Aunt Doris has had another nervous breakdown and couldn't cope at her age with a new baby. No one would ever need to know that he was really Violet's – and her reputation would stay intact.'

Daisy raised her head and looked at Tom straight in the eye, her steadfast, maternal conviction melting into the blue-grey steel of his resolve.

'I just know he was meant to be mine.'

Tom put his other arm round Daisy. 'You're not thinking straight, love, with Bill having been missing in action. Now he's coming home, you're all at sixes and sevens.'

'I *am* thinking straight. I am NOT giving him up to Auntie Doris. She won't treat him well; she won't cope and he'll end up being just as damaged as Violet. He deserves better than that after his rough start in life.'

'Look, Daisy. You keep him till after tea and then we'll talk about it again when our heads are clear. In the cold light of day, you'll see things more clearly.'

Outside the rain had stopped to be replaced by a heavy,

362

grey fog. As Tom strode up the garden path and shut the gate behind him, he coughed uneasily.

Inside, Daisy stood at the window, Oliver in her arms, watching her father walk away. She had never been so determined about anything before in her entire life.

Nothing, and no one, was going to take this baby away from her.

Bill Roberts stood on the station platform, heaving his heavy kit bag over his shoulder and looking up and down to see if there was anyone he knew milling about. There had not been time to let Daisy know he would be arriving early, having secured an extra couple of weeks' leave before the Ministry of Defence said his next posting would be considered.

He left the station quickly, his heart lightening with every step as he strode up Station Road towards the town, despite the cloying murkiness that swirled around him following the night's heavy rain. People raised their hats at him as he walked by and he felt proud of his uniform and for serving his country. On impulse he called into a corner shop, buying treats for Eileen and Daisy. The filthy weather could never extinguish the light that radiated from him at the thought of seeing his family again, and the relief at simply having survived when so many others had lost their lives.

A few minutes later he turned the corner into Windmill Avenue. He thought his heart would burst at the familiar and yet subtly different sight of his home. The trees seemed taller, the grass greener and the curtains in the windows brighter than he had remembered – even through the fog. Would Daisy be in? After all, she had no idea he was coming home that afternoon. He looked at his watch – it was ten to three.

He let himself in the gate, caressing the rough wood as he shut it behind him. He walked around to the back of the house and stopped momentarily to drink in the stillness and pure joy of returning home. He took a deep breath as he tried the door. It was unlocked, as usual. They hardly ever locked the back door, even if they were going out.

The kitchen was warm and he could smell the stew that was cooking in the oven. A saucepan of vegetables, placed on the top of the cooker, was ready for the gas to be lit underneath when Eileen came home from school. A wooden clothes horse laden with drying clothes stood in the corner of the kitchen, by the table. He put out his hand and touched it, remembering making it for Daisy when, as teenagers, they had lived in exile in a dreary back bedroom in an unscrupulous landlady's house after Daisy's father had threw her out. He breathed in the homely smell of clean washing mingled with the aroma of the food cooking and shut his eyes, absorbing the pure bliss of being home.

He could hear the wireless in the living room, where Daisy was gently humming along to Glenn Miller. He smiled and opened the door with tears of joy in his eyes.

She was sitting in an armchair, eyes closed, rocking backwards and forwards as she clutched a newborn baby, her face resting on its downy head in a pose that radiated motherhood.

A few seconds passed before, sensing someone was in the room, she opened her eyes with a start.

364

'Bill!' she cried out, momentarily forgetting the sleeping baby on her shoulder. Her face lit up in wide, happy surprise as she jumped up.

'What the hell –'

Bill's face fell in disgust and undisguised horror as he added ' – have *you* been up to while I've been gone?'

They stood, looking at each other, transfixed, the moment existing in an unforgettable hiccup of misinterpretation and confusion.

'Just whose is that.' He jabbed an accusing finger in the direction of Oliver, still sleeping contentedly.

'Don't be silly. It's Auntie Doris's baby – well not hers, but really Violet's. You remember? I wrote to you and told you? I know I did.'

Daisy put Oliver into his pram before flinging herself at Bill, her arms wound tightly around his neck. 'You don't know how much I've missed you.'

Bill stood, as still and rigid as a marble statue, an icy cold expression on his face as he stared at the baby in the pram.

'A Yank, was he?' he muttered, almost without moving his lips.

'Bill ... Oliver's not *mine!*'

'How do I know that? How do I know it's not some tale you and your crackpot, scheming father haven't dreamt up? Oh yes, now I see it. It'll be: *Oh Bill, can't we adopt him,* and there you are. Fait accompli. I'm no sucker, Daisy, You hear about this sort of thing all the time.'

Bill pushed Daisy away from him, stormed out into the kitchen and snatched up his bag.

'Oh, God ... Bill ... come back! You've got it all wrong.'

Bill ran down the garden path, tripping on the unfamiliar terrain. He raced blindly out of the front gate without shutting it behind him, momentarily disorientated in the dense fog, uncertain as to which way to turn or where to go. As stumbled along the road, his hand spread across his face in anguish, he stopped, paralysed by a familiar, never-to-be-forgotten little girl's voice calling out to him.

'Dad. Dad. Daaaaaad!'

He swung round. Running towards him out of the fog were the blurry silhouettes of two young girls, one trailing the other. Eileen had her coat open and it fanned out behind her, her gas mask box bumping noisily with each step.

Fire replaced the ice in his eyes and his voice broke with emotion. 'Eileen! My little Eileen. Just look at you. I can't believe it. You're all grown up!'

Margaret stood by, smiling at the reunion, as her Uncle Bill swung Eileen round and round in a big hug, her feet off the floor. She quickly kissed her uncle on the cheek and said her goodbyes before hurrying home to tell the family the good news that Bill had arrived home, two weeks early.

'Where are you going, Dad?' Eileen said, swiping tears of happiness from her cheeks with the back of her hand.

'Nowhere. I'm just coming home.' Bill buried his anger and confusion for the sake of his daughter. He put his arm around her. 'Just got here.' He forced himself to rewind time and, proudly clutching Eileen's narrow shoulder, he walked back to his house.

They entered the living room together, holding hands. Daisy was sitting in an armchair, leaning forwards, her elbows on her knees, sobbing through her fingers, her face covered.

'Mam. What's the matter? What's going on?' Eileen stared at the pram in the centre of the room.

Bill turned to his daughter.

'Whose baby is it, Eileen? Tell me the truth, now.'

'Well ...' Eileen looked at her mother who was drying her eyes with a handkerchief. She was a quick-minded, sensible girl and knew it was time to confess about hearing the conversation through the floor six days earlier.

She turned to her father and grabbed his arm. 'You'd better sit down, Dad. I'll tell you all about it. Mam's in no fit state.'

Eileen explained to her father about Violet's return, Doris's fake pregnancy, the fall, the broken arm and the failure of the baby to arrive on the train as planned. 'Honestly, Dad, we didn't have a clue – no one did until last Friday, even Mam.'

Eileen rolled her eyes for effect. 'We heard *everything* when Auntie Rose came round last Friday night, to tell Mam all about it. We were listening through the floor.'

'It's really Violet's baby then? Really and honestly hers?' Bill said to his daughter, stunned by how grown up she was.

Eileen gave her father an accusing look. 'Yes of course it is ... who else's could it be?' . Bill didn't notice the look, as he was gazing at Daisy, accusation and recrimination

367

replaced by compassion and pride.

'Oh ... love. I'm so sorry. It's the war. You wouldn't believe the tales we hear about this sort of thing, and it's usually the Yanks. So many soldiers have come home to find their wives and girlfriends with babies.'

He sat on the arm of the chair and Daisy put her arms around his waist as he kissed her hair and tear-stained face.

'It's all right, Bill. I know how it must have looked.'

Overcome with embarrassment, Eileen went into the kitchen to put the kettle on. She somehow felt she was glimpsing the first signs of the imperfect nature of adulthood. She didn't know what the uncomfortable feeling was, but as she grew up would realise that, at that moment, she had just felt very let down by the suspicions of her father, which had left her with the notion that grown-ups were really just big, duplicitous children, playing adult games of war, not with toys but with other people's lives.

Eileen carried in the tea tray and put it on the table by the window.

'Brew up?' she said cheerfully, interrupting her parents, who were deep in conversation and locked in an embrace.

Bill was shaking his head.

'We can't Daisy. No. We can't. I want some more children of our own. He's a lovely little chap ... but I just can't. People will jump to the same conclusion I just did and I'll be a laughing stock.'

'Where's Margaret?' Daisy said to Eileen.

'Oh, she went straight home after school when we saw Dad coming home. She'll tell Grandma and Gramp.'

'Grandma was supposed to give you both tea and then bring you back when she collected the baby. I wanted to keep him, Eileen, and adopt him. Would you have minded?'

'I'm afraid I'm with Dad on that one, Mam.' Daisy gave her mother an apologetic look. 'I'm sorry, but I want my own brother or sister now. This baby is not our responsibility.'

'He'll always be my responsibility. After all, I was the one who fetched him from the station.'

'Yeah ... and Violet's his mother! If he's anyone's responsibility he's hers!' Eileen retorted.

Later that evening Violet stared at the baby before her for a long time.

She was not worthy of being a mother. His birth shouldn't have happened, as it was never her intention to continue with the pregnancy. He should have joined his twin in the lavatory pan before his life had even started. But his life had burst forth from her body and he lived against all the odds stacked against him. She should have opened the door to a good life for him. She could have insisted, and let the doctor and his wife adopt him instead being sucked into the whirlwind of misplaced family ties and secrets, stirred up by Uncle Tom because he just couldn't bear not to be in control. There was no worse mother on this earth than her. She wasn't even worthy of being his sister, which was all she could ever be now everyone had been duped into thinking her mother had given birth to him.

She reached out and brushed his sleeping face with her fingertips.

He was beautiful. A perfect miracle. She fought back an overwhelming urge to pick him up, hold him close to her and never let him go. She almost did it. She almost scooped him up and ran out of the house, away from her family; far, far away from Kettering and into an uncertain future.

Just one thing stopped her. Once, she had a mother who loved her. Up until she was seven years-old her mother had filled her life with bright, sunny days; she had cooked proper meals and baked delicious cakes. She had cleaned furniture and mopped floors, filling the house with the fresh smell of beeswax polish. She had gone to church on Sundays, done the washing on Mondays, ironed on Tuesdays and cleaned the front step on Fridays.

Once, long ago, her mother had been normal.

Violet had been much too young to understand what "depression" and "nervous breakdown" actually meant, but had gradually become detached from her mother, embroiled in secrets, deception and lies. When she had reached eight years-old, she knew about things no little girl her age should even have to think of. That was when things had begun to go wrong. Perhaps this baby would be the making of her mother? Could this perfect little boy be her mother's salvation?

If she stayed to become part of his life as his older sister, there were no guarantees of a happy-ever-after. Violet's eyes filled with tears. She would be a bad influence on him, fighting with her mother for maternal control over his life in exactly the same way Uncle Tom had tried to control hers. She could not possibly bear to live her life, loving him at arm's length while all the time knowing that she had tried to terminate his life and flush him away in a lavatory pan, just like she had done to his twin brother or sister.

After staring at her son for a long time, her tears dripping onto the blanket that covered him as he slept, she had forced herself to turn away, pulled on her coat, stuffed her purse in her coat pocket and left the house to fetch some cigarettes.

When she came out of the corner shop, she sat on a low garden wall to count the money in her purse. Then, with no spare clothes and no belongings she walked the streets for two hours, unable to bring herself to go home. She finally ended up at Kettering railway station with the twin images of one perfectly formed miniature baby floating in the lavatory pan and one perfect, sleeping baby haunting her so completely that she knew she had to put as many miles between her and her son as possible. Although she hadn't planned to re-set the clock of her life on the day Oliver came home, Violet knew she now had no place in her family. She had to start again, somewhere else, and let destiny determine his future. She at least owed him that.

She was the worst mother ever to walk the earth and she knew she would never forgive herself for the terrible thing she had done to her twins.

Chapter Twenty-three
Catharsis and Determination

The cottage was built of brick and stone, with a grey slate roof which mostly blended into the sky. There was an attic room, with a tiny skylight; a white painted picket fence and a neat front garden with freshly dug borders. The cottage next door was forlorn in comparison as it stood, empty, waiting for new tenants. The only other house in sight was the farmhouse way down the hill, so distant its windows were now just tiny specks of black on the white render of its walls. It had taken almost twenty minutes to walk from the white farmhouse to the cottage, along a stony narrow road that wended its way along the contours of the wild coastline.

A West Highland white terrier yapped at the gate as the unfamiliar figure approached the cottage. Devoid of make-up, her hair bedraggled and dirty, and carrying a small, battered cardboard suitcase, the young woman was as weary and grey as the oppressive clouds overhead. Her journey had been long and tortuous, with protracted enforced breaks as she secured any work she could find to earn some money to feed herself and put something aside for the next leg of her long journey. Some of the things she had done to earn money had left her degraded and had sapped her sense of self-worth until she felt like a hollow shell inside, unable to feel either pain or joy.

She opened the gate and the little dog jumped up and down, yapping incessantly, excited in its welcome of an unscheduled visitor.

Hearing the dog barking, Walter Grey opened the front door, a pipe in his hand. He didn't recognise the young woman at first, even though it had been only a few weeks since they had spent a few hours together when he had signed her baby's adoption papers.

'Violet?' he said, squinting in the sunlight as she closed the gate behind her. 'Is that you? Oh my word, what on earth are you doing here?'

'Hello Dad.'

Walter picked up the little dog and then took the case from her. 'What the hell has happened to you? You look dreadful.'

Violet shook her head. 'It's taken me a long time to get here. I've walked for miles and miles and got lost hundreds of times. I thought I was never going to find you.'

'You should have written – we could have collected you from the station.' Walter nodded towards a black car in the driveway.

Violet shook her head. 'Too risky,' she said. 'I didn't want the authorities to track you down if anyone suspected anything after the adoption, so I've done the journey in stages, earning enough money to live on along the way.'

Walter shook his head. 'I think the authorities have far more to think about right now. The whole world is changing.'

'It's just that I didn't want to be the cause of you going to prison.'

'Come in, love. You're here now and that's all that matters.' Walter said, ignoring her remark. He showed her into a cosy, neat living room. 'This is such a surprise. I can hardly believe you're here.'

'Can I stay?'

'Of course you can.'

'Just for a while.'

'Stay as long as you like. But what's happened? Is your mother all right? And the baby? Has anything gone wrong?'

Violet sank down into an armchair, too tired to even take off her coat. She sighed and pressed her fingers into her eye sockets.

'Are you hungry?'

Violet nodded. 'And I could do with a cup of tea. I've had nothing today. I stayed in a guest house last night, but I was up early and left before breakfast because I knew it would take me all day to walk here.'

When Walter returned with a cheese sandwich, Violet had fallen asleep in front of the log fire. He covered her with a tartan blanket and quietly shut the door.

Deception continued to worship at the altar of respectability. It strained to prop up and maintain appearances whenever it could. It fed hungrily from Tom's yearning to recapture the past and keep a hold on his family and soaked up Doris's insatiable craving for someone to love her. But crumbling and decaying with each passing day, its secrets spread as easily as a small amount of water spilled on glass, running away quickly and uncontrollably. Whispers rippled around the town about Doris's sudden, farcical pregnancy and Violet's abrupt appearance and disappearance, which the family attempted to explain away using the cover of war.

At the centre of the controversy, the little boy whose conception and birth had caused so much inconvenience was tossed around the Jeffson family like a hand grenade with the pin removed.

Daisy quickly conceived a baby following Bill's return. The whole family was overjoyed at the pregnancy, not least Eileen and Margaret who seemed to spend all their spare time learning to knit, Liz patiently teaching them the skills they would need to make tiny baby clothes for Daisy's new baby. Bill softened towards Oliver and secretly harboured a growing affection for the good-natured baby with fine golden-red hair, pale skin and huge blue eyes. Oliver grew used to being passed around and tolerated the uncertainty in his life without complaint, sleeping right through most nights.

'I see Doris has abdicated her responsibility, once again,' Bill said one day when Oliver was seven months old. 'After all she went through to adopt him – now she's grown tired of being a mother and doesn't seem to want him at all.'

Tom had been pacing up and down, with a fretful Oliver on his shoulder. Bill took him from Tom, and put him over his shoulder, stroking his head.

'How about *we* look after the little chap at weekends,

Tom? I'll be posted again soon and I know Daisy and Eileen would love to have him. It's not fair on you and Liz. You should be taking it easy now. After all, you're not getting any younger.'

'It'd be a solution,' Tom said with a weary sigh. 'Everything has gone tits-up, hasn't it? I sometimes wonder why I bothered trying to help. All that money it cost, it's almost ruined me. What's the matter with her? She's craved for another baby for years – now she's got one she can't cope.'

'It would have been for the best all round if he'd been adopted ...'

'No!' Tom grabbed Oliver back from Bill. 'Never. Not in a million years. He's a part of our family and I am quite prepared to take responsibility for him while Doris is going through this bad patch.'

Bill sighed and rubbed his chin. 'Has anyone found out where Violet's gone? It's been months now.'

Tom rolled his eyes upwards. 'Gawd knows. I could kill her, buggering off like that. I know she made it plain she didn't want to keep the baby, but you'd have thought she'd have helped her mam out a bit, wouldn't you? No thought for any of us – no thought at all.'

'Daisy is worried to death about Violet,' Bill said. 'She just wants to know she is all right and keeps imagining she's got herself into some awful trouble. I wish she would get in touch with us. You would have thought that was the least she could do, considering how we looked after her when she was a little girl.'

Tom scratched his chin. 'I suppose I could ask around a bit. Perhaps I could try the Andrews boys? After all she was quite acquainted with them after she took up with Theo.'

Bill shook his head. 'No, I don't think they would know where she is. After Theo was killed and she went off the rails, they washed their hands of her. Daisy reckons they always felt she was bad for him. Once they'd heard she had cut off her hair and slashed her arms and legs when she was a child, they felt she was a bit of a psy –'

Bill coughed and curtailed his words, embarrassed as he almost blurted out the word "psychopath".

Tom sighed in despair, feeling the weight of responsibility for Violet's turbulent life pressing down on him. It was no wonder the poor girl had ran away.

'You're right, lad. She might have buggered off, but she's still a part of our family. I'll do my best to try and find out where she's gone, if only to put our minds at rest.'

As Doris fell deeper into depression, her best friend became the gin bottle. Alone and unable to cope with the baby, the weekends when she handed him over to heavily pregnant Daisy and Bill for a reprieve gradually spilled over to Tuesday or Wednesday morning and then started again on Friday afternoon, until Daisy and Bill were caring for Oliver almost full-time.

One day, another brown envelope from the Ministry of Defence plopped through Daisy and Bill's letterbox. Bill ripped open the envelope, apprehension quickly turning into a broad smile.

'Daisy! Guess what? I'm not going away – I can stay at home – I'm being posted to help the Yanks at Grafton

Underwood!'

Grafton Underwood air-base, home to the 8th US air force, was tiny compared to other bases in the country. Built in 1941, it was located only four or five miles away from Kettering. Nestled in the heart of the Northamptonshire countryside, it meant Bill could live at home and cycle there every morning. The armed forces had been kind to him, repaying him for his hard work, loyalty and the valuable intelligence he had gathered during his capture and eventual escape.

Daisy and Bill's marriage had flourished since he had come home, strengthened by the agony of separation. From their uncertain beginnings as a seventeen-year-olds, living in a filthy back room with no belongings, no money and a dismal future, they had developed into loving parents who cared deeply not only for their own daughter and baby Oliver, but also for Eileen's cousin, Margaret, giving her a sanctuary from an oppressive childhood, living as she did with ageing grandparents. Their home was warm and welcoming: their back door was always open to visitors and they were the most popular family in Beech Crescent, having won the trust and respect of their neighbours, despite their young age.

Although they had not yet officially adopted Oliver, Daisy was certain that Bill would relent once their own baby was born, smiling to herself as she watched Bill playing with him. Although Rose and George helped out too, taking him out for walks and buying him clothes and toys, it was her and Bill who provided the parental love and security which was crucial to the little boy's development.

'I knew he was meant to be mine the second I set eyes on him,' Daisy said.

'Aye,' Bill acknowledged. 'I feel that way too. Once our own baby is born, we'll see what we can do about taking him on. He needs stability in his life and the only way he is going to get that is if we look into adopting him.'

'What about Doris? And what about Dad? He'll never agree. He'll fight it all the way, and do you think people will think he's really my baby, just like you did when you came home.'

'Your dad will see it's for the best,' Bill replied. 'This way, we can keep him in the family, and that was all your father ever wanted to achieve. And I don't care what people think – we know the truth and that's all that matters.'

Two weeks later, Daisy bent over uncomfortably as she folded Oliver's clothes and laid them out on the spare bed, the smell of clean washing filling the room with fragrance.

'I'm really going to miss him, Dad. He feels as if he is my own flesh and blood, and I've felt it ever since that first night. I just can't describe it. It was as if I'd actually given birth to him at the station.'

Bill turned to Tom, who was standing in the bedroom doorway, waiting to collect Oliver to take him back to Cornwall Road to stay for a while. He put an arm around Daisy's shoulders in support of his wife.

'I love him too, Tom. I've been thinking – Doris is never going to be well at this rate – well enough to look after him anyhow.'

Bill picked up a pair of dungarees, folded them neatly

and added them to the pile. 'He needs a proper mam and dad. I know you and Liz are doing your best, but it's not fair on you – after all you're both not getting any younger.'

Daisy raised her eyebrows, looking at Bill. She hoped he would choose the right words to tell her father that, after their baby was born, they were going to go to the authorities and try to adopt Oliver.

'I'm sure I could cope on my own while you have our baby,' Bill said to Daisy. 'Eileen will help out. I know you think it's the best thing all round if your parents look after him for a few weeks, but I know I could cope. I just can't see why he can't stay here, with me and Eileen. What do you think, Tom?'

Tom rubbed his chin, deep in thought as Bill continued.

'He needn't be uprooted and it would keep him in the family, wouldn't it? And we could use the time to set the wheels in motion to make things more permanent. We all know this can't be allowed to go on. If we don't do something ourselves, as a family, the authorities will take him away from her and he'll end up being fostered out to someone else.'

Tom sighed, shutting his eyes, nodding his head slowly. 'We'll see,' he said. 'Let me just have a think about it. After all, you are about to have a baby of your own Daisy. It won't be easy looking after two babies.'

Daisy shook her head. 'I'll be fine, Dad. I love being a mother. Looking after two babies won't be a problem for me.'

'We'll have to pick our time carefully to speak to Doris. She won't want to give him up, even though she's totally incapable of looking after him,' Tom said with a shake of his head that underlined his deep despair.

Daisy flung her arms round Bill.

'It just feels so right. He *is* our son. He *does* belong here. I *am* his mother. I felt it was right from the first time I held him in my arms.'

'It's for the best all round, I reckon, bless his heart,' Bill said, beaming with pride as he watched Oliver crawling around the bed. 'He had such a rough start in life. Still, I reckon we can make it up to him. He's only a little 'un. He'll not remember.'

Tom put his hand on Bill's shoulder. 'Are you absolutely certain about this, lad? It's not every bloke could bring up another man's son.'

'I am,' Bill said. 'It will be better all round that he stays in the family – we are all he's ever known.'

'I still think he should go with Dad, now – just for the time being,' Daisy said. 'I'm due any day now and we don't want the added problem of getting him to Mam and Dad's, especially if the baby starts to come in the middle of the night. And what would happen if you were called to Grafton Underwood while I was laid up? After all, we don't know for certain how long it will be before you get your re-posting papers.'

Bill reluctantly capitulated. 'All right, then. But as soon as you're home from the hospital, we're having him back where he belongs.'

Violet was drying dishes in the tiny kitchen of her father's cottage. 'I *am* happy, Dad,' she said. 'Don't worry about

382

me. I'm quite contented here. You know I've never minded being on my own. I don't need company.'

Walter put an arm around her shoulder. 'Are you quite sure. Because if you're lonely and would rather live in a place where there's a bit more life, we can give up this cottage and find somewhere else. Perhaps we can do it when the war's over – surely it can't go on much longer.'

Violet shook her head. 'No. I'm fine. Honestly. And this place is just perfect for you and Noel. No one will ever find you here.'

'And you don't mind living with two men?'

'No. Why should I?'

'I wish you would let your mother know you are safe, though. She must be going out of her mind with worry.'

Violet shook her head. 'She doesn't care about me, not now she's got her precious baby boy to love.'

Walter reached up and put the clean plates away in the kitchen cabinet. 'You'll need a purpose in life, though. You can't just be a housewife for Noel and me, and spend all your spare time on the beach with the dog. It's no life for a young girl with the world at her feet. It's too isolated.'

'I'm happy doing housework,' Violet replied. 'It would be an ideal solution if I stayed here for good. You could go to work, instead of relying on Noel for money. I'll just stay at home and look after you both.'

'Well, if you are sure you're happy here, then I have something to show you. I can't keep it from you, love. It wouldn't be right.'

Walter walked through to the living room and withdrew an envelope from the bureau. 'Here, read this,' he said. 'It came a couple of weeks ago, but I couldn't bring myself to burden you with something else to worry about, and I suppose I was scared that you would take yourself off back to Kettering.'

Violet opened the envelope and extracted a letter, frowning slightly.

Dear Walter

I am sorry to have to contact you, but I am writing to you in desperation. Things have gone badly wrong. Violet has disappeared (I am hoping that you will know where she is), Doris is unwell again and I fear she is about to have another nervous breakdown and poor baby Oliver is being passed from pillar to post, being looked after by either Liz, Rose or Daisy for most of the time. It is a most unsatisfactory state of affairs.

Yesterday, Doris told me she can't go on. I am fearful for her state of mind. As you are Oliver's legal father following the adoption, we need your consent for Daisy and Bill to adopt him. They are expecting their own child any day now, but once they are settled they have said they are more than happy to adopt Oliver and give him a decent life as part of their family.

I think it is the best solution all round.

Please can you write back to me and let me know if you are willing to sign adoption papers. I'll then approach Doris and see what she says.

I am sorry to bother you with all this.

With regards

Tom Jeffson.

Violet exploded in anger. 'I just knew this would happen. My mother should never be allowed to look after children. I can't believe she doesn't want him after all.'

'What do you want me to do?' Walter asked.

Violet's eyes filled with tears. 'Do I get a say? I don't deserve to have a say, do I? After all I tried to get rid of him.'

Walter put an arm around her shoulder. 'Of course you get a say in your baby's future. He's your flesh and blood, after all, no matter what a stupid piece of paper says.'

Violet thudded down into an armchair, unable to speak. Since she had walked out on her baby she had felt a constant pain, just behind her breastbone. It was always there, making her feel empty, as if she was hungry. She read the letter again, and the sheet of notepaper shook as her hand began to tremble. The pain intensified and she shut her eyes momentarily. With a sudden clarity she knew what she wanted more than anything else in the world. She wanted to be his mother - the best mother a little boy could have. Her baby was over five hundred miles away and he desperately needed her.

'What I really want is to have him back,' she said quietly.

Later that evening, when Noel returned home from work, the three of them discussed what was to be done about Oliver.

'If Violet wants him back,' Walter said, 'then I am happy for them both to live here.'

Noel rubbed his chin, before a wide smile lit up his face. 'Well, this is a turn up for the books, but I'm happy to turn over new page in the book of our life. I have just one thing to ask.'

'Go on,' Walter said, sitting on the edge of his seat.

'When he comes to live with us, I'd like him to think of me as a grandfather, too.' He sat on the arm of Walter's chair and hugged him. 'We might never have been parents, but we sure as hell can be good grandfathers.'

Violet smiled at Walter, tears of happiness glistening in the corners of her eyes. 'You might not have fathered me biologically, Dad, but you have been my father in every other sense, despite everything. And I am so grateful to you both.'

That night, when Violet went to bed, she hugged a pillow to her chest.

Finally, the jigsaw pieces of her chaotic life were beginning to fit together.

The next day, in a tiny village post office in the Scottish highlands, Walter handed a letter over the counter, explaining to the post mistress that it was extremely urgent.

Five hundred miles away, Tom and Liz sat watching Oliver playing in front of the fireguard in their living room.

Doris appeared, having let herself in the back door. She had done her hair and make-up, but her lipstick had been applied with a shaky hand and had smeared slightly around her lips.

'I want my baby,' she said to Tom without looking at Oliver. 'He's mine and I want him back right now. You're all trying to steal him from me, and I'm not putting up with it anymore.'

Tom rose from his chair and drew breath through his teeth, the pain of arthritis biting into his hip. 'Well, we can't stop you, but it will be difficult for you, looking after him on your own – you know you're not well at the moment. Let's talk about this after our Daisy's had her baby. You can come across the road and see Oliver whenever you like, but it will be too much for you to look after him while you're poorly with your nerves. He's perfectly all right staying with us for a while. It'll give you a bit of time to get well again.'

'Tom,' Liz interrupted. 'Let her have her say.'

Tom sat down again and motioned to Doris to do the same. 'All right – keep your hair on.'

Doris still hadn't acknowledged Oliver, who sat holding two wooden building blocks, one in each hand. He banged them together and chuckled to get her attention.

'You been on the bottle again?' Tom sniffed the air in the general direction of Doris. 'You're definitely not having him if you've been drinking.'

Oliver looked from one to the other, as if trying to comprehend what was being said. He banged the bricks together again, and getting no response, threw one of them at Doris's leg.

'Ouch! Little bugger!' Doris bent down to rub her leg. 'We'll have none of that m'lad, when you come home,' she said, her voice slightly slurred.

She bent down and she slapped Oliver's little hand. His cheerful face crumpled and he began to wail, unaccustomed to being smacked. He held up his hand to Tom, showing him that it hurt.

Shocked, Tom pulled Oliver from the floor onto his lap

to comfort him. 'That was uncalled for,' he said, glaring at Doris.

'He's got to start behaving himself. He'll end up wild if he's not given some discipline. Your Daisy's too soft with him.'

'You're not having him,' Tom said. 'Over my dead body ...'

'Well – shall we just tell Liz what you've been up to all these years when she thought you'd kept your promise and stayed away from me?'

Tom waved his hand. 'Go ahead – she won't believe you anyway.'

Tea cups tinkled reassuringly in the kitchen. Tom knew Liz hadn't heard the comment.

'What the hell's up with you?' Tom said in a low voice as he shot Doris a cold glare. 'Pull yourself together, woman. For goodness sake.'

Tom stopped talking and the taut atmosphere relaxed slightly as Rose and George came home early from work, it being a Friday.

Rose took off her coat in the hall doorway.

'Hello, Auntie Doris. You look better today.' She smiled at Oliver. He rewarded her with a toothy grin through his tears and held out his arms to her.

Rose draped her coat over a chair, scooped him up from her father's lap and jiggled him up and down playfully.

'Horsey, horsey, don't you stop ...'

Doris interrupted her and joined in bouncing over-energetically up and down in her chair: *'just let your feet go clippety clop. The tail goes swish and the wheels go round – giddy up we're homeward bound.'*

388

She finished off the nursery rhyme, again without looking at Oliver, who gave her the hostile, unsmiling stare only a baby is capable of when someone has just smacked his hand.

Rose glanced at George and then at Tom. Doris was sitting on the edge of the chair, as if ready to take flight. *'The tail goes swish ...'* she repeated loudly giving an exaggerated sweep of her arm, almost knocking Tom's pipe out of his hand.

'And the wheels go round...' she rolled her hands around each other, swaying back and forth.

Liz, having heard Rose and George come home, stood in the doorway watching her sister, startled. 'Is she all right?' she said. 'Has she been at the gin again?'

'Giddy up, we're homeward bound.'

'Buggered if I know!' Tom stooped down to knock the ash out of his pipe into an ashtray on the hearth. He straightened up and began slicing off slivers of tobacco from a solid lump with a penknife. 'Gone doolally I reckon ... either that or it's the bottle again.'

Always the diplomat, George intervened.

'Shall we take Oliver to the park for half an hour? It's still nice out, Rose.' He gave an exaggerated look out of the window and took Oliver from Rose's arms. He walked through to the kitchen, with Oliver over his shoulder, to where his pram stood in the corner.

Rose shut the door behind them.

'What the hell's up with her?' Rose whispered to George. She pointed to her head with her index finger and circled it round and round, indicating that she thought her aunt had gone mad.

389

'Buggered if I know.' George echoed Tom. 'Let's just get this little lad out of here and leave them to it. Where's our Margaret?'

'Next door, playing with the evacuees, I should think.' Rose replied.

Just as Rose answered, the back door opened and Margaret stepped in.

'I was, Mam ... I went round to get out of the way when I came in from school. Aunt Daisy was here, talking to Grandma and Gramp about Oliver and they asked me to make myself scarce for a bit. Where are you going?'

'For a walk. I'd keep out of there if I were you.' George thumbed in the direction of the living room. 'Your Auntie Doris is still in there.'

'Oh, I know, I saw her come in and so I kept out of the way. She looks an absolute fright with all that make-up on and her hair all frizzed up like a clown,' Margaret said, pulling a face'. 'I'll come with you.'

George laughed.

'And she smells,' Margaret added as an afterthought.

Liz opened the door to the kitchen, raised her eyebrows and mouthed, 'Where are you all going?'

'For a walk,' Rose whispered. 'We thought we'd get little Oliver out of here until she has calmed down.'

'Good idea. I'll come with you. Perhaps if we all go out, she'll take the hint and go home. She's saying she wants to take him with her, but I reckon she's about to make her peace with the floor, as far as I can tell. I think she's been on the gin all afternoon.'

Liz poked her head round the living room door, her voice high and bright. 'I'm just popping out for a loaf of

390

bread. You don't mind, do you Doris? I don't think I've got enough for tea.'

Margaret pushed Oliver in his pram, walking slightly ahead of Rose, George and Liz. On the way they passed a new bakery that had just opened in the next street.

'I'd better go in here and buy a loaf,' Liz said. 'Especially as I used running out of bread as an excuse to get out of the house.'

'Can we get iced buns for tea?' Margaret turned around, still holding onto the pram handle. 'Please Dad?'

George put his hand in his pocket and tinkled his loose change, glancing at the new sign over the door. 'Have you got the ration book, Rose?' he asked. 'Have we got enough coupons to treat the children to some buns?'

The woman in the shop told George that she had acquired the premises with her daughter and son-in-law only a couple of weeks ago. By the time he had paid for a loaf of bread and two buns, iced with sticky, pink icing, George had ascertained that the woman was a widow, her husband, Frank, having died of the consumption in nineteen twenty-two.

'I never remarried,' the woman told George, adding that she only had the one daughter by her late husband, Frank Haywood, who had been a lovely man.

The woman's daughter appeared from the back room, her white apron smeared with pink icing. She stood on tiptoe to glance out of the shop window to where Oliver was sitting up in in his pram, laughing at Liz, Rose and Margaret who were pulling funny faces for his benefit. 'Oh,

391

what a pretty little girl and such a gorgeous baby – are they yours?'

'The young lady is my daughter, and the baby belongs to my wife's Aunt. We're just taking him out for a walk to give her a bit of a break. She's not been well, you see, and she had him very late in life, which means she's often tired.'

George smiled at the woman, studying her face.

No one else in the family knew the truth about Frank Haywood, but he did.

Chapter Twenty-four
Friendship and Revelation

Tom could hardly believe that Liz had gone out with Rose and George and left him alone in the house with Doris. He couldn't remember single time since Liz had discovered their affair twelve years ago that he and Doris had been alone in his house.

He gulped, seeing her through unblinkered eyes as he realised the innocent young woman he first took into his arms in nineteen twenty-one was unrecognisable, having aged twice as quickly in the intervening years. He spoke gently.

'Doris, love. Have you been on the gin again? It doesn't help in the long run. Believe me, if anyone knows, I do.'

'What do *you* know,' she spat at him. 'What do you know about being left by a husband and a daughter, and then nobody trusting you to look after your own baby?'

'I'll try harder to find Vi –'

'Don't bother,' she said with a wave of the hand. 'She's not worth the shit on the bottom of my shoe.' She fumbled in her bag for a cigarette, took out a lighter and lit it, blowing smoke in his face.

Tom put his head in his hands in despair. Doris had been a lovely young girl and now she was nothing but an old hag, using foul language and blowing smoke at him. Everything was his fault. If he could reverse over his life to the point where all this mess first began, he knew it would be to that dark, desolate day in the winter of nineteen twenty-one when he had taken Doris by the arm and led her into his allotment shed in an effort to give her a child to love. Even then he could have stopped, but once Violet had been conceived the following year there had been no turning back.

There was nothing he could have done about her marriage to Walter, but he knew that instead of liberating her, as he had intended when he agreed to their affair, he had stifled and suffocated her as surely as if he had kept her hidden away from the world in his dark allotment shed, stunting her growth and preventing her from blossoming into the strong woman she might have become had she not been his lover. No one knew the real Doris, because her life had been spent running around his legs like a puppy devoted to her master, howling when he had gone and then only able to think about the next time she would see him.

He should have resisted the urge to take control, kept out of things and not contrived to keep his secret grandson in the family. His idea for faking the birth was half-backed and daft, and had been the final straw for Doris, who had now completely collapsed under the weight of the deception. And to top it all, Violet had disappeared, and Tom instinctively knew it was because she was unable to face living under the same roof as her unwanted and unloved baby son.

He must have been completely mad to think his plan to

keep the baby in the family would work.

'You are a complete bastard, Tom Jeffson, ' he whispered to himself with tears of remorse glistening in his eyes as Doris wept and wailed before him.

Approaching dusk descended around them as they strolled back from the bakery, grateful for a few snatched minutes alone, which was something they cherished living as they did with Rose's parents.

Margaret and Liz pushed Oliver a little way ahead in the pram.

George threaded Rose's arm through his. 'Don't walk so fast. Let's enjoy the moment and let your mam and Margaret go on in front. Anyway, I've got something important to tell you.'

'What?'

'Remember your father's accident?'

'Which one?'

'When he fell down a drain and broke his leg and hip. Just before he tried to top himself in nineteen thirty-two.'

'I remember. That was the first time we met Quentin Andrews.'

'When Bill and I went to visit him in hospital one day, he was drugged up with morphine and strapped into contraptions to help heal his broken bones. He was rambling on a bit about your brother, Arthur, dying of the consumption. He mentioned that he had always loved his children and both his sons had meant the world to him.'

'I only ever had *one* brother. You must have been mistaken. Why didn't you say at the time?' Rose looked at

396

him with annoyance.

'I wanted to get to the bottom of it before mentioning it to you. No point in getting you all upset for nothing.'

They came to a junction and stopped to let a couple of army jeeps pass. Margaret and Liz strolled on ahead with the pram, too far away to hear their conversation.

'Do you remember when we went to visit Auntie Flo and Uncle Todge in Barton Seagrave one Sunday afternoon just before you had our Margaret?'

Rose shook her head. 'No, I can't say I remember. It was years ago. We went several times ...'

'Well, anyway,' George went on. 'Todge took me out for a ride in his car, and you and Daisy sat with Auntie Flo toasting crumpets by the fire. While we were out, Todge told me about something he had witnessed when he was a lad. Apparently, your father had a bit of a thing going on with a much older woman called Mary Haywood. They watched them in a field through a hedge, or something ...'

Rose tutted. 'How disgusting – in the open air as well. How old was Uncle Todge?'

'About twelve, I think he said.'

Rose shook her head in disbelief. 'Dad would have been sixteen, then.'

George nodded. 'Yes ... and then a while afterwards the woman had a baby, late on in life. It was a boy.'

'But that doesn't mean anything, it could have been anyone's if she was so fast and loose as to play around with a sixteen-year-old lad.'

'Ah .... yes ... that's what I thought, until a few months later, when your father actually admitted to me that he had another son as well as your brother. He was drunk as

397

skunk at the time ...'

'As usual in the bad old days!' Rose interjected. 'At least he's stopped drinking now he's turned over a new leaf.'

'Let the cat right out of the bag, he did,' George continued. 'He said that he'd had a secret son when he was only a lad, and then this son had died too, just before your Arthur. He swore me to secrecy. He was so drunk he wouldn't have remembered afterwards. So I never did say anything: I just reckoned it best to let sleeping dogs lie. God knows what it would have done to your mam.'

Rose screwed up her face. 'Why are you telling me all this now?'

'Because I think those two ladies in the bakery are your dad's secret son's widow and daughter.'

'How come?'

'Because of the name above the door – Haywood. The older lady said she was a widow, didn't she, and her husband died of the consumption in nineteen twenty-two? Well, that was when your Arthur died, and your dad had said he lost two sons in the same year.'

Rose walked on in silence, thinking about the relationship. If it were true that would make the older woman her half sister-in-law and the young woman her half-niece. She let out a low sigh. 'Oh my word, George, what if you're right? This is going to tip the apple cart right over – they are only in the next street, for goodness sake!'

Doris jumped up and stood in the kitchen doorway as George guided the pram over the back doorstep into the

398

kitchen.

Tom had forced her to drink several cups of weak tea and she had now sobered up. 'I'll take him, if you don't mind,' she said, glaring at Margaret, who stepped aside as she grabbed the pram handle.

Liz tried to stall her. 'He needs his tea, Doris. 'He's already late. Look, just wait until he's had something to eat and then you can take him home, give him his bath and put him to bed.'

Doris hesitated. 'I want to give him his tea. I *am* his mother after all.'

Liz spoke softly to Doris, stroking her arm as if she was a child, and told her that of course she could give Oliver his tea and, yes, she was his mother, only it would be really nice if they all had tea together.

With Oliver safely in his wooden high chair, messily trying to feed himself with toast and butter, Liz stepped into the kitchen, drawing the door closed behind her on the pretence of making sandwiches.

Tom, Rose and George stood, huddled together in the kitchen, worried.

'We've got to stop her taking him?' Tom said quietly. 'What can we do?'

'She's not capable of looking after him. And Daisy will go absolutely mad,' Rose said, a little too loudly.

'It's nothing to do with *her!*' Doris had been listening at the door and was angry and insistent. She yanked the door open. 'He's *my* baby not hers! And who are you, Rose Foster, to pass judgement on my capability as a mother?'

Tom stroked his chin and took out his watch. He turned his back on Doris and whispered to Liz behind his hand. 'How about we let her take him and get him settled for the night, then one of us can go over the road and check she's not been at the gin. He's had a walk in the fresh air, so he'll sleep well. Then I'll go over really early tomorrow morning and make sure all is well, and bring him back here.'

Liz nodded. 'That seems like a good plan. I'll go over about ten o'clock and check up on them to make sure everything is all right. Chances are, by the morning, she'll be fed-up with him again and hand him back to us to look after.'

After a few minutes Doris emerged from the living room, carrying Oliver defiantly on her hip. She brushed past Rose. 'Excuse me! I know you've all been whispering about me, but he's *my* son and it's about time you all realised that. I'm taking him home – for good!'

'Have you changed him?' Rose stared at her aunt accusingly. 'I bet you haven't.'

'He doesn't need changing.'

'Well, he hasn't been changed since –'

Doris interrupted her.

'*I'm* his mother. I'll decide when to change him.' Her eyes blazed with anger as she dumped Oliver back into his pram. He wailed, looking all around him as his bottom lip quivered and his eyes filled with frightened tears.

Tom made one last attempt to change Doris's mind. He stepped to one side to block Doris's exit and grabbed the pram handle.

'Doris – look love, you're not well. Let us keep him tonight and then we'll talk about all this in the morning and work something out.'

'No, Tom. He's mine. *Mine.* And I'm taking him home.'

With that Doris gave a wild stare, her eyes darting from side to side before turning and yanking the pram over the doorstep. It lurched dangerously to one side and Oliver cried in fear, holding onto the sides. He turned and looked back at Tom, who bent down to give him a kiss on his cheek.

Doris, without saying goodbye, strutted down the entrance passageway and into the street. On impulse she turned in the opposite direction to her house, muttering to herself. 'I'll take him to the park to see the ducks. Let all the nosey neighbours see me out with my son. That'll shut 'em all up.'

Oliver sat up in his pram, clutching onto the sides, eyeing up the mad woman who was pushing him without talking to him or entertaining him. He blew a raspberry – that usually got someone's attention. When that didn't work he said the only word he knew: *'dad. ..dad.... dad...dad ...dad.'* The strange woman looked at him.

'Huh! He's cleared off back to America and doesn't even know you exist. You can stop saying that word right now, young man. You don't need a dad. You've got me.'

'Dad. ..dad.... dad...dad ...dad.' Oliver, at last getting some attention, repeated the word.

'Shut up!' Doris shouted at him, and then muttered under her breath, 'little bastard'.

'Dad. ..dad.... dad...dad ...dad.'

Doris was getting annoyed now. She looked disdainfully at Oliver, who rammed his fist into his mouth and tried to smile.

'*Mam ... mam ... mam,*' she said, leaning forwards and shoving her face into his.

Doris carried on walking without talking to Oliver. After a while she stopped and reached into her handbag, which she had stuffed under the pram. She took out a new bottle of gin, unscrewed the top and drank a quarter of it in one go, straight from the bottle. With a furtive glance over her shoulder to see if anyone had been looking, she shoved it back in her bag.

Wicksteed Park was about half an hour's walk away, and when Doris and Oliver arrived there was no one around. The wind blew eerily through the trees and the odd bird gave a last burst of song before falling quiet for the night. Oliver began to cry. He was tired and cold, his nappy was both dirty and saturated and he wanted his bath, a bottle of milk and a warm bed. The pram bumped over the uneven grass as Doris made a detour from the concrete pathway.

'Shut up, you little bastard. I'm taking you to the park, what more do you want? See what I good mother I am?'

Confused and even more frightened by the approaching darkness, Oliver's screams became more frantic and insistent. Doris, swayed, swigging the gin with one hand and cruelly bumping the pram with the other to try and stop him crying. When, unsurprisingly, he cried even more, she walked round to the side of the pram and yanked back the covers.

'Uggh,' she said, wrinkling up her nose as she realised Rose had been right and his nappy did need changing.

She leaned over the pram, her face only a few inches

402

from Oliver's.

'You'll have to wait until we get home. I haven't got a nappy,' she said as she threw back her head and took another swig of gin.

She screwed the top back on the bottle and leaned forwards to give him a drunken kiss on the cheek. Unused to hot fetid breath laced with cheap perfume and alcohol fumes, Oliver wailed even louder.

Doris knew she was drunk but didn't care. They had walked only a few yards further into the park before she downed the last of the gin in the bottle and let it drop to the ground. She stopped and lifted Oliver out of his pram to try and stop him crying, staggering back slightly.

'Ooops! Nearly.' She gave a trill laugh.

The pram, unbraked, started to roll almost obscenely down the incline.

Doris stared at the runaway pram bouncing and lurching across the uneven grass, but a whole bottle of gin downed in less than twenty minutes had dulled her judgement and delayed her reactions. She eventually staggered awkwardly towards the lurching pram, as if in slow motion.

'Stop ... stop!' she shouted.

The pram was gathering momentum. Doris swayed and slipped on the wet grass as she ran after it, the alcohol deadening her senses and robbing her of a sense of direction. Oliver, picking up the vibes of the danger he was in, gave one last futile attempt to free himself. He threw himself backwards but Doris was not supporting his back and he hung upside down over her arm, his head banging against her hip as she stumbled forwards, chasing the pram. She stopped briefly to haul him over her shoulder.

His terrified screams pierced the chilly autumn night and wafted thinly on the wind, drifting around the accumulating mist on the lake like gossamer threads of a broken spider's web.

The pram finally came to a stop as it ran into a litter bin at the side of the concrete path beside the boating lake. It tipped over onto one side, spilling out the contents into a muddy puddle.

Doris felt her feet slide away from under her as she reached the pram, her still-weak ankle letting her down. There was a sickening crack as Oliver's head hit concrete.

With terrifying abruptness, his screams stopped.

She struggled to get up, squinting through the darkness to stare at him lying on the pathway beside the litter bin. She bent over to scoop him up, wondering why he was limp and unresponsive.

Eventually, she sank down on a park bench, clutching him to her, whispering into his hair, fighting to regain control of her mind and body. Her maternal instinct, barely intact through years of conflict and uncertainty was briefly triumphant in its victory as it burst forth and gathered Oliver to her breast, but his little body was floppy and silent. Tears welled up from somewhere in the centre of her chest and bubbled uncontrollably from her eyes, nose and mouth.

She stood up and staggered forwards, hesitating momentarily before she put one leaden foot before the other, drawn towards the seductive dark water of the lake as it danced and flirted with white flecks of weak moonlight and fronds of mist curling around her. Shadowy fingers beckoned and enticed her intimately, caressing her ankles with a lover's touch. She stood, looking out over the water, watching with fascination, as a lone duck paddled back and forth. A line of shadowy, bobbing rowing boats tethered in the distance momentarily distracted her, and drew her back into an uncertain reality. Surprised to find a baby in her arms, she looked down at Oliver. She needed to get this baby home: he was tired and needed his sleep. She was tired and needed her sleep, too.

So, so tired.

Doris hiccupped several times as she swayed around the edges of consciousness. Disorientated, she stepped forwards, trying to find the pram so she could tuck up her sleeping baby into the warm covers and get him home. She *would* be a good mother, if only everyone would give her a chance.

There was a moment of surprise as her foot made contact with a permeable surface. Gratefully, she allowed herself to become absorbed into a cloud, unable to distinguish whether it was warmth or chilliness that enveloped her as she slid into its welcoming but mysterious depths. A gentle, hypnotic sound lapped in her ears, enticing her to join it and become as one with it. As lovers, Doris and the water flirted for a while before desire overcame her. With a calm acceptance, she succumbed to its playful advances, realising too late that she had fallen for its charms.

The lapping noise drifted through the empty park and hung in the air for a few seconds as fronds of mist closed in over the bubbles.

The dark hand of Evil had won the challenge and claimed its prize. The infinitely repeated circle of birth, procreation and death had been enacted in one short scene as Oliver fell into its clutches. Evil momentarily let go of its prize and punched the air in victory, but the cheer of triumph was short-lived as Power and Glory snatched the prize away from it and reclaimed the red-haired baby boy angel to join its twin in Heaven, together with the tortured, lost soul of its grandmother.

Chapter Twenty-five
Deliverance and Divinity

A mile away, in Cornwall Road, Liz hammered on Doris's back door with her fist, the back of her neck prickling in fear.

'Doris! Open this door ... right now.'

The house was in darkness. Liz stepped back to glance up at the back bedroom window, where Oliver should have been sleeping. She tried the door knob again, although she had tried it twice before.

Panicking, she ran out into the street, crossed the road and hurried back home. She burst through the back door. Tom was filling a hot water bottle at the kitchen sink.

'She's either not there or she's blind drunk.' Liz said, breathless with running. 'It's only nine o'clock. She can't be in bed yet, and I knocked on the door so hard I hurt my hand. And I looked through the windows in the moonlight. None of her blackouts are drawn and I couldn't see the pram anywhere.'

'What? Oh, bloody hell!' Tom put the hot water bottle down on the draining board. 'Where can she have buggered off to at this time of night with a baby in tow? Are you sure she hadn't just gone to bed and forgotten to draw the blackouts?'

408

'Tom, I'm sure.... I'm positive ... what are we going to do?'

George jumped up. 'I'll come with you.' He pulled on his coat, with Tom in quick pursuit. 'I bet she's hit the bottle again and is passed out.'

'Be careful,' Rose shouted. 'It's a clear night and there might be German planes ...'

Rose and Liz stared at each other, helpless as the sound of the door slamming shook the house. Rose clamped her head in her hands. 'I should have stopped her.'

'No one could stop her, Rose. Don't go blaming yourself. I don't know where all this will end – things are just going from bad to worse.'

Liz flopped into an armchair and sat forwards, her fingertips digging into her eye sockets. Rose noticed her thin, blue-veined hands and, for the first time, realised how frail-looking her mother had become over the past year. She looked like an old lady, although she was only sixty-two.

'Mam.' Rose sat on the arm of Liz's chair. 'None of this is your fault; it was a daft idea of our dad's from the start. You know what it's like, we just can't do anything to stop him once he's made up his mind. We are just going to have to persuade him to admit that it was a mistake and try and put things right for Oliver's sake. If it comes to it, we'll adopt him. You know we have always wanted another baby since Margaret was born but there's never been any sign.'

Rose unconsciously twizzled her wedding ring as she thanked God for her placid easy-going husband and felt a pang of regret at their inability to conceive another child. 'George would love to adopt him, I know he would, and Daisy loves him just as much as we do. Either of us would have him like a shot.'

'We'll have the authorities on our backs soon if this goes on much longer and she doesn't pull herself together,' Liz sniffed, dabbing her eyes with a handkerchief.

'To be honest, Mam, that thought has gone through my mind a couple of times. It might be for the best. I know it's a gamble, but the authorities would most likely be grateful for us to look after him if we can prove Doris is insane.'

'Oh, Rose.' Liz stood up and looked in the mirror, pushing back her hair and grimacing at the heavy lines, hollow cheeks and sunken hooded eyes framed with thick straggly eyebrows. 'Doris is not insane, she's just ill.'

'She's drunk most of the time,' Rose interrupted. 'She's an alcoholic! Look how she carts a bottle of gin with her everywhere she goes? Look how George and Bill had to carry her back home when she was found slumped in the town in the middle of the afternoon? And she's dirty. I'm certain she never washes and just splashes on that cheap cologne she buys.'

Liz sighed. She knew Rose was right. Ever since they had first discovered that Violet was pregnant, Doris's health had spiralled downwards in spectacular displays of slovenliness. She thought back to how, as a young woman, she had envied Doris's youth and beauty, her quick-minded wit and the way men found her attractive. Liz stood up and glanced at herself in the mirror. She might be plain and she might be ageing, but at least she had held her family together through the worst things life could possibly throw at her: she had lived a good and honest life and could hold her head up high. *For better or worse,* she thought. *For better or worse.*

'Your grandmother on your father's side was a dirty beggar too, you know,' she mused. 'I'm wondering now if she suffered from nervous breakdowns, too. There are so many similarities with Doris.'

'Umm, you've said before,' replied Rose. 'What turned *her* into an alcoholic?'

'I don't know. By all accounts your grandfather was a decent man. He worked hard, according to Tom. All I do know is that Tom couldn't stand it. The filth and disorder in the house nearly drove him mad. They lived like pigs. He just had to get away when he was nothing but a lad.'

The back door opened and both women turned round expectantly. Tom's brow furrowed into deep lines, his usual neatly combed grey hair wild and untidy. 'I broke the kitchen window and George climbed in. She's not been home by the looks of it, the blackouts haven't been pulled and the house is an absolute mess.'

'Where can she have got to?' Liz wailed. She glanced into the mirror again, for a moment wondering who the old woman was who stared back at her.

'George has gone to try and find her. When he gets back, if he's had no luck, we'll have to fetch the police,' Tom said with a reluctant shrug.

'What will people think?' Liz said, absent-mindedly tidying up the living room at the thought the police might be called in. 'With all our business back in nineteen thirty-two being dragged through the mud, folk will have a field day with all this.'

411

'Bugger everyone else,' Tom said, pacing up and down the room. 'All that matters now is that little lad, and getting him back safely. I should never have let him go ...'

Rose jumped up to straighten antimacassars on the fireside chairs, like her mother spurred into action at the mention of calling in the police.

'Dad, you said yourself we had no choice – after all she is his legal adoptive mother – and anyway the entire town thinks she has given birth to him!'

George returned, breathless with sprinting.

'No joy,' he panted. 'I'll run and raise the alarm – we'll have to fetch the police – then I'll go and tell Daisy and Bill what's happened.'

Once George had caught his breath, he raced off again.

Half an hour later, Daisy, Bill and Eileen arrived with George. Agitated for Oliver's safety and panting with hurrying, Daisy had to bite her lip hard so as not to explode in anger at her family for letting Doris take Oliver.

The search went on until the early hours of the morning, with more and more police officers called in to help as the night went on. Hampered by the black-out, the search was laborious and risky. Periodically a policeman would return to the family home to report on progress, and to plead with everyone to try and remember any small snippet of information that might lead them to Doris. Margaret and Eileen sat huddled together in Tom's armchair covered with a blanket – no one thinking of sending them to bed. Tom paced up and down the garden path, chain-smoking his pipe, while now and then, Liz would stick her head out

412

of the back door and admonish him about the stray German bombers overhead seeing the light of his pipe. Several times, the air raid warning sounded, but no one moved into the shelter.

Daisy sat sobbing, inconsolable, her terror at Oliver's disappearance extinguishing all earlier anger. Bill tried to console her, his own face ashen with fear. At two o'clock in the morning an ambulance arrived to take Daisy to hospital as she had been experiencing some painful cramps. The midwife, who had been fetched out, was also uncertain and concerned because of Daisy's difficult birth with Eileen.

'Better to be safe than sorry, love,' said the kindly police officer who had arranged for the ambulance to take Daisy to the hospital, before announcing that the search would have to cease until first light, on the direction of the Home Guard.

Stuart Roberts was born at six thirty on the morning of Saturday, 14th October 1944. As his birth was taking place, a Bedford pick-up truck rattled noisily towards the entrance to Wicksteed Park. The truck slowly made its way over the bridge and along by the park's lake, where the driver stopped to investigate the curious sight of an overturned pram by a waste paper bin. As he stood, looking at the pram scratching his head, out of the corner of his eye he saw what looked like a bundle of rags floating on the misty water a few feet away.

The next few moments of the park keeper's life were to be replayed in his memory many times in the years that followed. A baby's body was floating, face down at the edge of the water. The park keeper lifted it out, gasping with shock at the child's cold, grey face. Horrified he stood, holding the baby and looked around the deserted park for help. A lone walker strolled in the distance, throwing a ball for his dog, too far away to hear his shouts.

The park keeper placed Oliver's body on the edge of the lake, his heart pounding at his shocking discovery. He set the pram back on its wheels. As he lifted Oliver's body into the pram with a sinking heart he noticed a woman's body floating in the misty water about twenty yards away.

'God Almighty, save their souls!' he cried out loud, and crossed himself, casting his eyes aloft.

Half an hour later the park was closed off, with a police guard at every entrance.

The knock on the door came at exactly eight o'clock.

The sun had risen triumphantly, ending a night that had seemed to last forever. It streamed in through the window of the living room and sparkled and glittered as it met the microscopic specks that swirled in the air.

Liz was in the kitchen making tea and toast for an exhausted Margaret and Eileen, who gazed at each other not knowing how to react to the knock on the door. Tom had fallen into a fitful sleep in his armchair, his mouth open with a dribble of saliva escaping from the corner of his mouth, and a half empty whisky glass in his hand, consumed only to coax his reluctant body into welcome sleep. Rose sat opposite him and for the second time in twenty-four hours realised with shock that her parents were getting old.

George was the one who eventually leapt to his feet to answer the door, the ominous knocks echoing in the silence.

'You'd better come in'.

The words were quietly solemn – not spoken in a tone conducive to the birth of a new baby. Everyone's hearts sank and Tom woke up with a start. He stood up, still cradling the glass. The police officer stepped into the living room, bringing with him a dark air of doom that filled the entire space and dimmed the sparkling early morning sunlight until it was a mere speck of light. He took off his helmet, coughed and nervously rubbed his moustache.

'It's not good news, I'm afraid.'

All the family's eyes were on him.

Tom exhaled and closed his eyes, as if in silent prayer. The hand holding the glass started to shake. He opened his mouth to speak but nothing came out.

'The lady – Mrs Grey – your sister, I believe?' He turned to Liz with a sympathetic glance. 'She was found in Wicksteed Park early this morning. I'm afraid the early indications are that she either took her own life or accidentally fell into the lake after drinking a large quantity of gin. We found an empty bottle, you see.'

Liz stared at him, not believing what she was hearing. She heard a strange voice that might have been her own say: *"and the baby?"*

The policeman shook his head and looked at his feet.

'Him too. I'm so very sorry.'

Margaret and Eileen stood in the kitchen doorway, arms intertwined in shocked disbelief at what they had just heard. Rose turned to look at them, feeling as if she had stepped outside herself and was watching the scene through disembodied eyes. The sunlight bothered her and she raised her hand to shut it out.

Tom was quiet and still. His free hand flew to his throat as it constricted, strangling any words before they could be uttered. He sat back down in his chair, and shrank into the cushion, his shoulders drooping with the heavy weight of conscience.

He started to cry silently, his head bowed in grief. The whisky glass in his hand shook and trembled and patterns of crystal sunlight reflected and danced on the wall opposite.

The policeman picked his way through the living room into the kitchen without uttering another word. He placed his helmet gently on the kitchen table, plucked the kettle from the stove and filled it from the tap.

Rose spoke first, in a heavy, thick voice. 'We should never have let her take him!' Tears flowed down her cheeks and she pulled Margaret and Eileen close to her, holding them tightly as if to shield them from both the horror of the news and the dazzling, too-bright sun.

Eileen broke free from Rose's embrace.

'I want my mam,' she wailed, her twelve years falling away until she stood, like a five-year old, alone and lost, crying for her parents. Margaret clung to Rose in comfort and both girls sobbed as the policeman make a pot of tea in the kitchen. In their awkward in-between age, they didn't know whether to make themselves scarce or stay with the grown-ups.

Before the policeman had the chance to pour out the

tea the sound of running footsteps pounded in the entrance passage before Bill burst through the back door.

'It's a boy! We've got a little boy!'

He stopped. His excitement hitting a brick wall of sombre faces. The policeman stood like a statue, the teapot hanging in the air, a thin wisp of steam escaping from the spout.

Bill's heart lurched into his throat. 'What ... oh, no! What's happened?'

'Are you the new father?' The policeman realised he had asked a silly question, but felt uncomfortable and embarrassed, not quite knowing what to say. He put the teapot on the table and didn't wait for an answer. He cleared his throat.

'I'm afraid it looks as if Mrs Grey has drowned in Wicksteed Park lake, although there'll have to be an investigation. The baby was drowned too. I ... I'm so sorry...'

His words tailed off as they failed him.

The colour drained from Bill's face and he slumped onto the draining board, locking his fingers over his head. 'No ... no,' he cried. 'How? What happened?'

In the sunlight-filled living room, no one moved or spoke. No one knew what to do or what to say as the strange paradox created by the marriage of a simultaneous death and birth fused in the air, crushing every single member of the family.

Tom sat motionless, the irony of the tragedy sinking into his troubled mind. Shocked, he realised he had lost one grandson and gained another within hours.

The heavy silence was rudely broken by the sound of a

417

smashing glass. Tom, cradling the half empty glass of scotch, having leapt to his feet, throwing it across the room with a force fuelled by shame, anger and grief. The glass smashed symbolically on the opposite wall, slivers of cut crystal spraying across the room in sparkling, glistening chunks.

For the second time in his life Tom wanted to die. For the second time he had thrown a whisky glass at a wall. For the second time, chunks of broken glass had settled around his feet in silent recriminations, reflecting prisms of rainbows amongst the broken dreams and agony of broken hearts. He thought back to the first time he had thrown a glass at a wall and shuddered. If only he had died that day, it would have spared all this shame and anguish.

No one spoke. The only person to move was Liz, shutting out the irritating sunlight as she closed the curtains.

In hospital, just a couple of miles away, Daisy sank thankfully back into the soft pillows and shut her eyes. The birth had been relatively easy, unlike the first one, and she had been in labour for only four hours. She shivered with excitement and mentally hugged herself, proud that she had easily given birth to perfect little baby boy with large dark eyes and a mop of black hair. The only clouds on Daisy's horizon were grim worries over the events of the night before. Had Doris been found? Was Oliver safe? Would Doris want to keep him? How soon could they start the process to adopt him? A thousand questions ran uncontrollably through her mind and she was ravenously hungry for news, as well as for the large breakfast she had just been given.

'Come on, Mrs Roberts,' a kindly nurse beamed, 'you should have some rest now you've had your breakfast. It's been a long night for you.'

Daisy levered herself up to a sitting position.

'I know,' she replied. 'I just need to find out if my aunt and her baby are safe before I can settle – is there any way you could find out for me, please?' Daisy gave the nurse a withering look. 'I won't be able to sleep until I know.'

The nurse sighed. 'I suppose I can telephone the police station for you. And then you must promise me you'll go to sleep.'

Daisy smiled. 'Thank you,' she said.

The nurse stepped into the office, thumbed through the telephone book, and picked up the heavy, black telephone to make the call. Her expression darkened as a police sergeant told her the terrible news. She replaced the receiver on the telephone and sank into the office chair, all colour drained from her face. After a moment or two, she stood up and composed herself before putting a bright, false smile on her face and walking back into the ward.

'No news, I'm afraid. You know what they say ... no news is good news. Now, you go to sleep like a good girl and we'll look after little Stuart if he wakes.'

Daisy sank back into the pillows, disappointed that her mind could not be put at rest before she allowed herself to get some sleep.

At two o'clock that afternoon, a fifteen year-old boy cycled laboriously up the hill between the white house and the isolated cottage, a telegram tucked into his pocket. Inside the cottage, Violet, Walter and Noel were packing a suitcase with a few items, ready to begin the long journey to Kettering the following day to finally reunite Violet with her baby son.

'It's a new life for us all,' Violet said, hardly able to contain her excitement at being allowed to love her baby without guilt. 'Once we have Oliver home with us, we can get on with our lives and put all the troubles in Kettering behind us. It's an ideal place for a little boy to grow up. I just love it here. It's isolated, wild and windswept – just like me, really. I just know we are all going to be so happy.'

Noel smiled at Walter, placing a proud hand on his shoulder. 'Who would have thought we would end up with a *family*,' he said. 'It's like a dream come true. No more struggles and having to fight our way through life for something we believe in.'

Violet giggled. 'I can't believe how the pair of you blackmailed my Uncle Tom into giving you enough money to set up home here,' she said. 'But I'm glad you did.'

Walter shook his head. 'We hated doing it,' he said. 'But we had no choice. We had to have the means of disappearing if we were to have any chance of escaping prosecution. Now, with you and Oliver joining us, we will be safe. The people in the white house at the bottom of the hill and folks in the village all think we are brothers. People already know you are my daughter, staying with us for a while, and now, with Oliver coming, it will be easier to escape any suspicions that folk might harbour about us.

The knock at the door made them all jump. 'Who on earth is that,' Walter said. No one moved as they all stared at each other. Noel shrugged his shoulders, palms upturned.

'I'll get it,' Violet said. 'It might be a parcel, or something.'

Noel shook his head. 'We're not expecting anything.'

Violet opened the door, surprised to find the telegram boy outside.

'Telegram for Mr Walter Grey,' said the boy as Walter appeared at Violet's shoulder.

Walter leaned over and took the flimsy envelope from the boy's hand. Shakily he signed for it before tearing it open.

With an ashen face he read the few words on the telegram.

'What is it?' Violet said. 'Why have you got a telegram?'

Walter handed it to her without speaking.

Violet read the few brief words and passed it to Noel, again without speaking.

Fleetingly, she wondered how a mother should react at the news that her baby had just died. Not only had her baby gone, but her mother too. Should she wail and fling her arms around herself in anguish? Should she sink to her knees and cover her head with her arms, shutting out the cruel world that, yesterday, had given her a whole life with one hand and then the very next day snatched it all back again?

She leaned back on the wall and slid down until she was sitting on the floor, watching, detached as Walter and

421

Noel clung to each other.

Violet felt the last vestiges of her spirit ebb away as she realised the truth was the worst lie of all. Her entire life had been lived under the burden of secrets and lies from the moment of her creation: her mother and Uncle Tom's affair; her piano, not bought for her because she liked to play, but to keep her within Uncle Tom's grasp while he moulded and manipulated her. In a grotesque act of deception, she'd endured having her most lovely asset – her hair – shaved off, week after week at her mother's insistence when, after being so violently shaken awake to the reality of her artificial existence, she had succumbed to the harsh truth and cut it off, her inner voice crying out for love and attention. Even her Auntie Liz, so serene and good, had a secret affair with her boyfriend's father. The American, too, had deceived her, impregnating her with one mouse-baby with fingers and toes, and one beautiful, perfect little boy with glorious red hair. Even the scene before her was a lie. Her father and Noel weren't brothers. They were lovers. Illegal and unnatural.

But worst lie of all was herself. How could she have ever believed she could be a good mother?

Walter helped her stand and then hugged her to him. 'Oh Violet,' he said. 'I can't imagine what can have happened, but no doubt we shall soon find out. I'm so sorry, love.'

Violet stared blankly over his shoulder. She should be crying at the death of her mother and her son. She should not be dry-eyed, only able to think about truths and lies. She should be mourning. This surely proved she was nothing but a monster with a psychopathic disorder – just like her Uncle Tom. She was not a young woman who, yesterday, had a family who loved her and a son to cherish and nurture. She was a cold, hard, evil hag and it was for the best her son had joined his twin in death, because surely should could not have been a proper mother to him, despite all her good intentions.

With a stab of pain she suddenly understood. There had been only two truths in her sad life. The first truth was her love for Theo Andrews and the second was her steadfast resolve to give her baby boy a good life in the highlands of Scotland, with a mother who would be the best she could possibly be and two grandfathers who loved him.

Now, with both truths snatched cruelly away from her, all that was left was lies.

The hunger in her heart that had been with her since the birth of Oliver suddenly turned into a ball of impregnable steel. Never again would she allow herself to feel love for another human being. It was just too much trouble for everyone. From now on she would not allow love to be a part of her life, because that way, no one else could ever be tainted by all the lies.

The Jeffson sisters and their husbands clubbed together to pay for a funeral for Oliver. Bill acted as the sole pall-bearer walking down the aisle with the tiny white coffin resting lovingly in his arms, tears flowing without shame down his face. He had, in a faltering, tearful voice, delivered a touching eulogy to the little boy, declaring that he had loved him like his own son and that in his eyes, he *was* his father. The church was packed, with three times as many people turning up for the funeral of the little boy who had brought so much love to everyone than for that of his grandmother, which was a depressing affair with few mourners. Even the two ladies from the new bakery turned up at the church for Oliver's funeral and sat at the back, touching Rose's arm in sympathy as she walked past.

Violet arrived in spectacular fashion for the funerals, heavily made-up, covered in expensive jewellery and wearing very high heels. She showed very little emotion or grief, but great interest in talking to the newspaper reporters and posing for the inevitable photographs, dressed in her new fur coat, a handbag over her arm and a cigarette in her hand, blowing delicate puffs of smoke up into the air.

'*I* was his mother,' she declared in a low, superior voice. 'He was my child. I was blackmailed by my family to give him up to my mother for adoption. You see these clothes, this jewellery? All paid for with the money I was given by my family to make myself scarce. But it was all perfectly legitimate, you know. My mother legally adopted him. She didn't want *me* hanging around to spoil things. Oh no, I was something to be swept under the carpet after I fell pregnant by that brutish American airman.'

Through real tears, Violet told eager journalists how she was bullied into taking part in the scam by her wicked Uncle Tom, who told everyone she was going to work in munitions and then sent her away in disgrace to a hostel for unmarried mothers to have her baby and then forced her into going along with the obscene lie. She related in gory detail how her mother had broken her arm just before

424

the faked 'birth' and how she, Violet, had, single-handedly, strapped it up on the instructions of her evil family to avoid them having to take her mother to the hospital.

'It was all against my better judgement, of course,' she added. 'It's no wonder my mother went mad and jumped into the lake, poor soul.'

Violet was offered a hefty sum for her story, which she accepted with a mercenary resolve and embroidered with skill. The whole sorry tale was dragged out in the local press, day after day, and even made the pages of one of the national newspapers, the scandal diverting people's attention from stories of war and giving them something to gossip about.

Later that day, behind the closed doors of her former home, Violet wept in Walter's arms, exhausted by the necessary public declarations of the truth. She thought she would feel purged, finally able to construct a new reality – a life that would feel clean, untainted by the past and free from lies and secrets. But the truth was all she could think about was her perfect baby boy and the windswept, wholesome life they would have shared if only she had followed her instincts and taken him with her on the day she walked out on her family.

Tom was broken.

Unable venture out of his house for months, he obsessively tended his garden until there was not a weed in sight, the edges of the lawn were razor sharp and the earth around his prized rosebushes was hoed to a fine tilth. Reporters from the local press eventually gave up asking for his side of the story and he became a hermit in his own home with only his family for company, staring bleakly into space with a detached absence so acute, Liz actually bought him a bottle of scotch to cheer him up.

Daisy and Bill were lost and bereft, the tragedy tempering the joy they should have felt with the birth of their new baby boy. By far the worst effect on Daisy and Bill, though, was guilt. They each blamed the other: Daisy blamed Bill for not allowing her to keep Oliver when he returned home from the war the previous year, and Bill blamed Daisy for arranging for him to be cared for by her parents instead of allowing him to look after the little chap while she had her baby.

Eileen, caught in the midst of accusing stares and could shoulders, cried herself to sleep many times because her parents were arguing. Eventually, in one long healing discussion of recriminations and mutual forgiveness, Daisy and Bill realised that neither of them could be blamed in any way for any of the disastrous events. They had given Violet shelter, when little more than children themselves, they had taken her in and showed her the true meaning of family love. They had also given her little boy happiness in his life and they came to realise that the seeds of the tragedy had been sown the day the conspiracy was born.

Six months after the tragedy, Rose shared George's hypothesis about the Haywood Bakery ladies with her sister, telling Daisy that she suspected that the two women who worked in the bakery were really their sister-in-law and niece. Daisy, although shocked by the revelation, was not really surprised – after all, the sisters had long suspected that Violet was really their half-sister and not their cousin. It was not unlikely, they agreed, that Tom may have fathered another secret child.

After much deliberation the sisters decided they there would be no benefit to telling the Haywood Bakery ladies they were really related. After all, hadn't the family had enough upset to last a lifetime? Journalists had pulled the family through the mill twice now, and wouldn't hesitate to do it again at any mention of the, by now, legendary and eponymous Tom Jeffson.

It was inevitable that Tom would find himself, once again, hauled before the inimitable Dr Ernestine Crabtree, Clinical Psychiatrist, after Liz had declared that enough was enough and made him an appointment herself.

Tom gazed in wonder around the smart newly furnished consulting room.

'Blimey,' he said. 'This is a bit posh, innit?'

He sank down gingerly into the comfortable armchair, running his hands over the smooth, cool damask upholstery.

'Crikey, swanky new armchairs, posh coffee tables, wallpaper and pictures on the walls? You've come up in the world, haven't you?'

Dr Crabtree smiled. 'I need to make sure my patients are comfortable. Even you, Tom.'

The doctor sat down and Tom's consultation began.

'So I understand that you haven't been out of the house

427

for six weeks. Is that right?'

Tom nodded. 'That's right. Ever since –'

He looked at his shoes and shook his head slightly. There was no need to explain what had happened to him. It had been splashed all over the *Northamptonshire Evening Telegraph* and had even featured in a full page article in *The Daily Mirror* entitled *"The Baby Snatchers"*.

'You should have come to see me, Tom. When I read about you in the newspapers, I knew I should be helping you through it all.'

Tom scratched his balding head, almost in tears.

'My wife made me this appointment, Doctor. She's really worried about me.'

Tom knew Dr Crabtree meant business when she extracted her glasses from a case and slid them over her nose before opening a folder containing his medical notes.

'I always feared something like this would happen, Tom; you did very well with your treatment, but I've never been totally comfortable about discharging you. After your wife came to see me, I took the opportunity to completely review your case and I can see how hard you've worked to make amends since your suicide attempt in nineteen thirty-two.'

'Aye,' Tom said. 'I've ticked off everything in my little red book, except that one thing. I couldn't tick off Doris – perhaps if I *had* been able to tick off Doris none of this would have happened. It was entirely my fault, doctor. I can't blame anyone else for the death of my sister-in-law and little Oliver, and for my Violet going off the rails. It's hanging over me like an executioner's noose and I can't face anyone. Liz is the only person who cares. I love her doctor. I love my wife with all my heart. She is the most special, incredible lady that ever walked this earth.'

Doctor Crabtree took off her glasses, folded them and set them down on the coffee table, alongside Tom's medical file, which she had just closed. She wiped the corner of one eye with a forefinger and Tom's mouth fell open slightly as he peered at her under his eyelashes. Was that a *tear* in her eye?

'I'm going to tell you something now, Mr Jeffson. I'm only telling you this because I think it will help you to come to terms with this dreadful tragedy. I don't usually discuss the technicalities of a patient's case with them, but it is clear to me that the biggest part of your psychopathic disorder has been your lack of conscience. The majority of human beings find it impossible to understand that conscience is not universal and not automatically built-in at birth. Most people can't comprehend living a life with no pangs of conscience whatsoever ...'

'But I'm different, aren't I?' Tom interrupted. 'I know I am.'

Dr Crabtree nodded. 'You *were* different, Tom, and I stress the *"were"*. But what you have just said to me, about blaming yourself for this tragedy and expressing so much unqualified remorse, it has just evidenced the fact that your odd and bizarre behaviour for most of your life has been down to the fact you have no inbuilt sense of restraint to speak of. You have been completely at liberty to exercise your chilling advantage and satisfy your desires for power and control unchallenged by your own conscience. After every single consultation you have

429

attended in the last thirteen years I have noted this deficiency in your psyche.'

Tom extracted a clean, white handkerchief from his trouser pocket, unfolded it and dabbed at his eyes. 'I am never going to be cured, am I doctor?'

'Talk to me about baby Oliver, Tom.'

Tom cleared his throat. 'The moment I clapped eyes on him in our Daisy's arms I knew he was special. The love that little lad brought with him filled the air with sunshine and goodness. I had never experienced anything like it before in my life, Doctor. It was much more intense than when I held any of my own children.

'I can't even begin to describe how much I loved that red-haired little boy. Everyone was drawn to him. He was such a happy little soul, despite all the chaos around him. He brought a calmness and serenity to us all, doctor, even though the times were troubled. Every single person whose lives were touched by Oliver felt it too. Even our Violet. She felt so guilty about everything, she turned and ran from him for his own sake. It took her weeks to make her way up to the Scottish Highlands to her father's house, with hardly any money for train fares, having to earn her passage wherever she could. She feared she would taint his life by staying. Walter confided in me at the funeral and told me that she turned up on his doorstep, filthy, exhausted and as broken as a snapped twig.'

Tom sat forwards, his head in his hands, mopping up the tears of remorse, shame, guilt and self-loathing that flowed freely from his eyes, nose and mouth. Dr Crabtree waited for him to compose himself sufficiently for him to continue.

'When the policeman told us how he had died, Doctor, I threw my whisky glass at the wall. It was as if I had to shatter my life, too, because I knew in that moment, what an awful, monstrous thing I had done to everyone and I realised that I had ruined all my family's lives. I've caused the death of a baby; the death of my sister-in-law; ruined my wife's life; all my children's lives; Doris's; Violet's – and even that nice surgeon and his wife who wanted to adopt little Oliver. I've ruined their lives too, doctor. Everyone who comes into contact with me ends up ruined. I should wear a sandwich board that says: *Keep Away From This Man: He Will Ruin Your Life.*'

Tom threw his arms around himself and looked up at the ceiling, tears streaming out of his eyes and into his ears.

'It's weird, Doctor. Way back in nineteen thirty-two, I threw a whisky glass at the wall in my allotment shed when I tried to end it all. It shattered and the last thing I saw as I lost consciousness was bits of my miserable life reflected in the shards and chunks of glass. This time, it was just Oliver, Oliver, Oliver, and the love he brought to my shattered family.'

Dr Crabtree leaned back in her chair and crossed her legs.

'Mr Jeffson – Tom – it is very clear to me now that your lack of conscience hasn't taken away your capacity to feel love, it has just meant that every time you have felt a connection with another human being – love for your wife; paternal love and romantic love – it has been distorted into something ugly and repulsive by lack of remorse for your actions.'

431

'It has also affected my daughters, Doctor,' Tom went on. 'Rose and George are paying the price every single day of their lives for how I am. Even though I finished paying them their money back years ago, they can't move out because they are still worried about leaving Liz all alone with me. At the beginning they daren't leave Daisy because of that time I got myself blind drunk and molested her when she was twelve, and they had to watch over her to make sure she was safe from anything else I might do to her. Rose gets terribly upset because my granddaughter, Margaret, is never in the house: she's always at Daisy and Bill's with Eileen and who can blame her? A young lady growing up in a house full of old people? It can't be much fun for a youngster, can it?'

'I suppose not,' Dr Crabtree agreed. 'It must be quite oppressive for a young girl as an only child living with grandparents.'

'Our Daisy is the light of my life, though. She's such a good mother, Doctor. So strong and reliable. I used to call her *headstrong*, because she was such a handful when she was growing up, but I realise now that Daisy's strength has been the only thing keeping my family together. She's a remarkable woman, and she does allow me to love her, but at arm's length if you know what I mean. I know she doesn't love me back, but she does care for us and comes round to see me and her mam every day.'

Tom bowed his head and began to cry again.

'But it's our Violet, doctor, the one who is the most damaged. She's the clever one. She could easily have been so successful in her life – a writer or a musician – you should hear her play – and yet she's thrown it all away. I

432

was shocked when she came back for the funerals. Utterly and totally shocked. She's gone off the rails completely. I can see now that it's entirely because of the terrible things that happened to her while she was growing up. It's no wonder she's turned out as she has. I need to make amends with Violet, Doctor. I want her back so that I can try again because the day I slept with her mother so that she could be conceived was the day I should have made sure the child I had procreated was happy and cared for, and I didn't do that, did I?

'I lost our Lily when she got married in nineteen twenty-one. She stays well away, Doctor, and has built up her own life that definitely doesn't, and never will, include me. She did come round a couple of months ago to tell me that our Violet is now living in London and has taken up with some undesirable characters and is living in seedy lodgings. She was furious with me, and said that Violet deserved better than to be selling her body for money. She wants me to go to London and fetch her home, but I can't. I'm too scared to make contact. Lily is furious, but I can't help it. I'm just not strong enough.'

Tom's final consultation lasted for almost three hours, but Dr Crabtree waived the rest of the fee for the time it had taken for him to unburden a lifetime of guilty conscience.

Eventually, as exhausted as Tom, she stood up and put her hand on his shoulder.

'Mr Jeffson,' she said. 'You won't need to come to me for any more appointments. I am completely happy that you have now brought your psychopathic disorder under control. I finally feel comfortable in discharging you. Go back to your wife and thank her for making this appointment. It is probably the most valuable thing she has ever done for you. But make no mistake, Tom, you owe your recovery to that red-haired little boy who touched your soul so completely he gave you back your conscience.'

'Am I cured, Doctor?'

Dr Crabtree nodded. 'As cured as you ever can be, Tom. I think you have to go home and learn to love yourself again. You are not to blame for your condition, but that's no excuse to ever fall back into your old ways.'

Tom shook the doctor's hand. 'I won't. I promise. I have a lovely wife and family and I am so grateful to you for helping me. Thank you.'

As Tom walked out of Dr Crabtree's new clinic, he could not have received more of a fanfare to celebrate the beginning of the rest of his life. Every single person in Kettering was out on the streets, waving Union Jacks, shouting, whooping, dancing and crying in each other's arms.

The eighth of May was a day to remember, destined for a special place in every history book to be written in the future. Not only was the nation set free in a triumphant celebration of the end of World War II, but on the same day, in a small town in England, an ordinary family also celebrated its own private victory as its patriarch, complete with his newly-found conscience, walked free and held his head up high, ready to prove that, even after all the mistakes he had made and the terrible things he had done, he could be a good man.

Chapter Twenty-six
Love and Forgiveness

So it was that, soon after his discharge from Dr Crabtree's clinic, a reinvigorated and happy Tom started to venture out to places where he could begin his quest to re-enter the world instead of indulging his usual daily routine of manicuring his garden, tidying his workshop and tending his allotment. He began to speak to neighbours, re-acquaint himself with friends and even do a bit of shopping for Liz, which was something he hadn't been able to do since the tragedy, for fear of coming into contact with gossiping townsfolk.

One sunny Saturday afternoon in the height of the glorious summer of nineteen forty-five, Liz, Rose and Daisy sat in deck chairs on the back lawn with Margaret, Eileen and baby Stuart. The girls were in the midst of a competition to see who could make the longest daisy chain. Tom was bored, having been forbidden by the women to let Margaret and Eileen play with his ferrets.

'Who wants to fetch a big jammy cake to cut up?'

'Me!' Margaret and Eileen shouted in unison.

'Don't you think that's a bit extravagant, Tom?' Liz said shaking her head. 'There's some home-made cake left in the tin and if we buy cake it will use up all the sugar ration for the next week.'

Tom gave a dismissive wave of his hand. 'Rationing will be over soon, now the war's ended. In any case, we have something to celebrate.'

'What,' everyone said in unison, suddenly interested.

'The end of the war.'

Liz laughed. 'That was two months ago. You're a bit behind the times, Tom.'

'Depends what war you're talking about,' Tom said, tapping the side of his nose and winking at the girls, who had each laid their daisy chain the length of the garden path to see whose was the longest. 'I reckon it's a dead heat. Anyway, there's something else to celebrate. This morning I had a letter from Violet.

'Really?' Rose said. 'That's fantastic. How is she?'

'Not good,' Tom said. 'I've written to her three times since Dr Crabtree advised me to contact her, but she hasn't replied until now. I'm going to see her in London. I've told her we need to make a fresh start, and I want to welcome her back into our family. I feel responsible for her.'

'She's been in contact with Lily, too ...' Daisy said.

Tom beamed. 'I know. I'm pleased. I reckon this family has turned the corner, eh? So let's go and buy cake to celebrate.'

Daisy sighed and turned to her mother. 'I suppose I'd better go with him, or else he'll use up all your sugar ration for the next six weeks.' She stood up and stretched her legs, rubbing her growing abdomen.

'We'll both go with him,' Rose said, and then added in a whisper, 'and hope his eyesight isn't good enough to read the new sign over the cake shop.'

Leaving baby Stuart with Liz, they all set off.

When they arrived at the shop, Tom stopped, dead in his tracks:

HAYWOOD'S BAKERY
FINEST BREAD AND CAKES
Prop: Mrs Sarah Haywood

'A bakery owned by a woman?' Tom said, squinting through eyes blurry with developing cataracts at the shop sign. 'Well, I never. I don't know what the world's coming to.' He peered through the window past rows of tempting cakes and freshly baked bread at two blurry women who stood behind the counter in the shop.

In the shop, an elderly lady sat inconspicuously in the corner behind the counter, her head on her chest, seemingly asleep. There was a small queue and Tom stood behind his daughters, speculating with Margaret and Eileen on the size of cake they were about to buy.

'Who's that?' Rose whispered to Daisy. 'I haven't seen her before.'

Daisy turned and shot a quick look at Tom's face. He was laughing with Margaret and Eileen, oblivious to the woman, snoring softly in the corner.

'You don't think it could be her, could it?' Daisy whispered to Rose, who shrugged her shoulders.

Tom straightened up, one hand on each of his granddaughter's shoulders. Daisy watched him squint at the elderly lady, and then his line of sight dart from the old woman up to the colourful poster on the wall at the back of the shop, which said *"Haywood's Bakery – Finest Bread and Cakes, Fresh Every Day."*

Rose and Daisy cast each other a silent look as ancient secrets passed briefly across their father's face like an old, silent film. Daisy did a quick calculation in her head and then put her mouth very close to Rose's ear. 'If it's her she's got to be very old – in her nineties I should think.'

'Who?' Rose mouthed.

Daisy whispered, so that Tom couldn't hear her. 'That woman asleep over there – you know, the one George found out about. The older woman he had an affair with when he was sixteen. Frank Haywood's mother.'

Rose tried to remember the woman's name. 'Mary Haywood?' she mouthed to her sister.

'What?' Tom said, cupping his hand behind his ear. 'What are you two whispering about?'

It was the sisters' turn to be served. The elderly woman stirred as Millie greeted Rose and Daisy. While the girls chose a cake to buy, they exchanged news.

Daisy felt a small but significant sense of fate at Tom's discomfort as she turned to introduce him to Millie. 'I don't think you've met our father before, have you?'

'No ... I don't believe I have.' Millie wiped her hands on her apron and held out a hand for Tom to shake. Her mother, Sarah, interrupted, a broad smile on her face.

'... but I have! Mr Jeffson – how nice to see you. I was wondering how long it would be before we finally met again.'

'Ummm ... do I know you?' Tom mumbled, going bright red and scratching his ear under his cap. He subconsciously glanced around for an escape route and put a grandfatherly hand on Margaret's shoulder. 'I can't quite recall ...'

Millie withdrew her hand, embarrassed that Tom had not wanted to shake it, but in his discomfort, he hadn't even noticed.

Sarah trilled, her voice animated and excited. 'Of course we have! You used to work with my late husband – you remember – Frank Haywood? You organised a whip-round at the factory when he passed away and brought the money round to me. You visited a few times, too, when Frank was ill and helped me out. Why – it must be nearly thirty years ago!'

'Nineteen twenty two,' Tom said, unable to take his eyes off the elderly woman, who was staring back at him, an amused, mocking look in her rheumy eyes.

Sarah nodded towards the old lady. 'Didn't you used to live next door to Mary in Broughton? My Frank said you used to be his neighbour, so you must have known her. Mother look who's here. MOTHER!'

Sarah shouted at the elderly woman who was obviously hard of hearing, but it was evident that she and Tom were already locked in a mutual antipathetic glare of recognition.

Mary spoke, a smirk quivering over her wizened, lined face. She had no teeth and her thin lips were drawn into something resembling an animal's anus. 'Well lad. Fancy seeing you here. I thought you were dead.'

'She rambles a bit,' Millie whispered apologetically in the general direction of the customers, motioning towards her temple with a circling finger, 'and she's away with the

441

fairies most of the time.'

A strangled cackle emanated from behind the counter, as Mary pointed her walking stick at Tom. 'Well I never. Little Tommy Jeffson! Who'd have thought you would still be alive.'

'Mother!' Sarah remonstrated, shocked, her face reddening with embarrassment. 'I'm afraid she's got a bit of dementia,' she said to Tom. 'She comes out with all sorts of odd things. We are looking after her for the week as her daughter is in hospital. She moved to Leicester years ago to live with her and we don't see her that often.'

Sarah attempted a smile as she apologised for Mary's outburst. 'I'm so sorry, Mr Jeffson.'

Tom took off his cap and scratched his head, eager to publicly disassociate himself with the elderly woman in the corner. He glanced round the shop. More customers – all women – had entered and the queue had grown longer. He began to wish he had not broken the habit of a lifetime and entered a cake shop, which was unmistakably a woman's domain.

'She's Frank's mam ... you must remember her Tom! I'm sure when you visited Frank you said you used to live next door to him when he was a child.'

'Oh ... yes. I do remember her now. I was friends with her son, Jack.' Tom's words failed him as he realised he couldn't wriggle out of the situation. He pretended to be in a hurry, grabbing each of his granddaughters by the arm in an effort to steer them out of the shop.

'We must be getting off, now. These young ladies ...' Tom's words were drowned by a loud leery cackle from the corner. ' ... want their cake.' His voice tailed off as he braced himself for the next revelation.

'What is it they call 'em?' Mary chortled. 'You know – bulls they put in a field to service all the cows. I know ...I know ... I know. It's a STUD.'

Mary, in full swing, was enjoying the attention from the customers in the shop, most of whom were finding it difficult to hide their amusement. 'Eeeyoore. Eeeyoore, Donkey Tom. He fell into the brambles and scratched his hand. Enjoy your blackberries did you, Tom? Were they nice and juicy?'

Mary was enjoying herself. She swayed from side to side as she swung her arm backwards and forwards.

Tom hid his hand behind his back, conscious of the scar he had worn like a macabre trophy all his life, evidence of Mary's seduction of him when he had been little more than a boy. Indeed, he *had* been a stud, because a baby had been all that she had wanted from him. Once she had achieved her goal and become pregnant, she had spat out his bones, having chewed every scrap of flesh from Tom's future conscience.

By this time Rose and Daisy were helpless with laughter and Millie had joined in. Sarah's mouth twitched at the corners. Tom could see she was trying hard not to laugh too, his indignant expression and obvious embarrassment in a shop full of giggling women exacerbating her mirth.

Tom's face burned hot with the women's laughter. 'Batty old mare!' he mumbled loudly to all the customers in the shop, who had no idea there was a thread of truth running through the old lady's ramblings.

He grabbed hold of his granddaughters' shoulders and

marched out, his face burning hot and sweaty. As he left the shop he realised with irritation he had forgotten to pick up the cake from the counter, but there was no way he could bring himself to turn round and go back in.

Mary had managed to stagger to her feet and, with the aid of her walking stick, had shuffled out from behind the counter into the shop doorway. She stood, her legs splayed inelegantly, waving her stick at the receding figure of Tom. Her hair was long, as she refused to have it cut, and it hung in grey rat's tails around her face.

Later, in uncontrollable fits of giggles, Margaret and Eileen would declare to an amused Liz that there was a real, live witch in the cake shop who was shouting rude things to Gramp in the street.

Having realised they had forgotten the cake when they were half-way home, Rose turned back to return to the shop.

Millie was alone behind the counter, Sarah having taken Mary off for a lie down.

'I bet she's a handful,' Rose said with a withering, sympathetic look as Millie marked off the sugar ration for the cake. 'But that was so funny! Our dad's face ... it was a picture!'

Millie sighed. 'Oh dear, I'm really sorry about your father. It was so embarrassing for him. You wouldn't believe it what a trial it is to have to look after her – we can't wait for her to go back home. She's a real nasty old woman. She's ninety-eight, so she does well really. The doctors say she has dementia caused by old age, but she's

444

been like it ever since I've known her. Anyway, I think I remember your father, too. I was only five when my dad died, but I remember him visiting Mam. He was so kind and generous to us. Mam always said he was an angel in disguise. If it hadn't been for your father looking out for us, I don't know whether Mam would have coped after my father died so young. After Mr Jeffson organised a whip-round in the factory for us, my mother used the money to set up a little business baking bread and cakes. She's done really well for herself. Of course, with the war and everything, she had to put her plans on hold, but her business is thriving now the government is relaxing the rationing a bit and the Council is giving grants to people like us to expand our businesses.'

'Really?' Rose said, faking an intrigued reaction. 'I had no idea. I don't remember him talking about a Frank Haywood and I'd have been eighteen then. What was your dad like?'

'Wait here a bit, I'll fetch a photograph.' Millie went out into the back room and came back with a sepia photograph in a polished, wooden frame.

Rose's heart flipped and turned as many somersaults as a circus acrobat as she took in the young man's dark eyes and hair. His resemblance to her dead brother, Arthur, was astounding. She felt a prickle of tears as she realised that she was looking at the face of an older brother she had never known. She handed the photograph back to Millie.

'He looked like a lovely man, Millie.'

'He was. I was the apple of his eye.'

Rose had a sudden urge to tell Millie the truth, to lean

445

over the counter and hug her tightly and tell her that she was her auntie

'Rose?'

'Yes.'

'All that business last year. You know ... with baby Oliver?'

'Yes?'

'I just wanted you to know that my mam and I came to the funeral. I know we had only just met on the day of the tragedy, but we both put two and two together and knew it you, because of the story in the papers. We wanted to come. That little boy was so beautiful, we shall never forget him.'

'He was. I often think that if I could turn the clock back, I would turn it back to that last hour before my Aunt Doris took him and we were buying iced buns in this shop.' Rose shut her eyes momentarily, remembering her first encounter with Millie and George's revelation on the way home. Should she tell her? Was it really fair to deny Millie her ancestry and the chance to know her grandfather?

Millie continued. 'I think your father was only trying to do his best for Oliver. After all is said and done, he was only trying to make sure he stayed with his family and was loved. It was just misplaced loyalty. I didn't really believe all that was said about Mr Jeffson in the papers, because my mother and I knew what a kind and generous man he really was.'

Rose rubbed her forehead, trying to erase the mixed feelings from her mind.

'Rose, I think what I am trying to say – I mean, what I

have meant to say since that day, but the time has never been right ...'

Millie wiped her hands on her apron and bowed and twisted her head so that Rose was forced to look her in the eye.

'I just wanted to say that meeting you on that day, and having the privilege of meeting that beautiful little boy just hours before he lost his life, it's been the best thing that ever happened to me. We've become such good friends since you've been coming in here for your bread, haven't we?'

Rose looked at Millie in the eye. It was cause for much regret because she and Daisy both now regarded Sarah and Millie as good friends, but as she said goodbye to Millie she knew she couldn't risk her father's hard-won recovery and her mother's new-found happiness by raking over the dead leaves of the past. She knew she would never reveal the truth to Millie or Sarah because it just wouldn't be fair on her parents.

Later that evening, Liz and Tom sat listening to classical music on the wireless. Tom was contented, watching Liz as she darned socks, her glasses perched on the end of her nose. That afternoon, prompted by his granddaughters to tell Liz all about the witch in the cake shop, he had tearfully confessed to his wife about his affair with Mary Haywood and told her the story of the day he had been out blackberrying when he had been sixteen and how she had stolen his conscience as well as his virginity. Liz had stroked the scar on the back of his hand. *"The past is in the past,"* she had said, placing a forefinger on his lips before he could reveal that Mary Haywood had given birth to his son.

'I love you, Liz,' Tom said, his words spontaneous, not expecting a reciprocation. After all, he had told her he loved her many times over the past thirteen years, but never once had she told him she loved him back.

Liz sighed, put down her darning and smiled back.

'I love you, too, Tom.'

Tom's eyes sparkled and filled with tears of happiness. He hauled himself up from his chair and shuffled over to her, perching on the arm of her chair. He slid his arm around her shoulders and she rested her head on his chest.

'You don't know how much that means to me,' he said. 'It's took us a long time, but we've got here, haven't we old gal. We've been through thick and thin together, but here we are.'

He bent his head forwards as Liz looked up and they kissed, briefly but tenderly.

Tom levered himself up. 'Wait here,' he said. 'Don't go anywhere.'

He walked slowly up the stairs to the bedroom and opened the drawer of Liz's bedside cabinet. Checking that the pressed rosebud and the poem were still inside her Bible, he went back downstairs.

Liz looked startled as he shuffled back into the living room, carrying her Bible, and sat down again on the arm of her chair. He opened the pages, extracted the rosebud and the poem and read it out loud:

"Gather ye rosebuds while ye may,
Old time is still a-flying;
And this same flower that smiles today
Tomorrow will be dying.
The glorious lamp of heaven the sun,
The higher he's a-getting,
The sooner will his race be run,
And nearer he's to setting.
That age is best which is the first,
When youth and blood are warmer;
But being spent, the worse, and worst
Times still succeed the former.
Then be not coy, but use your time,
And, while ye may, go marry;
For, having lost but once your prime,
You may forever tarry."

'It's beautiful and so clever, Liz. Did you write it?

Liz shook her head. 'No, it's by a poet called Robert Herrick. It's called *"To the Virgins, to make most of Time."* Have you been reading my Bible? You've never read the Bible.'

'No,' Tom replied. 'I found this just after Quentin Andrews passed away. I thought you might have written it. I just want you to know, Liz, I completely forgive you for your affair with Quentin. I've always known about it, you see. But I don't blame you at all.'

Liz bowed her head and covered her eyes with her hand.

'When did you find out?'

'Not until after he passed away, but it was finding this poem and rosebud that made me realise how much of your life I had stolen away from you. You met Quentin and he gave you something I never had. He valued you and made you feel like a proper woman. I might have given you four children, but he made you feel cherished and loved in a way I never could.'

Liz shook her head.

'No, Tom. You've got it wrong. I wasn't ever unfaithful to you. I never slept with Quentin, even though he helped me through probably the most difficult period in my life. But you're right about loving him. I loved him very much.'

Tom stared at her, relieved that he had been wrong about Liz's adultery but heartbroken that she had loved someone else.

'Really?'

Liz shook her head. We had arranged to stay together for just one night – remember the night you went to London with your boss to negotiate the order for boots for the troops?'

'Aye,' Tom replied. 'I remember. That was the day before he died wasn't it?'

'It was the night he gave me this rosebud and poem, which he had written out for me. He told me how much he loved me, but he didn't want me to carry the guilt of adultery through my marriage. Just at the moment we agreed we couldn't go through with it, Theo and Violet broke the kitchen window and we thought it was burglars. He ran downstairs and the shock must have brought on his heart attack. Of course, he was right. Quentin was always right. He was such a lovely man, Tom.'

450

'Aye,' Tom agreed. 'He was a nice chap. A far better man than I can ever be.'

Liz read out some words from the poem.

"That age is best which is the first, when youth and blood are warmer"

You can see the meaning now, Tom – can't you? Our time for love had passed us by; we were both fifty and Quentin didn't want to destroy the rest of my life with guilt just because we had been given an opportunity to seize the moment when you went off to London. He knew me better than I knew myself. And then he died. It was so hard to hide my grief, I had to pretend I had the flu.'

'The jewellery.' Tom whispered. 'He bought you the firework brooch, the necklace and the diamond ring for your little finger, didn't he?'

'Yes. He gave the jewellery to me at the same time he gave me the rosebud and the poem. After he explained to me the reasons he couldn't go through with it, he said I could wear the jewellery for the rest of my life and know that, had we met as youngsters, we would have had a wonderful life together.'

Tom's eyes were wet with tears, and an unexpected pain shot through him as he imagined Liz lying in Quentin's arms. 'It was all my fault, Liz. If I had been a better man, you wouldn't have needed to find shelter in the arms of someone else. I'm so sorry about everything – all the hard times and struggles we have been through – all the marriage vows I have broken in the past. It's no wonder you sought comfort elsewhere. I don't deserve you. I've never deserved you. I've caused you so much pain. '

They gripped hands in silence. Liz eventually spoke.

'Yes. I know all that. But you have faced enormous difficulties, and even though you have made mistakes along the way to your recovery, I know you only ever had the best intentions. You're a completely changed man now, and I *have* grown to love you again. I didn't think I ever would, but I have. For better for worse ...'

'For richer, for poorer ...' Tom continued.

'In sickness and in health ...' Liz whispered.

'To love and to cherish ...'

'Till death us do part.'

ଛଠ

"The confession of evil works is the beginning of good works."

St Augustine

An environmentally friendly book printed and bound in
England by www.printondemand-worldwide.com

This book is made entirely of chain-of-custody materials